Wife to
the Bastard

About the Author

Hilda Lewis was one of the best-known and best-loved of all historical novelists, known for her authentic application of period detail to all her books. She was born in London and lived for much of her life in Nottingham. She wrote over 20 novels and died in 1974.

Wife to the Bastard

HILDA LEWIS

TORC

To

J.C. HOLT

Professor of History in the University of Reading,
with affection and thanks

Cover Illustration: Cover photograph © 2006 Nathan Davis. Costume made and modelled by Melanie Schuessler http:www.faucet.net/costume

This edition first published 2006

Torc, an imprint of Tempus Publishing Limited
The Mill, Brimscombe Port,
Stroud, Gloucestershire, GL5 2QG
www.tempus-publishing.com

British Library Cataloguing in Publication Data.
A catalogue record for this book is available from the British Library.

ISBN 0 7524 3945 6

Typesetting and origination by Tempus Publishing Limited.
Printed and bound in Great Britain.

Acknowledgments

To Edith M. Horsley of Hutchinson for her warm interest and never-failing kindness and to D. Alice Clarke of Nottingham University for her valuable help, my warmest thanks.

The Young Matilda

I

She sat very still, respectful as was proper, upon the stool at her father's feet. But, for all that, the hands folded upon her lap trembled with anger that consumed her utterly; at this moment anger was greater, even, than fear—and that was great enough. But beyond the light trembling of her hands, she gave no sign. She was fifteen, old enough to hide her feelings, let them be what they might. She lifted an all-but blank face to her father and mother sitting there, each in a great chair. Although this was her mother's private apartment in the palace at Bruges, still it had something of a presence-chamber; Adelais that had married count Baldwin of Flanders was sister to King Henry of France—and not likely to forget it.

'He most deeply regrets...' her father was saying; and, though it was some hours since his messengers had returned from England, there was still surprise in his voice.

And still she listened; and still there was nothing but polite interest in her quiet face.

'He thanks us, most humbly, for the great honour...'

'And so he should!' the voice of my lady the countess rose sharp.

'...and regrets, deeply, that he should have given us cause to think...'

'Cause to think!' My lady's voice rose again, 'Surely, he did give us cause!'

Cause... and cause enough! The girl's anger was bitterness in her throat. She said, evenly, as though she, Matilda, princess of Flanders and niece to the King of France, had not been betrayed; had not been offered and refused, 'If he is betrothed, he is betrothed!' And managed to shrug.

Baldwin, that men called *the Great*, raised his brows. Cunning in politics he yet found this young daughter of his too much for him. It

7

was she, she herself that had urged him to set on foot negotiations for the betrothal. She had pointed out the wisdom of giving her in marriage in a manner that could, in no way, upset the courts of Christendom; neither the Emperor, nor the King of France, nor any prince in Gaul, nor yet any of the many princes of Europe. She had wheedled him—no doubt taken by the attractive young man from England who had, indeed, been more than a little attentive—and in the end she had convinced him. All Christendom waited to see how he would bestow his daughter; so much was true. Such a marriage must be a clear sign where he meant to show friendship; where he would, at need, raise his sword among the troubled kingdoms of Europe. So powerful a man, so strong his armies, so rich his resources, all Christendom must wait upon his choice. The English marriage—though not nearly as great as he had the right to expect—could give offence to none.

He had listened to his girl in some surprise; he knew her to be ambitious—as she had the right to be, not only on her father's account but on her own. She was beautiful, she was rarely educated, not only in all the ways of women; but she could outshine most princes in Latin, in writing, and in cyphering. They said of her that, young as she was, she had great wisdom; but her father preferred to call it a blessed commonsense.

My lady countess, having received no answer to her last remark, broke in once more. 'This Saxon fellow, this...' she stopped short, affecting to forget a name too lowly to be remembered. 'I, for one, am glad of the refusal, humiliating though it may be. It was a match never to my liking. We have been saved, all of us, from a great folly.'

I have not been saved. I threw away my virginity upon a cheap fellow. And still the quiet face gave no sign of fear.

'Brihtric Meaw,' her father said; and at the sound of that name her heart shook, remembering his Saxon fairness, the blue eyes and the hanging curtain of his gold hair, 'is no low Saxon. He's the son of my old friend Algar that holds the Honour of Gloucester, and many rich lands besides; a great inheritance. He comes of noble stock; a prince you might call him! Not the best match for our daughter, perhaps, yet it would have been well enough, or I'd not have offered it. I offered it because there was wisdom in it.'

'No wisdom, none at all! And it would not have done. And so I said at the time!' My lady broke in sharp and sour. 'But you would not listen.

My daughter is fit to be a Queen! There's no blood in Christendom so royal as hers; between us we have seen to it. Through you she comes of the line of the dukes of Normandy—your own mother was daughter to duke Richard. So easy-going you are, you have forgotten. But I do not forget, not I! Nor yet that I, myself, am from royal kings descended; daughter and sister to the Kings of France!'

He found her boasts distasteful; one should take gentle blood gently. 'Yet still the match would have been good!' For all his gentleness he was not to be put upon; nor was he minded to see his daughter shamed further by agreeing that the match was unsuitable. A fine young man—good blood and great promise; and, moreover, son to my old friend. It would have suited me well. Now our daughter's marriage must give us some thought; yes, and prayer, too, if we are not to quarrel with your brother in Paris, nor with your kinsman the Emperor, nor yet with Spain; nor indeed, with any prince of Christendom.'

'No need to trouble your heart,' Adelais said, waspish. 'Nor yet to importune God. Your daughter—' and it was no longer *my* daughter, 'has been refused by a low Saxon. I cannot think the bidding will be over-high for her!'

The crimson sprang into the girl's pale cheeks; her father looked at her with love. 'Your mother makes overmuch of this affair! What after all is it? The young man is already promised—so who's to blame?'

'You are to blame!' Adelais cried out. 'You are to blame that you took no better thought before you sent your offer into England. But the girl wanted it. You'd not refuse her any toy!'

He ignored her mockery; he said peaceably, since he could not entirely acquit himself, 'Well, now we know where we are!'

'Let us hope so!' My lady sent her daughter a thoughtful glance.

The silence was broken by a soft movement as the girl rose. 'Sir... Madam... if I might be excused.'

Adelais gave an irritable nod; but Baldwin, arm about his daughter, said, 'Do not trouble yourself in this matter. But in one thing your mother is right; some blame there is—and it is all mine. I should have made stricter enquiry. But for all that it is a good young man—still, we'll find you a better. You are young; over-young to marry. I care not at all for marriage between children; and I am glad to keep my daughter a little, yet.'

She took his hand and laid it against her cheek. He was surprised and touched; gestures of affection came rare to her. She passed through the arras, the gown of fine, bright wool trailing upon the stone floor. The little page, crop-headed, picked up the hem of her skirt as she passed; she twitched it away, impatient, lifted it before her in both long, fine hands and went, quiet, away.

Her father watched her still, loving the grace with which she walked. She was small-made—in that she took after his house, but she was perfectly proportioned—and there she took after her mother; himself and his sons were broad, shortish men, all. She was so beautiful, this young child of his! Those deep grey eyes set in the wide forehead, the fine oval of her face, the soft-flowing waves of her dark hair. She looked gentle, and her smallness gave her a fragile look; but, as he well knew, she was neither. Looks and nature, both, she had inherited from her mother. Her blood brooked no contradiction—inheritance from him as well as from her mother. Men called him gentle; but it was a gentleness he knew how to stiffen at need. Well, it was good she should have the strength to fight, to defy—if need be. A pity, though, she couldn't have the man of her choice, her life would have gone easier so; Brihtric was an easy sort of fellow—too easy, maybe. It was like having too many sweetmeats; she would, perhaps, have tired of him!

He sighed, a little, watching her out of sight.

Across the great hall she went and through the heavy doors fastened back now for carrying in trestles for dinner. At the heels of servants dogs fought and pushed and slank back from the well-aimed kick; then, kick forgotten, began their pushing and fighting all over again. So it is with men! Baldwin sighed a little.

Up the twisting stairs the girl went to the north tower of the great house. This last year she had demanded a chamber of her own; she would no longer share the women's dormitory. It was not fitting for the daughter of the house; the only daughter.

'A daughter of the house needs guarding more than most!' her mother had said. 'Oh, not your virtue—God forbid I should doubt it! But gossip. It springs from nowhere to bespatter the great; it has a way of spreading—and before you know it, there's a scandal on your hands!'

They had fought on the matter and had come to terms at last. Her own chamber she should have; but she must share it with Agnes her nurse. And to that she had agreed; one could always turn the old woman out.

The turret-door stood ajar; the old nurse seated upon a stool was darning a scarf of fine silk; Matilda had torn it carelessly passing. Agnes rose to her feet. Her young lady was white to the lips... frightened; she was very frightened. Agnes had never seen her like this before; the girl had a proud spirit. But Agnes knew the reason. Reason and reason enough for fear! She said, very gentle, 'What ails you, demoiselle, my darling?'

'The answer from England. He'll not have me!' Again the girl affected to shrug.

'What then? A pleasant young man and you fancied him. But young men like him—they grow on every tree!' Head bent upon the fine silk, she was concerned, it would seem, only with her work—under, over, went the careful needle; under, over.

Matilda said, at last, 'That isn't the whole of it!'

'I know,' the old woman said, 'I've known it these three months.' And seeing terror leap to the girl's eyes, added quickly, 'No-one else, though. No-one handles your linen but me.'

Matilda said no more. She did not ask for help; but *Help me. Help me.* The dark troubled eyes spoke for her.

Agnes shook her head. 'You must speak to Madam, your mother.' And seeing the girl stiffen and grow whiter—if that could be—said, very earnest, 'There's nothing I would not do for you, if I might, though it cost me my life. But the thing on your heart could mean *your* life, my darling—and that I could not do. In this affair your mother is the only one. Oh, she will be angry, and very angry; that you must expect. But her bark is worse than her bite. She will have her say; and then she will arrange everything—you will see! No-one will know; not even my lord, your father. I was your mother's nurse. I understand her very well.'

And, since the girl stood dumb and obstinate with fear, added, 'The thing is hard to tell, and hard to hear. Yet, I fancy, she has made some guess already; her eyes are sharper than most. Why else, do you think, she allowed the offer to be sent into England? She had other plans for you—that I know. Now she waits for you to speak; then she will do what must be done. But first you must rest; stay quiet awhile.' Already she was unlacing the close-fitting gown.

Standing there in her shift the girl looked childish, forlorn, so that Agnes thought, pitying, We forget, even I that know her body as my own, how small she is, how young! And now the girl was taken with a fit of trembling so that Agnes thought, I gave the right advice; the only advice. But still at the thought of the coming interview she was troubled—a great deal for her young lady and, somewhat, for herself.

Matilda lay beneath the fur coverings; gradually the shivering stopped, warmth crept back to her limbs. Safe for a little from prying eyes, she let the rare tears have their way. The afternoon sun, falling dusty through the window-slit, struck arrows of rainbow light into wet eyes. Anger was dead in her; she was racked with fear, she was sick with shame. But, for all that, Agnes was right. She must tell her mother; and certainly my lady would take everything into her capable hands. *Virginity is a valuable commodity in the marriage-market; it is, indeed, the indispensable commodity.* More than once she had heard her mother berating some demoiselle slipped from virtue. Yes, her mother would see to it that the virginity of her daughter was not called in question.

Her mother's help. It shone like a light in a far harbour—but first one must venture the stormy seas.

At the thought of that stormy passage her distressed mind shrank; drearily it went back to the past.

She had loved him, Brihtric the Fair, the Bright Chief. She had loved him before ever she had known it; at fourteen one does not recognise the face of love. Her heart had been given; but not her body. That was a different matter. Yet he had taken that, too. She had not wanted to give him either. He was a Saxon; and though of good birth, not as high as she had been taught to look. Well, her heart being gone, there was nothing she could do about it. But her body—she had fought for it. In spite of all the love leaping with in her, beating down her will, she had known she must not give in. Girls must be chaste; and especially a girl whose marriage is the affair of Christendom. Virginity lost, a girl be she never so fair, never so gifted, never so high-born and richly dowered, must waste in loneliness—if, indeed, no worse fate befall. There were tales of girls thrust by parents within a dungeon; or, at very best, within a nunnery—and the difference was not so great after all! Girls paid the rest of their lives for their sweet sin.

Yet in the end he had persuaded her. It was no sin. They were promised one to the other; in honour bound, husband and wife—a secret betrothal, but not the less binding. It wanted but her father's word. That *his* father should not speak that word, he had never for a moment considered. The match was very great.

Husband and wife, and within a few hours he would be gone. But he would be back at once, he swore it. Her father had but to make the proposal—as was proper because of his exalted position; but who could doubt the outcome? Let her be kind then; how could she let him go hungering and thirsting?

So in the end he had his way.

But how, if there should be no betrothal and no return?

It was a question she had not asked; and now it was too late.

Against closed eyes she saw him as she had seen him then, tall and white-and-gold and burning with love... He drew the bolts of the door, this very room where I lie weeping; he took the covers from the bed, the narrow bed, he spread them upon the floor. He pulled me down...

Again she felt desire shoot through her innermost body so that she must clasp herself, both hands between her thighs, to thrust it down again. But it was useless. If he were here now she must give herself again.

That day he truly loved me; he was honest—I must believe it. He returned home to find his match made. He could not dishonour his father's word—the word spoken for all to hear; could not dishonour the bride they had chosen. But what of the secret word? What of the bride himself had chosen; chosen and taken—and forsaken?

What of me? She turned twisting and weeping upon the bed.

And *What of Agnes?* For the first time she thought of Agnes that had been set to guard her, Agnes that had failed in her charge. *There is nothing I would not do for you though it cost me my life.* When Agnes had said that she had spoken the plain truth. Her punishment would be dire; dire enough to cost her life.

She was taken with fear for Agnes, for Agnes also. Anger sprang again, flamed yet higher. He had taken his pleasure. He had left an old woman no less than a young one to face the consequences. The fierceness of her anger gave rise, as always these past weeks, to threatened sickness. Trying to quiet herself she fought the sickness down.

Maybe he was not so much to blame. Maybe things had proved unexpectedly hard. In England there was unrest; things changed from day to day. Their King was not liked; they didn't altogether care for his piety; his peculiar, excessive piety. *The Confessor* they called him, half-deriding. And he was half-Norman, a foreigner. In all the five years since his crowning he hadn't learned to like his people. And they? They looked not to their King as leader but to Godwine their great earl. That family was altogether too powerful, her father said; they had the King under their thumb. Trouble was coming; her father said that, too. Great men in England must take sides, look to their position. They would, no doubt, marry their children to that end. Brihtric, she must believe it, had been a counter to suit his father's game. He could not, she thought, bitter, have put up too hard a fight! Had he shown some courage, dangled before his father's eyes the Flemish alliance, the great, the unlooked-for match, what then? But maybe it wasn't politic for Algar's house to marry a foreign bride. Well, but he should have thought of that before!

Shame of pregnancy, shame of refusal, threatened her once more with nausea. She dared lie no longer upon the bed. She paced the narrow room... up and down; up and down. She hated him now, this Brihtric, this easy maker of promises, easy breaker of promises. By the blood of Christ, give her the chance, and she'd spoil that handsome face of his, Brihtric Meaw, Brihtric the Fair.

But—her legs gave way beneath her so that she sat suddenly upon the bed—she would never be in a position to punish him. He'd come no more into Flanders; he'd not dare. And, for herself, never would she have occasion to set foot in that barbarous country they called England.

Ah, England. Once she would have been happy to live there for ever, in the sweet west country that Brihtric had spoken of; his father's manor set about with fruiting trees, and the blossom and birds' song. His father had promised him a house when he should be wed—the manor of Felstede. 'You will like it well,' he had promised. 'It stands upon a little hill where soft winds blow; hills as gentle as your own breasts.' And he had caressed them so that beneath his hands the nipples sprang upwards. Well, she would never see those hills, nor Winchester the lovely city—the heart of England he had said. Here she would remain in flat Flanders; she would never marry. She'd had enough of men!

Desolation and fear; and love turned to bitterness, rose in her like a wild sea. She lifted clenched fists and beat herself about the head; Matilda that men called gentle, driven by torment since she could not punish that other, to punish herself.

Hands held above her head, quite suddenly, she stopped. Why this torment? Why this despair? No man was worth it—and her mother would help her; her mother would know what to do.

The handle of the door turned sharply. Matilda did not hear it. Madam the countess Adelais looked down at the sleeping girl, the long dark lashes fringed with tears. Her own face did not soften. She reached out a hand and shook the girl awake.

The interview with her mother was not easy—she had not expected it; but she had not expected the coarseness, either. It was partly her own fault, Matilda must admit it. She had meant to conduct herself with becoming humility, but humility came hard to her; and, for all the wretchedness of her situation, the contempt in her mother's face, the harshness of her manner, stung beyond endurance. Yet she tried; she did try for humility.

'I am sorry, Madam...'

'You have good reason!' Adelais broke in grim. 'Well, we must clean up this mess before your father guesses that his daughter is a shop-soiled virgin—your pardon, mistress, no virgin at all!'

It was not only the contempt and the coarseness, it was the girl's own condition that pressed hard; the whole situation was too much for her extreme youth—she was but fifteen.

'All this talk of virgins; all this pretence!' she cried out trying to shield herself from further insult. 'As if we don't all know better! As if we don't know about the goings-on here, in this very house! As if we didn't know about...' *my father, even.* She had all but said it; she said, instead, 'my uncle's court in Paris!'

'Well, it's a dirty world! Must you make it dirtier? You're a fool, my girl, for all your fine learning. But there's one lesson you haven't learned yet; one lesson that's worth all the rest. If a girl cannot wait for a man until she marry, then she must carry herself like a virgin; she must never—do you hear me?—give rise to gossip that she's none. After marriage, she must, I suppose, do as she pleases; not that I hold with it. I leave that behaviour to the farm yard. A man should know his son's his own.'

Brihtric will never know his son...

Adelais answered the thought; it was clear in the desolation of the girl's whole body.

'But not in this case; not he nor anyone. Breathe a word, and by the body of God, you'll not live to breathe a second! I'll not have your father shamed, nor yet your brothers; no, nor me and my house, neither. You smeared my brother and his court this moment since; how d'you think he'd relish this scandal? You fool, you *fool*! God, it's hard to keep my hands off you! Yet I must take your burden upon me, must plot and plan and lie to keep you from scandalous tongues and from your father's anger, his very proper anger!'

And now it seemed she could control her hands no longer; she seized the girl and—she was a tall woman—shook her like a terrier a rat.

'...as though she would shake the child out of me!' Matilda told Agnes later. 'And by the holy name of God I wish she had!'

'Be thankful she didn't strike you! Me, I was not so lucky. Yet luckier than I thought; it seems she has some use for me. I got off with a whipping—though you might say I'm over-old for that!' She moved to ease smarting shoulders. 'It might have cost me a hand; and where would I be then? A useless mouth to feed; she'd have sent me away. The loss of a hand I could endure; but to send me away from you and from her—that I could not endure. I'd rather, believe it, die!'

'To go from *her*, would that grieve you?'

'To my death. She's my nurseling, also. She can be hard—and very hard; but at heart she's sound. Well, thank God we've taken the first hurdle. She's said her say and she'll say no more; that I promise you. For all her sharp tongue she's easy to understand; easier than you, my lady. With her it follows a pattern—fierce anger, harsh words, a blow, maybe. And then—all over! But you? Who can tell? What you think and what you'll do, there's no knowing. Very quiet you are, very gentle—so it would seem. But underneath's a different story. My lord your father thinks he has a loving, obedient daughter...'

'So he has.'

'So he has—so long as he's a loving, obedient father. But you'll never hurt yourself with obedience. Under all those gentle ways you're self-willed as they come!'

'Sly then? Deceitful?'

'I'd not say that! But you bide your time; there's a sort of silence in you. And what you'll do, no living soul can guess; not even those that know you best—or think they do! You have, I've thought it often, a root of darkness in you.'

The girl lifted a bewildered head; the old woman nodded.

'You are capable of dark deeds, my lady—though you don't believe it. Not often; once in a lifetime, or twice, or thrice maybe. Or, again, maybe, never. But come some great anger or some dark event—and the darkness in you will rise to meet it. It comes from that streak in your blood; they have it, all those of Rollo's house—the viking streak. Death by treachery, by poison, by a stab in the back; their history shows it plain. But if you are lucky and if you are wise—and it is for this I warn you—then, no dark deed; no dark deed at all!'

Agnes did, indeed, know her nurseling. Adelais had been distressed and furious; distress remained but the fury had gone. Her violent words, like a strong current, had carried it away. She spoke no more on the subject save to give Agnes her orders; to Matilda herself—no word good or bad.

Within the week those two had left Ghent.

'I have sent our daughter into the country,' she told Baldwin returned from a hunting party. 'The town is too enclosed, too noisy, too stinking-hot! Old nurse will look to her.'

He nodded satisfied. Certainly the girl had looked white and listless; the spirit out of her. Adelais remained in Ghent. She could safely leave all to Agnes that had brought the girl and her brothers into the world.

It was a hard life alone with Agnes; such stark living the girl had never imagined. A one-roomed cottage, isolated and, save for some sticks of furniture, bare. In this cottage Agnes herself had been born; and in the village where they went to buy food, they were accepted—an old woman returned home with her widowed grand-daughter. A hard life, indeed, a rough-and-ready life but safe; safe from spiteful eyes and spiteful tongues.

The summer days dragged and the autumn days. In late October Matilda's child was born.

A long, hard labour. She lay silent while the pains all-but wrenched her small bones apart. She had known it must be bad; but that it should be bad as this she had not dreamed. She lay drenched in her sweat; only her lips bitten through and running with blood showed the measure of her anguish.

She was free of her burden. Her desecrated body was her own again. It was her first thought; she thanked God for that. Agnes brought the baby for her to see; a large child, Saxon-fair. Brihtric's child—child of the man that had betrayed her. This creature had wrenched her bones apart in anguish. She commanded Agnes to take it from her sight. She did not so much as ask whether it was son or daughter.

Agnes distrusted this dislike. Sometimes it came with childbirth—she had experience enough to know it. But returning strength might bring an outburst of natural love, more passionate for first rejection. The girl, obstinate and proud, might refuse to part with her child. Heaven be thanked Madam countess had made all arrangements. Before Matilda could ask again for her child, it was gone.

She should be glad, Matilda supposed, that all was so happily arranged. But she was not glad. Now she wanted her child; heart and breasts ached for her child. Now, tears pouring down her cheeks, she asked incessantly about the little one.

'A little girl, my demoiselle,' Agnes said. 'A fine enough child; but you are better without it.' And when the girl pressed for news—where had they taken it? To what house? What people? What *kind* of people? Agnes lifted a closed face. She did not know. But she knew; she knew! It was clear in her face. Driven and pressed, the old nurse said at last, 'I went free of punishment once. I was spared only because I was of use. This is no matter of a whipping; for this I could lose my tongue.'

She was free of her shame; she was safe. But safety carried its own punishment—a punishment hard and unexpected. She was bound to the lost child as surely as if the cord had never been cut. She was unfree; forever bound.

'It will pass,' Agnes said. 'It will pass, you will see. You must stop weeping, my demoiselle, you will kill yourself with weeping.'

Matilda was back in Bruges. Her father, having remarked that she looked no better for the country air, said no more. He had his suspicions and preferred to know nothing. He intended his daughter to make a great marriage to tip the balance of power in Europe in his own direction; that she should be no longer a virgin was a disaster he could not afford to contemplate.

She had come back meaning to leave the past behind her, but she would find herself weeping in the solitude of her own chamber and there, Adelais, coming upon her, would scold her for an ungrateful fool.

She found, surprised, that there was sense in her mother's roughness; the more often she forbade the tears, the less often they were likely to threaten. Agnes, she found, was right, also. With returning strength her grief grew less; sometimes for days, together, she would forget the child she had abandoned. But when she told herself that soon, soon she would forget it altogether, she would find herself waking from sleep, her face wet with tears.

The winter days went slowly by and now it was spring. Down by the river they were cutting young willow-shoots for baskets and the primroses were out. A new spring, a new beginning—and she had not dreamed of the child for weeks. Returned strength had given her back her looks; indeed, she was handsomer than she had been. Always thin, she had rounded a little; and she had lost her childish look of obedience. She had learned a lovely carriage of the head; pride sat well upon her. She had been a pretty girl; now, for all her tender years, she was a woman and beautiful. They sang her beauty—which was clear to the eyes of all. They sang her modesty, her virgin chastity—to that she would listen with a small smile. She was chaste because she was cold, out of love with men. Of them and their treachery she had had enough, enough. She would never love, never willingly give herself again.

It was unfortunate that William of Normandy should choose this time to ask her hand in marriage. Unfortunate the time, unfortunate the manner.

The Young William

II

The fact concerning his birth was a cross he must carry all his life; a wounding and a pain that must go with him to his death. A pain that, sometimes quiescent, would fester and erupt and, like an abscess, burst into the most savage anger.

Through his father he was of that line of dukes derived from Rollo the Norseman and he was of close kinship with Edward King of England—the saintly King they called the Confessor. But his great lineage and high kinship was ruined—his mother stank of the tanyard and he was her bastard; and both these things his enemies never let him forget. Yet, of himself, he could remember no life but that of the castle; he could not remember, even, being taken from his mother.

He had never known his mother. He had never been loved nor comforted, nor even treated as a child. But that had its other side. Even as a very little boy he had been respected and, curiously, feared; it was because of his courage, his high temper and, above all, his strong will. He had never missed his mother since he had never known her; yet he had been aware of missing something. He saw other boys, son of count or swineherd, run to their mothers and there find comfort; himself he moved in isolation.

Before he understood the truth of his birth, he would ask this one and that, what had happened to his mother. *Dead*, one would say; *gone away*, said another. And his nurse that resented the fierce child, the peasant child, the little interloper, said once, *You'll know one day, little bastard!*

He was five years old then and didn't know what a bastard might be; so when he said he'd ask his father, she told him, very sharp, he'd better not—or it would be the worse for him!

His father was the one creature he genuinely feared; but he adored him, too—duke Robert so young, so debonair. Twenty-three and swift of foot and gallant on his horse; a strong arm and a keen eye and a laughing mouth. How should a child—or man or woman either—not be taken with the splendour of him they called the Magnificent, though there were plenty to call him a less flattering name—*le Diable*. And he could be a devil, too, William thought. When he was in one of his rages his eyes would go pale as water and blind-looking as if they saw nothing. That William himself had these same eyes, he didn't know as yet.

He was just five years old when the palace boys came into the castle at Rouen. William needed schooling, so in they came—a dozen little lordlings; tough, every one. He was not good at lessons—he had no time; he had to be the leader because he was his father's son—and he was the youngest of them all. And soon he was the leader; but he had had to fight for his position. When he fought and won, all was well and his father was pleased. But if he lost, though the other boy was older and heavier, then though he came from the fight with a black eye and bloodied nose, he was beaten by Turold who instructed him in the skills of the bow; though no other boy was ever beaten because William had bested him. It was not fair. He summoned enough courage—and courage it needed—to ask his father the reason.

'Because,' duke Robert said, hiding his love for the small, determined boy, 'you must always be twice as strong and twice as brave and three times as clever as any other in Normandy—or outside Normandy!'

It was a hard saying and he did not understand it. It must be, he thought, because he was his father's son. That there could be any other reason he had not yet learned. He was full seven—just before his father went away for ever—when he learned the truth of his birth.

One of the palace boys had defied him; William FitzOsbern whom he hated most and who later, turned out to be his best friend. William wasn't going to stand any defiance; and, since he did not relish a whipping into the bargain, he put his full weight behind the blows. The other boy, beaten but defiant still, hiccoughed through the blood in his mouth, *Bastard*. William's hands dropped. *Bastard*. It was the word his nurse had flung at him, daring him to repeat it to his father. It was the word he'd caught more than once, whispered behind his back; a troubling word. What had it to do with him? He had the uncomfortable feeling that it had much to do with him. Now—the other boy standing there beaten yet triumphant—the half-whispers, the wretchedness the word always brought, rushed upon him. Driven by anger whose cause he did not fully understand, he brought the weight of his fist smashing into that grinning face. And now, giving himself no time to hesitate, he ran, need driving him, straight to his father's closet.

Duke Robert was not there; in council, William was told. So to the council chamber he marched; though now his anger had had time to cool. It was a considerable thing to do. Unless he himself commanded it, duke Robert saw no-one; and, certainly not a small boy though that boy was his only son. To break in upon my lord duke when he sat in council, was a thing unheard of. He was cold as stone as he bade the boy wait outside.

Duke Robert conducted his business leisurely. He had seen at one glance how white and wild the boy, and the blood streaming from the cut that had laid open his cheek. It was only, in part, for the sake of discipline he had ordered the boy to wait; William needed time to recover himself.

When the councillors had gone, Robert beckoned to his son. 'It is ill manners to burst in upon your father and duke without being sent for. Well?' And he would not show, least of all to the tall, handsome child, his pride, his love of this, his only son.

William came to the point at once. 'What's a bastard?'

Duke Robert's eyes went cold as glass.

'You are one!' And he was as direct as the boy himself.

'It is a bad thing to be?'

'It is what you make of it. But all the same you must punish any man that calls you so to your face.'

'For telling the truth?'

'For telling the truth. There are some truths better left unsaid.'

'Then I had better know what a bastard is.'

Robert set the boy between his knees. 'Some men are married; and some are not.'

'You are not?'

'Unfortunately I am—or was when you were born. When a man cannot marry a woman but lives with her as his wife—you know what I mean?'

23

The boy nodded. Life in the castle was open to all; he knew exactly what his father meant.

'When a man sleeps with a woman—you know what happens.'

William nodded again. He had not helped with the dogs and the horses for nothing. And anything he might have missed the other boys had told him.

'Well then, I took a woman. But I did not marry her. You are her child and mine.'

'And does that make me a bastard?'

Duke Robert nodded. 'But since I am your father, it might make you something more.'

'What could it make me?'

'It could make you duke of Normandy.'

Well, but he had expected that; he was his father's son.

'So now,' duke Robert said, 'you know why you must be twice as strong and twice as brave and three times cleverer than any other man.'

'Because I am to be duke.'

'No. Because you are a bastard. Go away and think about it.'

'Did you know my mother?'

The nurse nodded; a fat woman, thin hair hidden beneath her wimple, the veins of her face branching purple beneath the skin. He had never come to her for comfort, even as a baby; he had sensed, even then, her unwillingness to be kind.

'Tell me about her. I don't even know her name.'

'It's best forgotten. Arlette they called her; and a pretty harlot she was!'

He caught the word *pretty*; the other he took to be some form of his mother's name. So she had been pretty! He was glad of that!

'A wench that stank of her father's hides.'

He could not take in the exact meaning of that; but it had a familiar ring. He would not ask her any more; plainly she had spoken in spite. When he was duke he'd cut out her tongue.

Reading displeasure in the boy's face she said, spiteful still, 'I'll tell you no more. There's plenty besides me knew your mother—and better qualified to speak!' And she was eaten with bitterness because she and Arlette were the same age; but Arlette was sleek and smooth and golden—a young woman still. But she herself? A servant worn with years

24

of drudgery dancing attendance on Arlette's bastard. Yet she'd been as pretty as Arlette once; but it was Arlette caught the young count's eye.

'Did you know my mother?' he asked Roger of Beaumont, his father's friend and his own tutor.

'Yes, I knew her.'

'Did she stink of the tanyard?'

'By God no! Your father would never have touched her. She smelt of fresh-cut grass and honeysuckle. And lovely to look at! Honey and cream and roses.'

'When did she die?'

'She isn't dead.'

'Then where does she live?'

'You must ask your father that.'

'I'd rather ask you.'

And, being pressed and prayed, de Beaumont said, at last, 'Your father gave her to a good gentleman.'

'*Gave* her?'

'In marriage. She lives beyond Falaise. She does not care for the court.'

'You mean my father does not want her here?'

'You may put it so.' And how quickly the boy was growing up! 'Yet it is not the whole truth. He loved her; and because of that he looked to her safety. A man like your father is forever at war; what would come to her if he should chance to die? So he gives her to a good gentleman to guard as his treasure. And, indeed, you are fortunate both. You, your father breeds as his son that might now be helping your grandfather in the tanyard. And she? She is a gentle woman commanding her servants, that might herself be a servant; she is delicate and fair that might be worn and gone to seed like that fat scold your nurse—they are of an age.'

And seeing the boy bewildered and dissatisfied still, he said, 'But these things—a man may long for a woman he may not marry, you do not understand; nor is it right you should. But one day you will understand; and you will know that, though many men breed their bastards, there's few to behave as well as your father!'

'I hate him!' And the boy was the image of his father, his eyes blind and pale with anger.

'Maybe at the moment. One day you'll feel different. Meanwhile keep your hate between your teeth; it might cost you a dukedom.'

'It could not. I am my father's son.'

'His bastard. It carries no right to inherit. For a man to put his bastard in his own high place would argue some courage... and much love.'

'What other son has a better claim?' And he'd not be grateful for his rights.

'There's no son but you. But there are others with a better claim. True-born. Your cousin Guy of Burgundy for one! There goes a young gentleman you should watch!'

So! There were true-born heirs. Young as he was, he knew the meaning of that! He must no longer take it for granted that he should one day sit in his father's place. Even should his father desire it, the councillors, the vicomtes, the nobles and the knights might well refuse—he saw that plain. He was seven years old; old enough to keep anger between his teeth. Though he bit his tongue through he'd say no word.

Robert the Magnificent whom men call *the Devil*—and not, as he was the first to admit, without reason—was weary body and soul. His life had not been unduly sanctified; and no man lived for ever. He was young enough, five-and-twenty; but a man couldn't live his sort of life—hard fighting, hard riding, hard drinking, to say nothing of less innocent pursuits—without paying for it. And if he left the account too long, he might pay overmuch. An accident, a stab in the back, a poisoned cup, or a simple fever might mean eternal damnation. He'd known strong men carried off in the winking of an eye; today lusty and full of life, tomorrow dead and in the grave. He must make his peace with God; now, while there was time. And he'd make it in the way of a Christian gentleman. He'd make his pilgrimage; in the holy places of Jerusalem he would pray forgiveness. Then, a better man, back he would come to rule in peace till it was time to lay his bones in the beloved soil of Normandy.

To Jerusalem he would go. But what of William? William, he meant to be next duke—and this was the time to make sure of it. There could be no better choice. He knew the boy's quality; strong beyond his age, and courage to match it. He could take a beating without whining and give back better than he got. He knew how to keep his mouth shut at need. He was a born leader of men. From the moment of his birth there had been signs and wonders and miracles foretold. From his conception, even—that first night they'd put Arlette in his bed. He hadn't been in love with her then; only hungry for her young body—as is the way with a lusty boy. And she? Proud to have been chosen. Gentle and loving, so that they'd taken their joy together. And then she'd gone off to sleep, peaceful as a child; but in the dark of the morning she'd awakened with a cry. There she was, bolt upright in the bed, both hands clutched upon her belly. She'd dreamed a dream. A great tree had sprung from her body; a tree that reached to the sky and cast its sheltering arms upon all Normandy, and upon England, too! Half-asleep, he'd scarcely listened; lazily, he'd reached out and taken her again. It was only later that he remembered her dream. He must tell William one day.

Next morning he'd sent her back to her father. He'd enjoyed her but he hadn't loved her then; and there were women enough to throw themselves at his head!

Arlette had been carrying his child but he hadn't known it. He'd been away fighting for his liege lord the King of France. The boy was actually born before he'd so much as known she was pregnant. And when he did hear he was not pleased. That year, the year of grace ten hundred and twenty-seven, was the important one in his life. It saw him—his brother having suddenly died—translated from count to duke; duke of Normandy. And, what he had thought almost as important, since it must secure the succession, he had just married. That the year was most of all important—and not to himself alone—because it had seen the birth of his bastard, he was not to dream. Instead he had tried to persuade himself that this bastard was none of his. But that Arlette had been a virgin that night, was certain; and, one look at the child, so he'd been told, was enough to show who was the father.

His marriage had not been at all important; it hadn't lasted long. To bed with Estrith had been a misery; so back she'd gone to her brother Cnut to make all England ring with her wrongs. Of his own wrongs no-one ever thought. A wealthy widow, Estrith—and mean; mean with her body, mean with her purse. Skinflint and shrew. In the end he'd laid hands upon her; she'd driven him mad with her clack. Let her thank her God she'd escaped alive to tell the tale!

It was only after she'd gone that he'd taken William into his household. Already he'd heard of the wonderful babe in the house of Fulbert the

Tanner; how the new-born child being set upon the floor—since his mother bled—he had clutched upon the rushes and would not let them go. And how the midwife, all amazed, had cried out, *Here's a little lord that takes his seizin. What he has he'll never let go!*

The first time he'd seen his son the boy was a year old—and crawling in the muck of the tanyard. He'd picked up the baby—flesh of his own flesh; himself in little, the thin child with the pale blue eyes and the dark russet-red hair. He had gone weak as water—a new experience that! He had actually trembled, holding the child. Ashamed of his weakness he had set it down again. In this moment he had spared no thought for Arlette; he had not so much as asked for her.

That night he had awakened crying out that someone had cut down the tree, the tree that was to shelter Normandy; nor could he sleep again lest some evil had already befallen the little one in the filth of the tanyard. He'd sent for the boy in the grey of the morning, not waiting for sunrise.

It was only then, when the child was safe, that he remembered Arlette. He would not share the mother of his son with any man. He had not brought her into the castle—it was not fitting; he intended to breed up the child as a prince of his house. He had set her up in a sufficient house; he had visited her when he chose; he had chosen, often.

Those early days he had not dreamed of marrying her; she was still the tanner's daughter, the washerwoman down by the stream. Later he would have married her—but his shrew still lived. So Arlette remained his darling sin; and his boy a bastard.

But, conscience forever troubling on her account, he had—though it had all-but torn the heart from his body—given her a dowry and married her to a good man far above her station. Three years ago he had done it and he hadn't seen her since. He had sworn to play honest with the good man her husband. On her bridal night he had lain awake restless with jealousy, but it had been nothing to the anguish with which he heard she had borne her husband a son; two sons she had by him now. And, though his own heart was set on holy things, still he would lie hungering for her body and burning with jealousy because she would bear her husband yet more children.

Well, maybe, his pilgrimage would cleanse him of his sins. But first he must look to the boy!

William should be the next duke. There'd be trouble about it; trouble with those that could themselves claim the dukedom—and no drop of bastard blood. And there'd be trouble with his comtes and vicomtes, too. For the most part they'd not relish a child for a duke—and a bastard at that! The first step was to call them together; to make them swear fealty to his son. The oath was but to set his mind at rest—that was perfectly clear. He was going a long journey; but he was young and strong and he would return. He would return to punish those that had broken the oath.

But even if they should, each and all, take the oath, it was a first step, only. He had still to reckon with his overlord the King of France. Well, one step at a time. He would summon the princes of church and state together with his vicomtes that held the reins of government in remoter parts; they should meet at Fécamp. He had been generous to the monastery there; maybe the monks would help him with their prayers.

III

He sat in his father's great chair. For all the cressets flaring upon the walls, it was dark this autumn afternoon. For all the great fires leaping each end of the great hall, and the braziers set against the walls; for all the press of bodies—knights and bishops and vicomtes and comtes come at his father's summons—the air was cold and stale.

The chair was very high; even though he sat at the edge of the seat, his toes scarce touched the floor. He knew exactly what he must do and what he must say. He had, of course, long known how the act of homage was taken; he had seen it a hundred times. But now he, himself, was to receive it—a very different thing. He took comfort from the thought that, but this morning, he had rehearsed his part and his father had been well-pleased. Now duke Robert stood by the side of the great chair; the fact gave him courage.

He was a little sorry for his father who was handing over his duchy. *I will never let go of anything that is mine, not as long as I live. A man shouldn't undress till he goes to bed.*

Duke Robert waited for the rustling of gowns and cloaks to stop—priests and lords settling themselves; then, in the silence he spoke. 'Sirs, I go a journey to purge me of my sins in God's Holy Places; and, also, to thank Him for the blessings of peace and plenty He has bestowed upon our land.'

'But—' and his voice sharpened a little, 'unless there be a duke in this duchy, there'll be neither peace nor plenty—you will be each at the other's throat; that is the nature of men. Therefore until you satisfy me that all will go well, I cannot leave. So I lose my chance of salvation and God the thanks that are His due. Therefore I require you to swear the oath to this, my son—to accept him in my place, your true lord till I return. And, that I shall return, make no doubt.'

He held them with pale, terrible eyes.

'You shall swear to take him as your lord; and I shall leave you such a council as shall please you well. How say you, sirs?'

They were not pleased. William sat there, very straight in his father's place and knew their thoughts... *A bastard to rule over us; a bastard and a child!*

Robert said, and the boy was shocked by the love in his voice, 'He is little, but he'll grow.'

They were whispering together, but in the end they would agree; his father had told him so. There were other claimants, but for all that, no real choice. There was, first and foremost, his father's uncle, Robert archbishop of Rouen, count of Evreux. He was rich and he was powerful; but he was a churchman and too old to change his ways. There was Guy of Burgundy and Alan of Brittany—both in true descent; but each through his mother. Good Normans preferred descent in the male line. And, besides, these two were strangers more or less, their first interest lay in the land of their birth. As for the rest—bastards all! To begin with there were his father's half brothers, Malger the sly bishop and William count of Arques—ambitious and greedy, both. If bastards were in the running, who better than his father's son?

The whispering lords had come to a conclusion. They were not pleased that their lord was leaving them to turmoil and lawlessness, still less pleased at the prospect of a little bastard as their duke. But they would swear—and wait for what the future would bring; a man could, at need, break his oath. A show of agreement would end the discussion.

The lord Robert archbishop of Rouen spoke for them all.

'Sir, we must still regret that you leave this land you have kept in peace. But a man's soul must come first. We agree to accept this your son; and are ready to swear the oath:' He knelt, the old man, and put his frail hands between the young small hands, and spoke the oath, *I become your liegeman for life and death and earthly regard. I will keep faith and loyalty to you for life and death, God helping me.* The boy in the great chair bent forward and kissed his great-uncle upon both cheeks and sealed the bargain between them. And, the others pressing forward, one by one, Osbern his father's kinsman and chamberlain, asked of each man his name and station and spoke it aloud.

'My lord William Talvas, of Belesme, of Alençon and Sées.'

There he stood, that same Talvas, the cruel man that had cursed the infant William in his cradle, but for all that, he must swear the oath, his bloody hands between the innocent hands of the boy. *What faith from you?* William wondered, those bloody hands still within his own.

'The lord Robert, count of Eu, the lord Alan, count of Brittany, the lord Guy, count of Burgundy, the lord Hugh, bishop of Bayeux, the lord bishop Malger, the lord Vauquelin of Ferrières St. Hilaire, the lord Robert of Grantmesnil, the lord William of Jumièges, the lord Tristan of Bastenbourg.'

On and on; and all kneeling and swearing and receiving the kiss. And, after them, the lesser lords, the vicomtes, the knights.

William was growing weary but still he sat upright and attentive. 'The lord Raoul of Toeni and Conche, the lord William of Bricbeque, Herlouin knight and vicomte of Contéville...'

He felt himself stiffen at that name. Even while the red-faced man knelt, William could not forbear his thoughts. *Is she here, with you, the woman that slept in my father's bed and bore him a son that, for all his glories, is still a bastard?* He felt his mouth shake but he had learned his lessons well. He leant forward and kissed the red cheeks either side.

And now Osbern himself, his father's kinsman, faithful friend and careful steward; a man to trust.

It was over; at long last, over. And now trestles were brought in for the feasting. For the first time William sat at the high table next to his father; and his cousins Guy and Alan served him on bended knee. Tonight he could eat and drink as much as he pleased; but he did not need Roger of Beaumont to tell him that a drunken man looks a fool; he had seen that for himself. Never in his life would he take too much to drink. When he caught sight of de Contéville at a lower table; he found himself wondering again about his mother. Had she come with her husband? If he met her, would he, unknowing, pass her by? Or, if he should know her at once—his blood answering hers—should he still pass her by? He had asked his governor. 'You will behave like a Christian gentleman,' de Beaumont had said; and what did he mean by that?

He was late seeking his bed; the old man, archbishop Robert, had told him, 'This day you undertake a great charge. It is fitting to ask God's help.' From the feast he had gone straight to the chapel; he had knelt and prayed, vowing—God helping him—to be a good man and a good ruler.

He must have fallen asleep, for he found himself tumbled side ways before the altar and very cold. He rose, a little stiff and rubbing his eyes. Time to seek his bed.

He heard, as he passed, movement from his father's room—a rhythm of noise; a sigh, a groan, a sharp cry. He passed into his own chamber. Darkness was lightening, a little. The cry had disturbed him, wrecking the peace prayer had brought. He had the fancy, now, not to sleep; but to watch this great day out. He was leaning at the window—when he heard it; the light tap upon his door. Before he could answer, the door opened gently and she stood there.

His mother. He knew her at once; because she *was* honey and cream and roses—as de Beaumont had said. She was young; a girl, almost. Her face was flushed and her eyes, her sea-blue eyes were shining; her golden hair hung careless and bright upon her shoulders. She was dressed—but only just; as though she had thrown on her clothes in a hurry. She was pretty, he'd not call her lovely—she was a little plump for that; he liked a woman to be delicate and fine. But she was pretty, she was very pretty.

He felt not the slightest quickening of his blood. She was a stranger. And there was something about her that offended him—the flushed cheeks, the hanging hair, the disordered gown. And now the meaning of those sounds from his father's room flashed upon him; these last weeks he had been learning fast.

They stood looking at each other—she, all love, all admiration; he all disgust. He could not like her—but yet he liked her eyes; they were honest eyes. And—Roger had been right—she didn't smell of the tan-yard; she smelt like any other lady of some sweet essence; it didn't quite cover the smell of woman.

She said, and her voice trembled a little, 'You know who I am?'

He nodded, noting that, although she affected the speech of gentle-women, she could not disguise the flat peasant accent. She waited, he saw, for him to speak, to say some kind word. There was nothing he could say. She was his mother; and she was a stranger. And, in spite of her honest eyes, she was not honest. Tonight she had dishonoured her husband; would she beget yet another bastard? The facts of his birth forever rankled. Yet she *was* his mother.

He opened his mouth but no words came. The whole thing was beyond him. He was, after all, but seven years old.

And still she stood looking at him; she made no movement to touch him or to come near him... *This is the child I carried in joy and bore in anguish; but the anguish when they took him from the womb was nothing to the anguish when they took him from my arms. Well, he is no longer that child, ...and there is nothing left...*

She said, softly, 'God be praised that sent this day!' And then, the wonder bursting forth, 'That my son should be duke of Normandy!'

He wanted to cry out, *Not yours; my father's.* He was angry that, on this great day, she must prick him with the shame of his birth. She was stupid, as her peasant speech proclaimed her. But he must say some-thing—something; if it were but one word. He could find no word.

She said, and, for the moment, he forgot her common speech in the sweetness of her smile, 'Well now you are a great gentleman. God keep you so. A bonny fighter, too, they say. Well, you'll have need.' She sighed a little. 'You are too small to be left to the violence of greedy men.'

He was angered still more that she had brought his greatness to the level of a little boy.

'Well,' she said, 'here's my wish for you. Be a good Christian and an honest man. But—' and she was unexpectedly bitter, 'you are honest, enough, already! For, if you cannot speak the truth to say you are glad to see me, at least you tell me no lies. Well, I think we shall not meet again. So, God be with you... and remember me sometimes.'

'I am not likely to forget you!' he said, a little spiteful and was sorry the moment he had spoken.

She said and now she was smiling a little, 'This way or that—so long as you *do* remember!' She took a step forward and, kneeling humble as a servant, lifted his hand and kissed it; and, not without her own dignity, was gone.

He stood looking at his hand and not knowing what to do. He began to tremble. He had thought himself unmoved; but, for all that, he could not stop trembling. And now, though this day he had been accepted in his father's place and though he was a big boy, all of seven years, this ending had been too much. He flung himself upon the bed not caring how he spoilt his fine new clothes. He longed to weep yet was unable to weep; for him there could be no easy release in tears.

They were gone—two—before he awoke in full morning-light, stiff in his crumpled clothes.

Robert was pleased with the boy. The long ordeal of swearing he had taken with untiring dignity; and, at the feast, had shown that same dignity. He had, as was fitting, gone thereafter to pray. He had not wept over his mother nor shown a silly sweetness; he had been quiet and self-contained. One might have wished a little more kindness; but to expect a seven-year-old to keep a perfect balance was asking too much. His behaviour in both difficult circumstances promised well.

They had sworn the oath, bishops and nobles, vicomtes and knights. But duke Robert was troubled, still. 'I do not trust them!' he told de Beaumont and Osbern, the three of them at their wine.

'Rebellion; that might not be the worst of it. There are some, sweet Christ forbid, would make an end of the boy altogether. I cannot risk it. I shall carry the boy to Paris; I shall ask King Henry to look to William till he's old enough to look to himself.'

'You must first make Henry accept the boy as his vassal,' Osbern said. 'Only so can he confirm William in his dukedom. Then, any man that turns against the boy, breaks two oaths; not only to you his lord and duke of Normandy but to his sovereign lord the King of France.'

'I know. I know! Do you think I haven't thought of that! But it will not be easy.'

'You must remind him of old friendship,' de Beaumont said, 'of help given him in his wars; without your help he'd not be on his throne now. He's touchy, though; dwell gently upon that obligation.'

'Offer to pray for him in the most sacred places!' Osbern grinned. 'That will fetch him!'

'Point out the advantage of having a child on the throne of Normandy—and that child his vassal and his ward. Make much of the fact that leaving William behind in Paris, you leave him under the King's direct control,' de Beaumont said. 'But, indeed, the boy himself is his best advocate—an ornament to any court—good looks, good manners; clever with hawk and hound, a fine horseman, and as promising with sword and bow as can be; I never saw so young a boy so skilled! It's odds but you'll have him accepted before Henry knows it.'

'God grant it!' Robert said.

De Beaumont was right, Henry had accepted the boy almost before he knew it—and William had been his own best advocate. Robert had explained to him the necessity of being accepted; it could mean life or death. William understood perfectly. He played his part well. He looked appealing and very small. 'Sir,' he told the King of France, 'I could learn very much from you. I could ask nothing better than to stay here, save it be to take you as my lord and serve you with my life!' There he had knelt, lifting two small hands as though he prayed to God. Before Henry knew what he was about, the hands had been taken; the oath and the kiss given.

Henry was much taken with the boy. William rode by his side at the hunt; he was cleverer than the King with his hawk—and cleverer still not to show it. Of all the pages he was the King's favourite and soon he was leader of them all. It did not need Robert's request that the boy be kept in Paris; it was Henry that asked for him.

And now, his plans accomplished, Robert was to ride away. Perhaps, this cold winter morning, some doubt did assail him as to his return. He spoke his last words to William.

'You must stay in Paris till I come for you; here you are safe. But God has His plans for us all. If within the year I do not return then you must obey those councillors I have chosen to have you in charge. If they summon you home, then home you must go. Now what word shall I say to you, yourself, how you shall carry yourself in life? Be strong always; be truthful when you can; be cruel when you must, be generous when there's need.'

And then he spoke of Arlette. 'Be gentle with her; be kind, because she is your mother—and because I loved her, and do love her still. Advance her family and honour them; humble they are but they have the virtues of good men. Never once did they seek to advance themselves—though most men would do so. They ask nothing but to serve me; and to serve you. Fulbert, my bedchamber servant, keep as your own. He is your grandfather and will serve you to the death. And Walter, the captain of my bodyguard—keep him also as your own. You may trust him with your life; and with more than that—your honour. He is your mother's brother and a truer man never drew breath. Honour them, advance them; upon these men may rest your safety. For, hear me, boy! Great lords look each to his own advantage; but these humble men look first to yours. Remember it.'

'I will remember.'

'And now your mother; I must speak of her now, for there may be no other chance. You are over-young to know the nature of a man's love for a woman. But remember this—and remember in kindness. She was not yet fifteen when first I saw her; and I, myself, not much older. And, in that same year you were born. She was loving and obedient; and there's no blame in her. What could she do? I was her lord. If blame there is, it is mine. But I was young also... and she was so lovely. And if our loving brought you into the world and into a high place, you must thank her that through her wit and character, far above her station, shaped you for that place; a Queen could do no better. And more; she loved you, boy, enough to part with you; for always she knew you were destined to a high place. She had dreamed a dream—a great tree sprung from her body cast its shelter upon Normandy; and, as I remember, upon England, too. That tree, she believed, was *you*.'

'Normandy—yes!' He was not at all surprised, 'But—England?'

IV

The months went by and it was summer. He was weary of Paris. King Henry was kind as ever, but for all that William was a foreigner and a vassal; and, worst of all, he was a child. In Paris he didn't count. He longed for his home and he longed for his father. Night and morning he prayed for both.

His father was dead. William could not believe it at first. His father! His father that could outride the fastest; that no man could beat in the chase or in the fight. How could he believe it? But soon he had to believe it. De Beaumont came to take him home; Normandy wanted its young duke. He questioned de Beaumont; but Roger knew little except that it had happened in Bythinia. 'The hot eastern sun killed him they say; but who knows? Whichever way it was, there he lies buried, God rest his soul.'

There was something else Roger had to tell; he did not find it easy. Yet the boy was duke now and must be told. And in this moment of change he would, perhaps, feel it less.

Roger said, 'There is something you should know. Madam de Contéville has sent to tell us she has borne a child; a daughter. She meant your father to have the news.'

William kept his eyes on the white road where the horses kicked up the dust so that it settled upon tree and grass. He had known... that night. He had heard; he had seen—seen her flushed and glowing. He could not trust himself to speak.

'Well,' he said at last, 'What is it to me? And what can I do about it?'

'The child is your full sister. And what shall you do? Nothing. For the present. But you must not forget her. When she is older you must, for your father's sake, see to it that she marries well.' And when the boy did not answer, said, 'And for your own sake, too. A brother, a sister, a daughter, or a son—these are tools in a man's hand; their marriage may mend or mar his fortunes. And there's your first lesson in the art of ruling.'

It was a sad homecoming. When they came again to the familiar roads he had ridden with his father, when he saw the towers of his home rise before him, he felt his heart must burst. But he knew he must give no sign. A still face; that was his second lesson in the art of ruling.

Duke Robert had left his affairs in order. The boy's guardian—responsible to Henry of France—was Alan of Brittany. William was greatly surprised. Alan had his own claim to Normandy—a good claim; he had not been willing to give it up.

'He will never claim it now. By showing trust, your father turns foe to friend. That trust Alan has accepted. He is a true man; he will honour it with his life.'

Trust may turn foe to friend; third lesson in the art of ruling.

'Still,' he said, 'I had rather it were you.'

'No need to win me. I am always and forever your friend and your father knew it. He desired that Fulbert and Walter stay in their same office; and Turold, also. He is to look to your practice with the bows; he is to be chief of your bodyguard when you ride. Your father chose well; these men you may trust with your life.'

A child duke; he had need of such men. Many of those that had, unwilling, sworn the oath, now held themselves free to break it. At the age of eight, when most boys were playing at fighting, he was practising with intent to kill—lest himself be killed. The need came with blinding force when Alan of Brittany, faithful guardian, died horribly of poison. William was wild for revenge. 'But who shall be punished?' de Beaumont asked. 'We do not know the killer. A wise man waits until he is sure.'

Gilbert, count of Brionne, chosen by King Henry, stepped into the guardian's shoes—and died no less horribly. This time everyone knew the murderer—Ralph of Gacé, William's own kinsman. Now William swore the murderer should be brought to justice. Again de Beaumont restrained him. 'Who in this troubled land dare punish him? Try it, and you may find civil war on your hands—if you should live so long. A wise man knows how to wait.'

Henry nominated no more guardians; he found none willing. Osbern, duke Robert's kinsman, the powerful steward that men called *Steward of Normandy*, took matters into his own hands. It was not the guardians the murderers wanted; it was the boy, the boy himself. He must be guarded day and night. But, whoever the watchers and however many, Fulbert his grandfather and Walter his uncle, kept their own watch; they took it in turns to guard Arlette's son.

A bad life for a boy. Anarchy and rebellion throughout the land; and, at his very hearth, murder and the constant fear of death. Robert of Montgomery broke into the boy's very bedroom and killed—and was killed by—Turold, defending his lord while Fulbert and Walter held the door against the rest of the murderers. It was only by a hairsbreadth of time that Osbern dragged the boy from the shambles and carried him off to his own castle at Vaudreuil. Now it was he that slept in the bedchamber of his young lord; and there William of Montgomery, avenging his father, burst in upon them, and butchered Osbern.

Young FitzOsbern, weeping and vomiting, was mad for vengeance. If no man moved in the matter, he would, he swore it, kill the murderer with his own two hands. But William had learned his lesson. 'You are too young; we are both too young. A wise man waits his time. Your father was a father to me, also; he gave his life for me. We are brothers now. Nothing shall come between us, ever.'

Murder and revenge, revenge and murder; no end to it. Osbern's death was avenged by a faithful vassal; and he, good, true man, was in his turn slain. And many a fearful night did Fulbert or Walter carry the boy, startled into instant wakefulness, through the dark night, hearts ahammer in their throats, to be sheltered in some hovel where good, poor folk welcomed their young lord and watched over him while he lay in the wet and stinking straw and the hunt went by—hunting down the nine-year-old, the ten-year-old, the eleven-year-old boy.

William was twelve and growing up quickly. One by one the guardians chosen for him had been murdered. Now he would choose for himself. He remembered that third lesson in the art of ruling.

'I choose Ralph of Gacé,' he told his council.

De Gacé who had murdered Gilbert of Brionne that he might lay hands upon the young duke himself! They stared at such foolishness; the lamb was putting himself into the hands of the slaughterer. 'This is no lamb,' de Beaumont said. 'You may trust our young lord in this!' And so persuaded them.

William had shown courage and wisdom beyond his years. He had turned one assassin into a friend. But he had not made himself safe. He was forever dogged by fear of being cast from his high place; of prison... of death. For Normandy, wasted by bloodshed and by fire, was all a stark disorder. A man killed his neighbour and ravaged his lands, to be killed in turn by his victim's sons. Friends rushed to take their revenge upon the avenger and started a long, deadly and ever-growing vendetta. The country was torn by such vendettas that grew steadily into private wars. William Talvas of Belesme and others of his house did unspeakable deeds of cruelty. He entrenched himself in Alençon, whence he sallied forth to do his deeds of blood. Thurston Goz, that evil man, took Tillières and there entrenched himself. It was the pattern. Castles and fortresses sprang up all over the land; and from them robber-lords conducted their warfare and performed their dark and secret deeds.

That the boy could survive these bloodstained years was a wonder and a miracle. Only through the devotion of those nearest—of de Gacé, now his friend, of Fulbert and Walter, had it been possible. But the years were passing. He was sixteen, he was seventeen... and he was sickened by this private warfare, this senseless cruelty in the land his father had left in peace; and where no man was safe. He would put an end to it, he swore it. A wise man waits his time—but he must not wait too long.

The year of grace ten hundred and forty-six; he was nearly nineteen, with a mind to match his strong body. Old enough to put an end to this vile disorder or die in the attempt... and he did not mean to die. He would ask help of the King of France. Henry had accepted him as duke of Normandy; Henry was his overlord. Henry must help him; it was his duty.

In Paris Henry kept eyes and ears open. Private warfare in Normandy was massing into solid revolt. From north to south, from east to west, the rebels were gathering. And what had William to set against them? A handful of loyal friends and his own courage. It was not much. How long before he asked help of his overlord? And would that overlord give it? It depended upon William himself. Courage was not enough. If he lacked other qualities—initiative, wisdom and wit—he would prove an expense, and a danger to his overlord. Henry would wait and see.

The heart of the storm is quiet. The first William heard of revolt was when he was hunting in Valognes—the very heart of enemy country, though he did not know it. And with him, all smiling friendship, his cousin Guy of Burgundy.

It was Gallet, the fool, keeping his wits sharp as fools must, that came bursting into his lord's chamber in the dark of the morning. 'Sir,' he cried out, 'you must fly. Your lords are in revolt. Grimbaud has sworn to murder you!' and all the time he was handing William his shift, his tunic, his riding-boots. 'They call him leader, but the one behind it all is your cousin of Burgundy—it was he persuaded you here.' And now he was fastening William's sword, was bringing his cloak, was stuffing money into his pouch.

Half-dressed, spurring at his horse, beating upon it with his whip, William regretted most bitterly that, in spite of their protests, he had left Fulbert and Walter behind in Rouen. Now he must ride alone; for the first time in his life, no friend at his back. At the thought of Guy he sickened. *You played the part of friend; we hunted together… now you hunt me to my death.*

Riding there in the moonlight he was desolate, less with fear—though that was sufficient, than with knowledge of friendship lost. But, for all that, he kept a watchful eye; it was moonlight and dangerous. At Vire he forded the river, his horse winded, and the enemy at his heels. With sunrise he was into the Ryé country. Hubert, seigneur of Ryé, saw his duke flying for his life. He brought forth his best horse; he sent his three sons to ride with their lord. By night fall he was safe in Falaise.

In Falaise he heard a piece of news that set the sun shining for him again. King Henry was in Poissy. To Poissy he galloped; and all the time he asked himself a question. *Will he help me?* And sometimes it was a question and sometimes it was a prayer.

Yes, Henry would help him—if William would help himself. William asked nothing better; his anger was great and the lust of battle consumed him.

He was gathering his forces as swiftly as a man might; de Gacé, de Beaumont, together with FitzOsbern lost no time, either. It was not an unimpressive force that joined King Henry a few miles west of the village of Caen.

Val-ès-Dunes. Whatever victories should henceforth be his, this was the battle William would remember to his dying day. First battle. First victory. First step towards making Normandy truly his own. And surely God was with him; surely God had sent a miracle. Ralph of Tesson, rebel peer, suddenly remembered his oath. Struck to the heart by the sight of his young lord, his true lord, he changed sides or ever the battle was joined; came over with all his men to fight for the right.

And now the combat waxed swift and fierce and bloody; horse locked against horse, man against man in hand-to-hand fighting. When the lances broke, then it was sword against sword. And, above the clash of arms, rose William's battle-cry *Dieu m'aide* and Henry's *Montjoye-Saint-Denis.* Wherever the fight was thickest those two were found. In William lust of battle was a madness; for long after minstrels sang of his deeds that day—how he had slain the greatest warrior of them all—Hardrez of Bayeux, striking between chin and breast so that the champion, impaled, fell dead. So wondrous a blow from so young a hand! And how

41

Randolph, lord of Bayeux, lost courage at that and fled the field—and the rest of the rebels after him; and how they fell beneath the pursuing horses and were trodden to death, or were drowned in the waters of the Orne so that the mills of Borbillon were stopped with dead bodies.

King Henry had departed; and now William must deal with his rebels. His first task was to deal with those that had headed the revolt—Grimbaud that had sworn with his own hand to take his duke's head; and Guy of Burgundy, false friend and traitor.

They were skulking in Brionne, the fortified city; too strong, William judged, to fall by assault. He had won his first victory in the heat of the battle; now, coolly and with patience, he must win his first siege. He knew exactly what he must do. He commanded wooden towers either side of the river on which the city stood. Now no food could come into Brionne. Hunger slow but very sure was William's ally.

Day after day, week after week, month after month. Encamped about the walls and seeing day-to-day little change; a hard lesson for an ardent young fighter flushed with victory. And at last, from the walls—the white flag of surrender.

He had won his first battle; he had taken his first city. When the hostages knelt before him, craving mercy, he was lit by glory, touched by compassion. Grimbaud that with his own hands would have taken his lord's life, he cast into prison. But Guy the traitor, he took by the hand, remembering the ties of blood and the years of friendship. But Guy's spirit was broken; he could not match the greatness in William. He turned his back upon Normandy for ever.

And William's mercy reached out to the rebels within the castle; and, most of all, to the humble men that, whatever their true loyalty, must follow, not their duke but their immediate overlord—it was the feudal oath.

He had won a battle; he had taken a city. He had done more than that. He had won respect—a most unwilling respect—from his rebel lords. They would, give them the chance, revolt again; he knew it. But it would be not lightly. Meanwhile Normandy should know a little peace; let the grass grow green again from the bloodshed and the killing.

V

Had he thought, even for a little while, to have peace? There was going to be trouble over Maine; and the trouble-maker? Geoffrey of Anjou, Geoffrey Mattel, *the Hammer*, the brutal, vicious fellow. He was pushing northward beyond his own borders, dangerously, slyly pushing. Now he had both feet in Maine—Maine that lay between Anjou and Normandy.

'And with some show of reason,' de Beaumont told William. 'The old count's dead and the new count's a child. Maine offered itself to Geoffrey—at least the capital did. Le Mans prefers surrender to a sacking.'

'And there's the bully posing as guardian to the child! And now he's on my doorstep. He's had the impertinence to garrison my bordertowns of Domfront and Alençon.'

'Only Alençon is yours. Domfront belongs to the count of Maine.'

'The castle at Domfront was built by permission of my grandfather; it owes me obedience.'

'You never asked it.'

'No need, among friends. Now it's full of my enemies.'

'Enemies, indeed! Sir, I must say it; you are not liked in either town. It is Belesme country. Talvas that should hold Alençon for you has set the whole district against you.'

'The more reason I should have both towns. And have them I will, by the Splendour of God.'

Domfront frowned high above him with its strong walls and fortified castle. Impregnable; and the only way to reach it a hard climb by steep and narrow paths. Men must go afoot in single file carrying the full weight of their harness; the defenders could pick them off as they came.

Not to be taken by assault. Again the long, the dreary sitting-down before the walls, the watchful patience; the sort of warfare William relished least.

It was longer and drearier than he had thought. Summer gave way to autumn; now it was winter and bitter-cold.

And still though there was little food and less firing, the city stood menacing and proud. 'We, at least, have all the woods for your firing,' William said, 'but the city grows cold and colder still. Yet, for all that it thinks itself untakeable.'

FitzOsbern shrugged. So it was proving!

'Well let them think so! I mean to strike elsewhere.'

'*Withdraw your armies?*'

William nodded. 'But they'll not guess. I leave part behind to make a show. Tonight we march for Alençon.'

Split his forces! Madness. FitzOsbern would have told him so; but William's face forbade it.

Through the long night of winter darkness William marched; a hazardous march with his small forces—and every inch enemy country. Sullen winter daylight brought them before Alençon. The bridge across the river, strongly fortified, kept him from the town. Kept from Alençon, his own town! Anger held him transfixed.

His surprise had little value. The town, looking down upon his small forces, greeted their lord with insult—the direst insult of all. They spread the walls with undressed hides; the morning wind brought the stink to William. They beat upon the hides, his own Normans within the city as well as Angevins, crying out *Work for the Tanner!*

FitzOsbern, riding beside his duke, saw the eyes drained of colour, lit and luminous, and blind.

The insult drove William madly on. He hurled himself against the bridge—the bridge that kept him from his own town. The bridge gave way; broken timbers and wounded men, together fell into the river. Now he stood by the moat that ran beneath the city walls. Jeering still, the men of Alençon watched while William's men cast tinderwood into the moat; but when they set it alight, then, too late, those within their city left their mocking. Now, wildly, they ran his way and that for water, for sand, for anything at all to put out the flames that licked ever higher. The charred gates fell from their hinges; in rushed the enemy, running through the town where houses burnt like torches and flames leaped to the sky.

The town was taken. William turned his back upon it and commanded the prisoners to be brought before him. Thirty-two he chose, kneeling white before him. He stood there impassive, staring with those pale eyes so curiously lit; he commanded that their hands and feet be struck off, himself stood by to see it done. It was as though he were possessed by a devil. Only then did he turn about to face the town. Behind him the mutilated wretches groaned and grovelled in their blood; the piles of severed limbs lay in a slippery heap. He ordered them to be cast over the walls; messengers with no need of words.

He had won his victory; proclaimed his prowess and his will. Rage left him; he was more merciful than they had hoped. Flushed with his victory he rode back to Domfront. Only once did he speak; to FitzOsbern he said, 'I did what I did. It will save bloodshed in the future.' It was not a justification; it was a plain statement of fact.

And he was right. Now it was a different story. Domfront had heard of Alençon; of his victory... and his punishment.

Not a blow struck; and there was William's standard waving over Domfront; city and castle. Now Alençon and Domfront, the great fortresses guarding the frontier and the river valleys into Normandy, were no menace—save to Maine; to Maine and to Anjou.

Back triumphant in his capital he found tales had preceded him. This duke of theirs had more than mortal powers. He could transport himself and his armies, at will, unseen. A miracle. God was in it, some said; but others murmured of witchcraft.

'Such tales are as good as a victory in arms!' William said.

And now at long last, a little peace. But peace is no resting-time. In time of peace a man strengthens himself. So, down with the castles that had tyrannised the land, the castles that had sprung up since he was a child; and down with those that had built them. A wise man strengthens himself with friends. Now he remembered his father's counsel to raise up his mother's family. Fulbert he made his chamberlain; Walter his captain of the guard. Nor did he forget his mother's Sons by Herlouin, his half-brothers; he kept himself informed of them—their nature and abilities. Odo was twelve or thereabouts; Robert a year younger. Odo looked to be that rare bird—scholar and soldier. He could read and write and cypher; and he knew his Latin. Already they spoke of his strength and his courage. A violent nature, they said; headstrong and could be cruel. Well, but who could not? And Robert? Well-grown and strong—strong will, strong arm, and very proud. His mother, he thought, must have had more than her share of pride. Proud and strong; useful virtues—and both of them his brothers.

The see of Bayeux had just fallen vacant; it was as if God Himself kept an eye upon his affairs. Odo should have it. He showed no leanings towards the church; he was first and foremost a fighting-man. Well, what of that? He had some learning and could acquire more. But he was less than fourteen. Well, what of that, also? The place should be kept warm for him. First this bishopric; then, if he proved worthy, the highest place in the church. As for Robert—he'd advance Robert as soon as might be. And there was the girl, his sister, the little Adelaide conceived that night, the night his barons had sworn fealty—the only time he had seen his mother. He must make a useful match for her; de Beaumont had told him long ago.

'She is scarce thirteen,' de Beaumont said now, 'and can wait awhile. You should do well to consider your own marriage first.'

'I have no mind for marriage yet,' William said. 'My hands are full. For the moment, we are at peace; but for how long? For fourteen years I have been duke of this turbulent, rebellious land. But have I truly won it yet? To keep myself secure I must still watch, still fight. I have no time for a wife.'

'It is your duty to marry, sir—and so your council will tell you. I speak for them!'

And so his council did tell him.

'Sir, it is your duty to continue your house. And it is your duty to marry one that shall strengthen your hand. A wife must have other virtues, naturally; but your wife must have them all.'

'And—the lady?' William was clearly uninterested.

'The count of Flanders has a daughter,' de Beaumont said. 'Her blood you know; the most royal in Christendom. Her father is rich, he's powerful; a great soldier and a good Christian gentleman.'

'It is the lady I'm to marry,' William reminded him.

'She is beautiful; she is gentle and obedient; she is skilled in all the work of women.' That she was a scholar also—since William was none—de Beaumont left unsaid. 'Certainly, sir, she is the wife for you!'

'There's a thing, sir, you have all forgot.' Voice of his uncle Malger, new-made archbishop of Rouen. 'They are too near in blood. It could be no Christian marriage.'

'A very Christian marriage—if the Pope approve,' de Beaumont said, a little sharp. 'And why should he not approve? The kinship is not so close; he has approved unions yet closer in blood.'

'I will think upon it,' William promised, reluctant still. When he examined his reluctance he understood it was because he must remember always the stigma of his birth. It was a stigma that, for very shame, he was inclined to flaunt. *William Bastard*, so he signed himself, wearing the name as it might be a decoration. Now the thought pricked within him: *Suppose I am refused?* Against the insult imagined—yet unimaginable—his jaw hardened.

Roger de Beaumont, his governor in boyhood, knew his thoughts. 'Sir,' he said, 'there's no prince in Christendom, nor King, neither, would not gladly put his daughter in your bed... so it be a marriage-bed.'

The marriage-bed it should be. He'd sleep with no woman save they were fast-wed. Never would he beget bastards that they should be taunted with their birth. But, mightn't his children, though lawfully begot upon the noblest blood in Christendom, be taunted still? For still they would be the children of the Bastard; great-grandchildren to Fulbert the Tanner. What princess of Christendom could stomach that?

Well, but his council advised and his council insisted; and young as he was, and self-willed as he was, he knew when he must obey.

Unfortunate the time of asking; unfortunate the manner. Unfortunate both.

VI

Unfortunate the time of asking; Matilda was not fully recovered from the shock of childbirth and grief of parting with her child. Unfortunate the manner of asking; no diplomacy, no compliments—the short, sharp request.

Count Baldwin was taken by surprise. He was flattered and not altogether pleased. He was disturbed and not at all decided.

'I met the young man a couple of years since,' he told his wife, 'and was much taken with him—though *taken* is perhaps not the word. Impressed

I should say. He is of striking appearance; taller than the most part of men; a noble bearing and would be handsome enough save for the hardness of the jaw; hardness that, if I know men, will deepen to harshness. A strong man and a fine soldier.'

'And the stain on his birth?' asked Adelais, daughter and sister of Kings.

Baldwin shrugged. 'There's greatness in him.'

'An alliance with him could breed trouble—especially in Paris,' she reminded him. 'I say nothing of Anjou and Brittany.'

'I know. I know!' No need to remind Baldwin that power in Gaul was delicately balanced. Nor that William, ruthless for every inch of his right, might well upset that balance. 'A man needs time to think! But, there's no harm in hearing what the girl has to say.'

She came into her father's presence; there he sat in the great chair that was like a throne; and her mother beside him upon a lesser chair, yet great enough. And it was all as once before, when Brihtric had refused her. Humiliation sickened her as she made her reverence, took her place upon the stool. *What now?*

'My child,' her father said, 'today we have received great honour. The lord duke William of Normandy asks your hand.' And when she did not seem to understand, so great the shock, he added a little sharp, 'He asks your hand in marriage.'

She stared at that, bringing back her thoughts from the shame Brihtric had thrust upon her, to this duke upon his slippery throne; this bastard duke. Well, now it was her turn to refuse, to make good the insult she had received.

She said in her clear young voice, 'Did you say... *honour*, sir?' And then, truly puzzled, 'An honour... to give me to a bastard?'

She saw the surprise in her father's eyes, as though he could not quite believe the thing he had heard; she saw her mother scarlet with anger... *She thinks I must snatch at any marriage. Well, I have no mind for it. Men—I hate them all.* And, indeed, at this moment she found the idea of marriage revolting.

But it was not refusal alone that made Adelais redden with anger, nor even the discourtesy that shamed the girl's breeding; it was because the heedless words might make a great mischief.

Now, looking from father to mother, she understood too late that her words might carry where she had not meant—a listening page, perhaps, his palm well-oiled. She understood now, that her parents had relied upon her gentle breeding, her sense of honour conferred. Surprised, she had surprised them all—herself not least. For intended honour she had returned insult. She was instantly sorry for that. *But they should have warned me, my father, surely; my* mother most certainly. Well, the thing was said. And, at least, she had made her mind clear in the matter.

Her father's nod dismissed her. She went down into her curtsey; felt their anger follow her as she pushed aside the tapestry that divided the closet from the great hall. The dogs sprang to greet her, all-but knocking her down, small and slight as she was.

Her parents' anger rekindled her own anger. Well, but was it such an honour to be asked in marriage by a bastard, she, the most royal blood in Christendom?

Anger went with her to the turret room. Here it was quiet; in all this great house the one place where she could be alone. In this refuge she was not to be left long. She heard feet firm upon the stairs; sighing, she rose to face her mother.

'I am sorry, madam,' the girl said. 'I should not have spoken as I did. But, indeed, it is not so much bastard blood that offends me, though when I marry I prefer—'

'*You...* prefer?' Adelais interrupted, apparently amused and wholly spiteful.

'—it was that I was all unprepared. The thought of marriage frightens me. I am not ready.'

'You were ready enough a year ago,' Adelais said in the same amused and spiteful voice.

'Everything has changed...' Her voice trailed off; she stood dumb with misery.

'It has, indeed!' Adelais said cruel and cutting.

'I need time.'

'Time cannot give you back your maidenhead. Well, it's a loss we can cover when there's need.'

'Go to my husband a lying bride?'

'Lie with him properly—and who's the worse?' Adelais mocked.

The girl's hand went to her breast to still that pain where still the milk welled. 'I need time,' she said, again.

'Time cannot alter the fact that you have borne a bastard and deserted it!' Adelais said, brutal. 'Time will not make it less hard to tell the truth—

if you're fool enough to try! I tell you, my girl, not to play the fool now; or ever.'

When her mother had gone, she gave herself to her thoughts. Save for lack of courtesy, she was not sorry to have put an end to this talk of marriage. Duke William, she had heard, was a proud man. He'd not ask again. She was glad of it. What she had said was true. If marry she must, she'd no mind to take a bastard.

It was evening before her father summoned her; they were there, mother and father, both.

'My girl,' he began—and though he was quiet enough, she knew his anger burned still. Well, she could not blame him! 'You have shamed us this day. I did not think to blush for my daughter.'

'Sir, I am sorry with all my heart—'

'Your sorrow does us no good at all,' Baldwin said. 'We may yet find ourselves at war with this duke you have so wantonly insulted.'

'War?' And she was plainly amazed. 'I did but name him as the world does; as, indeed, he names himself. He signs his decrees, so I have heard, *William Bastard.*'

'He forces the dagger into his own breast—lest others do it for him!' Baldwin said. 'To face such a truth is hard enough; to have it trumpeted aloud—'

'By an ill-mannered girl!' Adelais could no longer contain herself.

'By anyone at all!' Baldwin said, more gentle. 'This William has a great pride; his birth is a subject on which he allows no jesting. Surely, my girl, you've heard of Alençon.'

'Yes, I have heard. They called him by his name; and the river ran red with blood. And this is the man you would give me to!' But, underneath her horror she felt a curious excitement... of pleasure, almost. Did it come from that dark root of which Agnes had spoken? She said now, very meek, 'Sir, I would unsay it if I could. But I did not, nor cannot, think you would mix our blood with his.'

'It is already mixed. He is our kinsman. But kinsman or not, it was an honour,' Baldwin said.

'Sir, would you give me to the tanner's bastard grandson?'

'Hold your tongue, girl!' Adelais cried out. 'Who are you to judge? A bastard brat—' she said, very deliberate, 'it does happen, you know; and not always in a peasant's family. But a good marriage covers all—as the tanner's daughter could tell you. A good marriage—in such a case, it's scarce to be prayed for; and when God Himself sends it, should be accepted on one's knees.'

She saw her father look from one to the other. Soon he would come at the truth. She must speak, say something—anything at all to put an end to the barbed words.

'Sir,' she said, 'I am truly grieved for my ill-behaviour. It was surprise forced me to the words. I would not, of my own will, marry this duke; but if it be your pleasure—'

'The offer is no longer open. He would not look at you now!' Adelais said, acid. 'The envoys have gone home.'

She took in her breath with relief. She said, 'Sir, I am your most obedient, humble daughter...'

'From such obedient daughters, God save us!' Adelais cried out; but her father gave no sign of hearing. For all his love of his daughter he found her conduct hard to forgive.

She made her unheeded reverence, and took herself from the room. Up in the tower-room she found Agnes at her needlework frame; the old woman rose, sending the girl a side-long glance. It was clear that everyone in the castle, and, no doubt, beyond, had heard the tale.

'Oh my demoiselle!' She lifted her hands high, 'What have you done?'

Matilda did not, it seemed, hear the question. She said, looking at the work upon the frame, 'You are careless. This stitch is caught upon the one before; the wool pulls at the back.'

'There are few as skilled as you, my demoiselle. And, if the wool be caught—' she shrugged, 'it is no great matter. Such work may always be undone. But, my demoiselle, there's other work can never be undone. The whole house is abuzz!'

'And what does it buzz?'

'That you were offered for; that you refused... and the refusal not over-sweet.'

'And then?'

'That a bastard's no match for our lady—duke though he be! But you and I know better!'

'I cannot marry yet. I am sick, body and soul, of men!'

'Yet marry you must! And this duke—his birth; what of it? A duke's crown hides every stain. In all else he's a man fit for any princess of the world. Strong body and the will to match it. The thing he wants—that thing he'll get.'

'He'll not get me!'

'I'd not be too sure of that!'

'But still I'm sure. There can be no marriage between him and me, let me be never so willing. He's my kinsman; cousins, you might say! And that they have forgotten; all of them forgotten. My grandmother was own sister to his father. Such a marriage the church would not allow.'

'And still I say be not too sure!'

VII

She had spat upon the offered honour. She had named him *bastard*. Well let that word suffice! He would crown it with bay, make it prouder than the name of any King in Christendom. But, for all that, the word pricked him on to madness. So great his rage he had much ado not to strike the envoys kneeling abject before him. Pierce the ear-drums that had heard, cut out the tongues that repeated their lord's humiliation. But, for all his rage, he had still some sense of justice; his own will had pressed upon the men forcing out each unwilling word. He thanked them for their services, bade them hold their tongues and begone.

Left to himself he fought to control his anger; but still his fierce eyes blared; the iris, all-but colourless, gave him a blinded look. The ebbing of his blood had brought the cheekbones to stand out high against the bleached skin. He was flame-white; a man consumed.

He could not breathe, here in the cold dark room. He climbed to the battlement and looked out upon the city.

Caen lay before him; as always the sight calmed him. His new city, growing proud, growing steady, from the village it had been; Caen all of golden stone, sitting crowned upon the river, the Orne, winding amidst rich pastures to the sea. His golden city.

He took in his breath, let it slowly out; the colour was returning to eye and cheek.

Rouen was his capital; but this city of his own making was the city of his heart. He would make it the finest in Normandy! He would build fine churches to the glory of God, and a new palace to his own glory...

His thought snapped. There came to his ear, unmarked at first, the rhythmical clack of wood upon stone; now, insistent to be heard, it clamoured about his head and upon his heart. It was a sound he knew well—the beat of wood falling upon linen; he had heard it in the very womb. He could no more escape the sound than he could escape his own breathing—his mother washing just so, kneeling by the river the first time his father had seen her.

Again he was oppressed by his sense of bitter wrong. The words of the girl Matilda came back to sting at him.

Bastard. Bastard. Bastard. The word echoed and re-echoed in his ears. He had not, of himself, desired marriage; an unwilling suitor he had asked for his bride. And been refused; most shamefully refused. It was intolerable. Not to be borne! The thorn of his bastardy she had driven deep to draw blood. By the Splendour of God he could kill her! But—kill? It was not enough. Death ends all things. It was punishment she needed, a long, long punishment; humiliation for humiliation—and more, more!

Bastard. Bastard. Bastard. The word drummed in his ears, beat upon his brain, quickened his hot blood. A bastard had a strong arm to defend such tittle of honour as was left!

He was out of his chamber and roaring aloud for men, for horses, for all the necessities of a journey. Where he was going he knew well; what he should do when he got there he had no notion. But *Bastard, bastard, bastard!* It was the spur that drove him onwards.

He galloped the countryside, clattered through village and town; the handful of his escort could not keep the pace. The sharp spring wind stung eyes and mouth, blew dust into every crevice of skin and clothing; in the dust-plastered face agleam with sweat pale eyes glittered. Anger possessed him so that he felt no need to rest or eat. The hunk of bread and meat seized in the saddle was wood in his mouth; but for all that it sustained him.

Yet still he had no clear notion what he meant to do; but his hands itched to be on the impudent girl. She had asked for punishment—and that punishment she should have!

Himself had no need of rest; but the mare was growing distressed. He would stop in Rouen to change horses and to wait for the company to come up with him. And there it was that de Beaumont and FitzOsbern found him.

'Sir,' Roger said, 'where do you go and for what reason?'

'I am for Bruges. And, by the Splendour of God, the reason is clear! I go to punish an insolent wench!'

FitzOsbern said, 'She is no serving-maid to chastise.'

'Do you think that, without due ceremony, you'd get near her?' de Beaumont asked. 'And if you could—and, having insulted her, what then? Baldwin would hang you—and King Henry would approve; he had no pleasure in the match. Yes, you would hang, and every soul in Christendom would say you deserved it.'

At the thought of hanging him, duke William laughed aloud—though the laugh was grim enough.

'You may laugh now, but it's yourself will be the laughing-stock of Christendom,' de Beaumont said.

That last did halt him, though it did not cool his rage.

'You have been insulted,' FitzOsbern told him. 'Such insult must be wiped out in blood.'

'You are right, both of you!' William said, thoughtful. 'To lay the whip about the girl helps nothing. As for the insult, her father shall answer it.'

'Thereafter you may make what terms you will!' FitzOsbern grinned. 'Take the girl to wife—if you've still the mind. A pretty piece, they say! Then you may tame her—do with her what you will.'

When Baldwin heard that William was arming he laughed aloud; but in his heart he was not amused. 'I shall pull the bastard duke's crown about his ears and send him snivelling home!' And all-but cursed his daughter. He was too old for life in the saddle and the rigours of warfare.

'Now, perhaps, you are satisfied!' Adelais said when Baldwin had ridden out with his armies. 'Now the peace of Flanders is disturbed, her prosperity threatened—and your father may never return.'

'My father's the best soldier in Christendom.'

'*Was*... he's no longer young. But, let him be victorious, let him be beaten, let him be killed, even,' Adelais could not stop her tongue nor wished to, 'how does your honour stand then? *A woman with a mischief-making tongue. No wonder she was refused and by a mere Saxon chieftain. Ah but he had sense, the Englishman!* So they will say! And what man of worth will take you now? It will be a convent for you, my girl!'

A convent. Again her heart shuddered from the thought. Most bitterly she regretted her heedless words. Give her but the chance and she'd not so offend again; she'd learned her lesson. In future she'd bridle her tongue. But who, who would take her now?

It came to her—a sudden inspiration. One man alone could give her that chance; the man himself. Suppose she married this William? It could be done! The kindly word spoken and carried; the word of regret, of humility. To marry her all repentant, obedient—surely then the insult would be wiped out; surely it must satisfy his pride, add to his pride.

She would pay for it, no doubt. She did not like what she knew of him; but liking had little to do with marriage—she had learned that in a bitter school.

...A man of iron will; well, she knew the strength of her own! A man of wrath; a wise woman would see it did not fall upon herself. Ambitious; well so was she—no man nor woman more! She would play upon his ambition to serve her own, all the time showing herself obedient and gentle. A clever woman could manage him!

She would marry him. *I set my will upon it. Think of me, William; keep your anger bright against me; so you will remember me. Remember my pride to match your own; remember my blood better than your own. I am the only woman in the world for you. All others fear you; but I am your match. You and I, William; you and I.*

She did not love him; she doubted she ever would. But she needed him; needed him for her own honour, her own ambition. Together what might they not accomplish, what heights reach? William and Matilda.

Matilda and William.

Matilda and William

VIII

Baldwin lay with his armies on the frontier. William, regarding the pitched tents, the waving pennons, the general stir of war, was moody, dissatisfied. He had sufficient enemies without wasting time and strength on this! Anjou on his doorstep, trouble with Maine, and Brittany in league with both; and within his own doors, restless lords ready to rise. He could deal with them all because he must. One should have a clear aim in warfare; and that aim was not a woman. But there was no choice; the girl had insulted him. Had Baldwin any sense of justice, he'd offer to punish his daughter and close the whole affair. FitzOsbern had suggested marrying the girl; a jest. But, *was* it such a jest? To become her husband must add to his honour, prove him worthy of the alliance; and he could look for a rich dowry. She was, besides, a pretty piece; she needed taming. To tame a woman was man's work; he was, he hoped, a man. FitzOsbern's jest began to wear the look of sound commonsense.

Count Baldwin received William FitzOsbern with some surprise. To my lord duke's request for an early meeting, a request so courteous as to suggest friendship, he replied with equal courtesy and fixed the day. He, too, would be glad to lay down arms—if with honour it could be done. He was sick of the distasteful affair; he would offer his apologies, to proceed further in the matter would do his girl no good. He could not, in truth, hold himself blameless. A less indulgent father would himself have dealt with the matter and at once. A taste of the whip would have saved us all a good deal of trouble, his wife had said it more than once and it was true. The girl had shamed them all. For all her looks, all her skills, all her dowry, it would be hard to marry her now!

William stood in the opening of the tent. He was unarmed and, save for his squire, unattended; a man unafraid in the midst of his enemies. The girl was a fool, Baldwin thought; they would have made a handsome pair!

It was over several cups of wine that they came to their agreement. Bygones to be bygones. Peace between Normandy and Flanders; friendship and peace.

And something more.

Indifferent, it would seem, William threw out a suggestion—peace might be sealed with a marriage. Well, why not? There was Baldwin's little sister Judith; strangers took her for his younger daughter. She was gentle and biddable and altogether charming. But the young man was not interested in Judith; he was talking of that proud girl, of Matilda herself. Incredibly he was actually offering for her again!

When Baldwin had sufficiently recovered his breath, he said, 'For my own part I would welcome such a son. But as for my daughter—it is a thing you must settle between yourselves. Had things been other I would here and now pledge my word and she would honour it. But seeing what has passed—' he shrugged. 'My lord, an unwilling wife is a heavy cross.'

'Sir, you speak with wisdom. Let the lady, your daughter, know my mind. Whatever be the outcome of this meeting, I hold myself your brother-in-arms and your friend.'

Baldwin came riding into the courtyard; his wife waited to greet him together with the two girls. Judith was certainly a pretty child; but beside his daughter she was nothing. Matilda was a Queen... but Judith would be easier to wive.

It was after supper that he opened the matter with his wife and daughter. And now the girl's answer was so different, he could scarce believe eye or ear.

'A daughter is bound to obey her father.' And she was all sweet obedience, 'My wish, sir, is your wish.'

'Had my own wish been considered the thing would have been settled long ago!' He was a trifle sour. 'Now it has gone beyond me. Can you take the man? Can you like him?'

'If you wish it, sir.' Her face was blank as an egg.

'Then it is settled,' Adelais said quickly. She knew that blank look; a warning to push the matter no further. 'It is settled—and better than we could have hoped.' She was, it was clear, well-pleased.

By no means settled.

William had come to Bruges and he had seen the girl. She would do well enough! She was small and fine; so, he liked a woman. She had a proud air, becoming in his duchess; yet, in spite of her pride, how quickly she had come to heel! He could, he was certain, deal with her. For her part, she looked at the tall, handsome young man with little emotion save pride; pride in herself, her own will. In spite of her behaviour he had offered for her again; her will had brought it about. For the rest, he was well enough; she was grateful to him that he had rescued her from a difficult position. She would make him a good wife.

And then, in the midst of negotiations—settlements, dowry, morning-gifts and the rights of the bride—the bombshell.

No marriage. Forbidden by Holy Church. At the Council of Rheims—that great council before which the Kings of Christendom must bow, the voice of Rome had been heard. *Count Baldwin of Flanders is forbidden to give his daughter in marriage to William the Norman and he is forbidden to receive her.*

William took the decree badly. 'No reason given. None!' he cried out to FitzOsbern, to de Beaumont; and chafed inwardly that Baldwin had been given his title and he, himself, called simply *the* Norman. It was an insult; a deliberate insult.

'The Pope, I fancy, listens to the voice of Henry of France,' de Beaumont said. 'You cannot expect him to relish your alliance with a rich, powerful, all-but royal house—his own house!'

'Send for Lanfranc,' FitzOsbern advised. 'There's no man so able to advise.'

But, for all his wisdom, the abbot of Bec could suggest nothing; nothing but obedience.

'But no reason given; no reason at all!' William cried out again.

'The Lord Pope needs no reason,' Lanfranc said. 'His voice is the voice of God.'

'Yet a reason I must have; without a reason how shall I fight this decree?'

'You are not meant to fight it and you are best not to try! And, though I do not presume to give reasons where my master gives none, yet the reason is not far to seek. You and the lady are too near in blood.'

'The lady is my promised bride. She is mine. I do not give up lightly what is mine.'

'Dare you set yourself against holy church?' Lanfranc's tone was a warning. 'The church knows how to make herself obeyed. And, if you should dare for yourself and for the lady, what of the children? How shall men call them—born of a union that is no marriage?'

Lanfranc had him there, the wily priest.

'Had I slept with a dozen women,' William burst out into the quiet face of the Italian priest, 'the Pope would not concern himself, not though I sinned again and again. Now I would take a woman in holy bond, does the church deny me?'

'Sir, it does.'

He foresaw, now, the whole dreary business—the setting-out of arguments, the pleading, the sly bribes growing steadily larger until they were large enough to tempt the Pope. And even then, the endless waiting; God's Mouthpiece regarding his own dignity would take his time.

No help from Lanfranc. William raged with frustration; yet something he had gained from the meeting—knowledge of the man himself. An impressive man, this Italian; an almost royal dignity. A man to be watched; a man to have on one's side; *at* one's side. A man of prayer, a scholar; but equally a man of affairs. A man true to his master and for that master not afraid to speak. He would not forget Lanfranc.

Matilda found delay easier to endure. She was angered by interference but she could afford to wait. She was not hot for the marriage-bed; Brihtric had killed desire. When the time came she would do her duty. As a check to ambition it was harder to bear but it was a check, merely—William would never let go. In the end he would win, though half-a-dozen popes stood in his way. At sixteen, even ambition can afford to wait—but it must not wait too long. Calm and smiling, she made no complaint; even when it was clear that she must wait longer than she had thought, she carried herself with a sweet obedience. It won for her the name of the gentlest princess in Christendom.

Patience; it was a mask upon ever-growing frustration—frustration of ambition, frustration of womanhood. She would never give herself in love again but, for all that, she was a woman. And the years were passing, one year, two years, three years.

Four years; four long years since the Pope had spoken. To Rome and back again rode the messengers; William was fighting for his marriage as fiercely as ever he fought in battle.

Four years and he had done those things he promised himself save one, one only. He was no nearer his marriage. Odo had been installed as bishop of Bayeux; it had created a near-scandal, so young the boy. But William had had his way. The boy looked to be all the things report had promised—a brother to stand by a man's side. Robert he had sent for, also; the boy he treated like a royal prince. At the first opportunity he should be raised to a great position.

In the year of grace ten hundred and fifty, in the middle of William's struggle for his marriage, Arlette died. She was thirty-eight. He had always thought to feel relief at her death; how could he forget his birth while she lived? Her death shook him to the core. She was his mother and death could not alter the facts of his birth. And what, after all, had she done save give birth to himself—a glorious birth? In his softened mood he could scarce find room for blame. On the contrary; when he thought of Odo, of Robert, strong, quick-witted and brave, he could wish she had borne other sons—in marriage or without.

It was now he sent for Adelaide, his full sister; child of his father and mother. She was scarce fifteen—Arlette's age when she had gone to his father. His heart shook when he saw her; she was the perfect compound of them both. Blue eyes, honey-gold hair, rich, full bosom—she was all Arlette. Grace, elegance, quick laughter and wit—she was all duke Robert. He would make her match and not only for his own sake, but for hers—the lovely girl. She should wed Enguerrand, count of Ponthieu, worthy of her in looks and character; an honoured name and rich acres.

He had carried out his father's wish—and his own. He had raised his mother's house on high, her humble, faithful house. Now to cast down a second traitor of his father's house, that proud and treacherous house—William count of Arques, brother to Malger, archbishop of Rouen. These bastard brothers of his father were a continual thorn in the flesh. The man had made Arques a nest of robbers and the terror of the district. He was looting, he was burning—churches as well as farms; he was carrying off the peasants' crops so that they looked to starve. With fire he ravaged the countryside; with hunger and rape the homes.

William was on the march hot for punishment. It was pleasant to forget the long frustration of his marriage in the congenial and righteous business of warfare.

He stood before Arques, the great castle on the steep hill. He was unexpected; it was his one advantage—so formidable the hosts within, so small his own collected in haste.

Once again the long patient sitting-down before a town. But, as ever, starvation was William's ally. Arques fell, town and castle. Humbly the enemy knelt, saddles upon their backs like beasts of burden.

William was merciful. Even his uncle of Arques, the arch-rebel, might take the oath again, remain in Normandy, keep the best part of his lands. But, like that other traitor, he could not face his own treachery; like Guy of Burgundy he left for ever.

William was sorry to see the name of his sister's husband among the slain; but not for long. As soon as her first tears were dry he'd give her in marriage again—a more glorious marriage. Lambert of Lens should make her happy once more.

William's name shone brighter than ever.

IX

He had won every battle, every siege. He had put down the rebels of his father's house, bastard and true-born alike. He had raised his mother's house to stand by his side. He was, he knew it and relished the knowledge, living his own legend—William the Victorious, never to be conquered, never to be wounded. Now Normandy was more or less at peace; with God's help he would keep it so. But God helps those that help themselves; it was a thing never to be forgotten. Any slight spark could give rise to rebellion—but nothing to equal those he had put down. With God's help he would keep all between his two hands. Ruined churches he would restore, new ones build; religion he would cherish.

He had won every battle; save one. He had not won his wife. He was, though in the press of his affairs he did not know it, a lonely man.

Save for the kindness of Roger de Beaumont and the single-hearted FitzOsbern, he had not one true friend. He preferred it that way; the less one trusted, the less one could be betrayed. But a wife was a different matter. He was twenty-five and a virgin; he was minded to wait no longer. His betrothed was, at this moment, with her father in Lille; he would ride into Flanders and demand his bride.

He had forgotten how desirable she was; it was hard to be near her for the clamour of his blood. He wanted to enjoy her in his bed; he wanted to carry her off and take her there and then. But he wanted more than her body. If he took her by force—though she were helpless in the matter—she would lose not her virginity alone but something of his respect. And he would lose, also; he would lose the free giving of herself. So he must wait. He found it harder than sitting down to a siege. Hard, and hard indeed!

He found her cool and friendly; she did not appear unduly disturbed by the delay in their marriage. Women, he supposed, were like that! They must not admit to their appetites. It was seemly in a virgin; he would teach her better when they were wed.

She had news. Godwine, the great English earl, was in Ghent. Banished. Banished together with his sons. Her father had made them welcome. He was giving them, as he gave many English in trouble, refuge. It was old tradition born of friendship in the wool-trade.

William had heard something of the banishment and was uninterested. 'I came to talk of our marriage. Four years we have waited—and none the better for it! I'll wait no longer.'

She was shocked. 'You would not disobey the Pope! Without his word there can be no marriage.'

'Once the marriage is made he will accept it.'

'Who would dare marry us against his will?'

'I will find the priest.'

'My father will not hear of it!'

'He will have to hear of it!' And he wore the bleak look she was beginning to know. 'Once we are wed the Pope will lift the ban. We'll hear no more of the matter.'

And, that affair disposed of, he was pleased to hear news of England where, after all, his cousin was King.

'It was time to banish the house of Godwine; time my cousin showed himself truly a King. He's more the stuff of saints than Kings.'

'Could a man not be both—saint and King?'

'Best not to try! I saw a good deal of him when I was a child; he took refuge in my father's court; Edward and his brother, both. Athelings— English royal princes—and they went in fear of death from England! And who shall say they were wrong? Alfred, the younger brother, went into England to visit his mother—and there he died...

'I know,' she said. 'All Christendom knows.' And shut her mind against the horror of the tale. A young prince kindly received at Dover by this same earl, this Godwine; and taken by treachery and blinded horribly; and set upon a horse, naked, his legs bound beneath him... and tears and blood streaming from those ravaged sockets; and driven to Ely—and there he died. A hateful story.

'Some said, and do say still,' William told her, 'Godwine himself planned it. But they couldn't prove it. As soon as he heard of the murder Edward left our court; he went into a monastery for safety. And just as well! It was just after my father died. I couldn't protect him—nine years old and being hustled from place to place. It was as much as I could do to save my own life. He was a strange young man; twenty-four or so at the time. Slow to move; a dreamer; yet he could be violent, too—but afterwards he'd be drained of strength. He'd be quiet and listless till next time.'

He was silent, thinking about this strange cousin of his.

'Of course,' he said, 'I saw him often; but I never knew him. Fifteen years older than I was—and like no other man I ever saw. He always seemed so *old*; and not because I was a child; my father was the same age and he'd always seemed young. But Edward. He was thin and frail and bleached. Not pale, you understand, but bleached; bleached as a bone. His hair was white; white as snow—he was born with it! And his skin—translucent; you could see the pale blood flowing beneath it. And his eyes; rimmed with pink and a pink light to them. I had a rabbit like that once. But Edward wasn't a rabbit; not by any means. You should have seen him at the hunt! He had a passion for hunting; and still has! He's like a hound then; a lean, white hound.'

'The English don't like him!' Matilda said. 'So Godwine tells us. They offered him the crown because they were heartsick of Danish Kings.

But, for all that, they don't like him; for all his English blood he's half-Norman—a foreigner.'

'I hear the voice of Godwine there!'

'Yes; but a true voice, my father says. The English King is overpious; he spends too much time in prayer; he's withdrawn from life.'

'That should suit Godwine well!' William was not greatly interested. 'He meant the royal crown to fall into his own family. My cousin had barely turned round in his English bed—and there was Godwine presenting him with a bedfellow! The King of England found himself married to Godwine's daughter. But no grandchild of Godwine's house will ever sit upon the English throne. In all the years of their marriage Edward's never slept with his wife—nor any woman; nor ever will. A vow of chastity they say. And maybe just as well! Impotent, I'd swear. Maybe he took the vow to save his face. Well, so Godwine's turned from hearth and home; the sainted King shows himself human at last! What was the trouble? Does Godwine say?'

She shrugged. 'Who knows? There's been bad blood a long time.'

He nodded remembering a tale of the eldest son Swegen; the impious fellow had raped a nun!

'This is only the end of the tale; some trouble with the King's kinsman, Eustace of Boulogne.'

'He's my kinsman, too. A troublesome fellow; bad manners. What's he been doing now?' And almost he found himself in sympathy with Godwine.

'A disturbance at Dover. The English wouldn't find lodgings for him and his men.'

'The King's visitors; it was their duty.' William's sudden sympathy was gone.

'Maybe. But this Eustace—nothing, it seemed, was good enough for him. He provoked the citizens with his insolence. Up went fists, out came swords. The King ordered the men of Dover to be punished. Godwine's their overlord and he refused. They were not to blame, he said. And he didn't mince words. The King called a council, a witan... witan... some odd name.'

'Witenagemot. It means a meeting of wise men. A barbarous tongue this English.'

'Godwine was commanded to attend; and he did attend... with armed men at his heels.'

'The man's a fool.'

She shrugged. 'He says he feared for his life. You can guess the rest.'

'Easily. Even a saint was not likely to endure that piece of insolence!'

'So now Godwine's banished and his sons with him. And there they are in Ghent. And not only does my father shelter them; he means to give his young sister to one of the sons; to Tostig, I think. This Tostig; I don't like him. Not to be trusted! Sly and jealous; a violent man. Big and strong. Very fair; with a great ragged moustache and long shaggy hair... a wolf of a man. I tremble for my little aunt.'

'So this Tostig will be your uncle—a pleasant addition to your family! But why Tostig? Why not Harold? He's older, he's richer and more powerful. A better proposition I should have thought.'

'Harold's in Ireland.'

'I wonder why? It could mean trouble for my cousin King Edward. This Harold—he could return with an army of wild Irish savages; and there's the Danes, too, thick as bees in a hive on the east coast of Ireland. He's not the sort to let insult to his father go by!'

She nodded at that. 'A fighter; but unlike his father, his tongue will not betray him. A pleasant man, they say; a charm to win all hearts.'

'Yet with all his virtues my cousin doesn't like him,' William said. 'He believes Harold had his hand, also, in Alfred's horrible murder. Of all Godwine's sons Edward likes Tostig best.'

'And now Tostig is going to marry my father's sister. It could mean more than I thought.'

He sent her a sharp look.

'It could be,' she said, very slow, 'my father means to help Tostig to the English crown. Edward is childless...'

Edward is childless and we are of kin... and there are ties of gratitude. Edward is childless and we are of kin...

For the first time the thought was in his conscious mind; quite deliberately she had put it there. The English crown shone golden before his eyes.

'We are to be wed in six weeks,' William said, a few days later. 'Things have changed in Rome.'

'I have heard it. Pope Leo that forbade us is in prison—the proper place for tyrants. But still we are near in blood, and still—'

'You may leave that to your father and me!' he broke in, impatient. 'The matter is arranged. I trust you are pleased.'

'Yes, I am pleased.' And pleased she was; pleased to be done with the endless waiting, to take on the dignities of marriage and the full, new life that lay before her.

'Then all is well. Meanwhile I am for England. I have no fallals and fripperies to trouble my head.'

'England?' She pretended to surprise; but that two-and-two make four she knew as well as he!

'I have never been in England,' he said.

'It is not so different from your own Normandy, I believe. The court as Norman as your own; the same dress, the same tongue.'

'Yet still different. In England there is also my cousin the King.'
She waited.

'He's frail; they say he looks an old, old man.'

'He always did—or so you say!' she reminded him. 'How old would he be?'

'Not above forty; but he'll not make old bones.'

'What do you hope to gain?' she asked softly. And she must make him speak his purpose; once he had spoken, he would not, for pride, go back on his word.

'A promise... perhaps.'

And still he could not name it, so daring, so undreamed of, so glorious the thought; that it had come to him through her, he was unaware. He said instead, 'The English court is Norman, as you say. My cousin is childless... and the English are used to Norman rule.'

'It was to have been English rule,' she reminded him. 'They were weary of foreigners—have you forgotten?'

'They're used to it now.'

'I doubt it. Your cousin has a Norman heart; and because of that they do not like him.'

'Like him—no! But they respect him; venerate him—a near-saint. He is their King; they accepted him and his Norman rule. And they must go on accepting now Godwine is gone and his sons with him.'

'They are not gone for ever,' she said. 'Godwine is not a man to lay down his power. I have seen him—and I know.'

'It has been taken from him. I think they will live and die in exile.'

'Then,' she said softly, 'you do not know them. But my father knows them. Do you think he'd give his sister to a hopeless exile?' And now she had dropped all pretence to not knowing the thing on his mind. 'They are not men to be turned aside. As for the son in Ireland, this Harold, I hear what men speak of him. All praise him for a kingly man—except Tostig that for jealousy cannot see straight. A man above all men, they say. In battle a hero; no man can stand against him.'

'There no man so strong but I am stronger!' he cried out quick and angry; and she smiled inwardly that her taunt had stung him. 'But let us not talk of him; let us talk rather of my cousin that has no heir.'

'Has he not?' she asked gentle; but within she was all triumph because she could lead this invincible young man, this legend of a man, any way she chose. 'Godwine mentions a royal prince of England—an atheling in exile.'

'Who thinks of him?' William shrugged.

'The King of England might; and the English people might.'

'I doubt he'd be in haste to answer any invitation they might send. He'll remember his murdered cousin—his and mine; maybe he's too young to remember it himself, but he'll have heard it, the filthy tale! And he'll not forget it. And by the Splendour of God I'll not forget it, neither! Their great Godwine had both hands in that; *and* their Harold. A golden tongue maybe; but bloody hands I'll swear! As for the atheling himself, call it exile if you will! But he's lived in Hungary from childhood and, for all his English blood, he's as foreign as myself; I have no word of English on my tongue and I doubt he has, either. No, they'll not ask him; nor would he come, well-settled as he is; married to a princess of Hungary, I believe. He'd be a fool.'

'To win a crown?'

'To lose his life.'

'And you?'

He threw back his head and laughed. 'No man has bested me, ever. In no fight have I received a wound, a scratch, even. Ah well, we concern ourselves too soon in the matter. Maybe I am wrong and my cousin of England will live a great while yet; a creaking gate, they say, hangs longest. And, by God, I hope he may!'

'And when he dies... since no man lives for ever?' she asked, softly. 'Then the English will speak. They will call one of their meetings with the barbarous name and they will choose a King. It is their custom and their right. And what man will they choose?'

'The house of Godwine is finished,' he said.

'I'd not be too sure of that! They are men to reckon with.'

'And what am I?' She saw him set his jaw; again she smiled to herself. Yes, always—if she were clever—she could lead him.

'Listen!' he cried out, 'I'll not rest until I put the crown of England upon my head—and upon yours that well deserves to wear it.'

He saw her lift her head at that as though already she wore a crown.

'Well,' he said, 'now I am for England. When I return I will bring your marriage-gift in my pocket—the crown of England.'

'You can bring nothing but a promise,' she said very quiet above the triumph in her heart. 'And what would it be worth? You may bind the King of England; I cannot doubt but you will. But can you bind the English people with a promise that's none of their making? Can you bind the will of the English and the power of their witan?'

'Let me but have the promise. I will do the rest. And there's an other promise that I claim. When I return from England I shall have my wife. In six weeks we shall be wed—though twenty popes stand in the way.'

X

But still she was troubled at the breaking of the ban. Surely it would be well to send to Rome. 'We have considered the matter—and least said, soonest mended!' her mother said. 'Pope Leo lies in prison and can do nothing; and there's no-one in Rome with authority to speak. The risk is small and worth taking. But there's another risk we dare not take. Suppose your duke tires of the whole affair—and who could blame him? Suppose he calls the bargain off—where are you then?'

The wedding-preparations broken off four years ago were resumed. Matilda was glad of it. She was not meant for a celibate life. She did not love William; she thought she never should—not him nor any other. But he was enough of a man to promise enjoyment in the marriage-bed; and she respected him—the great duke, the unconquered. She would wear a ducal crown... and, maybe a royal one.

One thing troubled her—she was no virgin; and he was a bad man to try and fool. Conscience and fear both driving, she asked her mother's advice.

Adelais stared. 'Do you propose to tell him? Have you taken leave of your senses? He'd never marry you; not he nor any man! How would it be in the eyes of Christendom if he refuse you at this last minute and for such a cause—for cause he must give? Do not think your father would keep you here at his court! Nor would any convent receive you, except, with luck, as a lay sister—lowest of the low. To tell him would be the act of a fool. The thing is over and done with!'

Not while the child lives, the child I bore.

'Of him,' Adelais said, 'you need have no fear. You're no virgin, true. But he is—so they say! He'll not know the difference.'

'He's never slept with a woman, maybe; but surely he must know the difference between a virgin and... one that is not!'

'It depends upon yourself. And it is simple enough. You must cry out at the right time. You know very well what I mean—it won't be the first time you've bedded with a man. And, before he comes into bed, scratch yourself on the buttocks—a good, deep scratch. And, to make matters more certain, he will, I don't doubt, have drunk freely.'

'He drinks but little at all times!'

'Any man may be forgiven for being a little drunk on his wedding-night,' Adelais said. 'And, with your careful drinker, a little goes to the head. We'll keep his cup well-filled.'

William was back in Rouen, well-pleased; things had gone better, even, than he had dared hope. He must wait to tell Matilda of his success; he cursed Pope Leo heartily that had caused the delay—a delay, however, that soon must end. Meanwhile he told FitzOsbern and de Beaumont, those two alone, of this success.

'My cousin has promised me the crown. I had scarce to hint, even; he was eager. He cannot endure the thought that all things Norman should perish from England. And, after all, I am his own kith and kin. He could not make enough of me! He's old—beyond his years; and frail. And he knows well the Saxon earls wait like a pack of wolves for his death. Their leader's in exile; but he fears their return. And that my cousin will not have at any price. He cannot endure the house of Godwine and its arrogance. Oh they show him the respect due to the King; but never the respect due to himself—a man. He feels he should have dealt with them before; but he hasn't the will and he hasn't the strength.

'So there's the King of England on my side. And, curiously, the Queen also—Godwine's daughter. She's no friend to her husband. And can you blame her? He has never once slept with her. She should have had children of her own and she has nothing. She scorns all things English; she has no love for her father or her brothers—except Tostig. She's a Norman in her thinking and in her dressing; he speaks our tongue rather than her own, she favours our countrymen—and yet her husband doesn't trust her; he doesn't trust her an inch.'

'Then he's no fool for all his holiness!' FitzOsbern said. 'An English heart should be English!'

William nodded. 'My cousin's an odd bird. Concerned about his kingdom, true; but much more concerned about the church he's building. I went to see it; across the river to the west, on the site of an old church there—St. Peter's it's called. I saw the stone-mason's plans. A fine building it should be!'

'A man may build a church out of a thankful heart,' de Beaumont said slow and thoughtful. 'But, save he be a priest or a mason, it must not be his life's work. To leave his kingdom well-found and strong—that is a King's work. And since God has called him to it, that, also, is to the glory of God.'

'God has called me also to a King's work,' William said. 'And I shall make England well-found and strong.'

'What use a promise made in secret—and such a promise?' de Beaumont said. 'Who shall believe you?'

'My cousin will make all clear before his death. It is understood between us.'

'And, if the English will not accept the promise?'

'Then my sword shall speak for me.'

'And mine, also!' FitzOsbern's eyes lit with joy of adventure and lust of the fight.

'To take the word of a frail old man,' de Beaumont said, as if neither young man had spoken, 'to build your life upon it! Sir, I must speak plain—it is madness. Believe it; I was your father's friend and now am yours.'

71

'To build my life upon England would be madness, certainly. Normandy with me is first and always must be. It was my father's inheritance and his father's before him. But England shall be mine also. I have left good friends behind; and not the least of them Godwine's daughter, the King's wife.'

'Can you trust her?' de Beaumont asked.

'I can trust her. Her heart is Norman; and her hands open for gold—her father's daughter there! But come and see the gifts my cousin of England gave me—English horses and hounds, there's none finer in Christendom; embroideries for which English women are famed; and a great jewel for my wife. But, greatest gift of all—his goodwill and promise.'

Godwine had returned to England. He had returned in defiance; he had returned in triumph, and his sons with him—all save one; and he was in the Holy Land to pray God's forgiveness. They had sailed up the Thames; Harold had come from Ireland to join them. The people had gone mad with joy.

William spoke no word when he heard it; only the colour drained from his face; behind blind-seeming eyes his fury raged.

'All London stands firm for the earl,' the messenger said, kneeling. 'And the whole of Kent and Sussex, also. Yet he will not, he says, shed English blood.'

'Will he not?' William startled them all with his laughter. 'Then why does he come in arms?

'For justice,' he says, 'for that and that alone!'

'Pray God he gets it... at the rope's end!' William said. 'As for the raper of nuns, God is not to be cozened; and so he will find!'

The next news came from the heart of the conflict, itself. Robert of Jumièges, kinsman to William and archbisop of Canterbury, arrived with blood and dust and sea-stain upon his robes.

'Sir, the peace is made. The King has taken them back—the man of blood and his sons; the King restores their honours—every one. Now godfearing Normans must run to hide in all the corners of England; or, like myself, must fly across the sea. Outside the walls of London a great meeting was held; with one voice it pronounced Godwine innocent.'

'Innocent, that slayer of princes; of the King's own brother?'

'Innocent, sir. The earl laid his battle-axe at the King's feet—a token of submission; and the King picked it up with his own hands and restored it. Then the King gave him the kiss of peace. It was then honest Normans knew they must flee. I made for the coast... and just in time!' And he pointed to the stains of blood upon his gown; but he did not say it had come from urging his horse through the streets trampling down men, women and children as he went.

'I found, sir, an open boat; a cockle-shell. By God's Providence we crossed the open sea...' And he did not say that his life and the lives of other Normans had been safe and that he had fled for very cowardice.

When de Jumièges had gone William called for his horse; restless with rage, he could find no peace save in the swift motion of the mare; and all the time his thoughts flew swifter than the galloping hooves. *What of your promise, my sainted cousin? What of the crown? Godwine will see that it come not my way. But God, by His Own Splendour, shall see that it come to the rightful head.*

Within a few days de Jumièges appeared again.

'Sir, this accursed earl has cast me from my office; he pronounces me outlaw. He has put, yes, he has dared it, another in my place—Stigand the English priest is declared archbishop. And how can that be? He has not been blessed by the Pope; he has not even received the bishop's pallium. And if he had? No bishop may be put from his place once the Pope has received him. But this Godwine, this impious dog...' He choked upon the words.

'You should go to Rome,' William advised, very smooth. 'Lay your wrongs at the Pope's feet. All good Christians are with you.'

He knew well that this de Jumièges was a bad priest and a bad man. But his tale was good; and would lose nothing in the telling. Let Christendom ring with the tale of his wrongs; it could benefit William... one day.

XI

The marriage was to be celebrated at Eu; William had desired it. Now, the two processions were converging towards the castle. It stood within his own borders and was now his own; he had taken it after a long and heavy siege. In this castle, so long with-held, he would take his bride so long with-held; the symbolism pleased him. With his train, and all in bridal array, William rode in first; now, at the great door, he stood ready to receive his bride.

Encouraged by her mother's assurances that all would go well, Matilda had set out cheerful enough; now, the castle frowning above her, her spirits dropped. She cast a sideways look at Adelais riding by her side. Easy enough for her mother to promise all would be well—but her mother had not to deal with this man, this hard, proud man. For a taunt against his birth he had taken a bloody vengeance at Alençon; for that same taunt, foolishly spoken, he had prepared for war against her father. His honour demanded it. What would his honour demand if ever he found she had stained it? Disgrace published in every court of Christendom. Poison, perhaps—it was the Norman way. Panic-stricken, she longed to turn the mare, to fly from him that stood, all knightly courtesy, unbonneted to greet her.

She had not, upon this journey, for one moment escaped the thought of the child she had borne. After the birth she had wept; then she had dried her tears. She had known nothing of the child—where it lived, or in what circumstances; or even whether it lived at all. It had been her mother's command. She saw now it had been wise; save for a few bad dreams, grief had faded. It was as though the child had never been.

But now it was different.

Last night Agnes had spoken. 'My demoiselle, there is something you should know. I am old and will, I think, not see you again; and there will be no-one to tell you what has become of your child. For, be very sure, madam your mother will never speak. God, praise be to His Name, has smiled upon the little one. She is daughter to Maître Gerbod, the advocate of St. Bertin in St. Omer. A good man of gentle birth and rich; he has much honour. He has one child of his own, a boy—at that time a year old. The lady had lately lost her baby at birth; a little girl—and could look to have no more children. They were happy, my demoiselle, to take your little one. They did not know, nor do they know, whose child she is. How old would she be? My wits fail a little.'

'She is four years old.' And in that moment memory began to wake.

'They were so happy to have a daughter of their own. And, though no word is said, here in this house, upon the matter, madam your mother sends every year to enquire of the little one; they call her Gundrada for the child they lost. She is as lovely as an angel; fair as a lily, they say.

74

The little boy, Gerbod—he is called after his father—is her most loving playmate and faithful servant. Yes, truly, God has been good.'

The old woman stopped. She said, 'My demoiselle, you are best not to see the child—she is happy; it is enough. But we none of us know when ill-fortune may strike and the little one need help; and for that reason I speak now. Well, goodbye my demoiselle, my nurseling; and God send you happy.'

Matilda had bent to kiss the old cheek; she had found her way from the little dark hole off the kitchens where the old woman lay, and up the winding stairs to her own chamber—and all the time her eyes blinded with tears. A child fair as a lily; fair as the man that had begotten her.

That night she had dreamed of Brihtric; and dreamed of the little one. And when she awoke, the tears running down her cheeks, it was as though he had just deserted her, and the child new-taken away. Henceforth she must remember Brihtric with hatred; remember her child with ever-growing sense of loss. The child had a name; had become a living person. How should she fail to remember, as the years passed, that Gundrada was five, was six, was seven, was marriage-high, was living, growing... and her own?

The procession had come to a halt; she felt strong hands lift her from the mare; she saw the harsh lines of William's face soften at the sight of her. She thought again, *If I am wise, and if I show my self loving, I can hold him in the hollow of my hand*. She would follow her mother's advice; with God's help all would go well. She smiled a little wryly for expecting God's help in this matter.

She knelt with him at the altar of Nôtre Dame at Eu; she listened to the solemn words, made her responses, swore to be a faithful wife. She was deceiving William; but she was not deceiving God.

They sat together, crowned, upon ducal thrones; for the first time she sat above her parents. It gave her some satisfaction. There were, she could not but notice, no high princes of the church present; Malger, she thought, had set the example. William would not forget it. Her eye ranged among the noble guests. Arlette had been dead these two years, but the pretty girl, William's sister, stood behind Matilda's chair. She was seventeen; and, her first husband being dead, William had given her to Count Lambert of Lens. Behind William stood the two half-brothers—Odo, bishop of Bayeux, twenty and stalwart, and Robert, a year younger. The fighting bishop they were beginning to call Odo; and, indeed, his strength lay less in the cross than in the sword. A proud man; and Robert, equally proud, his young face fierce even in this moment of rejoicing.

William, Odo, Robert and Adelaide—so noble, so handsome, all four; they drew the eye. Arlette, she thought, must have been a remarkable woman; but for all that she was not sorry Arlette was dead; matters would go simpler. The old man, the tanner with the strong arm, was dead also; but somewhere among the lesser guests stood Walter, brother to Arlette. She would seek him out, thank him for his past care of the child William.

The child. Her thoughts went off to another child, a child she must never acknowledge, whose name she must not speak. In this moment she yearned for the child so that her glory dimmed and blurred. Forget. She must make herself forget. Because of this child she must act the virgin on her wedding-night; well, it should not be too difficult.

She watched William; as usual, he drank sparingly. FitzOsbern, more than a little drunk, was teasing him, holding out a cup of wine and laughing at his lord's refusal.

'Tonight of all nights a man may drink!' FitzOsbern cried out and offered the cup again.

'Tonight of all nights a man needs his wits!' William answered; and he did not laugh.

She took the cup from FitzOsbern, and, with her own hand offered it. 'Pledge me, my lord,' she said.

'Do you, also, seek to befuddle me?' He spoke in jest; and, though she took it with a laugh, she felt the moment's fear.

'Yet drink to me, my lord!' She set the cup to her lips. William took it from her hand and drank it to the dregs.

The feast had come to an end; some of the guests had fallen beneath the trestles where, among the rushes, the dogs fought for scraps.

And now it was the time.

She let them undress her; she pretended that their jests went by her. She displayed nothing but virgin modesty; the jests, she knew well were to rouse the bride to willingness. And, indeed, they had aroused her. She did not love her husband; but he was a man and she was a woman. Her duty in bed she knew; Brihtric had been her teacher. She had but one concern; to carry the night through as though she were virgin.

76

She lay in the great bed; the cressets cast a warm glow upon arms and breasts; upon the dark hair flowing upon the pillow. They stood about the bed—her mother and the young Adelaide and as many women as the chamber could hold. They were wishing her good luck and a lusty lover; they were wishing her a handsome son. She smiled, accepting their wishes; only her mother could guess at her fear.

She heard the ring of feet. In came William magnificent in bridal bedgown. There was laughter as his gentlemen led him to the bed. His eyes were bright with desire, his bearing a triumph. FitzOsbern took away the bedgown and he stood there in the splendour of young manhood, so that the women cried out she was a bride to be envied.

Adelais threw back the bedcovers and bent to kiss her daughter; in her shadow the bride's hand stole out and took the pin.

For all Brihtric's teaching she was not prepared for William. Brihtric had coaxed and pawed and whispered the words to rouse her. But William threw himself upon her, and, direct as an animal, took her. He hurt her more than a little, so that she did not find it hard to cry out; but, already roused, the pain was pleasure.

She had been well and truly taken; her sheets—examined according to custom—proclaimed it. The bride-night was over and she was safe.

Nothing more to fear.

XII

Duke and duchess rode the summer-countryside in splendour. William had planned his progress that all Normandy might behold his bride. Fifty years since there had been a duchess in Normandy—duke Robert's short-lived marriage no man remembered. But such a duchess as this, so young, so fair, so kind, surely had never been seen.

Crowds stood bareheaded for hours in sun and rain to welcome her; flowers were thrown before her horse, gifts poured in upon her—rich gifts and homely ones. And all alike she received with most sweet looks; everywhere she showed herself debonair and kind.

Everywhere fêted, everywhere blessed; and, if there were few princes of the church, there were humble priests a-plenty, together with rich citizens in chains of office and humble peasants, all kneeling with a most joyful respect; and from their castles came the great lords riding, to bring her in with love and reverence.

But when they reached Rouen it was a different story. On the surface the same love, the same respect, the same joy. But beneath the surface? There were many to question the marriage—the Pope's ban stood; there was no-one to lift it. And it was a righteous ban the people said. All children born under it must be accounted bastard—as if their own duke were not one bastard too many! Nor were the ladies, for all their smiling, best-pleased. Their duke, that had never cast a hot look upon anyone of them, was in love with his wife! And though their lords affected to find charm in the small creature, they themselves could not but laugh at such a dwarf ensnaring their lord. There were plenty of lewd jokes on that score.

Loudest of all was Adela, wife to Hugh of Grantmesnil. A beauty in the admired fashion—full breasts, long limbs and high colour. Once she had cast her eyes, her fine dark eyes, upon the young duke. He had not been interested. She thought he might be interested now; now that he had slept with a woman; she did not think his wife could hold him long. Once more my lady tried her charms on William. He looked upon her—the fine, willing woman—and with a few coarse words sent her away smarting. Thereafter he asked her husband to keep her from the court—and no reason given; it was kinder than sending her away. There were words; and Hugh found himself dismissed together with his wife. Thereafter, if not entirely stilled, tongues were quieter.

In October they heard the ugly news. Malger, archbishop of Rouen, highest prince of the church in Normandy, had publicly denounced the marriage. If the duke did not come to his senses and put away his wife, he would excommunicate them both; he, himself!

'He's not dare!' William said, white and furious and guttural with his anger. 'But he allows his tongue to wag—that is enough; it is more than enough! This bastard uncle of mine, this bad priest that lives fat and keeps the church lean! I have long borne him and his ill-doings in mind. Let him have a care or I'll have him stripped and on his knees.'

'He stirs the whole business, keeps the pot aboil!' she said. 'But for him the matter would have been forgot. He forgets his obedience towards you. This excommunication that he threatens—what does it make me but your harlot?'

'It is his revenge because I cast down his brother, the traitor of Arques. Now he shall himself be cast down; but not for revenge. His crimes are sufficient. But first I must gather my proofs.'

'What proofs, my lord? That he sleeps with women and begets his bastards? All Normandy knows it—that he robs the churches to adorn his own table; that he concerns himself not at all with the business of his flock but gluts himself with meat while his sheep starve! My lord, he should be put from his place.'

'And shall be!'

'Then do it quickly,' she said.

'It is not in my hands. It is for the Pope—'

'There is no Pope!' she said, very quick.

'There's a Pope-elect; soon he will wear the triple crown. Meanwhile I must gather my proofs. Then a legate must come from Rome to sit with my council of bishops. By that time the elect may be truly Pope—'

'And, if he is not?' she flashed at him. 'If things do not move fast enough, then punish him yourself! Quieten his tongue lest others echo him. Punish him, my lord, at once!'

She stood there small and taut as a steel spring; for the first time he caught a glimpse of the iron beneath her softness. It disturbed him but it pleased him, too.

And now Lanfranc spoke also, against the marriage; and that was worse. Lanfranc, good man and good priest whose honesty no man, could question, Lanfranc to whom more than once he had turned for council. With Lanfranc he would deal at once.

Lanfranc, since he could in no way persuade to silence, he banished from Normandy; in no place within the duchy must he be found. His abbey farms and orchards William commanded to be burnt.

And yet he had Lanfranc back and forgiven—won, in spite of himself, by the quick wit of the man.

Hunting, he had reined horse at the sorry sight of the great scholar jogging humbly on a broken-winded nag. 'What, not yet gone?' he cried out enraged. 'Get from my sight at once!'

'Sir,' Lanfranc said, mild, 'I go as fast as the nag will carry me. She goes, poor thing, upon three feet. Give me a nag with four and you'll not see me for dust!'

William could not but laugh; and laughter carried away his anger.

'Back to your abbey, priest! I'll make good all damage. But, in return, you must plead my cause at Rome.'

Lanfranc lifted his troubled face. 'Sir, I will do my best; but to defy the Pope is no light matter.'

'To defy me is no light matter, neither; moreover there is no Pope.'

'There is always a Pope!' Lanfranc said.

'Does it not occur to you,' Matilda said when she heard the tale, 'that he planned the whole affair? There are horses and to spare at Bec! And, isn't it odd that your paths should cross? And wasn't Lanfranc's road taking him not out of Normandy but towards Rouen—towards Rouen, itself!'

'It could be; and I'd admire him the more—so gently to get his own way! We could send no better messenger to Rome.'

But for all that it was a mission to take seven long years.

To William and Matilda it was the bitterest of blows—this ban upon their marriage. With the marriage, itself, both were content. She saw now that she could never have been content with Brihtric; beside William he was trash. William had greatness above all men. She had deep pride in him; but still she could not love him—not him nor any man. Brihtric had poisoned the spring of passion.

But she was still a woman; and William all of a man; in his lovemaking, direct. She preferred it so. If she could not return his passion, she could take him with satisfaction; he fulfilled her needs. If she had not love, she had a kindness for him; and a deep concern for his well-being—which was her well-being, also. That he had come to love her with passion gave her great satisfaction; it added to her power over him.

They could have been happy; were, indeed, happy—to a degree; but true content they would never know until the ban was lifted.

For William the ban was yet more bitter. He had wanted her for her royal blood, to pass it on to his children; now he loved her for herself. A chaste man long denying himself a woman—lest he beget bastards—he found sleeping with his wife a joy and a duty. But it was not only that. She was not only his wife and his love, she was his companion and his friend. She had not only beauty and blood; she had a clear wit. Some learning he suspected too; but it did not take from her graces. He would like to lay the crowns of Christendom beneath her feet. Yet he could not even call her *wife*.

In October she said, 'I am with child.'

Elation swept him head-to-foot; such joy, such triumph he had never known.

'The ban is not lifted nor Malger punished. Do you wish it to be said—' she stopped short. *Bastard begets bastard*; he knew well what she had meant to say. Had she spoken out of a troubled heart; or had she meant to lire his anger? Whichever way it was she had spoilt his joy.

'Have patience a little...' and he heard his own voice, as ever, guttural with anger. And then, more gentle, 'When?'

'In May... or so I think.'

'We have all of seven months,' he said. 'Lanfranc shall go to Rome once more.'

He came to her bower a few days later and stood by the brazier holding chilled hands to the warmth. He said, 'Good news; no, not from Rome, there's not time. But still good news, let us take it for an omen. Godwine's son, his eldest son, that raper of nuns, is dead; he died on his way back from the Holy Land. God is not fooled. God does not accept a show of repentance. He knows the hidden heart.'

God does not accept a show of repentance. She took in her breath. Was the ban upon her marriage punishment for the thing hidden in her heart?

The child grew in the womb. She carried it with pride; that she carried it with difficulty, small as she was, she let no-one, not even William, guess. In June it would be born—and still no word from Rome. William that longed to lay the crowns of Christendom at her feet, could not even save her child, child of her royal blood, from bastardy.

In mid-April William brought her further news of the house of Godwine. The willows were out along the river-bank, violets filled the air with green fragrance—and Matilda was heavy with her burden.

'Godwine is dead. And his death—' satisfaction blazed in him, 'all Christendom, save, maybe, the besotted English, will say he deserved it. Through him my cousin Alfred came to a violent death; now God has sent a violent death to him!'

She listened eagerly. Did the death of the great earl further her husband's ambition, or hinder it? For all her eagerness she kept her needle steady, embroidery was her skill and pleasure. Head bent upon her work she weighed one chance with another.

'It was at Winchester,' William said. 'The King was keeping the easter festival there, it is his custom. He was holding the gemot there; that is also his custom. And both customs I shall keep when I am King. Godwine was there with all his sons—all of them dining at the King's own table—except the eldest that is himself dining-table for worms. And now his father is in that same state. It seems that Godwine rose in his place and called aloud to the King, *Sir, I think you still believe I had some hand in your brother's death. I swear by God I am innocent. If I lie, let this bread choke me. So now God be my judge.*

'And then God was, indeed, his judge. For he lifted the bread to his mouth and fell choking to the ground. He never spoke again. So let God deal with all murderers!'

Amidst the tears of the English, Godwine had been buried with highest honour. 'Buried in the old minster at Winchester—the burial-place of Kings!' William cried out enraged. 'When I am King I shall drag his body from holy ground and throw it on the dunghill where it belongs and there the dogs may lick his bones!'

The old enemy was dead; but a younger, stronger stood in his place.

'Harold succeeds to his father's honours. Now he is earl of the West Saxons in Godwine's place!' William cried out. 'Now he stands next to the King. Now he will be—in all but name—the King himself; my cousin does little but pray and watch his church grow. He has won the King that till now had little liking for him! Well, if God stand with me, I am content. And stand with me He will; He has no love for the breaker of promises.'

'Harold made no promise,' she reminded him.

'He must know of it. He stands close to the King—too close for my liking. It is the same thing.'

'The King of France is mustering against me,' William said and knit dark brows, 'Since Alençon he has become my enemy; yet I was always his faithful vassal. What have I done to arouse his anger?'

'You married me; he's afraid of the alliance. And he's jealous; you've been successful in everything you set hand to, your name is greater than his—and will be greater still. There's your answer.'

Henry was on the march. He had called upon his vassal-lords, north, south, east and west. First to come was Geoffrey the old enemy, the men of Anjou and Maine behind him; and with him the lords of Brittany and of Blois. From every corner of Gaul they came, eager to pull down the arrogant Bastard of Normandy.

William called upon his own vassals; and every one, highest to lowest, answered the call.

'I do not take this as loyalty to myself!' William said, grim. 'It is to save themselves; their property, their lives, their very skins.'

'They acknowledge you as leader and protector,' Matilda told him. 'Whatever the cause, they acknowledge it. Every man willingly performs his vassal's duty because he trusts in you. Sir, you have come far, indeed!'

'You strengthen me more than an army of soldiers,' he said.

Evreux had been invaded and pillaged. The stink of burnt fields, burnt cattle polluted the air before William's forces were gathered. Now he was ready. With FitzOsbern steel-true, with young William of Warenne afire to serve his lord and many another, William marched.

Marching swiftly, marching slyly under cover of night, as was his way, they came upon half the French forces scattered in pursuit of pleasure and all unprepared. William, on the march, had heard of these same pleasures—rape and murder!

At Mortemer the hosts of Normandy fell upon them with great slaughter. 'Their commander, caught with his drawers down—and exactly that!' William said afterwards when there was time for laughter. 'You should have seen him run! He and his men after him. I've found a new captain; young William of Warenne. The lad's a fighter. He gets Mortemer castle for himself; and well deserves it! Well, now we can sleep in peace... for a while. We're not through the wood yet!'

'With God's help we shall be; He guides us,' Matilda said. 'Everywhere they sing your praises—the people, the song makers and the sober monks writing their chronicles. There'll be trouble again—it's the nature of things. But the worst is over.'

'Henry asks for peace,' William said a little later.

'Make your peace but—'

'I know. I know! I trust Henry no more than I'd trust an adder underfoot.'

XIII

The year moved on towards June, And still Lanfranc besought the Pope-Elect and was still refused. 'Leo still lives,' he had said, 'I cannot revoke the ban.' But in the matter of Malger he promised an answer as soon as might be.

William's joy in the coming child was spoilt; but, for all that, he put a good face on the matter. 'It will be a boy,' he told Matilda. 'For him I shall take the crown of England. He shall be a King—after his father. And you I shall make a Queen.'

But all his cheerfulness did not deceive his wife. Restless with pregnancy, she urged Lanfranc to further efforts promising, promising… rich gifts for his abbey at Bec; and for himself, whatever he chose to ask.

He needed no bribes. While the duke lived in what must be accounted sin, what hope of clean living from lesser folk? Yet even though it was now June and the birth expected mid-month, she could not believe that her child, her ducal child, her royal child, should be born out of wedlock. Day and night she besought God with her prayers.

In mid-June the child was born—out of wedlock.

Labour had been hard, as for her, it must always be; but at no time, not even in the supreme moment of birth, did she cry out. When they put the child into her arms, a passion of love and pride over threw her for the tiny creature she had carried in the womb. Let Rome say what it would, she was duchess of Normandy and this child the heir. But there was guilt, too; his parents had defied the Pope, the babe might have to fight for his birthright.

A dark baby with a long back. 'He will be tall like his father,' she told the midwife. The wise woman said nothing; with such short legs he could never be tall. 'He will be sturdy and strong,' she said.

'Certainly he will be strong like his father,' Matilda said, insistent, 'yes, and he will be the handsomest prince in Christendom.'

William was disappointed when he saw the child; he was not like the house of Rollo, he was not like a Norman at all. He was the image of Baldwin—a little Fleming. Disappointment, intensified by guilt that the child could not be regarded as true-born, persisted; it was to colour all relations with his eldest son. To his wife he said no word; but, for all that, she knew his mind. Resentment pricked in her; it took from her satisfaction in her husband, it added to her worship of the child.

And, indeed, he was a laughing baby with a chuckle to catch at the heart; a winning little creature. And it was not only his mother that was won; he had charm enough for twenty! 'I shall call him Robert, after my father,' William said. 'By God's grace here is Robert the third of Normandy.'

And Robert he was christened, according to the rites of holy church, for Malger—the case building up against him and wishing already he had not interfered—judged it wise to hold his peace in the matter of the threatened excommunication.

The year wore on; the child grew into all the endearing tricks of a baby's first year—a bright, friendly, laughing baby. But still William could not love him. The fault was his own, he admitted it; he was no lover of children. When the child was grown a little, then, maybe, he would come to care for it as a father should. And Matilda, the small dark head against her breast, would remember another child whose fair head had never rested there, and she would weep for the little lost one.

Robert was a year old and she pregnant with her second child; but still the ban lay upon her marriage.

Her second child was a boy, also; a handsome child. In build and colour he was all his father. 'A true son of my house,' William said and named him Richard after William's grandfather, Duke Richard the Second. His pride in this child was great; he had begotten a son in his own image. It had been hard enough to endure the slur on Robert's birth; but this little one so like himself! He could not endure it. Again Lanfranc must go to plead Rome's clemency. But, for all Lanfranc's prayers, Rome answered as before—the Pope that had laid the ban still lived; no other man in Christendom might break it.

'Two little bastards begotten by the prince of Normandy upon the princess of Flanders of the royal house of France!' Matilda said, bitter; and it was but what others said—and did not whisper it, either. William himself said no word; but anger ate into him like acid.

Pride he had for this second son, but again—and to his own surprise—no tenderness; he could find no interest in children. He was never to be easy with them; not even with the child he truly loved—his third son. But still he wanted children; more and more children. 'Sons are a weapon in a man's hand,' he said.

'Weapons may be two-edged,' she said, fretful with her third pregnancy. 'Sons have been known to turn against fathers!'

'Not my sons!' William promised, grim.

This third pregnancy she could take more easily; not in the body but in the mind. For now Pope Leo by the grace of God was dead; dead at last. His Regent was Pope now; Victor the Second. Surely he would show mercy; surely they had been punished enough! Whatever penance was laid upon them they would willingly and perfectly perform. Let him but speak! Lanfranc must go to Rome once more; he must go at once!

The Pope had listened, at least, to that other plea upon which they had set their hearts; and from that they took hope.

My lord archbishop of Rouen wished, with all his heart, he had never meddled in his nephew's marriage. At the council of bishops William's charges were proved. By the Pope's authority Malger was deposed; by William's, banished. He betook himself to the Channel Isles and there he lived his agreeable life—feasting and drinking, wenching and begetting his bastards, till he came to his death by drowning and troubled William no more.

They took much comfort from this casting-out of Malger; the new Pope was a man of understanding. They counted the weeks and then the days before Lanfranc's return. Which would come first—the lifting of the ban or the birth of their third child?

Matilda was already in labour when Lanfranc returned.

Pope Victor confirmed the ban. They had chosen to defy God's Word together with His Vicar on earth. He desired to be no more entreated.

They looked at each other without a word; between them lay the new-born babe. For this moment they had prayed and waited. Now the words had been spoken and nothing was altered.

'I shall make Christendom too hot to hold him!' William cried out at white-heat. 'Let him not forget Pope Leo that died in prison. And who put him there but my own countrymen? Normans settled in Italy that have no truck with tyrants!'

'This Victor is no tyrant; you can do nothing there!' she said. 'But, he desires to be no more entreated. And there lies our hope. We shall entreat and entreat again; we shall batter upon his ears until for weariness or compassion he give way at last.'

Her third child was a boy, also—a child restless as flame and his hair bright yellow. 'Even more than my second son this is a true child of my house,' William said. 'By the colour of their hair you shall know the sons of Rollo! Already he is a little bull; I shall name him William. Two sons I have named for my house; this one I name for myself.'

A strong little boy, plump like his brother Robert and self-willed; a little red face that grew redder with his frequent angers—for this was a passionate child. The little red one they called him; and, to distinguish him from his father, *Rufus* he became. William, though it was not in him to show it, doted upon his yellow-haired son, his true son of the house of Rollo. Matilda thought this third son well enough; but he had not the winning ways of Robert nor the high and handsome look of Richard. *Curthose* they were calling Robert now—*Shortshanks.* His father had found the name, laughing between gritted teeth that the child was not growing tall, as his long back had promised. His mother resented the nickname, the child was sturdy and he would grow! It was wrong for a mother to have a favourite child, she knew it. But Robert was her darling. She loved Richard—he was her little son; but not with that same passion she had for her eldest. Her third son, she found hard to love he was a greedy baby, biting at the breast, nipping and pinching.

When, in the next year, her fourth child was put into her arms she knew again that same uprush of passion she had known for Robert. This child was a girl, a daughter; hers to keep. She would, she promised herself, grieve no more for the lost one; all was well with her—beloved only daughter of a rich household. This child, this little Cecilia, together with Robert, crowned her life.

The three little brothers came to admire the baby. Three-year-old Robert, laughing, tried to close the tiny hand about his small wooden sword. William was not pleased. 'Here's one,' he cried out, harsh, 'to give with too little sense!' Matilda defended the child. Robert was himself a baby; he showed a generous spirit. Little Richard allowed his hand to be guided gently upon the baby's head; but Rufus went scarlet with rage when he saw the little one at his mother's breast—his own place. They had to drag him away before his clenched fists fell upon the infant head.

'He's one to take his own!' William said laughing.

'He takes what is not his own also, the greedy little creature!' his mother said.

'He also is a baby,' William reminded her. 'But he'll make a man to have and to hold.'

'We must give our thanks to God for these children,' William said.

'I will give thanks—when the Pope speaks,' she answered.

He said nothing; but he was thoughtful watching mother and daughter. He had his own notion of the proper way to give thanks; he, also, must wait until the time was ripe.

That same year William ridded himself of yet another bastard of his father's house—Malger's son; and gave his rich lands and titles to his brother Robert. Justice there was none—save that he had always distrusted the man... one would be a fool to wait till the adder bites! Now Arlette's youngest son was my lord count of Mortain; and William had two brothers, rich and powerful, to stand by his side.

In the next year, the year of grace ten hundred and sixty-seven, Henry of France broke the peace he had sworn after Mortemer; for three years he had brooded over his revenge. In August he came riding with Geoffrey, that Hammer of Anjou, into Normandy by way of the Hiésmois; behind them streamed their armies, spears and pennants black against the summer sky. The countryside, where the harvest had stood golden, lay beneath a pall of smoke.

Rage took William like a madness. His orders were immediate. All castles and fortresses to be strengthened; the open country left to the enemy. Falaise he would make his headquarters.

Bitterness burned as he rode at the head of his forces; he tasted it, sour in his mouth. And it was the more bitter because of the nagging concern over his marriage; now he must bite upon a new and most grievous disappointment. Pope Victor that had desired to be no more entreated was dead and Stephen sat in his place. Once more, with fresh hope, Lanfranc had been sent to Rome. Once more that hope was dead. This new Pope, too, refused to acknowledge the marriage. But for Henry of France there would have been no ban, ever; of that William was certain. Henry had not played an overlord's honourable part. William that had vowed never to beget bastards found the curse of bastardy hanging over his children.

He rode through the blackened fields, sickened with the stench of burning and the ruined crops. Well, Henry should pay; he should pay for all!

Falaise, itself, he found well-defended. He strengthened it still further, and set himself to wait patiently for news. Hourly his spies rode in.

The enemy were avoiding Falaise; they had no wish to stick their noses into a nest of hornets. They were making their way north to Caen.

Hornets have wings to fly! William moved quickly. A few miles out of Falaise, fresh news met him.

'Sir, they have burned Caen. The city is wasted; a ruin!'

Caen. His little growing town, his small cherished city sacked and burnt; wantonly destroyed—wantonly, since as yet, it held little of value... except his plans and his hopes. They had destroyed the little town since they had not dared attack Falaise.

He vowed revenge for Caen.

'Sir, they are making for the Dives—the ford at Varaville. They mean to cross; they mean to sack and burn the lands on the other side; Lisieux is to be given to the flames. They have sworn it!'

And, while he stood stark and white with passion, there came further news.

'Sir, they take their pleasure before they cross the river. They are glutted with food and drink; their pack-horses can scarce move for weight of their plunder. They take their ease, while behind them the fields go up in flame.'

Mortemer all over again!

He gave orders to march through the dark night. By daylight they were hidden in the marshes by the river—marshes he knew well, he and his men. And so hidden, heard the news for which they waited.

'Sir, they are beginning to cross the river—the vanguard together with its captains. Already the King of France and the count of Anjou are on the other side. The rest follow.'

'Let them!' William knew the river; the river would do his work for him.

Half the forces had crossed; on a hill King Henry stood and watched them. All going well! But... so well? The river was surely running swifter, running higher. Surely the men were crossing now with some difficulty; they were losing foothold. Some were actually swimming and some were going under—the harness was heavy. Some were turning and swimming back again. The rest of the army must wait. To cross now—impossible!

William, too, watched. The river, truly, was doing his work. It was the time! With his men he burst forth to the attack. Now, taken by surprise, the enemy were being driven beneath his spears, his swords.

Back, bath again into the swift-flowing river. The river running with blood, was choked by floating corpses. Those that tried to escape in the opposite direction were caught in the marshes, were bogged down, were sucked under. Driven by the lust for killing, which he mistook for righteous anger, William ordered every man to be put to the sword.

From the heights on the other side King and count watched the slaughter. 'We must cross again; we 'must go to their aid!' Henry cried out, and would have ridden down the hill.

'The river is impassable,' Geoffrey told him. 'You will add to the slaughter.'

Henry gave way; he was an old man now. 'My heart, I think, is broken,' he said. And certainly, later, that same year, he had young Philip his son consecrated to be associated with his father, according to the habit of the Kings of France when they felt their end was near.

'Not a battle but a massacre!' William told Matilda, gleeful. 'Now Henry, false friend and false overlord, must sue again for peace.'

Henry did sue for peace. Without asking he gave back Tillières, proud town and castle, long lost to Normandy.

'Now we are out of the wood!' an exultant William said. 'Now we have finished with trouble from France. Now if there's to be war, it is I that shall decide it, I that shall take the first step. I shall watch; watch my good friends of France and Anjou. At the slightest sign—I move!'

That same year brought another event; not to Normandy but to England—and yet it was an event to shape William's future and Normandy's future.

'The stars in their courses fight for me!' William said, coming into Matilda's bower; she sat suckling the new-born child, the little head golden against her breast. At her feet little Robert sat; he went quickly to hide behind his mother's skirts. He had learned by now not to try to come to his father; baby as he was, he sensed his unwelcome.

Matilda looked up from her nursing.

'The atheling is in England together with his wife and children. The English sent for him into Hungary; they sent—and he came. A thing I never thought to see!'

'How do the stars fight for you? This must take you further from the crown.'

'I think not!' William said softly. 'The atheling is not on English soil; he is in it; in it! He's dead.'

She looked up startled. A young man—and *dead*!

'Harold shows his hand,' William said. 'For five years he's ruled in the shadow of the throne—and not so much shadow neither! Do you think he means to give up that power? By the Splendour of God, no! And more; he means to rule—and no shadow at all! When my cousin dies, he means to set the crown on his own head!'

'But it was Harold himself invited the atheling; he had no need. He's master of England.'

'He both invited—and put an end to it; put an end to the atheling, too! The atheling never saw the King. He never left Dover; Harold's Dover.'

'But *die*? How?'

'Some say this and some say that. Some say a natural sickness others—poisoned by Harold. But this way or that he's dead and buried. And still in the shadow of the throne, Harold rules England.'

'But the children; what of the atheling's children?'

'Two girls and a boy; and all very young. If the English choose the boy to succeed, which I doubt; and if the child should die? How easily such a child may come to his death! Then Harold takes the crown—or so he thinks. To bring the atheling and his son to England, and to take them off at his pleasure—a master-stroke! Well, we must watch Harold, that wicked devious man!'

XIV

Matilda was pregnant with her fifth child. And still in the eyes of Christendom her marriage was no marriage.

Life, she thought, had played her a hateful trick. She was duchess of Normandy and might one day be Queen of England—a possibility she never lost sight of. She was young—just twenty-five, she was accounted beautiful, she was well-liked and her husband loved her... perhaps too well; already she had four children and was carrying her fifth. But the success of her marriage was flawed. She could not reconcile herself to the ban; nor accept that her children were bastards.

Five pregnancies in five years. She loved her children; but she did not love her pregnancies. She was so small and her children so large. She longed for some rest, a respite for body and mind. But though William was often from home—making visits to his provinces to see that justice was done, putting down small insurrections with much profit to himself, keeping constant watch upon his enemies of France and Anjou—she could not escape conception. She did not love him but increasingly she admired him; and his lovemaking she had learned to enjoy—the swift taking and the deep peace that followed; save that it was always clouded by fear of pregnancy.

Pregnancy she could, at any time, have ended; the old nurse had whispered in her ear. But she understood the need for children; and she had her own need to play fair with William—she had deceived him enough.

Her fifth child was another girl. Even as a baby Agatha was beautiful; not pretty, merely, like Cecilia but beautiful. Her hair was deep gold, her eyes deep blue; William, when he looked at her, remembered his mother, the beauty that had won a count's heart and kept it.

In the first year of the little girl's birth Pope Stephen died; for one short year he had reigned. 'God gives us another chance!' Matilda said.

But it was a chance she did not choose to take.

'I would not sue Rome now, not if I were certain of the answer for which we long,' she told William. 'Half Christendom does not recognise this Benedict, this usurper that thrusts himself upon St. Peter's chair. What use his sanction? Our enemies would still brand our children.'

'And our friends, also—if it suit them!' William said, respecting her fore-sight. 'Well we have waited so long; we can afford to wait a little longer!'

That year they could hope again. Benedict, the usurper, had been put from his throne and Nicholas sat in his place.

'Now we can ask again; ask and ask and go on asking!' William said. 'Thank God we waited. Had Benedict said *Yes*, it is odds that the new Pope would say *No!*'

'Eight years we have been wed,' she said soft and bitter. 'Eight years—and our marriage not recognised. Five children we have—and our marriage not lawful!' Suddenly she could bear it no longer. 'Lanfranc must go; he must go to Rome at once. He must deafen the Pope with his clamour, melt him with our humility. Whatever the Pope demand, we shall do; no penance too great if he will lift the ban!'

She sent for Lanfranc. 'Tell the Pope—*tell* him! Ask him what—the ban unlifted—I must do! Must I go back to my father dishonoured and my children bastards? And how would my father receive me? Ask His Holiness that! And my husband—what of him? Must he be left wifeless, childless? Punishment we deserve; with a full heart I admit it. And punishment, God knows we have had! And further punishment will take; and no murmur. But let not the little ones suffer. Christ is merciful; he would not wish that the sins of the parents fall upon the children. Tell the Pope; tell him, I beseech you!'

'And tell him more, also,' William cried out, 'Tell him that this ban threatens the peace of Christendom. For, if I put my wife away, if I so dishonour her—it must mean war between me and Flanders and between me and France also—my wife is of the French royal house. And where would there be an end? If he show himself merciful, like Christ whom he serves, we shall accept with joy whatever command he lays upon us. There can be nothing too costly or too hard.'

Lanfranc had gone. Matilda was restless as never before. 'It is the last chance!' she said. 'We have seen four Popes come and go; how many chances will God see fit to give? This fifth Pope may outlast us all!'

The Pope had consented to their prayers. The threat of bloodshed in Christendom had moved him. The ban was lifted, the blot erased. The children were to be recognised as born in holy wedlock.

'The ban is lifted,' she cried out, joyful, the tears running down her cheeks.

'The penance is just; and after my own heart. I rejoice in it!' William declared.

'The penance is no light thing,' Lantranc reminded them. 'But it is worthy of him that set it and them that shall perform it. You are to build to the glory of God. You must build, each of you an abbey together with you, sir, a monastery, and you, madam, a convent; and each with a hospital for the blind, the sick and the aged. So you may wipe away your sin.'

'Until the work is begun, neither of us shall know peace,' William said.

Now they must forget the long bitterness; now she would enjoy her children. Lanfranc that had so successfully pleaded their cause should become their tutor; or, if he had not time, since William had made him responsible for the building of the abbeys, he should name their tutors, and watch the children's growth. She admired him most that, for all his goodness, all his real love of God, he had firm knowledge of people and events.

It was early August of that same year that William said, 'Henry is dead—the old enemy, dead; and I do not know whether to be glad or sorry. It could mean an end to peace with France.'

'It should mean closer peace,' Matilda told him, 'I have heard from my father. He's to be guardian to the young King; the old King willed it so. Now my father will have both hands in French affairs. He will watch our interests you may be sure.'

Three months later, on a cold November day, William said, 'It is my lucky year. My second enemy is dead—the old Hammer of Anjou, God rest his soul. I shall not know what to do with so much peace on my hands.'

'There are always enemies, and there is always... England,' she told him.

It was truly William's lucky year. The ban lifted, his two formidable enemies dead; and now a further piece of luck.

Young count Herbert, the true heir, had been driven from Maine when his father died. Now—Geoffrey of Anjou safely dead—he was back again demanding his rights; without help he could not possibly regain them.

'Be my friend,' he implored William, 'and seal our friendship with marriage—a double marriage. My sister shall marry your Robert; they are of an age. And give me, for myself, one of your daughters.'

'Well enough—as far as it goes! But if you should die without children? A man cannot look too far ahead!' William said.

'Then Maine shall come to you; and thereafter to Robert and his heirs.'

'A good bargain!' William told Matilda triumphant. 'Daughters are indeed power to a man; what did I tell you?'

'Cecilia is but four, Agatha three—'

'He's little more than a boy himself; a betrothal, only. Who knows what time will bring? As for Curthose, he's lucky, indeed! The little Margaret is a pretty child; and gentle, so I hear. I shall require that she be bred in Normandy—its future duchess; and that her brother provide a household suitable to her station. I tell you the advantages are too many to count! The promise of Maine for myself or my son, Herbert bound to us by ties of blood; and my own hand directing Maine—Herbert's too young;

Maine that has been a thorn in my side all these years! To win power by peace—it's a rare thing.'

Matilda was carrying her sixth child; she hoped it would be the last. But William joyfully declared that he was brisk enough to beget a dozen more! Of late he had been disturbed. Three years and no child! He had began to question his virility; now that virility had been triumphantly proved. 'A man can never have too many children. I've said it before and I say it again. Sons are weapons in a man's hand; daughters are power; power to bargain with. You have seen for yourself!'

Two years since the Pope had spoken.

In the small dark castle at Caen that was little more than a rude fortress, one could hear the hammers and the picks and saws at work; see the two great abbeys rise slowly stone by golden stone. Matilda, anxious to have her penance done, impatient to see the lovely thing the master-mason had conceived, take solid shape, hurried on the work. But William preferred to take things more slowly. The work was begun—earnest of his sincerity; it must take its time. It would be greater, nobler than Matilda's—a man's aspiration in stone. Two great abbeys to glorify God—hers the Abbey of Holy Trinity; his St. Stephen's.

'I mean to build a house for us, also, a new house, hard by St. Stephen's,' William told Matilda, 'so we shall have God's House always before our eyes.'

'No other reason?' she smiled, knowing his joy in magnificence.

'The old house is mean and lacks all comfort; it still bears the scars of Henry's burning. It is not worthy of you.'

Three great houses in Caen growing apace—the two houses of God; and the house of William and Matilda. Caen, itself, was growing. William's favoured city; the gentry began to follow the court. Merchants set up their counting-houses and built their mansions; craftsmen followed them.

For the first time in years there was peace throughout Normandy. William was master now and so intended to remain. Those castles he had not destroyed were strongly garrisoned; he watched that, save for his own, there should be no new ones. He saw to it that his vicomtes—his sheriffs—did justice; he would appear unlooked-for to put fear into them. Since no men knew when to expect him, justice was, by and large, done throughout the land. His punishments were severe; though men acknowledged them just. Never a man to punish for love of cruelty save when rage drove him, he saw to it that his laws were obeyed. The worship of God he held in true reverence. It was not only his great abbey that he built but new churches also; and old ones he repaired.

Where there is piety and where there is peace, trade flourishes; and the arts. Slowly Caen was growing into beauty with its fine buildings, its rich carvings in stone and wood. In castle and in nunnery new embroiderers were at work with their silks, their wools, their gold thread; and in the monasteries illuminators worked in gold and fine colour; and the scholars at their chronicles made their libraries.

Throughout Christendom he was held in esteem. He was enlarging his cities, making safe his borders; above all he was watching his enemies. His eyes and ears were everywhere; and certainly they were bent upon England. The Channel was a highway; messengers were constant with the news.

'Things move,' he told Matilda. 'But not, I think, in my direction. Well, a wise man knows how to wait.'

She sat at her embroidery-frame, attentive, listening.

'Harold still carries himself as though he were King; and his brothers stand by him. Between them they have the best part of England in their hands.'

'Not all the brothers,' she said. 'There's Tostig.'

'Yes, there's Tostig! My cousin of England prefers him to his brothers—the lone wolf. I think my cousin fears the pack; not the one that runs by itself.'

'Of all men Tostig is the one to fear. Not to be trusted! A wild and jealous nature. I saw enough of him at my father's court. It's little good anyone will get out of him; least of all his wife. When I think of Judith I could weep!'

Daughters are power, William had said; yet he was not overjoyed when this sixth child was born—a little girl. Three daughters, one after another. They christened her Constance; a pretty child with dark eyes and carnation cheeks. She shall marry a great prince, William said. Matilda knew his disappointment, understood it, and, in spite of herself resented it.

Herbert, count of Maine, died. 'Two years since we made our treaty,' William said. 'And he is dead. A boy, only, and dead. And your fears about your daughter marrying a man older than herself were useless. And so I told you! Now everything arranges itself. Maine is mine.'

'You'll get nothing without fighting for it.'

96

'I have a strong arm; and I have the little Margaret for hostage. We shall see.'

You'll get nothing without fighting. And fighting promised to be hard. Certainly Herbert had promised Maine to William; but the Mayennais thought otherwise. There were heirs closer in blood. They chose Walter, count of the Vexin, whose wife Biota had the strongest claim.

'If they will not give me Maine, then I must take it!' William said.

In time of peace he had not forgotten the old tricks of war; now he was at the old game of reducing Maine.

He had no mind to destroy the capital—le Mans that rich and prosperous city; he destroyed the countryside instead. Burning field and farm, reducing castle after castle, he edged nearer and nearer to the city. So quick, so stealthy his march, no man knew where he might be found—only a long trail of ruin led directly to the city.

Without a siege, without a blow, even, the city surrendered.

'Le Mans is mine—unscratched, fortified and strong!' William told Matilda, returned in triumph. 'And I have left my castles ringing the land. If I go into England... *when* I go into England, I shall have my own men and not an enemy at my back.'

XV

In England the King grew ever more feeble—his one desire in life to see his minster finished that he might take his last rest therein. Across the sea William watched; watched Harold grow ever more powerful.

At home Normandy grew rich in peace, grew strong in peace; and Caen, the golden city, grew with it. Matilda's abbey, though not yet finished, was growing towards its consecration; William's, growing more slowly, promised more splendour. Lanfranc had charge of both great buildings. He handled the workers with tact; with cunning one might say, were he not so holy a man. No setback could trouble him; a seeming disaster would send him away to pray and back he would come, the remedy clear. A practical man yet a man of vision; a rare combination.

William kept a thoughtful eye upon him.

Matilda was carrying her seventh child to William's pleasure rather than her own. This time, he declared, she must give him a son—two or three if she chose; three at a birth—such things had been known. There were times when she looked at him with dislike. He loved her, he honoured her—but he spared no thought for the increasing difficulties of her pregnancies. On one thing she was determined; after this there should be no more. Her children, growing fast, took much anxious thought. Lanfranc though he had not time to teach the children himself, watched over their growth; he appointed tutors and reported progress.

Robert, at eleven, was a plain, square boy with a charm to whistle a bird off a tree. He was lazy, he was generous; he would give his last sou away. He was strong and quick in fight or sport. He could beat any boy two years older than himself with fist or stave or with his blunt light sword. He could not see the use of lessons, though he could read and write well and make his little poems. I wish he would see fit to praise God, therein, Lanfranc said, but he's no priest, that one—a little trouba- dour. He was inconstant in mind, though not in affection; he found it hard to obey. If he will not obey then he must be whipped, Lanfranc said. But advice and whipping were alike useless; whipping he took without flinching and went his lazy, good-natured way.

The tensions between his father and himself had grown with each increasing year. William, himself a shapely man, was mortified by the boy's shape and stature. Such a one to be his heir! And, in his turn, he mortified the boy. Robert would never forget that it was to his father he owed the nickname he detested—*Curthose... Shortshanks*. He resented the name; resented, even more, the father that had given it.

Richard, for all he looked like his father, tall, high-coloured with dark red hair, a high nose and a pale eye. For all his courage and strength, was a born scholar. He was gentle and patient. He would fight if he must but he had no mind for warfare and he sickened at cruelty. A great prince of the church, Lanfranc said, to glorify God and bring honour to his family.

Of all his children William loved his third son best—his yellow-haired namesake, the little red-faced Rufus. Like Robert he was short and plump; but his father found no fault with his stature—the boy would grow. A fierce little fellow that obeyed no-one but his father. A plain vain child that would drench himself in essences stolen from his mother, but cared not at all whether he were dirty or clean. He wore his hair long and curled which looked odd amongst the close-cropped nape-shaved Normans—and provoked some speculation. Once he wore flowers in his hair but once, only. His father laughed him out of it—the only one that dared. Laugh at him and he would spring vicious as a wild cat. He was mean, he was untruthful; he mocked at things he did not understand and screamed like a mad thing when deprived of a pleasure. At nine years old he knew well how to take his sly revenge—the quick stamp upon a bare foot, the sharp nip, the handful of hair torn from an unwary head. He talked too quickly, stammering and stuttering; when he could not get the words out fast enough he would beat his fists upon whatever stood nearest—a wall, a chair, or on his mother's breast... but he never struck himself. Childish faults, his father said, though he could find few of them in Robert and none at all in Richard. Childish faults must be cured, Lanfranc said, grave. The boy is able, we must watch which way his abilities grow. Like his brothers he was physically brave and a daring hunter. He was quick to attack and when rage drove he would hurl himself against those stronger and older than himself, he would hang on savagely biting and savouring the taste of blood. Like a rat, Robert said. There was little love between the brothers.

Cecilia at eight was a pretty, graceful child. She was gentle and merry and obedient. Tutors reported that she would creep in upon her brothers' lessons and outstrip them all three! William gave orders that she should take regular lessons with the boys. Already she could read and write and cypher; she knew her prayers by heart and went to church as to a feast. Matilda would wonder that William who disliked learning in women should encourage Cecilia. And, if Cecilia—why not Agatha?

Agatha was a golden beauty of a child; more than ever she reminded her father of Arlette. If ever a daughter represented bargaining power, William thought, that daughter was Agatha. Like Cecilia she was gentle and merry; but even at this tender age, she had a clear sense of right and wrong. Then she would set a firm chin and it was not easy to turn her from her purpose.

Constance at three with her dark eyes and cheeks like picotees was the spoiled darling of the family; an imperious little creature yet honey-sweet and easily won by a word of kindness.

Three little girls and each a bunch of sweets. 'Three daughters— and each fit to marry a King,' their mother said.

'Aye!' William said. But for Cecilia he had a special King in mind.

The year of grace ten hundred and sixty-four.

William paced restless about Matilda's bower, brows drawn and dark.

'I do not like it; I do not like it at all!' he cried out. 'The young son of the dead atheling—the English treat him like a royal prince.'

'He is a royal prince; the natural heir to the English throne. You must expect it!' Matilda sent him a sideways glance to see how he took it.

'I do not expect it. A little foreign child, his mother an outlandish Hungarian! What can England do with so small a King?'

She drew the bright wool through the canvas. 'It is clear. The English will choose the little foreign prince and Harold will rule England in the shadow of the throne... as long as the child lives; which, like you, I doubt will be long. English athelings have a way of dying young.'

'So! Whichever way it goes, Harold, it seems, must win; and I must lose! No!' he pounded fist against palm. 'I'll not lose; not I! My cousin promised me the crown; I'll let no man turn him from his given word.'

'Who knows of this given word?'

'I know. And my cousin knows. That Harold also knows, I must believe. He'll try, no doubt, to keep King Edward from his word. But, for all he's weak, Edward is pious. A promise is a promise; upon that promise I stand.'

'Shall you meet all England in arms?'

'If need be. But there'll be no need; it's a land divided. And there's Tostig. Have you forgotten him? He could be a good friend to me.'

'A good friend? A man that would betray his brother—and that brother the head of his house?'

'Then let us say a tool; a useful tool to be cast aside when it has served its turn.'

And when still she looked doubtful, said, very cheerful, 'Tostig has been given a great earldom in the north. He does not understand these northerners—from the south. Nor does he intend to learn. He oppresses this new ear of his; he wrings from it every drop that may be wrung. How it must end, any man can foresee.'

'They will turn him out.'

He nodded. 'And Harold will do nothing to stop it. He'll talk with a loud mouth of justice—and justice it will be; but justice won't be the reason. Harold means to get rid of his brother because he *knows* of the promise made to me. Tostig's your uncle by marriage; what more natural than he should help us? Harold will not risk it. He'll drive Tostig away. That's as far as he sees. I see further. Tostig will nurse his revenge; and that where I come in.'

Midsummer. William came striding into his wife's bower. Cecilia sat, fair head bent upon the Latin of her book. Agatha, upon a stool, sought to bring into some order the coloured wools that Constance tangled with small inquisitive fingers. Matilda sat, weary, on her chair, her bright beauty dimmed; she was near her time.

William scarcely looked at her. He was deathly pale and deeply moved. Yet, she thought, it was not anger. When Cecilia and Agatha had made their curtsy and departed taking the little one with them, she raised her eyes to his. It was not anger; it was triumph, a most passionate triumph.

'Heaven looks to my affairs.' And his voice was like a trumpet. 'God Himself will see the promise kept. He has delivered my enemy into my hands.'

The child within her leapt; she laid both hands upon her belly to quiet it.

'He is here. Harold is here; here in Normandy! So near I have but to put out my hand to take him.'

'No!' Her voice came out soundless. It was not possible! So shrewd a man, this Harold, he'd not venture—not if he knew about the promise.

'Yes!' And again the trumpet sounded. 'An accident; if you can call it that! Myself I call it divine Providence.' Some of the whiteness was going out of him; it was she that was white now with knowledge of what this could mean.

'He was taking a pleasure trip, sailing at ease round the English coast. Three ships, no less; with hounds and hawks to hunt at any point they chose to land. Well, God turned the wind, I am the hunter now; and he... and he the hunted. A storm. And Harold's ship blown from its course; and the hunted is in the trap. There he is, sitting pretty in a dark dungeon with fetters about his feet.'

'But... *fetters*?'

'They keep a man safe. He's at Beaurain.'

'Guy of Ponthieu, then! Now I see why the fetters. He knows the worth of his prisoner; he means to hold him to ransom.'

'A King's ransom!' William said, grim.

'Guy of Ponthieu...' she was thoughtful. 'Your vassal, my lord.' He nodded.

She said at once, 'We must have Harold here—in Rouen. Command de Ponthieu; if he hesitate, use force.'

'Hesitate—he'll not dare; he knows the strength of my arm! But, better command him to make an end of the man; what should I do with him here?'

'You could set him free, my lord; send him home in honour with gifts and loving words.'

At advice so unexpected his brows drew together.

'Bind him to you in bonds of friendship,' she said, softly.

'Freedom, gifts and friendship; the giving all on my side?'

'You give to get, my lord. Show yourself generous and you may get from him all you need.'

'Even the crown of England?' And at the absurd notion he laughed aloud. 'But, to have him under my hand is something; it could be very much. The advice is good.'

Harold of England was William's honoured guest.

When they met—the one that was to deal death and the one that was to receive it—they could not forbid the instant respect, one for the other. A good man, each thought, to stand by one's side in peace or war. In other circumstances they would have sworn blood brotherhood.

William saw the tall fair Saxon looking every one of his forty-two years. Shrewd eyes set about with crowsfeet in a tanned and weather beaten face... honest eyes; a kindly mouth and a chin like a rock. In spite of all the tales William could not believe this man guilty of treachery, much less murder. However the two athelings had died, Harold had had no hand in the business. On that William would stake his life.

Strength and command; it was Harold's first impression. A second glance showed him the proud, cold eyes set in the high forehead beneath the cropped dark red hair. A man some six or seven years younger than himself, he judged. A clever man that would not hesitate to scheme and lie; to snatch his advantage where he could—and having snatched it, would never let go. The mouth proclaimed it, the mouth that smiled now while William held out a welcoming hand. The whole man showed a sort of geniality; of such geniality, Harold thought, one had best beware.

When Harold was presented to Matilda she took in a sharp breath; she was all-but overthrown with anger—anger as unexpected as fierce. It pierced like a sword in her breast. The man reminded her of one she had believed forgotten; as if, she thought bitter, a woman can ever forget the man that took her virginity and got her with child.

Behind her gracious smiling she wondered about their visitor. Was he an unwilling guest here in Rouen? Would he prefer the dark cell where, at least, his captor's intention was clear? Did he guess he'd not return home—if ever he did return—without some damage to his prospects, to his honour? And did his shrewdness teach him to disguise dismay?

Certainly there was nothing but courtesy in his charming manner. A handsome man her woman's eye assured her—perfect Saxon; red-and-white beneath the tan, she'd swear, the hair hanging fair, the eyes a sturdy blue. A match for William! Tall above the common run of men, both of them; strength in mouth and chin, strength in the whole athlete's body. William would need all his cunning—and hers—to get the better of the Englishman.

XVI

She had been astonished by the uprush of anger at the sight of the Englishman; she was yet more astonished, as the days went by, at the shifting backwards and forwards of her emotions. This shifting, she supposed, was less because of him than because of herself; her condition. In a few weeks her child should be born. She would find herself wishing him well, this Harold; would look at him almost with love. How could she not? He was good to look at—all of a man! He was strong but he was gentle, too; with herself, with the children, very gentle. And then, the wind changing, she prayed that William should get the better of him, deceive him, crush him. She hated him, the fair Saxon. A love-hate relationship.

And Harold? He would look at the small, queenly woman with six sturdy children and wonder how she had found the strength to carry them. He liked to talk with her, always she showed herself smiling and friendly; of the angers that rocked her he had no notion. He thought he was learning from her—about conditions in Normandy, in France, in Flanders; and so he did—as much as she thought fit. That she picked his brains, that she was building up knowledge of England, never entered his head. So kind she was, so gracious and accomplished, he found affection for her growing, as it might be for a sister. No, scarcely that! He did not care for his sister Edith that had married the King of England; he did not trust her. But this woman, a man could trust.

He was a good guest, willing to please and be pleased. He rode with William and hunted with William; and so well-matched they were, it was hard to say which were the better.

He liked the children and the children loved him. Robert was forever at his heels; when they rode together or hunted, the boy had the praise he longed to hear from his father—and never did hear. Richard would question their guest about England. He liked best to hear about the churches, and the monasteries; and about the scholars that wrote their chronicles. Yet when they rode or hunted, he would outstrip the most part of the riders and even Harold found it not easy to keep up with him. A rare lad, Richard, active and contemplative, both.

But Rufus would have none of Harold. At the very sight of him he scowled and stuttered with anger, jealous that the man took up so much of his father's time. This discourtesy Harold appeared not to see so that the boy stuttered yet more; and, though Matilda raised her voice in gentle but firm reproach, William offered neither punishment nor reprimand.

The little girls had no fear of him. Cecilia would greet him with affection; but Agatha would come running, the little Constance at her heels. Sometimes, Matilda thought, it seems that the child in the womb leaps towards him, also. It is true; he has the gift of winning hearts, this Harold.

'We shall have to give you one of our little girls for a bride,' William said, one day, careless and laughing; and Matilda joined in the laughter.

Which shall it be? Harold took up the joke... but he longed for his mistress, for Edith of the Swan's neck whom he loved above all women, the mother of his sons. 'I choose Cecilia.'

Matilda saw the child flush rosy.

'Not that one!' William said, very quick—too quick? Matilda wondered. Was this a jest? Or did he mean some kind of betrothal? Then why not Cecilia? She was the eldest girl; and no match could be better than the duke of England, as they called him here—except that she was not yet nine and Harold past forty. But Agatha was younger still and Constance little more than a baby. Still that would not deter William if he saw his advantage there. But what advantage? He could never mean to give a daughter to the man he intended to put from his place whether as regent or King. It must certainly be a jest!

Harold thought so, too. 'Then here's my bride!' and he picked up the baby and tossed her into the air.

'Too small!' William laughed more than ever. 'What do you say to Agatha?'

'Agatha it shall be!' And, laughing still, Harold set Constance on the floor and held out his arms.

The seven-year-old came running and he kissed her gently. 'You must grow a little before we are wed!' he told her. She smiled and nodded and kept her arms about his neck and would not let him go until her mother called her back; then she allowed him, very gently, to unlock her arms.

'A pretty jest!' Matilda said later alone with her husband and sent him a sideways look. 'But—I thought, perhaps, the child took it for earnest.'

'What then?'

'She's but seven.'

'Margaret of Maine was younger.'

'But Agatha, young as she is, has a true heart. She is not one to forget.'

'She'll forget—if need be!'

'So! It is a jest or not—as you choose. You will use it for a solemn betrothal if it suits your purpose. If not...!' she shrugged.

'You have it exactly!' William said.

Harold was wearying of Normandy; he longed for England. What was happening there? How did it fare with the King? And with the young atheling? Was Tostig still oppressing the north? And how long would the north endure it? Not long if Edwine and Morkere had their way. Of all English earls these two were the most troublesome—greedy, untrustworthy; in one thing, only, constant—to seek their own advantage. Tostig was only partly to blame for the trouble in the north; some of it—and not a little—was due to those two brothers making their sly trouble for the southerner, the Saxon Tostig.

He was increasingly troubled by affairs in England; he wearied of this court whose splendour had, at first, so impressed him; Whose friendliness had won his heart. Now he desired nothing so much as to be back in England.

William would not hear of it. Harold began to wonder how true that friendship might be. Loaded with honours he was, but—he began to think—a prisoner? No fetters, no locks; but, for all that, securely locked within Normandy at William's will. Let him take one unauthorised step, and would not William's hounds be upon him? Now he wore chains of gold about his neck; would he not be in worse plight to exchange gold for chains of iron?

But still William had no mind to let his captive depart. Did time hang heavy? He would show Harold some very pretty fighting.

Matilda knew the reason for that. 'You mean to warn the man with the might of your fighting forces; to show him that you are, indeed, the Conqueror!'

William nodded. 'And one other reason. I must watch the man in battle, know with what I must contend!'

William carried him off to Brittany with whose duke there was grave dispute. They returned both of them with high honours—and Harold's was the greater. The duke of England, with his own hands, had plucked men from the quicksands beneath Mont St. Michel; with his single strength he had raised them and set them upon firm land. In the fight he had showed utmost valour; beneath the walls of fallen Dinan William had knighted him.

That last troubled Harold. Accepting knighthood did it imply that he had become William's man? Or had the honour been a courtesy, merely? He was beginning to find William over-subtle; he longed more than ever to leave Normandy; this land which, for all its friendliness, he was beginning to find hostile... sinister.

He must go home. The King was in poor health, he might die any day; if, indeed, he were not dead already! How should a man know—if William did not wish him to know? But why should William not wish him to know? How should it concern William? Maybe it did concern him, concern him very much. There had been that surprising visit into England when Godwine and all his sons were banished. They had been over-close—the weak King and his strong cousin. What had taken place between them? Edward himself had never said; but Tostig, taunting, had hinted... a thing too monstrous to be believed. But Tostig himself had been in Flanders at the time; what could he know? Malice; malice on Tostig's part, that was all.

But whether Edward were dead or not, whether there were any grain of truth in Tostig's malice, Harold must be home again to keep his hand upon affairs. When he had left on this ill-starred hunting trip, the witan was already raising the question of the succession. Some few had spoken for the young atheling; more for himself. During this tiresome absence of his more might go over to the atheling's side. If they did, Harold would stand by their choice. Useless to pretend disappointment wouldn't go deep—he had it in him to be a good King; a strong King such as the country needed. Yet, if they chose Edgar, then Harold would choose a council to rule for the boy; and he, himself, would lead it. An anxious and thankless task. It would mean unending vigilance lest the boy come to a sudden death like those other athelings his uncle and his father. For those deaths there had been many to blame the house of Godwine. Of the first, he had known nothing at the time; and preferred to know nothing now. Who could, after all this time, hope to get at the truth? Compurgators had sworn to his father's innocence—but for all that his father had taken the smear; and he, himself, had not wholly escaped. And for the second? The atheling had been ailing when he landed—a sickly sort of a fellow; a natural death. Yet once again Harold Godwineson had taken the smear. This third time there should be none!

William would, at times, talk casually of England. Once he mentioned the King's ill-health with some regret; and once he asked about the atheling—had the King seen him yet? All very careless—so it seemed; but Harold had the notion that William was not at all casual. And once William said, with seeming candour, 'When my cousin dies there may be trouble about the crown. Many will want the atheling; I know well how you English hold by descent. But others know well there's danger to a country with a boy-King. They will choose a man; a strong man, with experience both to rule and to fight!'

'Who then?' Harold spoke with apparent candour. *You mean yourself, You are wrong, wrong! We would never take you; we've had enough of Norman rule.* 'One thing is sure—the English will choose no more foreign Kings.' And he had spoken plain enough!

And still day followed day; and still William with smiles and courtesies held him. And still Harold sickened of the chase, sickened of the feasts, sickened of Normandy. He'd have no more of it! When would William allow him to leave? He put the question blunt and straight.

Matilda, bent upon her needlework, was, it would seem, both blind and deaf; it was as though she were not there. But she was there; eye and ear set upon the outcome.

'Keep you here, my lord?' William's amused brows did not hide the wariness of his eyes. 'I had thought it was your pleasure to stay, as well as mine to keep you! I had thought we were friends.'

'Friends, sir, I do hope it. And, for your kindness I thank you with all my heart. But life is not all pleasure and there's work for me at home.'

He could see wariness sharpening in William's eyes; see the smile fading in the set of the jaw. It was William's *pleasure* to keep him here; the word was two-edged. He lost patience suddenly. He said, very blunt, 'Sir, if it be a matter of ransom—'

'But... *ransom?*' William spread his hands. 'I had thought we were friends.'

'Friendship must be equal. The giving has all been yours. What may I do in return before I go?'

There was a long silence, each man taking the other's measure. William said, his tone a little too careful, 'Very well. Let us be frank. You would prove your friendship... before you go? There's one thing you may do.' And now he was careful, indeed. 'You know, surely you must know—he will have told you—my cousin has promised me the crown.'

So that was it! The rumour, scarce to be credited, was true—if, indeed, William was speaking the truth.

Harold said, careful and courteous, 'He has said nothing. But, sir, he could not give you the crown. It is not his, nor any man's, to give. Only by full assent of the people can it be given.'

'Nevertheless the promise was given. Shall you break the promise of so holy a man?'

'Sir, I did not make it nor did the English people. We did not make it; therefore we cannot break it.'

He had expected some outburst from William; he was not prepared for the sudden silence—which, when he looked at the man, he knew to be more passionate than any outburst. Such a passion of anger he had never seen. The whole man was white with it, blind, unseeing.

It was Matilda, turning heavy in her chair, that brought William to himself. 'What the English promise is not the question,' she told Harold, smiling. 'What you yourself promise—that is the question. Your King, whom you are bound by oath to obey, has given his word. Will you honour that word when he cannot honour it himself? You cannot make my lord, here, King of England. But you can raise your voice for him; and your arm, too! Will you do that?'

She had pinned him down; the little, smiling woman was as dangerous as William himself. He took a turn about the room; the air seemed to stifle him.

'It is too heavy a matter for me to decide now, sir,' he said. 'Give me leave, awhile.'

'All the leave in the world. But, till your word be given, here you shall stay. And it could be...' William said, thoughtful, 'that the stay may not be so pleasant.'

Harold walked, restless, about the pleasant chamber William had assigned his unwilling guest. He wearied of it; he wearied of the countryside beyond that was like his own England—and was not England. But would he not weary more of the dark dungeon where soon he might find himself; a dungeon from which he would never escape?

His first desire was to serve his country, free it from the Norman yoke. But for that, himself must be free. How could he serve England here in Rouen, still less chained in a dungeon? And time pressed; it pressed. *And any hour the King may die—if he be not dead already*. He groaned aloud.

Suppose he added his own promise to the King's—if, indeed, the King had promised; there was no trusting William! Would God require it of him? God knew his unwillingness; God knew his love of England. God knew. And to God he must leave it. Since other way there was none, he would make his promise. The rest he must leave to God.

'He will make the promise!' William said, grim, triumphant.

'But he will not keep it,' Matilda said.

'He is a man to keep his word.'

'Not the word given under duress. Would it not be simpler to put him out of the way?'

He stared at her. Coming from this small, quiet wife, the advice was amazing—the more so that it was exactly opposite to her first advice. *Send him home in honour, with gifts and loving words.* And now, after all the companionship between Harold and himself, all the courtesies and compliments, here she was calmly suggesting putting the man to death. He could scarce believe his ears.

'I might have done it at the first,' he said, 'but not now; not now. Harold is my guest, my unoffending guest. He has stood with me shield to shield, my own hand knighted him. If I kill him I shall have all Christendom about my ears; yes, even this Normandy of mine. Moreover I need his help; I need his strong right arm and the goodwill in which he is held. And, above all, I need his promise.'

'A promise is not enough. If you must keep the man alive then bind him with an oath; so great an oath, that, breaking it, a man risks to lose his soul.'

'I am ready to promise,' Harold said.

'Then let us waste no more time! You shall go with me into my great hall and, in the presence of my council, you shall swear the oath.'

An oath? So it was not to be the private word between two men; well he had hardly expected it! But—*an oath!* He had not expected that, either!

In the great hall the assembly waited—princes of church and state. Harold felt the air about him heavy with triumph; to himself triumph most shaming. His face, grave with the occasion, gave no sign as he walked with William towards the two thrones. On one Matilda was already seated, her three sons stood behind her. Before the thrones stood two chests covered with cloth-of-gold.

William ascended his ducal throne; and, from its height, addressed Harold in a voice for all to hear.

'In these chests are the most precious relics of our Norman saints. To break an oath upon their bones is blasphemy. Every saint in heaven will testify against you; every saint hound you to your just damnation. Are you ready to swear?'

This, this he had not expected and his heart shook. He must take this greatest of oaths knowing full well that he must break it! He tried to thrust down his fear, his anguish; but for all that his face blanched, his hand trembled.

'This is the oath,' William said. 'I shall speak it; and, that you may understand exactly, the interpreter shall say it in your own tongue. Now are you ready?

'I Harold Godwineson, earl of the West Saxons...'

The loud commanding voice, a trifle guttural as always with emotion, reciting the words; the clear voice of the interpreter... and the low halting voice repeating them.

'...my hand upon these relics, in the sight of God and in the presence of this assembly—in the belief that my liege lord Edward King of England whom I am at all times bound to obey, has bequeathed to William, duke of Normandy, the crown of England—do swear that, as soon as King Edward shall die, I will accept William as true King of England. I swear to take up arms for him, at need, when he shall come to claim the throne. All these things I swear, so help me God. And, if I break one tittle of my oath, may those saints upon his blessed bones my hand now rests, bring me to eternal damnation.'

'Now you shall have safe conduct home,' William said.

XVII

Harold was gone; and William was well satisfied. All had been made safe. Matilda was satisfied, also; Harold had stabbed her too often with memories best forgotten. But she did not believe that the oath would be kept.

'Let Harold break his oath,' William said, 'and he shames himself. He shows himself to all Christendom as a perjured, impious man.'

She nodded at that. 'Certainly he would set all Christendom against him. So much we should gain!'

But the children missed him. He had given each one a gift; to Agatha, half-jesting, he had given a little ring. Now she fretted for him. Harold was her lord; any day now he must come to fetch her away. She had tied up her treasures in a piece of linen and would allow no-one to touch them. Cecilia, too, missed Harold; she could not, it seemed, keep his name from her tongue. And there would be, at times, a quick turn of the head as though she heard a footstep, or a listening look as though she waited for the sound of a voice. What was there about this Harold, Matilda wondered, to win all hearts?

In early autumn her seventh child was born. It was, like all the others, a difficult birth. It was a girl; William not altogether genial said, 'You must do better next time!' And she, drenched and cold with sweat, promised herself that this child should be the last.

The child was christened Adela. The little girls adored the baby, even the three-year-old Constance; but the boys took little notice—except Rufus who would have tormented it, given the chance. Girls are easy, their mother thought; but boys! Except for Richard she found them difficult.

Robert and Rufus troubled her equally. Before Robert's birth William had talked much about him... too much. *My son... my little duke of Normandy*. He had never got over his disappointment at the first sight of *the little Fleming*. At twelve, Robert was still undersize and, with humiliation, knew it; knew also his father's disappointment in the fact—a disappointment that not all a boy's increasing skills of hand and eye could sweeten. *Curthose*. It was not a name to raise a boy's pride. He was lazy and feckless as ever. If he were not careful with sweetmeats, he would make a fat man; and so his mother warned him. A plain, plump boy, he relied over much on his undoubted charm. He was forever kind, forever generous. There was no cruelty in him; no sign of the old dark streak that William had, that she herself had, that Rufus undoubtedly had. In all his twelve years he had punished no-one; not even a servant when punishment was deserved. And that angered his father, too. A prince should know his place and see that others knew theirs. But punishment never did any good, Robert always said. Well, he should know, his mother thought, sighing! The first time she had wept over his small back. Five years old he had been, and given away something or left something undone. Who could remember the sum of his small naughtinesses?

'I shall put an end to it; time he learnt better!' Black with anger William had turned upon herself. 'He's spoilt; and you, madam, have spoilt him! This is no common boy. This is Normandy's next duke—and my son! Spoil your girls to your heart's content; husbands shall discipline them. As to the boys—'

'The boys!' she said very quick. 'Leave picking upon Robert, his faults will mend with time. Consider Rufus instead; his faults will not so easily mend.'

She sighed. An insolent child and cruel with it. Young as he was, he beat his servants. But that only amused his father—*my princely boy*! And he took what he wanted—if not by hook then by crook; a little thief. But William only laughed—*my clever child*! And there were other things. He was always running about with boys smaller than himself; not playing but hiding with them; a sly sort of hiding. What they did behind those bushes she thought she could guess. Of this she did not speak; for all his love, William would half-kill the boy. William frightened his children and was not unproud of it. Robert showed his fear in insolence; Rufus by lickspittling. Richard kept out of his way.

She said now, 'You beat Robert for a small fault—or for none; but if ever a child deserved beating it's your youngest son!'

'My little Rufus is well enough. But Robert! He's insolent; he cares nothing for a beating.'

'Medicine loses its taste.'

'Then we must give him something stronger!'

She ignored the threat. She said, 'He fears you and he'll not admit it, even to himself. But fear is there; and out it comes in the shape of insolence. No, it's Rufus you must watch!'

'He's well enough; would God he were my eldest! When I think of Robert, lazy, wasteful of all he has—weapons, clothing, coin—giving here and there and everywhere, knowing that whatever befall he'll not go short, I tremble for Normandy; for Rufus I have no fear.'

'Nor need have—if vices be virtue!' she said drily. And then, 'Be a little gentle with Robert; he respects you, greatly; you are—did you know it?—his hero. Give him a chance, and you'll find him everything you can desire.'

'All *I* desire? Why trouble your head in the matter? He's all *you* can desire, all you *do* desire!' There was an edge to his voice. Was he jealous of the boy, his own son? The thought winged like an arrow and, like an arrow, left its wound. Well, if it were so she must bear some blame; she was too honest not to recognise it. She was proud of her husband, she was grateful for the love he showed, the dignity he accorded her, yet still she could not love him; the man was too stark. But Robert was her son, her eldest son born of her body. She loved him better than anything in life; better than life itself—with one exception; Cecilia, the daughter given to her in place of the lost child. She loved all her children, even the troubling Rufus; but Robert and Cecilia she loved the wrong side of idolatry.

October had passed and the leaves were fallen and gone; the Orne had carried them away. Matilda looked from her high window over the golden city. Against the pale sky rose the high bulk of the two abbeys; her own would be ready soon for consecration; she must discuss the matter with William...

Her thoughts broke; William himself came in.

'News from England!' he said. 'And it has happened as I thought! The men of the north have risen and Harold takes their part. Tostig has lost his earldom; he's fled to Flanders; your father gives him protection. Now let Harold break his oath—and I could use brother Tostig.'

'Not to be trusted,' she said. 'Not a man but a wolf!'

'I must see for myself. I am for Flanders.'

He was back within two weeks bringing her news from home. Her father was well but ageing; her mother handsome and hard as ever. Her brothers were cold one to another—each with his eye on the succession. Judith looked sickly; she was expecting another child; her husband was unkind to her. 'The man is a wolf—as you said. But still I can use him. He's poisonous with his wrongs and jealous of Harold that rides so high. He means to win his earldom back though all England swim in blood. We can help each other—he and I!'

'Can you trust him—a man that seeks to stab his brother in the back, his brother and liege lord?'

'To a point—and no further. When I need him no longer I shall know how to deal with him.'

Tostig trusted William no more than William trusted him. He would use William if he must; but he could do better. Harald Hardrada, King of Norway, there was his man! And Edith, wife to the too-holy King, would help him. She, also, had quarrelled with their brother Harold. He was too English for her Norman tastes, she said; but the real quarrel was over something quite different. Forced to lead a virgin life and resenting it, she was bitterly jealous of Harold's mistress. It was she who had, in the first place, suggested the Norwegian King, a giant of a man; hard fighter and fierce sea-pirate. A man without pity: of restless ambition, his own inheritance insufficient for his need or his greed. 'He had long cast a lustful eye upon England, coveting her rich farms and pasture-lands.

He would send into Norway, and at once. A Norwegian King for England, why not? Were Norwegians worse than the Danes? He would offer to share England with the Norwegian; divide the land between them. Promise him the entire crown, if need be—anything; anything at all, so that Harold was cast down. Then, if the Norwegian showed himself difficult, one could always call upon William to help drive him away. A perfect plan!

He had not long to wait for his answer. The adventure, Harald said, was after his own heart. He and Tostig must swear blood-brotherhood; and Tostig must persuade his brother-in-law to join the invasion of England.

Baldwin refused. He had had enough of Tostig! He was growing old, he said; too old for the discomforts of war—the smell of blood, the stink of mud. If it were needful, for Flanders he would fight—for no other reason. Let Tostig invade his own country; Baldwin would help him, with money, maybe with men.

'I'd give much to clear him out of Flanders,' he told his wife, 'if only he'd leave my sister behind. I like neither the man nor his company; and more than all I do not like the way he treats my sister! He treats her like a child; not a child one loves, but a stupid, somewhat disgusting child. Sometimes she bears the marks of his bruises—our Judith!' He sighed deeply. 'When we gave her to Tostig, when we allied ourselves with the house of Godwine, I thought to do my own house some good. But this Tostig! There'll be no good from him ever. The sooner he goes the better!'

William said, striding about Matilda's bower, frowning and disturbed, 'Harold means to play me false. He's married.'

She took the news calmly; her calmness exacerbated his anger.

'And to whom? You do not ask. You sit there as though it concerns us not at all. It does concern us—and very much!' She could hear in his thickening voice his crescent anger. 'For, whom does he take to wife? Who but the sister of Edwine and Morkere? And who has got brother Tostig's earldom; who but brother Morkere? Now the best part of England lies in the hands of these three, bound by ties of blood. And more. In such a marriage he begets true-born sons; so far his bastards have sufficed. Can you doubt he plans to take the English crown?'

And since she still said nothing—for what was there to say? A man has a right to wed where he will—he cried out, 'He has slighted his betrothal, he has shamed our daughter!'

Almost she could laugh at that, save it was no time for laughter. 'A betrothal!' she said. 'You cannot take that jest for earnest!'

'Can I not? He gave the girl a ring.'

'He gave all the children gifts.'

'But not one of them a ring. He gave her a ring of gold and kissed her and set it on her finger. What is that but betrothal?'

'Had it been betrothal,' she said, 'there had been a ceremony, a formal exchange of rings in the presence of the council, a setting out of conditions—'

'It was all to follow!' He interrupted, harsh. 'The man was in haste to be gone. He has slighted my daughter and I'll not forget it.

Useless to argue with William deliberately whipping himself to further anger, seeking any stone to cast at Harold.

Agatha went about forlorn. Seven years old; and the whole of her child's heart set in love upon Harold. Matilda was gentle with the child, but William was rough and encouraged her in her grief. 'Harold is false, is perjured. You have been ill-used. Well you may trust your father to settle your score.' Then the child would run to her mother in fear for Harold, her blue eyes darkened with tears. And Matilda would tell her it had been a jest and that her father jested still. But jest or earnest, Harold was too old for such a little girl!

And now it was early December. The wind whistled through bare branches; and in William's new castle at Caen, fires blazed high. But, in spite of them, in spite of the great wool curtains and furs spread upon floor and bed, they shivered.

The year was dying. In his new palace of Westminster the King of England was dying, too. Hearing and sight were failing; yet to his all-but deaf ears came the sound of mallets, of spade and chisels, picks and saws. Day and night, by the flare of torches, men worked to finish the great new church. And, the faint sound reaching him, the King would smile and nod. This was the thing he desired most in the world—that the minster be finished and he buried therein. Not even the thought of his kingdom and his successor, nor the good of this foreign people he had never made his own, could stay long in his mind; a mind filled with the dedication of his great new church and his own coming translation to heaven.

Christmas was passed and the minster finished. On the twenty-eighth day of December, in the year of grace ten hundred and sixty-five, his church was hallowed... but he was not there. That strange woman his wife whom he had never known, knelt in his place while he lay, his eyes filled with visions of heaven.

From those visions he was called to name his successor. All England waited upon the words of the dying man. The one he named—let it be what man soever—that man they would make King; for the sanctity of a dying man and that man a King already held as a saint, was not to be gainsaid.

He had been lying in stupor unseeing, unhearing. On the fifth day of the new year he opened his eyes upon Harold on one side of his bed and Stigand, archbishop of Canterbury, on the other. He knew them and to Harold he spoke, slow and low, but sensible and clear.

'Harold... my brother. I commend my wife, your sister, to your patient love, bidding you forget the ill she has done you by secret plotting with your brother Tostig. See to it that she lose nothing of her honours, nor any gift I have given her. Hold her in reverence still... she was the King's wife.'

He lay back taking in hard, rasping breaths so that the room rattled with the sound. When he could speak again, he said, 'My good Normans that left their own land for me, I commend also to your kindness. If they are willing to stay here, see to it that they are protected. If they are not willing, let them put together their goods and return home...' *home*. It was pitiful to hear the longing as the sick man spoke of the land he should never see again.

Harold put his strong arm about the dying man and said loud and clear, 'I promise.'

'Send for my council,' the King said.

When they had gathered, the King said, 'I have had a dream... a vision and it troubles me greatly. For the sins of her princes God has put a curse upon the country. Within the year enemies shall stalk the land; they shall harry it with fire and sword...'

His voice died away; he sought in his troubled mind... *Enemy? What enemy? My own doing? Something I did... something said...*

One man, alone, held the clue—Harold remembering a promise made by the dying man seventeen years ago.

There was silence now; nothing to be heard but the hard, tearing breaths warning them that, for the dying man, time was almost run. Each man, kneeling, prayed God the King would speak once more, name his successor.

And, God listening, the dying man stretched a wasted hand towards Harold where he knelt by the bed.

'To you... Harold... I commit my kingdom.'

And Harold, his hands between the wasted hands of the King, in the manner of the feudal oath, accepted the gift and the burden.

XVIII

William was hunting in his park at Quévilly, across the river from Rouen, when he heard the news. It was a crisp morning in early January, such as he loved. In his hand he carried the great longbow he alone could bend; he was about to fit the arrow, when a man came forward and knelt at his feet. Something in the man's face—a wariness; fear, perhaps, warned William. He handed the bow to his squire and took the man aside.

It seemed to the watching company that the lord duke did not perfectly understand, nor know rightly what he did. There he stood, tying and untying the cord of his cloak.

But he had understood... he had understood.

They saw his face begin to change; saw the stiffening of the jaw, the paling of the eye, saw the white and rigid aspect of the man. For a full minute he stood thus; he spoke to no man nor dared any man speak to him. Suddenly he turned his back and strode alone along the forest path. To those that watched, the very trees, it seemed, shrank back to let him pass.

He had come now to the river where the boats lay waiting their return. He untied the first that came to hand; and he, that had come in joyous company, took himself alone across the Seine. And all the time the words the messenger had spoken, beat within his head. *The King of England is dead. Earl Harold is raised to the crown.*

When he came into his great hall, his limbs suddenly failed. He fell upon a bench and covered his face with his cloak; and there he sat, leaning his head against a pillar. From a distance men watched and dared not come near to ask what ailed him; he sat alone in his bitterness and the very dogs feeling his anger slank noiseless away.

On the sixth day of January, the day after the King's death, two great ceremonies took place—the burying of a King and the crowning of a King.

'The dead King hurried into his grave and the false King hurried into his crown. He could not wait!' William cried out in a terrible voice. 'He could not wait to put the crown of England on his head—the crown that belongs to me! Enjoy it, Harold, while you may! You'll not enjoy it long. You, and all England with you, shall rue your crowning with blood and tears!'

They were assembled in William's closet—the wife he loved best in the world, Lanfranc that subtle counsellor, FitzOsbern his closest friend, the wise old man de Beaumont together with William de Warenne and Richard of Evreux, two young men that had proved their valour in the fight. Trusted counsellors all. Odo he had kept from the meeting; he had a great jealousy of Lanfranc and was, besides, a man of choler. Odo should hear when all was decided.

William began quietly enough. 'Harold of England, you know well, is my sworn vassal. You know, for you heard it, the oath he swore to accept me as King of England and to take up arms for me.'

'Only,' Lanfranc said, 'only in the belief that the sainted King promised you the crown—and that no man can prove. Sir, you must find a better reason!'

William opened his mouth in anger; they saw the effort with which he controlled himself. He said, quietly enough, 'Then put aside that reason... for the present. I am still the man's lord; he swore, when he took knighthood from me, to become my man. Yet he regards not me, his lord; nor my daughter to whom he is betrothed. No; but he sets her aside. He has wed the sister of Edwine and Morkere; he has insulted my daughter—an insult to be wiped out with blood.'

'For Harold to take the crown is no proof that he breaks his feudal oath,' Lanfranc said. 'If you, sir, should take the crown of England, it would not make you any less the vassal of France. As for the lady, your daughter, there was no betrothal ceremony. No man saw it, nor heard of it; there is no writing.' He saw his lord's lips whiten and said slowly, 'There is a better reason, sir, to put Harold from the throne; a reason with which no good Christian can quarrel.' He paused, he said, 'Harold of England defies the Pope. He has cast out a true archbishop.'

'De Jumièges left England of his own accord,' Matilda reminded them.

'He left as archbishop of Canterbury,' Lanfranc said. 'Now he would return. And when he returns it must be as he left—archbishop still. No King on earth can make or unmake a bishop. If de Jumièges chooses to return, Harold must accept him. But this Harold refuses to do. So he makes schism in the church. Such a wounding in the peace of Christendom is abomination; it is a thing no good Christian can allow!'

'That Stigand is no true archbishop Harold knows very well!' William burst in. 'For who put the crown of England upon his usurping head? Not Stigand. No! Stigand is good enough to bury a King; but to crown him—no! Such a crowning would be null and void; it would stink throughout Christendom—Harold knows it. No! It was the archbishop of the north that crowned him—the impious dog that calls himself *King* grovelling before the high altar. God's own wonder he was not struck dead!'

'I think,' Matilda said in her small, clear voice, 'God saves him for a worse fate.'

'In the great new church my cousin built, this bishop of the north asked the people if they would take Harold for their King; so great the haste, the earth is not yet smoothed upon my cousin's grave. And all the people cried out, *Yes!* But soon they'll sing another tune! And Harold made the great oath, swearing to punish wrong done to any man. He and his oaths! What of the wrong done to me—his overlord? A crowning with prayer and all holy rite! Well, it shall not help him!'

'It shall help him not at all,' Lanfranc said, 'though this archbishop of the north is a good man; there is no fault in him. *This Harold makes a schism in Christendom*; must I repeat it? *He wounds the peace of Christendom to the heart*. Therefore go into England, my son. Go as a servant of God, to restore His archbishop; and the Pope shall bless your cause!'

William looked almost with love upon this subtle man. When he was King of England Lanfranc should be his chiefest adviser.

'But,' Lanfranc said, 'we must not rush upon a war, however blessed, without due cause; a cause accepted throughout the Christian world. First you must send to demand the crown.'

Demand the crown! What foolishness was this? What waste of time!

'We ask... and he refuses,' Matilda said softly. 'So we put ourselves in the right; so we gild our cause!' *And gilt it needs! You will give your reasons—and not one of them true. You will take the crown to which you have no right because I want it and because I have made you want it.* She shadowed her face with her hand lest the others read her thought.

'I have been betrayed, yet you would have me ask for the thing that is my own! No! I will fight until right be done and the English crown set upon my head!'

'Sir, your right comes second. God's right comes first,' Lanfranc told him, smooth. 'Heal the schism in Holy Church and God will see you do not lose by it!'

Mid-January, in the year of grace ten hundred and sixty-six, William laid formal claim to the English crown and received his answer; his expected answer.

He had gained the ear of the Pope; or, rather, Lanfranc had gained it for him. 'England,' Lanfranc wrote, 'stands outside obedience to your Holiness not only in the matter of Jumièges, archbishop of Canterbury, but in every matter. She makes a show of obedience but always she takes her own way. Her priests, great and small, are obedient, not to you, my lord Pope, but to their witan. England, once serviceable to God and to you that are God's Mouthpiece, now turns a deaf ear. My lord William, true son of Holy Church, asks nothing but that he may right this evil. It is a holy war.'

Who could refuse so subtle a tongue? William had won the blessing of Rome. Now he must win the consent of his people.

He was surprised to find his lords, for the most part, unwilling. His brothers were willing enough. Odo, the fighting bishop, scented the battle from afar and the rich smell of plunder. And Robert of Mortain was no whit behind his brother; he, too, was a fighting-man first and foremost. FitzOsbern, de Warenne and some half-dozen others would have come from loyalty alone; how much more when loyalty promised to be well-gilded? He had willing promise also from the old men—from Roger de Beaumont and Walter Gifford. Hugh de Grantmesnil wrote from banishment praying for recall and Robert of Montgomery, son of that Talvas who had cursed the infant William, came hurrying. And that was all. The rest, summoned to Lillebonne, were unwilling. Some, they declared, were too old for fighting; above all for fighting beyond the sea. Some were in debt from their lord's earlier wars, too poor, therefore, to follow him into a strange country. Plunder? Land? Honours? The offer left them unmoved. What hope to keep England, should they ever win it? England was too rich, too strong; renowned throughout Christendom for valour. What army had their duke? What ships, even, to carry such forces as he might scrape together? Had he forgotten the miseries of war—the bloodshed, the danger, the poverty? He had brought peace and prosperity to Normandy; let him not endanger it by leaving the country unguarded. The blessings of peace; he and they alike deserved them.

'My armies have never yet been beaten in the field, nor shall be!' William told them, fierce beneath his quiet air. 'As for ships, we shall build them; we shall build a fleet such as Christendom has never seen! Within the year we shall be ready. And God fights upon our side!'

But still his lords were unwilling; nor were they any more willing when, the next day, William FitzOsbern addressed them. Sweet reason dropped like honey from his tongue.

'We are bound to our lord's service according to our oath; it is our plain duty. But men of honour do not wait upon duty.'

'We are bound to his service *but not across the sea!*' Fulk the Lame interrupted. 'We fear what we shall find on the other side.'

'What shall you find but men like yourselves?' FitzOsbern let out in a great laugh. 'Or rather men not like ourselves, since they are not so brave, nor so well-ordered! You'll find no leader but a handful of earls each at the other's throat. And the army? We could break it with one hand! Save for the King's own housecarls—good fighting-men, but not enough—naught but a rabble of peasants taken from their homes, their eyes cast back with longing upon their fields.'

He stopped. 'And what shall you gain? Riches and glory beyond count. Earls you shall become; lands shall be yours and gold; the riches of rich England as much as you can desire! Offer yourselves then to our duke's service. How shall it be, if in after times, men should say, *England would have been ours but our fathers were cowards?* Now, therefore, run to offer the service that is his due. And more. Double that service. If you should furnish ten knights then offer twenty; if twenty—then forty. Fifty? Then a hundred. Do so and our duke will not forget. And I, myself—I practise what I preach and more. I owe my lord no ships yet I will give him sixty; sixty ships well-found, furnished alike with sailors and with soldiers. A free gift.'

They shrugged such munificence aside.

Cross the sea! Offer twice the amount due! Let FitzOsbern give what he would; he was hand-in-glove with the duke! But let him speak for himself. It was a mad adventure; they'd have none of it!

William began calmly enough. 'They are in the right. Service across the sea. is not in the oath. I cannot force them to go!' Suddenly his calm snapped. 'Must I be hindered from the start because these fools are unwilling?'

'Unwilling men, if you could force them, are useless—worse than useless,' Matilda said. 'Where there is no good will, you will find anger and discontent. But you could, I fancy, bring them to good will; to some belief, at least, in their willingness.'

She sat thoughtful, the bright wool dropped in her lap. She said, 'When men speak in council, they find safety in numbers.' She startled him with a laugh. 'Why, my lord, it is the old story of the bundle of sticks. The bundle, for all your strength, you cannot break. But the sticks—you may break them one by one.'

He burst into laughter at that. 'There was never a woman like you for ready wit!' He wiped away the tears of his mirth. 'I must win the crown if only to lay it at your feet.'

One by one he summoned them and one by one they came into the presence of their lord. And one by one he dealt with them according to each man's nature—to this one promising honour, to that one riches, to a third power, persuading yet another by promise of his duke's love, driving still another by fear of his displeasure. In the end he had his way.

And more than his way. For now, driven by a general madness, they promised what was never in their oath; what was never in their wildest dreams—nor in William's neither. Afterwards they regretted the rash promise, many of them; but this William had foreseen and it was too late. For, each man speaking, the scribe had written it down and the whole company assembled, the promise was read aloud. And how, in such an assembly, could a man go back on the word given, the word written?

'The lord Robert of Mortain, gives to my lord duke one hundred and twenty ships, fitted complete with sailors, with fighting-men, provisioned and armed.

'The lord Odo, bishop of Bayeux, gives one hundred ships, likewise fitted, manned and provisioned.

'The lord William of Evreux, eighty ships, complete as aforesaid.

'The lord Robert of Eu, sixty ships, complete; my lord William FitzOsbern, sixty ships likewise.

'The lord Hugh of Montfort, fifty ships complete with sailors, soldiers and provisions; with arms thereto and sixty knights.

'My lord Fulk the Lame offers likewise.

'My lord Gerald the Seneschal, forty ships complete with arms, men and provisions and adds thereto one hundred knights.'

And so on down the list, to those that could give one ship only; or would share the giving of a ship. Two thousand ships in all; the clerk counted them. And the number, William promised himself, would grow; it would grow.

He had gained the men of his own duchy, the nucleus of his army; but it was not enough, it was not near enough. He was to invade a kingdom, he was to win a crown. He sent his messengers the length and breadth of Gaul. From Anjou, from Brittany came fighting-men; from Poitou and Acquitaine; and from the Norman settlements in Italy they came—wild and undisciplined, hot for the adventure. Well, William would shape them to discipline.

From Paris, alone, the response was cold. Philip was hunting in Beauvais, a few miles across the border. William went to plead his cause.

'Help me in this great enterprise that has the blessing of God upon it and I will hold the English crown for you—my overlord. I will do homage to you for whatever my sword shall win!'

Young Philip laughed within himself at that! *Help to make you a King!* He said, 'I do not approve of putting an anointed King from his throne. And, moreover, you are not wise, my lord duke, to leave Normandy. All is well enough now, I grant you. But what when your back is turned?'

'God has blessed me with a wise wife and loving subjects. Together they shall keep the land in peace.'

Philip was more than ever cold. He would, if he could, be a hindrance. Well, William could manage without him! Eustace of Boulogne was coming with a sizeable army, Alan of Brittany was leading his Bretons, the lord of Poitou his Poitevins. And more important than any King of France, Pope Alexander had sent a sacred ring enclosing the true hair of St. Peter. Nor was this all. In Rome, a banner was being worked bearing a great cross; it should be blessed and sent to William, servant of God.

And one thing more. The Pope had declared Harold a usurper. He, and all England with him, lay beneath Rome's displeasure.

XIX

For Tostig he did not have to send. Tostig came of his own accord, mad with spite against his brother. He was forever pricking William with a question. *Shall you let the usurper keep your crown?*

'He's hand-in-glove with Harald Hardrada;' Matilda warned him, 'but that he does not mention. The Norwegian King has his own eye on the English crown—but Tostig doesn't mention that, either. I have it from my father. Tostig you know for yourself—a mischief-making traitor. Something you know of the Norwegian also—a thief with no pity in him. Why should either of these bad men put themselves about to serve you?'

'I can deal with them both,' William promised.

And still not enough men! William sent into Flanders for more. Surely his wife's family would help him!

Her brothers sent their answer at once. The messenger knelt before William and Matilda.

'Sir, my lords your brothers ask what share of England they shall get should they furnish you with your requirements?'

She saw the hardening of William's jaw. Yet it was a fair question; William, himself, would certainly have asked it. But William, she could see, did not intend to commit himself; he was searching in his mind for an answer both friendly and guarded. Well, she would answer for him!

She beckoned the scribe that knelt, parchment upon his knee. She took the roll as yet untouched; she rose in her place and held up the parchment, blank, for all to see. Every eye upon her she folded it in four and called for her seal. The blank sheet sealed, she sat again in her place and, using the scribe's knee, wrote in her clear hand. When she had finished she read her writing aloud.

'Brothers, of England you shall win
As much as this letter shows within.

'Which is to say nothing!' she said in her small, clear voice and handed the sealed parchment to the messenger. 'Tell my brothers that to fight for God is my lord duke's glory and it is my glory also. If they take no part in this high adventure they shall be the losers. And the glory they lose my lord shall gain. He will take England without their help.'

Never did man have such a wife! William said it far and wide. Beauty, wit and kindness—she had them all! For her sake, alone, England must be won. He must make her a Queen.

And still William must scour Christendom for men. From Germany, from Austria and Spain his broom collected the sweepings. These, too, he would wield into a disciplined force. But it was not only finding men, it was not only disciplining men, nor finding them arms and goods; it was a question of transporting them across the sea. And, most of all, it was a question of transporting cavalry—a more difficult matter. Men must put up with the conditions they find but horses were another matter. They were valuable; and what should he do with frightened animals, sick animals in a rough crossing? The answer was ships and more ships.

Some ships he had; old ships. They must be made seaworthy—fresh-caulked, sails repaired. But, even with the new ships promised, there were not enough. When he came to enquire he found the size of ships promised had been unspecified. Some, it was clear, were to be small ships for towing provisions or for carrying craftsmen. More ships must be built.

All through spring and summer, axes rang in the woods of Normandy.

But it was not only the building of ships he must look to; a man had need to look to his spirit, also. What of his vows? The abbeys he had promised were not yet finished but the church of Holy Trinity, at least, could be made ready—must be made ready—for consecration before he sailed.

Day by day the masons toiled. Now it stood proud and beautiful, earnest of the completed whole. The golden stone glowed in the sunshine, seeming to gather warmth and to garner it; within lay rich vestments, plate and jewels. He had fixed the day for consecration.

So far, so good. But what of the other vow, the secret vow he had made the day of Cecilia's birth? A fortnight only to consecration, and he had said no word to the child nor to her mother. Of the child he scarcely thought; a daughter's part was obedience. From his wife he feared little; a wife's part, also, was obedience, and she had scanted nothing, ever, of a wife's part.

But, for all that, he did not relish the telling.

Already he had planned with Lanfranc the consecration to the last detail. Here Matilda should sit—foundress and benefactor; himself at her side, the children on footstools at their feet. Here the churchmen, the nobles and the foremost burghers of Caen; there the builders, the masons, the glass-workers that had carried out the great work.

Discussing the matter with William, Matilda was aware of an omission among the children; one place was missing. She was about to point this out, but he spoke first.

He was, she could see, embarrassed; he wore his obstinate look. He said, 'God has prospered us exceedingly and for that I have returned thanks. Now I ask for more at His Hands; I ask for victory in England. And for that I would offer yet more gifts.'

'Yes,' she said, 'if more must be given—'

'It must be given. Stone and gold—it is not enough. We must give something dearer yet.' He paused; he said, 'We must give our own flesh and blood.'

She looked at him; she did not understand.

'God gave His Son,' William said. 'I give a daughter—our eldest daughter to God.'

She cried out at that, pushing the thought away with both hands. 'It is not *your* flesh you offer; it is your child's. You cannot offer another's flesh and blood.'

'It is already offered. A man's child is his own to do with what he will.'

'You cannot give her to God without her own consent and that you have not asked. How can she endure, young as she is, the comfortless life of the convent? She is a child, a child; she has only a child's small strength.'

And when he made no answer she sought to move him by those things he understood. 'When you fill your belly with good meat, shall you think of her eating the wretched fare of the convent—the thin gruel, the salt herrings? When you lie warm in bed shall you remember her upon the hard, cold pallet?'

And when still he said no word, she cried out, 'You have denied yourself no lust of the flesh. You have bred your children upon me whether I would or no. *Woman's duty is woman's pleasure; God has made her so!* How often you have said it! Well then, must our girl go unwed... barren?'

'She weds Christ.'

'And if she cannot consent?'

'The vow is made.'

'When was it made?'

'At her birth.'

She stared at him then; she said, 'Ten years; ten years—and you have kept this thing in your heart! Ten years—and no word to me, the child's mother!'

He said, 'I did not think you would show yourself a niggard in giving to God. As for not speaking!' he shrugged. 'It was early days. God might have taken the child to Himself—who could say?'

'Maybe,' she said, soft and bitter, 'you thought to spare me some grief!'

'Giving a child to God, there can be no grief. Well, the vow is made and all your tears cannot alter it. Nor her tears neither though I think there'll be none. It is blessed to offer one's self to God.'

'But—to be offered?'

'It is all one. See to it that she does not mar the vow with useless tears; and you, also, do not mar it with a bitter spirit!' He turned about and left her.

She paced the room beating her hands together. Cecilia, her lovely girl! Her mother had dreamed of a kingly husband; she had not thought the King of Heaven should be that husband. Ten years old. Ten years, only; in all the eagerness of her unlived life to be given to the empty embrace of a ghostly groom! That William should do this thing! Ten years... ten long years and no word; nothing to prepare the child for that strange and lonely life, bearable only if the soul was willing. Daughters strengthen one's hand by marriage, William always said. Now he sought to win God's favour, to strengthen his hand by this ghostly marriage...

Anger rose in her so strong, she felt it bitter upon her tongue. If she were not to hate William for ever, she must make herself see his side of the matter.

To give a daughter to God was no uncommon thing. There was scarce a great family but that a daughter or a sister was given to God. But to be given or to give one's self—there was the difference. She was not unwilling to give a child to God, if the child were old enough to be fully consenting to understand what she offered, what sacrificed. But—*sacrifice*. Was that a word to use when a soul offered itself to God? She saw now that she was not truly devout; in spite of her fine church she was not devout at all. Devoutness had been a façade in which she herself had believed. Now the façade was down she looked within herself. She saw, to her horror, that she did not love God. She believed in Him; she feared Him; but she did not love Him.

What sort of woman was she then, that loved neither God nor her husband? She was a woman that loved her children—and she had lost two daughters.

The wound in her heart began to bleed afresh. Past grief came shockingly to reinforce new pain. Beneath the double assault she was taken by a nausea; she ran cold with sweat.

In her turmoil and bitter anger she needed guidance but there was no-one, no-one at all. Head in her hands she found herself wondering what her mother would have said to this, the cold shrewd woman.

You make too much of the matter. Almost she could hear her mother speak in the quiet room.

Is it so small a matter to lose a daughter? And what of his long deceit?

It ill becomes you, child, to speak of either; the punishment is just.

I have been punished enough.

So the coward always says.

I will never forgive him though he crown me Queen of the world.

Forgive or not as you choose. But always play your part—the loving wife.

Give gossip no cause to say your husband tires. And remember this. Beauty wears thin with the years. Have a care lest you wreck your marriage.

Her mother's very thoughts! She understood, suddenly, she was more of her mother's daughter than she had thought.

That night William took her grimly, purposefully; it was as though he must seal her to him so that there could be no escape. She made no resistance; but hatred was a poison in her throat when he said, I take one child; I give you another. Well, she had not been unprepared; she was not that ignorant girl Brihtric had taken. She would punish him for Cecilia. There would be no more children unless she, herself, desired it. She did not think she would ever desire it.

Cecilia stood before her parents, a child obedient, innocent and igno-rant of her fate. William, for all his righteousness, did not find it easy to speak.

He said, at last, 'When a man has been blessed by God, it is right he should give back a gift the best he has.'

'Yes, sir.' It was but commonsense; but how did this concern herself?

William's tongue halted. The child looking from one to the other—at her father's cold face, at her mother's fixed look—knew a moment of fear. She tried to smile. Matilda, since she could endure it no longer said, harsh, 'Your father offers you to God. You are to take the veil.'

Cecilia put out a hand to plead; or, maybe to steady herself. She said, 'Does he take me from my mother and from my brothers and sisters? Will he shut me up in a cold place from the sight of the world? I love God... but not, I think, so much.'

'I have vowed it,' her father said.

The child turned, and quiet as a moth, was gone. Her mother did not follow. She had no comfort to give.

Cecilia spoke no word on the matter to her father; what use? Nor to Agatha or any of her brothers—they were already cut off from her. To her mother, only, she spoke. 'The sworn oath must be kept. Harold broke his oath and for that he must lose his life and his soul with it—so my father says. There is nothing for it but to obey.' She understood, though not very well, something of what she must renounce. Her one hope was that, since her own mother was helpless, the Blessed Virgin would lean from heaven to shape her spirit not only to acceptance; but to willing acceptance.

She went about white and silent; in her smiling she was infinitely piteous.

Sixteenth day of June; day of her abbey's consecration; day of her daughter's sacrifice. Walking in procession with William down the arched and pillared aisles of her new church, Matilda felt her heart cold as the stone itself. Not even Robert in this moment could bring her comfort. Today he looked subdued; he loved Cecilia. Richard, walking with him, looked, as always in church, serene; he would miss his sister, but he could not be sad for her. Behind them Rufus, unimpressed by the solemn occasion, darted his eyes here and there, weighing the richness of his brothers' clothes against his own. Eleven years old; and he had not yet learned to behave with decorum in church. Behind the boys came Agatha, the eldest daughter now, hand-in-hand with the five-year-old Constance; and, in the nurse's arms, staring in wonder, and better behaved than Rufus, the baby Adela.

All there, her boys and girls, all except Cecilia... except Gundrada.

Of all her girls, Gundrada, she thought, had the best chance of happiness; no considered policies would shape her marriage. Of all her girls, Cecilia must bear the hardest part—obedience, humility, poverty and chastity. When they laid the first stones of this abbey she had not dreamt of the grief she should know therein. Like Cecilia she would pray for an accepting spirit... but her own unwilling heart she knew.

And now came the procession. First the bishops leading the priests, and then the nuns already dedicated, behind them the novices. And, at the end, my lady abbess leading the child by the hand. So old they looked, even the novices, beside the child—Cecilia in her white gown and the pale gold hair that one day must be cut and hidden.

And now the choir was singing the paean and the white child prostrated herself before the altar.

Prayer and psalm, hymn and praise; and now it was over. Behind William and Matilda came the children walking; but the child, the flower of them all, left behind. It was the sacrifice; and the child with her weak strength must accomplish it. With courage, with pain, with endeavour she might win to contentment, to joy; even. But what of the years between then—and now? And what of the years that should be?

Never in this life would her mother be reconciled.

XX

The vow had been honoured and God smiled upon him.

The number of his ships grew steadily; they lay crowding the harbour at Dives and the small sheltered inlets as far as Lillebonne. But this was only the beginning. Armourers must be found and carpenters, stone masons and workers in metal; bakers and brewers and cooks. There was meat to pickle and fish to salt. Later the armies would live on the country; until then they must be fed. Through the gates of Rouen, of Caen, of Lillebonne, came the long line of carts carrying wood, carrying iron; carrying flour and meat and fish.

William was everywhere; from his headquarters in Caen his eye missed nothing. No man knew when he might not suddenly appear to inspect this store or that; to judge of quality, of price, to check amounts and see that all had been safely bestowed. He would at times ride out himself to choose and to order; he had been known to question farmers and tradesmen to see that they had been fairly and immediately paid. He'd have no thieving, no cheating; no discontent to smoulder into trouble. Nothing too great for him to encompass, nothing too small. He seemed to have the old magic attributed to him—the power to be immediately where he willed. Upright on the great mare he seemed more than his own great size, more than a man. He was like a statue to himself, a heroic statue symbolising strength and victory.

Never a duke of Normandy so strong. He had won his vassals great and small; he had won the nobles of Gaul; not only the lord of Ponthieu and Eustace of Boulogne, not only the old enemy of Brittany but Anjou and Maine, bitterest of foes, now marched beneath his banner. Now he could command every harbour in northern France as far as Flanders. Now he had fighting men from every land in Christendom; and, most of all, he had won the Pope. He had made the name of Harold stink in Christendom. The man that called himself King of England lay still beneath the Pope's ban; and all England with him.

These days William saw little of his wife. There had been no quarrel; but a small unhappy ghost stood between them. He had not, as yet, noticed it. Her courtesy was unfailing; that it was also unsmiling, he had not as yet, noticed—his days were overful. There were constant councils of war with his captains; with FitzOsbern, with his fighting bishop, with Richard of Evreux and William of Warenne. There were frequent discussions with de Beaumont and with Lanfranc upon the ordering of Normandy when he should be absent. These nights he rarely slept at home and when he did he would fall into bed and lie like a log.

Lanfranc alone, shrewd and subtle, watched lest some small affair flame suddenly to show William the truth concerning his wife. For, William angered was capable of leaving Normandy in other hands than hers—to the hurt of its duke, its duchess and the whole duchy. Discreet and devious, the priest made his suggestions to Matilda. 'My lord duke has yet to arrange for the conduct of Normandy; and who better as regent than Madam the duchess, whose mind has always been her lord's in every enterprise; head and heart at his command?' Head... and *heart*. He dwelt lightly upon the word. 'How seldom can any husband command both? Fortunate, indeed, my lord duke that can embark upon his greatest enterprise, secure alike in your wisdom and your love! And, it is the more fortunate since he has not yet named his heir—a proper thing when a man goes upon such a venture.'

'Proper it is; but my lord is not willing,' she said. '*I never take off my clothes until I go to bed;* his favourite saying.'

'Yet he could be persuaded.'

She understood what lay beneath his words. If she wanted something from William she must first give something. And with her whole heart she wanted to be named regent with Robert as heir.

She forced herself to smile again, to ask her questions concerning the enterprise, to visit his ships and speak with the men. In bed she showed herself loving. It was hard, at first, this show of love; but soon it became not so hard. She would never wholly forgive him; but the bitterness was less.

Harold went quiet and steady about his preparations; his crown and his country he would defend with his life. He had few ships; the sainted King had cut down the number needed for defence—he had preferred to build churches. More ships Harold must have; many more to meet attack from Normandy. There was, too, threat of invasion by Tostig and the King of Norway—a threat he could not ignore. To get money for ships was not easy; and time pressed. No time to ask or beg; he must command—command money, command wood, command iron, command service. Care sat heavy upon him. He had been elected King by consent of the witan but the whole of England was not with him—he knew it. Kent and Essex and Sussex—the lands of the Godwine earldoms were loyal but what of the north where little except his name was known? There he'd find a hard core of resistance. Edwine and Morkere; could he count upon them? He had married their sister, he had given them Tostig's lands. Surely they must fight since Tostig meant to snatch at his earldom again; Tostig and the dreaded Harald Hardrada.

The army, at least, he could count upon. FitzOsbern had been wrong in his estimate. A rabble it was not; nor yet undisciplined. Only a liar or a fool could hold it in contempt. The standing army—the King's house-carls—was small; so much was true. But they were all picked men bound to his service at all times; no army in Christendom more disciplined, more brave. For the rest, the army was composed of peasants—their thoughts turned, naturally, towards their farms. There FitzOsbern had spoken some truth; but a half-truth, only. The fyrd were disciplined fighters; and they would fight to the death. When fighting was short and sharp they were dogged and enduring; but, let the fighting be long-drawn, then they must return home for planting and for harvest lest the country starve.

And now it was planting-time—April in the year of grace ten hundred and sixty-six. The month had begun badly—storms and darkness fallen at mid-day. And not in England alone; all Christendom endured unnatural weather—and feared it. Now, in this last week of April, fear deepened to terror. Over all Europe the sky hung ablaze; a hairy star trailed three fiery tails across a bloody sky. It was as though the whole firmament swam in blood. Men could not sleep for the unnatural light; and for fear of it. Nine days, from midnight to dawn, the bloody star flamed and good Christians, everywhere, remembered the words of the saint-King that, dying, had prophesied doom upon England.

It is upon Harold, profaner of oaths, that doom shall fall; upon him and all that fight his cause. William said it loud and long for all Christendom to hear. And Christendom heard and applauded; for Harold lay beneath the Pope's ban.

Harold, too, made use of the hairy star. *Our sainted King prophesied evil upon the land. If the foreigner bring his armies, evil will, indeed befall. And will remain as long as one of them remain upon our sacred soil.*

The bloody star foretells blood; and a new dynasty, William said.

The new dynasty is my dynasty, Harold said.

The wild star foretold a new dynasty spawned by blood; all men were agreed. But—whose dynasty?

William's preparations were complete. Ships and men stood ready, every arrangement for the government of Normandy made. Now Matilda reaped the benefit of Lanfranc's counsel. She had been appointed regent; and William had declared Robert his heir. He had commanded his vassal-lords to take the oath of allegiance to the boy. He had done it with misgiving. 'If I must name my heir,' he had said at first, 'then I name Richard. He is dependable. It is unusual not to name the eldest, I agree; but it has been done and it can be done!'

She had fought for her eldest son as she had not been able to fight for her eldest daughter. Here was no question of vow but of simple justice.

'You cannot pass Robert over; God, I think, will not allow it. You would shame him and me and yourself, also. For men will ask why you pass over your eldest son; and there'll be but one answer. They will name him *bastard*.' She flung the word at him noting with satisfaction the paling of his lips. 'To be passed over—he does not deserve it. He's strong and brave and skilled in arms. He can read and write—which in a ruler does not come amiss!' And let William relish that himself, that without labour could not sign his name. 'He takes things lightly, I grant you; but that's a boyish fault. Give him his rightful place and he'll honour it.' And did not add that, William being absent and the boy no longer frustrated, Robert might well grow into the son William longed for him to be.

Lanfranc, too, had put in his word. 'Madam the duchess is wise. You cannot pass the lord Robert over. If he should prove unworthy—and not for a moment do I believe it—then the council shall tutor him until you return.'

So he had declared Robert his heir; but further he would not go. Robert should have no place as regent; but he should learn his lesson in statecraft by sitting with the council. The council William had chosen with wisdom. Lanfranc himself; Roger de Beaumont, the wise old man that had been his father's friend; Roger of Montgomery, valiant fighter and wise in the strategies of war; Hugh, son of Richard of Avranchin than whom no man was more loyal, together with Maurilius, the saintly archbishop of Rouen. At the last moment he added de Warenne, to advise with Montgomery if revolt should raise its head in Normandy. This council the duchess must consult on every matter of state; Roger de Beaumont, on all matters domestic.

By the mouth of the Dives and all along in little bays and natural harbours, William's fleet stood ready—so many ships a man lost count; as many as three thousand, some said. Each gift of a ship, as it arrived, had been listed together with the name of the giver and checked with his promise. All save one. She had appeared in no list nor had William commanded her.

She came sailing into harbour at Dives, a woman at the helm; the finest ship man ever saw. Shining sail and trim hull, she was shaped for speed. As she drew nearer he saw with amazement, the woman was his wife. The *Mora* was beautiful within as without; a shining example of the shipwright's craft. The figurehead, a golden boy, lifted a trumpet of ivory to his lips; the other hand carried an arrow—to hurl against England.

He could not speak his thanks; there were no words. Never was a man so blessed in his wife! Such a ship must cost a King's ransom. Had she pawned her jewels to pay for it? He would not ask. But he would, he vowed, pay her back in lands and gold; and with the royal crown of England. 'The *Mora* shall be my flagship,' he said. 'The golden boy is my little Rufus!' And, indeed it was not unlike—the craftsman knowing his passion for the child. 'The golden boy shall trumpet us to England.'

It was to be many a day before the golden boy was to trumpet them to England.

Day after day the ships waited... but never the favouring wind blew.

Summer was passing. It was August. It was September.

William moved his fleet to St. Valery across a hundred miles of sea; and, to avoid the wide estuary of the Seine, some of it open sea. But the new position had advantages; he would save time on the shorter crossing;

and, in addition, the farms about the Dives having provided what they could, he would find it easier to provide food for his men.

Even on this journey along his own coast, the winds proved his enemy still. Ships were blown from course and badly damaged; the very sailors were seasick. Into the harbour at St. Valery the fleet crawled; and waiting still for a favouring wind, William ordered all the damage to be made good.

The damage had long been made good and the men recovered; but still he waited for a favouring wind. With all his forces he knelt facing the church at St. Valery. He prayed to God; but he could not keep his eyes from the weather-vane.

Day after day Harold with his armies awaited an enemy that never came. With his brothers Gyrth and Leofwine he guarded the coast of Sussex and Kent, of Essex and East Anglia; Edwine and Morkere had command of the coast from the north to the Humber. Harold prayed that they prove trustworthy; they must, surely, protect their own earldoms—that, at least!

Corn stood knee-deep and golden; on the trees apples reddened, plums swelled—signs of ripening significant to the farmers of the fyrd. To William—his armies composed of warlords commanding their fighting men, and of mercenaries with little thought beyond their pay—passing time neither struck at the harvest nor threatened famine. It was an inconvenience, an annoyance; nothing more.

Leaves were turning, leaves were falling. No longer must the harvest go ungathered, already it had waited too long; already Harold had kept the fyrd under arms for weeks—and no battle. The men were restless. No sign of the enemy... and the harvest not yet brought in. When, in the first week of September, Baldwin sent to say that William could not sail until spring, Harold sent the fyrd home.

Then it was that Tostig struck.

Tostig and Harald Hardrada were in Scotland both; that harbourer of England's enemies, Malcolm of Scotland, made them welcome. The Norwegian had brought with him his wife, his mistresses and his children. He had brought all his treasure, including the fabled ingot of gold that took—so they said—twelve strong men to carry it. England is a fair land, he said; I shall never leave it!

Nor shall he! Harold agreed, grim.

Harald and Tostig had left Scotland; they were sailing south. They had one hundred ships, two hundred, three hundred, they had a thousand ships. Their armies, like their ships, swelled with the telling; from their settlements along the Yorkshire coast, yet more Danes were marching beneath their banner.

Edwine and Morkere made no move.

The invaders were harrying, were plundering; the northern harvest was going up in flames. They had no respect for man or God; not for God, even. Those that fled to sanctuary were burned within that sanctuary, women and children, even; rats in a trap.

Harold, the soldier, was hard put to it not to march north, to sweep the enemy from the face of England. Harold, the King, must stay where he was, his part to defend the east and south-east coast; to defend his capital.

The enemy had fired Scarborough; the whole north-east coast had submitted. They were marching on York.

At last Edwine and Morkere moved; and moved too late.

Two miles from York the armies met.

A bad day for the English, outnumbered and cut to pieces. Those that could crawl from the field must step upon a solid causeway of corpses—their own English dead.

York had surrendered; the capital of the north in the hands of the enemy.

Now, in spite of misgivings, Harold must move at once. William could not come until spring—Baldwin had said it; and the north must be saved. Harold, at this moment, was a sick man, racked with gout; but a man must do no less than his best. He called upon his housecarls and summoned such of his fyrd as he could reach. His army was small but in good heart. And, as he marched northwards, his courage rose higher; more and more men came to join his forces.

Marching by day and night, snatching a little sleep where it could, the ever-growing column marched north.

XXI

Harald and Tostig were feasting. Food had grown scarce in York—an army cannot live upon air; but in the King's House nearby, there was food aplenty. There they had retired to feast; to await the coming of Harold, to inflict upon him the beating that he sought.

Harold was in York. He had been welcomed with joy—the deliverer; had been implored to rest awhile, so strenuous his march. But, beyond a brief hour, he would not tarry. He must deal with this enemy before the more terrible appear.

In the last week of September, at Stamford Bridge, the armies came face-to-face. Harold at the head of the dreaded housecarls, a brother at either hand, rode in the forefront. Tostig and Harald, the wild Norsemen behind them, sat their stallions.

Three brothers facing the fourth, the traitor... and yet the son of their father, the sharer of their childhood.

It was Tostig that shot the first arrow.

It was the signal. Arrows rained like hail; the two-headed axe of the English rang against the shields of the Norsemen, the double-edged sword of the Norsemen against the bucklers of the English.

A battle hard and bitter... and short.

This time it was the invaders that fled the field; that made a high way of packed corpses upon which the English pursued. And dead upon the field lay Tostig; and with him the giant of the north Harald Hardrada.

Harold rode back to York. He had won. But he had left his own men—housecarls and thegns and men of the fyrd—lying together with the enemy. He had lost good friends. And he had slain his brother, slain Tostig with whom he had learned to ride and to shoot; Tostig with whom, throughout boyhood and manhood, he had quarrelled and made friends. Now they would never be friends again. Behind him in a cart Tostig was being carried to York for burial.

The city poured out to greet their King; the banquet was prepared. The banquet he refused; but rest a little, eat a little he must, before he marched south. His men needed time to cleanse themselves from the filth of battle; to dress their wounds, to stretch their stiff limbs, to sleep after the long, hard march, the short and bitter battle. He would rest a little, because he must.

With prayers and with promises, William still besought God to change the wind.

When Harold sent home the fyrd, *Now is the time, God of Battles* he had prayed.

And still the wind blew from the north.

When Tostig landed and Harold marched to meet him, *The time is better, better still. My enemy has withdrawn his armies, he leaves his coast defenceless. God, my Captain, send me the wind, the favouring wind.*

He prayed as never before, beseeching God as one soldier to another.

And still the unfavouring wind.

He sent Matilda home. She must wait no longer; she must take up the reins of government too long laid down. She was not unwilling. In spite of the patched-up kindness between them, she could not forgive him for the loss of Cecilia; it was a loss all too new. More than once, while he prayed for the south wind, she must bite upon her tongue lest she cry out *God does not listen. You have sacrificed our daughter in vain!*

Now, back turned upon the sea, Robert beside her, all-but standing in his stirrups, so great his elation to be free of his father, they set their faces towards Rouen. And, as they rode, the wind catching her veil sent it streaming seaward. Hand up to bring it back, she cried out, *The wind! The wind!* and reined in the mare. With all her company she watched the embarkation—the speed, the perfect order; no minute lost.

Through the daylight hours they watched, and through the dusk; by nightfall all was finished. They saw the darkness pricked by hanging lanterns, every ship bearing its light. 'They mean to sail by night!' she said all amazed; and crossed herself.

Now they saw the *Mora*, her great lantern casting a pathway of light across the dark waters, move out to lead the way. At that, some of the hardness in her heart melted; she knelt where she was in the cold dew and prayed for William's success.

A long and stormy crossing; wind and wave high and wild. The *Mora*, because of her build and the skill of her captain, flew across the dark waters. At dawn William bade the lookout climb to sight the others; on the dark waste of heaving water—no sign of any ship. Nor, in the near-dark could he know how near England might be. He was alone with his one ship and his handful of men! He gave no sign of his fear; he bade them cast anchor and serve supper. Calm as though he had been safe at home he ate and waited. At length, from the lookout, a cry of joy; and now they saw the fleet, canvas spread, crowding the quietening sea. In close formation the fleet sailed steady, and, in the broadening light, saw the glimmer of England's coast. Between white and beetling cliffs a wet pebbled beach flung arrows of light towards the sun; and there, the *Mora* leading, William commanded the fleet.

The twenty-eighth day of September, in the year of grace ten hundred and sixty-six, a golden day, bright and crisp, they beached at Pevensey; and, like the Vikings their forefathers, ran their ships upon the shelving beach—the unguarded beach.

First came the fighting men—the knights leading their horses that, for all the pebbles sliding beneath their careful feet, whinnied with delight, knowing themselves to be on land again. And then the infantry, bows at the ready to protect the carpenters and masons; for upon these depended the safety of the enterprise. Axes were ringing, saws singing, planes whining upon wood, when the leaders came forth—Guy of Ponthieu, Alan of Brittany, William FitzOsbern, Robert of Mortain, Odo and with him many another fighting priest. Last came William. And, as he came, the beach being slimy with cast-up seaweed, he stumbled and lay upon the stones.

Ill-luck! Ill-luck! Men whispered one to another; but before the words had breathed upon the air, he was upon his feet, both hands clutched fast upon sand and pebbles.

'By the Splendour of God, I have taken England into my two hands!' he cried out in a great voice, stretching forth his palms that all might see. 'With your help I shall keep it!'

Impossible not to be moved, not to be heartened, not to believe in the star of this tall man, undaunted and laughing, this man with the look of a hero. They answered with cheers that rang out upon beach and sea, and came ringing back to delight all hearts.

'First we must thank God for his especial mercies to us, thereafter we shall eat!' William said, knowing that prayer puts courage into famished souls as meat into famished bellies.

Dreaded mace laid ready at his side, Odo knelt upon the wet stones in the autumn sunshine; and with him knelt every man from greatest to least. Thereafter they sat down to eat—each man his weapon at the ready. So they ate and drank and were cheerful, tearing at their food and washing it down with the rough cider of Normandy. And each man, having eaten his fill, went about his appointed task. Knights mounted their steeds to spy out the countryside—a countryside happily, but scarce surprisingly—undefended, since Harold had taken his fighting-men north.

Now the carpenters brought from the ships sections of the wooden fortress already prepared and these they set up within the ramparts of the old Roman fortress that stood sturdy and serviceable still. All lent a hand, soldiers and sailors as well as craftsmen; and the duke, himself, walked among them saying here a cheerful word, lending here a willing hand, so that all men wondered they had ever feared so companionable a man.

That night they slept within the fortress under the stars, having commended themselves to God that had kept them safe within His Hand.

Dawn had scarce whitened the sky when William commanded the ships into Hastings Harbour for better safety; and to be at hand if need should be—though in so empty a countryside he could not imagine it.

Empty the countryside; but not so empty. Watchers in the scrub had kept their fearful guard. When steady snoring mingled with the rhythm of the sea, messengers went posting throughout the night to York.

Harold was at meat; feast he could not for grief of good men slain; for grief of one bad man slain—grief for Tostig. Dust-covered, grey as their mantles, the messengers knelt before him.

'Sir, William of Normandy has landed; it is three days since. So quick their fortress rose, the devil must surely be in it! Sir, they make for London.'

He had lost so many men at Stamford Bridge, and those left were stiff with weariness, were dirty and bloodstained, many of them wounded and in pain. Yet, for all that, he must march; he must get to London. He must command more men, men he had set to other duties—summon the last earls from their earldoms, the last thegns from their manors, and such men of the fyrd he had hitherto spared. Let the women bring in the harvest! Men and men and more men!

Marching south, a third of the army left to follow so great his haste, he heard the news. Wherever the enemy marched, field and city was given to the flames. And not only the houses of men; but the houses of God, also, this pious son of the church had sent up in flame. Would the Pope bless this, also, Harold wondered, bitter.

Harold was nearing London. And, as he marched, from every shire men fell in to join him. Edwine and Morkere had not come; they had sent their excuses—affairs to settle, vassals to be called upon, forces to muster. They would be with him, they swore it, before he marched again.

Men not to be trusted. They sought their own good first and always; the need of their country scarce concerned them. Let them stay quiet and William would not trouble them—the north was too far away; there they would stay, in peace, lords of their earldoms—so they thought! Fools! Harold could teach them better! William would leave no man in peace until he was lord of all.

Along the highways of England—from London, from Huntingdon, from Cambridge, men came marching; and, in the midst, high in the early autumn air, two standards floating. The *Golden Dragon* of the Kings of Wessex; and the King's personal standard—the *Fighting Man*.

Four days; four days, only, since he had had the news—and Harold was in London. Edith, his wife, was not there to greet him; she was with child and he had sent her from danger to Chester, the strong city of her brother Edwine's earldom. But that other Edith, his true love, hastened now to greet him; Edith of the Swan's neck, and the mother of his sons. They had not married because she was already wed; and since she no longer shared her husband's bed he had thought it no great harm to take her to his own.

And now, for all his haste, Harold must wait for his forces to muster—for those he had left behind to join him, for his brother Wulfnorth rallying the west; must wait, hoping against hope for the men of the north with Edwine and Morkere marching.

But it was hard to wait when every hour brought news of savage, wanton destruction.

And now came messages from William, from the man himself! Harold, robed, crowned and throned, received them at Westminster.

'Sir,' and the man made no movement to kneel nor to unbonnet, 'you know, and all Christendom knows, my duke's right to the crown of England; your sacred oath confirmed it. Therefore, yield it to my master; and yours. Thereby you shall save bloodshed and misery of which you, that wrongfully call yourself King of England, shall be judged guilty.'

Guilty! He, Harold of England by the English elected... and William burning and slaying in the quiet countryside! So great his anger he all-but leaped in his chair; but Gyrth, his brother, hand upon his shoulder, held him back.

His anger thus restrained but not less dire, Harold spoke.

'Your master has no claim. For that oath exacted by force and cunning, I regard it not. As for the late King's promise to your lord—no man may give this crown away. And if he could? Still the promise would be null and void. It is our law that a bequest has no force till he that bequeathed it be dead, lest, dying, he change his mind. So it was with our late, good King; for, dying, he changed his mind. He named me King. And, by that naming, revoked his early promise—if, indeed, such promise was ever made. Your master has no claim. If he will go in peace, I will give him gifts and my friendship with it. If not, I am ready to meet him in battle. If he choose to fight, I name the fourteenth day of this same month. He has above a week! Go, tell him so.'

When the messengers were gone Gyrth said, 'Sir, you make too much haste. Wait yet a little; wait for the army from York; wait for those men our brother raises in the west and south.'

'Not one day longer. This Norman duke inflicts untold cruelties upon the land. My people have suffered enough. They have made me their King; shall I fail them that trust in me?'

Harold was on the march. Steady by day and night, his armies marched, the *Fighting Man* and the *Golden Dragon* flying free—free as Englishmen.

In his high entrenched camp William waited. Harold must attack from the valley; such an attack was foredoomed.

But already Harold had chosen his place. He knew his Sussex, play-ground of his childhood, as he knew his own hand. Seven miles from Hastings he halted. Senlac Hill. This was the place.

XX

And now it was night. Tomorrow the two greatest captains in Christendom must stand face-to-face. In the darkness English and Norman kept watch upon each other.

William stared, moody, across to the camp on Senlac Hill where, late though the hour, the English worked in the flare of torches. They were putting a palisade about the hill; on the south side they had finished making a ditch. Harold had chosen his site like a great captain—William was great enough to appreciate it. He had been forced to leave his high camp at Hastings where the English could find no shelter; and where, in the harbour, his ships lay ready at need. He had been forced to come seeking Harold. Encamped now on Telham Hill William stared grim.

The more he brooded, the more he understood how magnificently Harold had chosen his ground. Senlac Hill commanded the valley on one side; on the other, broken ground made it difficult to approach. Two rivers flowing into the ravine between the two hills had turned the ground into a bog—a snare, alike, to horse and man. Yet, even without the bog, the hill with palisade and ditch was strong as a castle to withstand a siege. Harold had neglected nothing. The English fought on foot. Never, on equal ground, could they hope to stand against a charge of Norman cavalry; this disadvantage Harold had turned to advantage. Across that bog the Normans must move to the attack. As long as the English stood to the defence they were unbeatable.

Then they must be forced out. It wouldn't be easy but it could be done. He would win; he, God's soldier, with the sacred banner. He had never lost a battle in his life; and, God helping, he'd not fail now.

Well, it was late; he must go within, snatch a few hours' sleep! But still he sat staring into the darkness. Save for the sentinels, his men were for the most part, asleep. They had prayed and been shriven; they had commended their souls to God—which souls must, many of them, stand before Him on the morrow. The English camp was quiet now; quiet and dark. The English, he had heard, drank deep before battle, carousing to keep their spirits high. This night there had been no singing. After the long, forced march there had been no rest. He had seen them getting to work at once, throwing up the palisade, digging their ditches. They must be dead-beat. Well, weary men make easy prey!

His careful mind took him over his campaign for the morrow. That high fortified camp across the water-logged valley might force him to alter his plans. Of his own Normans he had no doubts—they were disciplined to last-minute changes; but what of the Bretons, the Angevins, the mercenaries? Well he must leave that till the time came; leave it to God that had never failed him yet.

And now he must sleep. And, since his squire lay already sleeping, full-dressed upon the ground, he spread his cloak upon the pallet; and, having knelt to pray, lay down. His thoughts before sleep took him were of his wife; tomorrow should win her the royal crown of England.

Dawn, Saturday the fourteenth of October. It was Harold's birthday and he was forty-three. He had slept well; and now, clear-eyed and confident, he looked younger than his years. He was already armed when his brothers Leofwine and Gyrth came to his tent. 'The camp yonder is already busy,' Gyrth said; 'but our men are scarce stirring. They are dead-beat!'

'Rouse them!' Harold commanded. 'Let it never be said we are laggards in the fight!'

William had risen long since. When he had knelt and prayed, he came forth from his tent, sniffing the damp air that blew from the sea and putting on his armour as he went.

'Sir,' said the young squire, very pale, 'what have you done?' for his captain wore his hauberk back to front. William saw those about him equally troubled; dearly they took it for an ill-omen. Unless he rallied them they would not fight this day.

He threw back his head and roared with immense laughter.

'By the Splendour of God, this means a changeabout—and a changeabout, indeed! This day shall see me changed from duke to King!'

So they gave him a rousing cheer and thereafter Odo led the forces in prayer, the men all kneeling; and William, in the forefront, knelt, too. Then they set to their breakfast and, fortified body and soul, went each man to his appointed place.

Now they stood in battle order, in three divisions as William had commanded. On the left, Alan of Brittany commanded his own Bretons, together with the men of Poitou and Maine. On the right rode Roger of Montgomery and FitzOsbern commanding the mercenaries—dogged men and brutal these mercenaries, that fought not for glory but for plunder. And, in the forefront, rode with them one that had caused trouble enough in England; through him the house of Godwine had gone into exile—Eustace of Boulogne, burning with revenge upon Harold—the danger were not too great.

In the centre, commanding the flower of the army, his own Norman fighting-men, rode William. He sat his steed, a beast as noble as himself. So heroic William's look, so strong in purpose, the men cried aloud their faith in him—a man born to be King: and should be if the strength of their arms could make him so.

And so sitting his restive horse, quietening it with a touch of his hand William spoke to the armies assembled. He spoke of his right to England and of the treachery of Harold. And now he pointed to his breast that all might see the necklace that he wore—those same sacred relics upon which perjured Harold had sworn. 'We march to victory,' he cried out. 'And when by the Splendour of God that victory is won, upon that very spot where false Harold's standards fly, I'll raise a mighty church to God—the God of battles!'

Every man knew the order of attack. It was to follow three lines. In each division the bowmen first—men of the dread Norman crossbow; and with them the slingers. These wore no armour but leather jerkins stout enough to turn aside the most part of weapons. Behind them the infantry in close-fitting mail to knee and wrist, the face uncovered save for the nose-piece of the cone-shaped helmet; each man carried his shield, his javelin and his sword. And last; to rush the charge and make an end—the cavalry.

Above them all, where every man might see, towered the mighty figure of William, the sacred relics about his neck, in his right hand the great double-edged sword. On his left rode Odo, carrying no cross now but his heavy mace. A bishop may carry no cutting weapon to draw blood, but he may bring his club smashing upon the helmet so that bone may splinter into pulped flesh and yet no blood be seen. On his right rode Robert of Mortain. Three brothers; two of them to serve the third—and that third, the greatest soldier in Christendom—Arlette had served her lover well. A little in advance of all three, Ralph Toussaint carried the standard; the great cross worked upon the banner the Pope had blessed.

Eight o'clock on a fine autumn morning. The English, too, were settled now in battle-order. On the heights of Senlac, Harold knelt also, among his kneeling men. Thereafter he rose and standing upon a mound for all to see, spoke to his men.

'We fight to keep our country; but this duke comes from a foreign land to bind us beneath his yoke. Our cause is holy. God will give us the day; but only if we play our part. That part is to stand firm. No man must leave his ordered place. Upon that, under God, depends our victory. For, heed me well, it is for us to defend—to defend only; not to attack. Never to attack. So long as we stand firm to the defence, no force however great, nor any charge of horse can move us.

'But, let your ranks be drawn from their place then the enemy will reach the palisade. They will take it; and their horses will trample you down. Stand firm and their lances cannot help them; the upward thrust is weak. But our javelins striking downward are strong to pierce them as they ride; our stones and arrows can dislodge them. If any of their men should reach the palisade our axes shall cleave them head to foot.

'Therefore no attack. Stand to our defence so that they hurl themselves against us in vain. And remember our battle cry *Almighty God*. Cry it aloud that in the fight God may hear us and confound the enemy.'

So steadfast he looked, so humble standing there on foot like the least of his men, yet every inch their undoubted King, the English cheers went thundering across the valley from hill to hill echoing and re-echoing. Now the two standards were raised on high—the *Fighting Man* and the *Golden Dragon*, aglitter both with jewels and precious work in gold.

Nine o'clock. And the two armies waiting, tense. Now Taillefer the duke's minstrel whose name means *Iron cleaver*, valiant in war as in song, spurred ahead, throwing his two-edged sword into the air and catching it again; and all the while he sang loud and clear the hero-song of Roland, that with his friend, had held the pass of Roncevalles against the hordes of Saracens, nor thought death too high a price to pay for glory. He rode, a solitary figure, urging his steed up Senlac Hill, while the two armies watched, motionless. He lifted the sword he had so lightly thrown and caught and a man fell dead ere he, himself, fell beneath the English axes.

William gave no sign of grief. He had loved the man; but his courage he loved more.

First bloodshed; first death.

Now came the rain of Norman arrows. The English answered with a rain more deadly. It was as Harold had promised. Hurled from above, gathering momentum, they did great damage; hurled from below they lost strength, fell, for the most part, harmless.

Dieu nous aide. The Norman battle-cry went ringing. And, *God Almighty!* the English cried; and then, rage overcoming them at the sight of foreigner encamped upon their sacred soil, *Out!* they yelled. *Out! Out!*

Like waves against a cliff the Norman charge broke; always axe and javelin, stone and arrow, drove them back. Now the cavalry went in to the attack, William, himself, leading his men to the palisade. It was hard-riding uphill; man and beast slipped and slid and fell beneath the arrows of the English who kept firm to their positions. Some few Normans that, like their leader, managed, at long last, to reach the top of the hill, found their labour useless. The palisade was untakeable; for should a man force his way through the wooden wall, there stood a second wall—interlocking shields; immovable wall of living men.

William's armies were beginning to lose heart. It was the Bretons on the left wing that, horse and foot, turned and fled down the hill. It was too much for the defenders. What need to keep place when the enemy ran? The English right wing rushed from its appointed place, raced full tilt after the enemy.

William's disordered troops fled to left and right, throwing their own central force into confusion. Now the whole of the invading army was seen to fall back. There came to those English still upon the hill the long wail of grief. It could mean only one thing.

The duke is dead! But now, above the wailing, sharp and clear rose their captain's voice. *I live!* And there he was, their duke, their leader, nose-piece of his helmet lifted that all might see his face.

His face, his voice, had worked their miracle. The flying Normans turned again and cut their pursuers to pieces.

Now, men again in due order, William spurred once more up Senlac Hill; on either side rode a brother, behind him pressed the flower of

Norman chivalry. It was for the English standards that they made. Hurl down the *Golden Dragon*, lay low the *Fighting Man* that soon should fight no more!

Harold, also between his brothers, all three on foot, faced those other three brothers towering upon their horses.

It was the moment.

Up went William's great mace; up went Harold's two-handed axe. But before the blow could be exchanged, Gyrth had struck. William was unhurt, but the shock unseated him. At once he was on his feet and hand-to-hand, those two engaged. It was Gyrth that took the death-blow. And, in that same dreadful moment, down went Leofwine beneath the mace of Odo.

Two brothers dead within the same split second. Between his two standards Harold stood alone, then, like a man possessed, he lifted his axe; but William had already been carried away in a wild sea of fighting. Now the men of Essex and Kent rose to wreak vengeance for their dead earls. Savage and grim they fought; and, in the forefront of the battle, faithful to his post between his standards, Harold stood in the midst of his dead.

Carried high on the tide of fighting, William dealt blows right and left, urging his steed towards Harold; but they were destined to come face-to-face never again, not the long day through to exchange one blow. Three times was William unhorsed; and three times was up again spurring a fresh mount into the heart of the battle. Wild and terrible his look, peerless and unconquerable; his men burned with their pride in him.

The long day wore on towards noon. For all William's great deeds and the pride of his men, the English stood immovable. They had advantage of the ground Harold had so brilliantly chosen; they had enduring courage—and they fought for their freedom. Some men they had lost; but the Normans many more. Save where the west wing had pursued the Bretons the palisade was unbroken. Within it, shields interlocked, the housecarls stood unmoved. Against that living wall every mortal man must die.

Yet still the cavalry essayed the hill, some there were to reach the crest, but, for the most part, the riders went slipping and sliding upon the bloody grass; and, stumbling upon dead men, the horses fell breaking their bones and those of their riders.

And all the time Harold stood in the forefront of his housecarls dealing death with each stroke of his double-headed axe. Above him lifted the *Golden Dragon*, lifted the *Fighting Man*. The royal standards, the mocking standards enraged William. He must have them down—Dragon and Fighting Man together; and with them *the* fighting-man—Harold.

Again and again the Norman armies flung themselves against the English; but English hearts were high and English bodies strong. And Harold was their King, their chosen King, their English King. They had submitted overlong to the Norman yoke; they'd die to a man before the Norman bastard ruled their English land.

To take the hill by assault was impossible. Already the tired horses were beginning to refuse. These English fought like men possessed, William thought; his own armies were, for the most part, adventurers and the value of that adventure they were beginning to doubt. He must change his plan of campaign, resort to strategy before their courage failed altogether. And now was the moment.

The English, weary but undaunted, saw, at first, unbelieving, the Norman cavalry wheel about, the Norman infantry turn their back. It was true, true! The enemy—horse and man—were on the run! Carried away by exultation out poured the English in wild pursuit. Broken and deserted the palisade, the royal standard and the Fighting man, the King himself unguarded. Suddenly as one man, those that fled, wheeled about, the horsemen trampling upon those that pursued, trampling, stabbing, spearing, hacking them to pieces.

The English had lost their ground. But not their courage.

Back within the palisade, those that were left gathered about their King where still the royal standards flew. No longer a living wall, they yet stood in dose formation to the defence. Again the Normans rushed the hill, William dead-white in the flame of his anger leading them on to where the standards mocked him still.

The long hard day was passing; it was three o'clock in the short afternoon, and still Harold was not to be moved nor a breech made in the ranks of those that surrounded him. And still the standards forever mocked.

William felt the discouragement of his men. He must make an end now, crush the indomitable English before daylight should be gone; darkness, an advantage to those that knew the terrain, must be yet a further enemy to strangers in an unknown country. And now there came to him the most formidable, the most simple, the most subtle plan. He commanded his bowmen to shoot upright into the air so that the arrows might rain down as if from God's own Hand.

It was the end.

Down came the deadly hail, piercing helmet, piercing eyes and ears and throat. Between his two standards the King of England stood, his brothers dead at his feet. Above his head the two-headed axe went whistling. Wherever it circled men fell. And, as he stood, arm uplifted, an arrow in downward flight struck him in the eye. In mortal agony, clutching at the shaft to pluck it forth, he sank to the ground.

Seeing the fallen King, a band of Normans tried to rush the standards; before they could so much as lift an arm, sixteen of them had fallen about the dying King. But four were left—and one among them, Eustace of Boulogne, that this long while had thirsted for revenge. He feared no dying man, not he! Harold tried to rise, to meet them standing upright; but they fell upon him, all four, and hacked the dying man to pieces.

Between his standards he had got his death.

Their King was dead. But it was not the end. Norman victory must be paid for in Norman blood. Dogged, desperate, the English fought on. When axes broke or dropped from weary hands, when javelins snapped at the haft, then stones were picked from the ground and flung.

On the field the flower of Englishmen lay slaughtered; not only the high earls, nor the proud housecarls and thegns of gentle blood, but the simple men—the peasants that would never again sow nor reap nor bring in any harvest.

Night had fallen; the groans of the dying still troubled the air when William came to look upon his victory. Upon that hill where the English King had stood, the dead lay thickest; and the proud standards, the mocking standards, lay beaten into blood and mud.

'What do they call this place?' William asked.

'They call it Senlac, sir. Here the soil is red; they say that when the sun shines upon the water it seems to run with blood.'

'Now it runs with blood, indeed!' William said. 'So still we call it Senlac. Well, a man must eat and drink after such a day! Set up a table and bring me meat and bread and wine. And give each man as much as he can eat that all may feast with me!'

Then he commanded that a chair be brought and the bloody standards set behind it; and, having knelt to thank God that had given the victory, there he sat, high in the chair where he might see the field of carnage.

All through the night the victors feasted; grey morning spread upon the trampled hill with the once-green grass clotted now and black; and upon the stiffened bodies of dead men.

William rose yawning from the feast. 'Today is Sunday. It is the day of grace. I give it to the English that they may bury their dead.'

And now came the women—mothers and children, sisters and wives of the English, looking for their dead that their men might have Christian burial. Among them searched the old woman, mother of Harold, that had in one day lost three sons. She pushed her weary feet among the corpses. Gyrth's body she found and that of Leofwine; and, for all her grief, shed no tears. They had fallen, heroes of their house, their lives freely given for their King.

But the body of Harold she could not find.

'Sir,' the soldiers said when, at William's command, they had searched the field, 'no man can say which is the man that called himself King. There's neither crown nor ring nor chain to mark him.'

'The face!' William cried out. 'By the face and the shape you should know him!'

'Sir, soldiers will have their way. There is no face nor any shape. Sir, they have hacked him to pieces!'

'By the Splendour of God!' William swore, 'it is ill done! This Harold, though he wrongly took the crown, was yet hallowed with holy oils. That should have kept his body from those that despoiled it.'

Gytha, the old woman, went still from body to body, peering into fearful faces stark in death. But still she could not find the one she sought. It was a grief she did not know how to endure. Three sons she had lost; but two, two only should have Christian burial. But the third, the flower of them all—no Christian rite for him that had so loved God; that had hoped to lay his bones, one day, in that great abbey he had built at Waltham. She could not give him this last thing to show her love nor know, even, that his wandering soul rested in hallowed ground.

And now, breaking in upon the low continuous wail of women seeking their dead, came a cry that rose and spread upon the air, a long, high wail rising and falling and again rising and falling.

It was Edith of the Swan neck. She had found the body. Headless it was and limbless; none other could know it, not even his mother. Yet by the mark she had so often kissed she knew it. Now she cried above it, wild with grief because of the thing they had done to that fine strong body her own had known too well.

'God be praised,' the old woman cried. 'Now the body of my son shall have Christian burial.'

William looked upon the woman that stood before him. She was not fit through age and grief to kneel... but still she knelt, going down heavy upon old bones, asking that she might ransom the body of her son, let the price be what it might. Yes, even to the full weight of it in gold.

'Not for all the gold in Christendom,' William said, 'I cannot give him Christian burial; he lies beneath the ban of Rome. Nor of my own will would I do it. He is a perjured man; he has broken the sacred oath. Through him has come slaughter and his own death.' And then, more gentle, 'Yet he shall have honourable burial; if not of a Christian, then of a hero. These shores he guarded in his life, he shall guard still in death. He shall lie upon the cliff-top at Hastings. We shall raise above him a high cairn that all men shall know he was a man of might.'

And with that she must make herself content—for the present. She would know, at least, where the body lay. It should not lie there for ever. Before God she swore it.

XXIII

Madam the duchess was at prayer when the messengers came with news of Senlac. She knelt in the chapel of Nôtre Dame in the priory of St. Severs; and, though her heart fainted for news, she must not rise until she had finished praying—she feared to anger Our Lady.

When at last she rose to her feet and took the message and understood the message, she said, 'Thanks be to God and to Our Lady. Henceforth this chapel shall be called *Our Lady of Good News*,' and commanded alms for the poor; and gifts for the priory and especially for the chapel in which she had prayed.

She was back in Caen which she preferred to Rouen. Here her abbey grew into steadfast beauty; here the child Cecilia, forever lost, lived still; her mother, unseen, might yet catch a glimpse of that beloved little face.

In Caen more messengers were waiting with the full story and with them a monk of Bayeux whom Odo had commanded into England; the man was a skilled limmer.

'Madam,' he said, 'my master the lord bishop is minded to make, as it were, a picture book that shall tell the story of the English earl's perjury; and the victory that God gave us in England. I have begun such drawings, Madam; my lord Odo begs that you will keep them safe till he return.'

He brought from his robe a roll of parchment in width twice the measure of a man's foot. When he unrolled it, the pictures, roughed in with charcoal, rushed out lively upon the white surface.

'Has my lord duke seen them?' she asked.

'Madam, there has been no time. But he sent me a message. He desires everything to be set out with truth for his children to see; and for their children after them.'

'Then we shall send for the children,' she said, 'and look at them together.'

The monk had begun at the beginning. There was Edward the holy King sending Harold into Normandy to make firm the promise of the English crown—Odo's story of the shipwreck; the horses and hunting dogs were presents to William. Had Odo any foundation for his tale, she wondered. Now Harold lay in prison...

Picture after picture.

The great battle. The monk had certainly been there; if he had not used his hands, certainly he had used his eyes.

The drawings had come to an end. 'The rest will follow,' the monk promised.

'I like them well,' she said. 'But you must make the lord Odo a little smaller and my lord duke a little larger. And that there be no mistake you shall say which man is which. Also, each picture shall carry words to show what has befallen.'

She stopped. She said, thoughtful, 'I am minded to set these pictures down in stitchwork; so they will last longer. I shall put my women to the work. So you must space the letters for the needle to pick out. Now for the pictures you are yet to make. You must show how my lord duke stormed the hill again and again; and especially you must show how the arrows were shot into the air and fell again, as it were, from God's own Hand. And you must show Harold pulling the arrow from his eye; and you must write above it that here Harold got his death.'

Agnes, the gentle child, had been quietly weeping. Now at the brutal words of death, she shook with sobs, head to foot. Rufus, that knew well how to drive pain deep, told her, laughing the while, not to blubber. 'Now my father is to be King of England he will give you a finer husband than Harold!' he cried after her as she ran blindly from the room; they heard her sobs die down the well of the winding stairs.

Rufus grinned his triumph so that his mother longed to whip him but she would not spoil, further, so joyful a day. More and more the boy needed a firm hand; even William must see it now. She was finding her husband's absence hard to bear. She was enough of a woman to need a man in her bed; she missed the sight of him and the strong mind that treated her own with respect. The duchy ran smoothly, he had chosen her council well; and de Beaumont was wise, besides, in her domestic affairs. But her children troubled her; all of them; even Richard, needed a father's authority to guide him.

Robert was not, as she had hoped, improved by his new duties. Always inclined to arrogance, he bore himself now—*the young duke*—so that for all he was her heart's darling, she was hard put to it at times not to strike him with her own hand. He was tiresome and he was lazy. Yet he had but to smile, and her heart melted; nor was hers the only heart.

Richard was a comfort—kind, understanding Richard. In looks he was all William; but, save for passion in the hunt, there the likeness ended. Pious, gentle and scholarly he was more like his kinsman the Confessor. He needed his father to stir him into other activities. William, for all his piety, was disappointed; piety for him was gilt on the gingerbread. When he spoke of his sons and the inheritance he should leave them, he would say of Richard, I shall make him a prince of the church and he shall pray all our souls to heaven. Was William jesting? She could not be sure. Richard was, after all, the second son and stood next to Robert in inheritance.

But Rufus. Her troubled thoughts returned again to him. He was more than ever a liar and clever with it. He had made himself his father's favourite by a show of obedience; by running to obey. He would listen with grave respect, though she had seen him strut, and mock at his father when he thought himself unobserved, except by his toadies—friends she could not call them that cringed before his spiteful ways. And, dear God, how spiteful he could be! Spiteful habits had grown with him. He was not clever—except to lie and to work his mischief; and there he was clever enough! She guessed now what his newest ploy would be and sighed for Agatha.

Of Cecilia she tried not to think. She had not seen the child, save from a distance, since the convent door had closed upon her. It was better so; better for them both. The child was settling well, Madam abbess said, though now and again she had been found in tears, which was but natural. The child had a clear vocation, Mother abbess said; but like a child she missed her home.

Missed her home—the place where she should be, Cecilia, her child, flesh of her flesh! And what of her mother that must go forever missing her voice and her face and the touch of her hand? And, brooding upon this lost girl, she must remember that other daughter torn from her—the girl that called another woman mother. One day, soon, she must make a journey to St. Omer, see the girl for herself. She might, if the girl's looks told no tales, give her a place at court; make a match for her suited to the grand-daughter of Baldwin of Flanders. Gundrada would be all of eighteen now; it was time. And now William was away no time could be better.

As for her other girls, Agatha, she thought, a little sad, must always suffer, even though life went gently with her. So faithful a hear, so delicate a nature! For Constance, with any luck, life must go easy. She was pretty and gay; and she had a will of her own. At present she was biddable; she had, indeed, the habit of cheerful obedience. She would marry well. Of Adela it was too soon to speak... a baby...

The children were with her when she heard how they had found Harold's body and how his mother had been refused it for Christian burial. Rufus could not sit still for glee in that mutilated body. He had but one fault to find. 'My father should have taken her gold and then refused the body!' He was indecent in his glee; his mother ordered him to his chamber before she turned her attention to Agatha. *Cruel. Cruel. Cruel*, the child was saying and went on repeating it as though there was no other word in the world.

'Your father is not cruel at heart,' Matilda said. 'He would do no cruelty unless he was forced. He gave back the English dead to all that asked; but Harold—you must see it—was a different matter.'

Robert nodded. 'To give him Christian burial would turn his grave to a place of pilgrimage.' He was neither cruel nor vindictive; but in war ugly things must happen—it was the way of wars. He considered this refusal from a soldier's point of view and found it admirable.

Richard said nothing; but his eyes had a sick look.

'And a centre of rebellion, also,' Robert added.

Matilda turned to Agatha, 'So it was needful; do you understand?'

But Agatha would not, by so much of a nod, admit right or need. *This is Harold of whom you speak, Harold to whom my father refused Christian burial. King Harold that gave me a ring.* She said nothing. She went away, as so often these days, to weep her heart out; the lonely one, the only one of them all to whom war in England had brought anguish.

The messenger had yet a message for my lady duchess. 'My lord duke is well-pleased that the pictures be stitched; so they may hang forever before his eyes when he comes home again. Yet he desires them to be sewn not in Normandy, but in England. Let English women stitch the story of their country's shame.'

She approved of that; but sorry, too. She would have wished to set her women to the work, to take a needle to it herself, to see the work grow. But there had not been time even to lay colour against colour; a regent has little time for women's pleasures!

News could not come regularly. With the press of events and the difficulties of the winter crossing, it was bound, at times, to be delayed. Yet she must go about calm and confident, giving no sign of fear. But she knew well that, for all the glory of Senlac, he was in constant danger; in a hostile country, *the* man to mark. A man, a man only; and not a god. For all her pride in him, all her belief in him, still she must fear.

Senlac had crowned him with glory; now he looked to a more substantial crown. In his camp at Hastings William waited for the English to come and submit—earls and thegns, bishops and abbots, sheriffs and portreeves; he expected them all. One battle does not make a conquest; and he had yet to learn the English. No English came.

He sat alone in his tent while every Englishman of any consequence went hurrying to London; even the laggards Edwine and Morkere from their northern fortress.

In London they had held a great witan. They had chosen a King. And it was not William. Not William but the weak boy with the royal Saxon blood. Edgar the Atheling.

Edgar had been chosen; but he had not been crowned.

'They wait for Christmas,' the messenger said. 'The holier the day, the holier the crowning.'

'Then they wait too long,' Robert said. 'By Christmas my father will be crowned; and, whatever the day, it will be a holy crowning.'

'I think it, too,' Matilda said. 'Edwine and Morkere did not help Harold their crowned King, not though he was their own sister's husband. Do you think they'll help this uncrowned boy? These English earls—it's each for himself and the devil take the hindmost!'

It was growing to the end of October now. For five days William waited for submission that never came. It was not time wasted; reinforcements came daily from Normandy. On the sixth day, fresh forces behind him, he marched.

He had reached the busy port of Romney, burning and plundering as he went. 'Madam,' the messenger said, 'I saw some of it with my own eyes. Men and women and children running like rats. There was a woman ran through the flames; she had a baby in her arms. The baby was dead but she didn't know it; not at first. She was blistered and scorched, but she was alive. Then she looked at the baby and she ran straight on to the men's spears. And that was as well; for, Madam, you know soldiers! They'd have had her, burnt as she was!'

Richard looked sick, and Robert subdued; even Rufus, for the moment, was speechless. Matilda said, on a sigh, 'If your father commanded it, there was need. The monk of Bayeux must put it in his picture. We must speak the truth as we know it. I'll not be little my lord with lies.'

William was striking terror wherever his men set foot; yet still the men of Romney fought; in the blackened shell of what had once been a thriving port he left his garrison—a heel to grind any resistance that might yet flicker in the still-hot ash.

Next day he was at Dover, the strong castle guarding the narrow seas. 'Here he might have expected resistance. The heart of Godwine country;

but the fear he had put upon the people wherever he passed—the ruin of Romney and the savage punishments—had done their work. Without the shooting of a single arrow both town and castle surrendered.

'Because of that, it has pleased my lord duke to be merciful,' the messenger said.

'He shows his wisdom,' Matilda told her children. 'He is harsh to those that resist his will, but to those that submit he is a gracious lord.'

Robert nodded; it was the sort of sense he understood. Richard was glad of mercy shown for whatever reason; but Rufus was angry—it was clear he thought his father a fool.

William had shown grace to Dover. But his men had tasted blood. Not have their way with the enemy; what new thing was that? They burned and raped at their pleasure; and, though William made good what losses he might, there was misery and there was terror that could never be mended.

He was marching for London at last, marching by way of Canterbury; terror marched with him.

William's policy—cruelty when opposed, mercy for the submissive—was doing its work. Before ever he reached Canterbury the city had submitted. On the road he met the procession; the fathers of the city together with their hostages, their tributes and their gifts. In Canterbury itself, William made the archbishop's palace his headquarters; Stigand, himself, was in London attending the witan—which was well for him!

And now all Kent came to kneel in homage and to kiss his hand.

'They'll kiss his arse if he tells them to!' Rufus said with more coarseness than truth.

The next news was not good.

'Your father is sick,' Matilda said. 'He vomits. Pray God it be not poison.' And went to pray for the sick man in a strange and hostile country.

He was so sick he could not, for all his trying, rise from his bed. These days his wife was near despair; the elder boys were subdued, even Rufus forgot some of his teasing and Agatha wept no longer for Harold only.

The news was a little better; and then better still. Soon William would be on the march again.

Sickness had delayed him a month but in his sickbed he had wasted no time. He had sent to Winchester, till late the capital; he had demanded submission. And got it. Edith that had been wife to the sainted King, for all she was own sister to Harold, hastened with submission on behalf of her city; her own city, her husband's morning-gift. She had no mind to risk her comfort for the unknown atheling.

William's deliberate policy—savagery and clemency as occasion demanded—had done its work. He'd had Dover and Canterbury submitting without a blow; he had Kent and Sussex—Godwine country—beneath his heel; and, in his hands, Winchester, equal capital with London, spearhead of the west country.

XXIV

And still London would not submit.

'He takes the old Roman road straight to the capital,' the messenger said. 'He intends, Madam, to teach London a lesson; that same lesson he taught at Romney.

'He kills and he burns, he burns and he kills! All London's burning; and the people are running and screaming and blazing like torches!' Rufus spoke in the strange voice of ecstasy; behind shut eyes he could see the blood and the flames and the charred bodies.

William had reached Southwark; from his camp by the river he looked across to London—strong walls all about; except on the south side where the Thames was wall enough. A city hard to take! But for all that he would take it.

'He sits down with his armies by the Bridge,' the messenger said.

'When does he cross the river?' Matilda asked.

'Madam, he cannot cross it. A wooden bridge; it would not bear the weight of armed men, to say nothing of the engines.'

'And if it could, still it would be too narrow,' Robert said. 'A handful of English could hold it. He cannot use the Bridge!'

'Nor the river neither,' Richard said. 'He has no ships; they are still at Hastings.'

'Yet my father will find the way, of that be sure!' Robert said, and his mother was startled by the pride in his voice.

'Sure. Sure. *Sure!*' Rufus cried out. 'He'll punish and punish and *punish!*' He took in his breath with pleasure.

William had burned Southwark; his men had behaved with a most bestial savagery. So far there had been some appearance of discipline; now he allowed them unrestrained licence. The sky blazed red further than eyes could see; the air hung heavy with the stench of burning; charred wood—and worse.

He had left Southwark burning; but he was not attempting London. Not yet. He was marching westward. Destruction marched with him.

'Turn his back on London!' Robert cried out in agony. 'I would not do so!'

'No,' Matilda said. 'You would not. But your father knows better! Look!' She unrolled the map the monk of Bayeux had drawn and showed him how his father intended to ring London about with destruction.

'Yes, he is right.' Robert traced with his finger the wide lands that would be given to fire and sword. He accepted it. It had to be done. Robert, she thought, could not take in the full measure of the pain; his mind could not compass it. The smell of burning flesh, the shortage of food, the starving wretches huddled in bitter weather among the cold embers of what had once been their home—a necessity of war. A pity, he might think; but war was war!

But Rufus understood well enough; he built upon his own small experience of pain. Once he had caught his finger in a candle-flame and that helped him; that and his diabolic imagination. Now he was at his horrible chanting, *Pull out their eyes, tear out their tongues and burn, burn, burn!* Sickened, she wondered what changeling she had brought forth.

Agatha looked as though she were about to vomit. Matilda asked a pale Richard to take her from the room; it would give him time to compose himself. She resolved to keep Agatha from such news in future; but Richard, must, alas, learn to bear the cruelties of war.

Through Surrey, burning, plundering, raping and mutilating, marched William's armies. Through Hertfordshire, through Berkshire; at the Walling Ford he crossed the river, no one barring his way. From Oxford came the sheriff to kneel in submission among hostages and gifts. He passed into Mercia, once Gyrth's earldom, then south again to Berkhampstead. He was marching steady, marching purposeful, towards London. And now it was submission all the way; submission, hostages and gifts.

'The ring round London is all-but complete,' Robert said. 'My father holds all the land; holds it south and east and west of the Thames. Dover to Wallingford, it is all his. Now he will take the land to the north and then—then he will take London!'

London had submitted.

'To fall like this, without a blow, I cannot, I dare not believe it.' Hand at her heart, Matilda turned to Robert. The triumph in his face assured her she might believe; from Richard, also, she might take assurance; Richard head bent, hands clasped, praising God where he stood. But When she looked at her youngest son she must turn away her eyes. His face showed a sick disappointment. *London taken; and no burning, no punishment, even!* His thoughts ran clear.

To Berkhampstead they came, the greatest in the land, kneeling before the foreign duke; my lord archbishop of York to speak for the church—Stigand not being acceptable. But not Edwine, not Morkere, nor any man of the north—well he would remember it! But, surprisingly, young Edgar whom the witan had chosen as King. He had come, the royal stripling, at the head of those that had once chosen him, to beseech the conqueror take the crown.

Matilda took in her breath at that. But Robert cried out, 'No need to offer! It is his to take!'

Patient, she explained the matter again. 'Your father cannot take the crown by promise; not he nor any man. Nor will he—though he could—take it by right of conquest; that would breed bitterness and rebellion. No. He will take it because the English people offer it; offer it of their own free-will.'

'If he waits for that, he waits till Judgment Day!' Rufus gave his high-pitched laugh; and for once he spoke the truth.

'This way or that—who cares as long as my father is King?' Robert asked, impatient.

'He is not King yet, sir,' the messenger said. 'He has not accepted the crown. He must wait, he says, until he consult his council.'

Not accept the crown for which these many years he had dreamed and schemed; for which he had spent both treasure and lives! Making a show of considering the matter while the English knelt beseeching him to accept the thing he'd always meant to have!

Matilda bit upon her lip to forbid the smile.

William had called his council. To Caen came messengers posting with the news.

'My lord duke is not yet willing for the crown. Better to wait, he thinks. He says the south and south-east, alone, are his; his arm, he says, reaches no further than Winchester. And what of the north, he asks; the north to which his arm has not reached at all?

'All this is reason enough to wait for a crowning, he says. And then, Madam, he said, There is one more reason. When God sees fit to honour me with the crown of England, I will have my wife crowned, also. A wife so loving and so wise must share my crowning with me.'

She listened; and some of the hardness of her heart melted; for the first time there were tears on that still face of hers. In this moment, almost she loved him—save that he was not a man to be loved. A man to be honoured—yes. Honour him with her whole heart she did. Respect she could give him, obedience, at need; affection, even. Everything but love.

'So,' she said, 'he refused the crown?'

'Madam he did not; they talked him down!'

So he had not refused, not for all his fine words about her crowning! Some of her admiration died.

'It was, Madam, the lord Haimer of Thouars that spoke for all. He said, "It is the wish of every man in your armies that you be crowned at once. And it is the wish of the English also, the wisest and the worthiest. They know what best befits their country's good. When we desire it and they desire it—it is your duty to accept."'

'He meant to accept it all along!' Robert burst out. He had prayed for his father's success; and now that success pricked him. He could not rejoice until he had somewhat belittled that overpowering man.

'The English have done well for themselves,' Matilda said as though he had not spoken. 'They have chosen the chiefest man in Christendom and the best soldier of the world; they have no man of their own people to lead them. Since your father accepts the crown, they must surely look upon it as the work of God.'

'Yet my father is still that same foreigner, strange to their laws and customs,' Richard said, thoughtful. 'Do they think to change the foreign enemy into an English King?'

'The holy oil should work that trick! And, if it does not—then so much the worse for England!' Rufus grinned.

Twenty-fifth day of December, in the year of grace ten hundred and sixty-six William went to his crowning—and there was no-one to share his glory. He had not sent for Matilda; the times were not safe. When things had quietened he would have her crowned—he swore it—as no King's wife in Christendom ever before.

A crisp morning with frost outsparkling the jewelled robes; and all the bells of London and beyond, pealing. And, if they pealed less for the new King, the proud man, the foreigner, than for the little King of Heaven, no-one was the wiser. The streets were gay with garlands himself had commanded; and crowds stood to see him walk from Westminster Palace to the Abbey—a silent, sullen crowd that could not forget the cruelties this man had done, the stark man with the high Norman look... or yet might do. Cheering there was; but it came from the foreign soldiers that stood in front keeping the crowd back.

It was several days before the full account reached Rouen. Matilda sat enthroned to listen, her children about her. The great hall was crowded—council and courtiers, priests and merchants, household servants and such common folk as could squeeze through the doors; and, each upon his knee, two clerks set down the story.

When all was silent the messenger spoke. 'The lord duke walked beneath a canopy of blue silk a-jingle with bells; it was carried by the chiefest lords of England. Beside him walked my lord archbishop of York; a little behind them, walking alone, the priest that calls himself archbishop of Canterbury.'

Wise William to give the man a lesser place; not to discard him yet, not to court the anger of his new people. Matilda listened with a quiet-smiling face.

'Before him went the priests, holding their crosses high; there after came his own council. First and foremost his brothers; and then following close, my lord FitzOsbern leading the princes and captains of his armies, all richly clad; but, Madam, beneath the long gowns you could catch, as they moved, the glint of steel. Bound for a crowning; but who could say what the day might bring? For, Madam, the witan chose the King; but the common people had no voice—ignorant as beasts they are and as savage.

'After our own lords, Madam, came the English earls, very fine and grand.' But he did not say how, at the sight of them the English, watching, turned aside to spit.

'So they came within the church all bright with torches, that glorious church their sainted King built and where he lies buried.

'And then, Madam, in came our duke, very proud; yet humble, too. He went to the King's seat before the High Altar—that same seat where false Harold took the crown. And there, upon the altar, as it might be an offering to God, lay the orb, the sceptre and the crown. It is a new crown, all set with jewels that, in the torchlight, leaped like living fire.

'Then my lord the archbishop of York cried out, *Nobles and Commons of England, here is William, duke of Normandy, come to ask this crown by hereditary right, being of that same royal blood of our late sainted King; and also by right of election seeing you have chosen him. Are you willing to take him as your King?*

'And all the people cried *Yes*. And Harold the false-swearer was forgotten. And then, Madam, my lord bishop of Coûtances asked that same question again, in our own tongue; and again all the people called out *Yes*.

'And so loud they cried that those without, fearing treachery within, whether of our men or theirs, no man can rightly say; but to my mind it was the English that, hating our duke and our lords, and hating their own lords, also, that had given him the crown, set fire to the wooden houses that stand by, trusting to smoke them all to death, English and Norman alike. There was a wind, Madam, and smoked filled the abbey.'

Knowing all was well, she yet could not avoid the small movement of alarm.

'Not to fear, Madam,' the messenger said, 'all is well. Those within did not wait to be smoked; out they came with less decorum than they went in, pushing and fighting—bishops and lords, sheriffs and priests, Norman and English alike. Out they came in their coronation garments and with their own hands helped the soldiers to put out the fire.'

She sat upright, smiling a little; but all the time the question beat in her head, *Was he truly crowned with every rite of ceremony; so truly crowned that nothing could undo the deed?*

'Inside the church, Madam, scarce to be seen amidst the heavy smoke, a handful of monks stayed yet in their places. By the high altar unmoving in his great robes stood our duke, the King; on either hand the two archbishops; and, behind him, his two brothers and the lord FitzOsbern. And I, Madam, stood by the door where I might breathe easier yet see all; for my lord King gave me my duty to bring you the news.

'So the crowning went on to the end. And it was a true crowning, not one thing forgotten. Then our duke swore to be a righteous King; to protect God's churches and to govern all men with justice according to the old, good laws of the late sainted King. He swore, also, that deeds of violence and unjust judgments should be punished, and so fine and proud he spoke, Madam, my heart all-but burst for my pride in him.

'But it was not yet finished. The smoke was a little less now; but still it was enough! My lord archbishop of York anointed him with the holy oils, put the sceptre within one hand and the orb in the other; and the man Stigand passed this thing and that. And then, Madam, my lord archbishop of York lifted the crown and put it upon his head.'

Clever William to have York crown him, not Canterbury, not usurping Stigand. Now no man can question the sanctity of the crowning.

'And we that had witnessed all this cried out *God Save the King!* And, Madam, he is as truly crowned as any King that ever went before.

'And now, Madam, he must show himself to the people. Out he came; but first my lord FitzOsbern took a cloth and wiped the soot from the King's face; and so did each man for himself as best he could. The smoke from the fire had cleared in the wind and the sun was shining. It shone upon the crown that made, as it were, a halo about him. And the men that had put out the fire stood with their blackened faces and sent up a cheer to the sky; and, Madam, if it came for the most part from our own men, it was none the worse for that!'

Elected and crowned; accepted and acclaimed!

She turned to her children. God save the King she said.

'What became of those that set fire to the houses?' Robert asked, stern; and Rufus pushed forward an eager face to hear.

'He'll not punish them, sir. My lord Odo urged him to it; but the lord King said, I cannot find out the wrong-doers; and I'll not let innocent folk suffer. Today is Christ's Day; and it is my day. Time enough for punishment, if need be!

'Need there will surely be! the lord Odo said, very quick. You are over-gentle, sir. Already the English blame our men, saying we fired the church ourselves to toast the English pigs within.

But the lord King only said, 'When men blame each other, how shall we come at the truth?'

'The truth is plain!' Robert cried out angered. 'The English are beaten and dispossessed——'

'To find out the truth is not possible,' Richard said. 'My father was right. Christmas day and the day of his crowning—he had to keep it a day of peace.'

XXV

Five months in England; and three of them wearing the crown, the glorious crown; the heavy crown. Three months labouring to win the English; the stubborn English. And now he longed for his home—his own land and his own tongue; not the speech of the court, which men made an instrument to serve their own purpose, but the rough country tongue of Normandy, the greeting, the friendliness that came from the common people. But more than that he longed for his wife; he had been chaste five months. And he had a fancy to see his children—whether Curthose had grown nearer the desired pattern and whether Rufus had learned any more monkey-tricks. Of Richard, whose virtues he took for granted, he thought less and of his daughters less still, except to wonder, with a lively curiosity, how all his children regarded their kingly father.

And now England—such part as had come into his hands—if not at peace, was subdued enough. He had sworn at his crowning to be both merciful and just. And such a King he would be—when it was possible. But mercy and justice; these are not light things. They need a people disciplined to accept them; such discipline takes time. He could not, at present, afford too strict a justice nor too lavish a display of mercy. He had shown both over that disgraceful affair at his crowning and he'd pleased no-one—neither the English nor his own Normans.

He was King; but only over that corner he had won—the wedge that runs from Dover to Winchester. What did the north know of him, the wild, rebellious north? True the northern earls had come swearing allegiance; but what did such lip-service mean? The north was far away. And nearer home in the west—in Exeter, in Gloucester, in Chester what did they know of him? And nearer yet; in the midlands, what was he but a name? A name maybe; but the name was *King*. By the Splendour of God, let any man rise in revolt and he'd learn what that name could mean!

Meanwhile Kent and Essex were his own; Sussex and Surrey, Berkshire and Hampshire. Winchester was his also, the old capital; and above all the new capital was his—London. He lived in Westminster palace. Londoners bowed to the ground when he passed. And well they might! He had given London a charter; the first charter of his reign. A fine charter that said everything. Himself had conceived it; had thereafter weighed each word as it was translated into the outlandish English tongue. He had little enough English, but he was learning; and this charter he knew by heart.

William King greets William bishop and Geoffrey portreeve, and all the burghers, French and English that be in London, in a friendly spirit. And I would have you know that I will keep all the laws that were in King Edward's day...

And he had ignored the name of Harold, wiped out the usurper.

...and I will that every man inherit from his father. And I will not endure that any man offer you wrong. God keep you.'

Beneath his name he had made his mark, the strong cross. Londoners should be satisfied! If they were not? Commanding the river rose his tower; he could, at need, starve the Londoners out. Between Thames and tower he held London between his hands.

These English had no leader—and that was his luck! Their earls fought each for his own hand. Harold, alone, had fought for England; and Harold had been a danger. But these? Troublesome merely.

He smiled grimly remembering how they had come offering submission; it was after his crowning and before his charter to London. One by one they had come, those that had not already submitted—and not only those from such parts as knew the strength of his arm. And chief of them all, proud Edwine and Morkere humbly kneeling. And from the wild north came Copsige that had been Tostig's friend and captain, and with him Siward and Thorkill, leaders all three of this savage rebellious people. And from Huntingdonshire had come Waltheof—their friend and ally in every cause. One by one they had come. As for the rest—those that had not yet submitted? One by one he would put them down; bit by bit take the whole of England into his own hands.

Till then, was it safe to go home? He thought it was; but, for all that, he summoned his council.

'Sirs, you know I am minded to go home for a while; I have still my duties there. England, I believe, I can safely leave in your hands. The most part of estates forfeited by those English that opposed me, I have given to you my councillors and to my captains, hoping thereby to strengthen myself and to please you!'

He paused; he was not at all sure he had pleased them. The Godwine lands—Kent and Sussex and Surrey he had kept for himself, appointing his earls to hold it for him; to build their castles—but only at the King's command. He knew that they grumbled among themselves, asking one another if this were some new form of feudal, service. They preferred, naturally, complete ownership of such lands. Well, he'd seen enough of that in Normandy!

'There remains,' William said, smoothly, 'the estates of those English that gave early submission. I have not yet dealt with them.' And it was almost as if he promised them more land.

He felt the air of expectancy and smiled inwardly. He knew well that he had satisfied few of them. He had rewarded them all generously. They were lords of many estates; many—but not vast. Their lordships were scattered here, there and everywhere. An earl in revolt would find it hard to raise an army against the King! And that was the intention. William had seen enough of revolt in Normandy.

And he had taken further precautions. He had raised fortresses and castles all over the country; and every one strongly garrisoned for the King. And he would go on building them; as many as were necessary.

'High offices are also in your hands,' he told them now. 'And I have built my castles to keep the English down.'

Again the faces were unsmiling. They knew, all of them, it was themselves he meant to keep down; to make them understand that strong as the King had made them, he had made himself strongest of all.

'England, then, is safe in your hands; do you agree that I should go?'

And when they had given their assent he said, 'You, Odo my brother, shall sit in the King's place. Deal justly with these people but watch for signs of revolt. Yet revolt I do not anticipate; what can the English do put from their land and places of power? And the church will stand by you; the church, also, I have strengthened to my cause.'

And, indeed, he had, he considered, done well by the church. Such priests as had stood out against him, disobedient to the Pope's commands, he had, very properly, punished. He had burnt their churches and carried off their treasure. Of that treasure he had kept nothing for himself. Some he had given to loyal churches in England, some he had sent to Normandy for his churches there, but the best he had sent to Rome. To Rome, also, he had sent the dishonoured *Fighting Man*. Surely God must prosper His obedient son!

And now, the council being agreed, he summoned his captains to give each man his duty. From the rebellious north came Copsige, new-made earl of Northumbria and, for that, much bound to his King; and with him Siward and Thorkill. And to these he spoke; and to Waltheof, also, seeing the closeness of friendship between all four.

'You have sworn the oath; you have answered, all of you, for your people. See to it that the promise is kept. If they are fools enough to rise—which I cannot believe, seeing how little has been asked of them and how great a punishment they would merit—I look to you to deal with them. And I must warn you, such a rising would be no longer lawful resistance; it would be treachery to your King. With such treachery, by the Splendour of God, I should know how to deal!'

And now he dealt with the others, one by one.

'Odo, my brother, you are earl of Kent and Dover castle is in your charge. You will keep the south-east obedient.

'My brother of Mortain, you shall deal with the west country—with Devon and Somerset and the furthermost point of land that men call West Wales. You have lands there aplenty; I doubt not you will guard your own.

'FitzOsbern, my friend. You hold Winchester, my second capital, spearhead to the west. You hold Norwich, also; you will guard the land whereon it stands and set a watch upon the coast.

'My lord bishop of Coûtances, you have many lands in the west. The people are proud and rebellious; stand by my brother of Mortain at need.

'My cousin of Evreux...'

To every lord his clear command.

And now he had looked to all and he could go. He was sick for home with a sickness nothing could cure but the sight of his cider-orchards breaking into bud, and the face of his wife and the rough speech of his countrymen.

William was coming home. Five months of fighting, scheming, threatening, conciliating; five months of rewarding, punishing. And all this in a foreign land, where a man must watch his own shadow lest it turn and strike him to the heart. And now he was coming home expecting to find peace in his family; and a fair and smiling land.

The last he would certainly find. 'He chose my council well. And you have been my mainstay and my guide,' Matilda told Roger de Beaumont. 'But—within the house?' She sighed. 'There's my eldest son and my youngest forever at odds!'

'Their father will deal with it.'

'But how will he deal with it? He's forever at Robert; the boy is always in the wrong. And the ridiculous name *Curthose* doesn't help. He needs a word now and then—encouragement to quicken his laziness, advice to curb his arrogance. But continual fault-finding—it rouses a devil in him!'

She had not meant to criticise William; it was not her way. Nor was she one to give confidences or seek them. But she was troubled and old Roger was secret and loyal. If anyone at all loved her husband it was the old man that had known him as a child.

And now, having started, she could not stop; she had kept things to herself overlong.

'As for Richard, his father takes his virtues for granted. He'll more or less ignore my second son, you will see! Yet, of all my children, Richard, I fancy, loves him best. The others are afraid of him.'

The old man nodded. 'And my lord Robert most of all.'

'He fears constant humiliation,' she said. 'Richard, quiet though he is, fears no-one; he has a wisdom in him. But Rufus; of all my children it is Rufus fears his father most. My eldest son hides it beneath arrogance; my youngest beneath a smiling face. My lord sees the smiling obedience—and little else! He spoils the boy when he should whip him. I fear for both Robert and Rufus when my lord comes home!'

She had another cause for fear; it was on account of another child. But of this child she must say nothing.

She had Gundrada with her now. In the misery of Cecilia's loss she had not been able to withstand the longing to see her first-born—her daughter. She had gone, under pretext of making an offering to St. Bertin. At St. Omer she had been well entertained; there among the rich burghers she had met Gerbod and his wife together with the younger Gerbod, the dark young man their son. And she had met Gundrada.

The first sight of her daughter had been a shock. The girl was all her father—sturdy, long-limbed, high-coloured—English red and white and gold.

In that first moment there was nothing but anger; anger deep and bitter and overwhelming because the girl was her father all over again. After that had come thankfulness; the girl had no trace of her mother. Nothing in those English looks to tell a tale.

She had gone home thoughtful. The girl was nineteen; and unmarried. Gerbod and his wife had not, it seemed, found a man worthy of their treasure. Some inkling of her high birth they had; but how high it was they did not know. A little later, when the young Gerbod came to Rouen to join reinforcements volunteering for English service, she had sent to St. Omer offering the girl a place at court. The old people had been glad to let her go; Madam duchess had promised her a good marriage.

A pleasant girl; a little slow, Matilda thought. She could not, she found to her grief, love Gundrada. Impossible to believe that in her own body she had conceived the stranger, and within that body carried her for nine frightened months. And, from that same agonised body, had brought her forth; had all-but wept herself to death for this alien flesh. The loss had long been healed. She had thought with Gundrada to comfort herself a little for the loss of Cecilia; but it was no such thing. For the loss of the child she had nursed at the breast, had watched grow from babyhood to girlhood, she could never be healed; it was a wound that must forever bleed. For Cecilia she would give her life; for Gundrada she would do what she conveniently could—see to it that the girl married well. Again she thanked God that nature had kept her secret. William could have no suspicion; neither he nor anyone, anyone at all.

And now he was coming home, their duke that should bring the royal crown of England to lay at the feet of Normandy—England, vassal to Normandy! Throughout the duchy there was exultation. But in Paris, the King was not pleased. Well, no need to consider his feeling now; the shoe was on the other foot.

'My lord duke plans to spend easter at Fécamp,' Roger of Beaumont said. 'He brings with him a great company; and we must find lodgings for them all.'

She nodded. 'He brings not only our own people that fought with him and won the glory, but the foreigners, also—the English. He brings Edwine and Morkere; and the priest that calls himself an archbishop, and the young man they call the atheling.'

'He carries away, under the face of friendship, all those he cannot trust—or so it seems!' Robert said, a little scornful.

'So he leaves a quiet land behind him.'

'But does he leave—peace?' Richard asked.

XXVI

William, together with a great company, had left Pevensey, the same quiet beach that had seen his landing. Now he was returning glorious; the great men of England forced to wear the yoke of his friendship. In old Rome such men had been marched through streets as slaves; but a proud slave might wear his fetters proudly. These men wore fetters also; the heavier that they could not be seen. Forcing them to accept the fetters of his friendship he had reduced them to less than the stature of slaves.

Hourly his messengers rode into Rouen.

My lord's ships are on the move; such a fleet has never been seen! The sails are white. Yes, every ship great or small hoists the white sails of victory.

The Mora leads them all. The golden boy looks towards his own land; he lifts the ivory trumpet in sign of victory...

He had landed. He had landed at St. Valéry whence he had sailed. As he rode the countryside, all Normandy came out to honour him—his comtes and vicomtes to bring him in triumph to the castles they held of him, the burghers to kneel with rich gifts, young girls and children to strew their flowers.

Rouen was crowded with Normans from every remote spot come to look upon their duke that was now a King. Several miles beyond the city processions came out to meet him—flying banners, fife and drum; music and garlands everywhere.

At the head of all the processions rode his wife and his children.

He had not fully remembered how fair she was; nor how small, how exquisitely fine. All these months of chastity—and this was his wife. Desire leaped in him. He could scarce take his eyes from her! By the Splendour of God he'd have her crowned, take her back with him; let all England look upon their queen!

His first sight of Robert brought at once the familiar pick of annoyance. The boy was too fat—too little exercise, too many sweet cakes. But, for all that, he sat the mare well; William was forced to admit it. In spite of his short stature and his plumpness he had a gallant air. Yet, as always, the boy's looks must always annoy him; William knew it and regretted it. But the thing was beyond him.

He liked the look of Richard, the long, lean rust-haired boy so like himself when young; yet in his ways so different. He sighed a little. But in little William that was named for himself—his little Rufus—he could find no fault. Of all the children, the most loving, the most obedient; the one that did not fear his father. As soon as the processions met, Rufus sprang from his mare and came running to fling both arms about his father's neck. William bent to lift the boy to the saddle. His youngest son riding high before him they entered Rouen together. Riding thus, William found himself wishing that this youngest was the eldest so that his father could give him Normandy and England and whatever else his sword might win.

At his girls he had scarcely looked. Agatha, he had seen in his first quick glance, was already a beauty, and Constance a pretty child. For Adela he spared no thought. She was not there and he had forgotten her existence. When she should be useful he would remember her again.

Yet something was missing; he knew it as he rode within the gates. What it was he could not, at first, think; it was not until he lifted his eyes to the spires of Holy Trinity that he remembered Cecilia. Well she had done with an earthly father; she was part of his bargain with God.

Matilda did not like Edwine nor yet his brother Morkere—their history she knew too well. Nor could she like Stigand—good priest, good scholar. She knew he was to be discarded as soon as might be; she could not face him without some pricking of guilt. The boy Edgar she liked, the fair and gentle prince whose crown William had taken; she treated him with especial kindness.

Rouen was full of strangers—an invasion of English, it would seem; for William had also brought his English bodyguard. Long haired, fair and ruddy, broad-shouldered and handsome, they drew the eye. The Normans looked upon them part-admiring, part-scornful—the vanquished.

William had brought rich presents home. First and foremost, as becomes God's soldier, yet more gifts for the churches of Normandy—taken for the most part from churches that still proved obstinate. For St. Stephen's, growing beneath Lanfranc's watchful eye, he had brought the great gold ingot of Harald Hardrada. It had been found in the King's House near York; and though it had not taken twelve men to carry it, two could scarce lift it. A kingly gift and worthy of the King of Heaven.

For his own household he had brought dishes of silver and gold; he had brought cloaks and gowns, the borders worked with famous English embroideries; and for Matilda, a girdle woven of gold thread encrusted with jewels. And he had brought her, also, a gift beyond compare—a new crown of finest craftsmanship. 'It is not only beautiful,' he told her, 'it is not only costly. It is important and it is unique. No such crown has ever been made before. In England the King's wife has never before been crowned nor borne the name of Queen. The Lady she has always been called. Now we shall teach them—as in other things—a new way. You shall be crowned Queen. Never did woman deserve it more nor so well become a crown.'

She was deeply moved; she bent and kissed his hand. Her eyes were full of tears; but they were not tears of joy. He had been away five months, five dangerous months. He had come back loving and kind—and she could not love him. The crown could not comfort her for Cecilia.

In the praises of his countrymen, in pride of his children that was pride in himself—he the bastard had sired lawful children, princes and princesses all; and, most of all, in the companionship of his so-loved wife, he healed himself of his weariness. He was so proud of her; of her wise government, of the graciousness that had allowed no quarrel with the council so that all had been friendly and smooth. He was proud of her looks and her charm; he could not wait to get her to England and have her crowned.

Nor, it would seem, to get her to bed. And she? She was proud of him, she was grateful; yet she could not freely give herself. Despite her own will she was closed to him. Once she had found pleasure in the marriage that she could find it no longer was yet another item in the count against him. He was intrigued with her withdrawal; modesty, he considered, an essential part in women. To win her again after fifteen years of marriage—it was an interesting experience.

They were to spend Easter at Fécamp; but first he took her on progress that the chief of his cities might see them both—the King and Queen of England. On such high occasions he decreed that they show themselves crowned.

In Caen they stayed several days. William went to visit Cecilia; but Matilda could not be persuaded. To see her child and have to leave her behind was pain enough; but to leave the child, knowing, perhaps, she was unhappy—mother could not endure it. William reported that the girl was well; a little pale, he must admit, when Matilda pressed him.

'A quiet child,' he said when still she pressed him, 'but so she was always.'

'She was a gay child,' her mother said; and, at the pain in her face, he said, 'Yet, she is happy, believe it.'

'*Happy!*' The pale, quiet child that once was gay.

'She asked after you all. Her first question and her last was of her mother,' he said, answering the question in her eyes. That the child's tears had spilled unchecked he did not say.

And still, though she must fight herself, Matilda refused to see the girl; ten months was too soon.

Satisfied about Cecilia, William put her out of his head. He had come home partly on Lanfranc's account; he wanted Lanfranc in England.

'They mean to offer me Rouen when the time comes,' Lanfranc said.

'Already they've put out feelers. The archbishop's an old man; he cannot last much longer.'

William gave no sign. That Lanfranc should be invited to Rouen had come as a surprise—an unpleasant surprise; as the good abbot had meant. He understood his duke's plans very well. Now he answered the question William would not ask.

'I shall not accept. I am a simple man,' said Lanfranc, of all men the most subtle. 'I have no wish for glory. I have work here to last a life-time. I count it a privilege to watch God's House rise stone by stone and know I have played my part therein. I like the quiet life best. The coming and going, the troubling administration, the bowing and scraping before an archbishop's throne—I am not ambitious and I do not want it.'

'You are right,' William looked full into the thin Italian face of this most ambitious man. If Lanfranc knew his duke, equally the duke knew his abbot. He did not mean to lose Lanfranc to Rouen; he meant to have him in Canterbury—when he should be rid of Stigand. And Lanfranc would accept the offer when it came. For this reason he would refuse the see of Rouen and for no other. They would wait, both of them, for the right time.

They talked much of England, Lanfranc asking many questions yet showing himself so well-informed, William could not but think the priest intended the right time to come soon.

'Yes, London is content—as indeed it should be!' William told him, 'And also all those parts over which I have closed my hand. The villeins at least, are satisfied. Why not? They live as they always did; they work their same strip of ground. Their masters are, perhaps, more strict; but a strict lord spells peace. It is the English earls and thegns that are not pleased,' William shrugged. 'They have lost their land—or shall do so. It is all forfeit to the King.'

'A wise King,' Lanfranc said, 'shows his wisdom when he disposes of it. All those that opposed you—their land is forfeit and rightly so. But those that have not borne arms against you—let them keep their lands.'

'Many that crossed the sea with me go still without reward.'

'There will be land enough—because there will be revolt enough!' Lanfranc promised, grim. 'If, sir, you make no distinction between friend and foe, you do but encourage revolt. Every man with nothing to lose becomes your enemy.'

'All lands belong to the King!' William repeated, obstinate.

'True. And it must all return to the King. Call it in sir; every rood of it. But let those that have shown themselves friendly redeem it with gold—some of it at least. So you get good will and gold, both.'

An excellent piece of advice! He needed Lanfranc's counsel at all times; certainly he must have this wisest of men in England.

He needed advice on one other matter, also. Neither Edwine nor Morkere did he trust; was it possible to bind them in closer bonds? He had marriage in mind—Edwine and Agatha. He had, indeed, made a half-promise to the young man—a secret between them; but not so secret that Lanfranc's sensitive nose had not already smelled it out. He disliked the notion and said so, very plain.

'Sir, do not do it. Those two brothers will cause you bloodshed, yet. Do not give them such a hostage. Harold, as I remember, married their sister; but they turned their back and left him to his death. Sir, I beseech you, leave your daughter out of it. Wait, at least—' and now he must tread delicately, 'until you have spoken on the matter with Madam the duchess.'

He had long been troubled about Matilda's attitude towards her husband. While all Normandy and beyond, rang with her praises, Lanfranc, alone, sensed coldness beneath her graciousness, and guessed that some of it was on Cecilia's account. It was good to give a daughter to God. A man need not consult his wife on the matter; but with a woman like Madam the duchess it would have been wise. A show, at least, of consulting her about the other children might, a little, soften her resentment. Lanfranc could see how she turned more and more towards her eldest son; knew, as all the court must know, the growing antagonism between the boy and his father. Unless William trod delicately he bade fair to lose his wife. Whether he himself guessed this, it was hard to say; he was not given to talking about his private affairs. Doubt cast upon his wife's affection was a thing he would never forgive.

XXVII

William had cast off care; such a casting-off was not for Lanfranc. To his listening ears came rumours. Odo and FitzOsbern were making trouble. They were grinding the face of the people, they were growing fat on a justice that was no justice at all. Thieving, arson and rape on the part of their own men they allowed to go unchecked. The country was restless.

He would say nothing to William until William should speak to him. William had his own information and would act on it as he saw fit.

In the third week of March, shortly after his return, William had news of trouble in the north. But he made no movement to return nor to alter his plans in any way.

'This is not revolt against me, the King of England,' he told Matilda. 'It is Englishman against Englishman—a private quarrel. Copsige was murdered because I made him earl of Northumberland. The dispossessed house, the house of Oswulf, did not, it seemed, relish being turned out—though they well deserved it! They drove Copsige away; they smoked him out of the church where he'd taken sanctuary and killed him. Now they're in possession again!'

'They insult God and the King!' she cried out. 'Shall you let this pass?'

'God, be sure, looks to His own. And for the King—you should know me better! And moreover the family of Copsige is out for revenge; they'll do my business for me. If Englishmen choose to kill each other—!' he shrugged. 'When the time comes for me to deal with the north my task will be that much easier! But now it is near Easter and time for rejoicing. Let the matter ride!'

In the cider orchards trees were putting out coral buds; willow and hazel flung gold dust upon the air; one could smell the green freshness of violets.

Duke and duchess, together with their elder children and all their train, English and Norman, rode in holiday attire to Fécamp; and, always, upon occasion William and Matilda showed themselves crowned. Once when she complained of the weight, he reminded her that she must accustom herself to a crown, how else would she fare at her crowning? She should be crowned with ceremony equal to his own; he never tired of telling her so.

'Greater, even; my crowning was a hurried affair, but yours shall be worthy of you.'

Useless to pretend she was not pleased. But it could not make up for the loss of her child nor ease the smart because her husband had not consulted her on the matter.

He glorifies me into a Queen; but he slights me as a mother. Lanfranc had read her aright.

So they made their royal progress. She was Matilda, Queen to great William that men were beginning to call a new name; *Bastard*, no longer; but *Conqueror*.

And so they came to Fécamp and into the abbey that William venerated above any other; for here was kept the most sacred relic in Christendom; a phial of the precious Blood. Before ever they gave themselves to pleasure he saw to it that the festival was fully honoured. Reverence to God must come first.

In Rouen the old archbishop died; and, Lanfranc, as he had foreseen, was offered the empty throne. Very humble, he declined. He preferred the archbishop's throne in England. He desired nothing better than to serve his God, his duke and himself.

The Easter celebrations were over, the court was back in Rouen; now for the feasting, the hunting and all good cheer. The lines of care were smoothed, a little, in William's face. All summer he spent his time between his favourite sport and his duties as Normandy's duke.

When he rode out to see that law and order were being maintained he would not take Robert with him—a sluggard given over to pleasure, he said; and since he could not publicly shame his eldest son by taking a younger, he rode alone. Here, in the remote parts of his realm he would sit; himself hear pleas, himself dispense justice. Though it was never in him to be easy, he was in these days an accessible lord; everywhere, in village and town, open to all. Nor did he forget the churches. He rode the countryside making his public prayers, offering his gifts, affable if not genial with priests wherever he went. He was, perhaps for the first time in his life, a rested man. He must, he knew, enjoy this peace while he might. It could not last for ever; and who knew whether it would come again?

It was August; in the orchards cider apples shone red. There was still feud between the house of Copsige and the house of Oswulf. 'When they have made an end of killing each other, the affair will settle itself,' William said.

But now there was news of another outbreak; this time in the west country. He discussed it with Lanfranc and Matilda.

'This also is no revolt against me—the King,' he said.

'Is it not?' she said very quick. 'Your new-made earl of Hereford, your FitzOsbern—it is against him they rise. And is he not your deputy in the west? Does he not stand in your place?'

Lanfranc could not forbear his admiration. While he sought to make that same thought palatable, she had put it plain.

'They revolt against him; not against me,' William said, obstinate and frowning. 'They have never so much as seen my face; but let them continue to make trouble—and they'll see it sooner than they like!'

Hunting, making his public acts of worship, feasting, dealing with the day-to-day press of his duchy's affairs, he yet kept his fingers upon the pulse of England. He was troubled by the uprisings; but not too troubled. He had known well enough that neither west nor north was conquered. They had not, as he said, yet seen his face. But, in the north, blood feuds were doing his business for him; and FitzOsbern in the west was a strong man; to his enemies harsh, to his King true.

William stood rigid; his eyes wore their blinded look. To that terrible face, the messenger dared not lift his eyes. The message spoken, it was Madam the duchess that gave him the nod to go.

'This is different; it is utterly different!' William's voice rose graving and guttural. 'This is revolt within my own conquered realm. When the men of Kent rise against my regent, they rise against me—their King.'

'Sir,' Lanfranc said, 'the lord Odo is your regent. But before that he is God's regent; a bishop hallowed and blessed. When such as he spills blood—sir, as a priest I must say it—the sight is hateful to God and man.'

Fearing in this moment for Lanfranc, for him, even, Matilda said, very quick, 'Sir, do you sail at once?'

'No! I have a duty to this duchy of mine; until it is done, here I shall stay!'

'For no other reason?' She dared to smile in his face. To Lanfranc's astonishment the smile was returned; tight-lipped but yet a smile—unwilling tribute to her knowledge of him.

'One other reason,' he said. 'I have to see what happens when my back is turned. I must wait awhile; I must show no fear of those I have conquered; I must show faith in those I have appointed in my place.'

'There is wisdom in that!' Lanfranc said. *But do not wait too long.*

When he received his next news she knew, as he knew, it was time to go.

It was no longer revolt; it was full-scale rebellion.

Essex had joined the men of Kent; and the Londoners had risen, too—ingrates to whom he had given their charter. Essex and Kent; Sussex and London. Revolt where his foot had passed, his face been seen! This he had not expected.

The next news was even worse.

They had sent for help, his rebellious English; for help to Denmark. Let Swegen come to their aid and he should wear a double crown; his own—and the crown of England.

It was a double, an unexpected disaster.

That the men who had sworn faith with him were in rebellion was a sufficient blow; that they should prefer another foreign King to himself was deepest insult. He was white, not with the flaming whiteness of his anger but as though inwardly he bled to death.

'Now all England lies open to the Danes!' He spoke through stiff lips. 'The east is already in revolt; and from their settlements in Ireland the Danes will sail to attack the west. And always there's danger from the north.'

'God send he'll refuse!' Matilda said.

'He'll not refuse. He's of kin to the house of Godwine.'

'God grant, at least, that he delay.'

'He will delay because he must. Winter will close down before he can gather his fleet. Fearless he may be; but not mad. To cross the sea in winter with all his ships would be madness.'

'So you gain time,' she said. 'For which grace we must thank God; thank Him again and again!'

XXVIII

On a bitter day in the first week of December, William took the road to Dieppe. Horses' hooves rang on the frozen earth; behind him streamed reinforcements for his armies, including a brisk young fellow Gerbod who looked to make a likely captain.

Riding between Robert and Matilda, William was not well-pleased. He had, all-unwilling, named the boy co-regent; now he could not look upon either of them without annoyance. At first he had refused to hear of it, 'Heir I must name him; but co-regent, no! The boy is sufficiently arrogant; he dares set his childish opinions against mine. I could spew if I did not laugh.'

Matilda did not tell him that the boy was resentful because the great father that once he had worshipped, showed no respect for his boyish dignity; that he resented his nick-name; that when his father was away he was different—frank and free; and, though never humble, a good deal less arrogant. As for that arrogance—time would surely cure it.

But, for all that, he had discussed the matter with Lanfranc.

'Name him, sir. A young lord like any other must learn his trade,' Lanfranc said. *Madam is not yet healed of loss for her daughter. It may serve to heal the breach which I doubt you know exists.*

'I have named him co-regent,' an ungracious William told Matilda. 'One day he must take my place—and so much the worse for Normandy. I doubt he'll have more sense then, than now.'

She had won his consent however grudging. Now, riding by his side, she prayed he would find it justified; prayed, also, that he would treat the boy with the dignity due to his growing years. Such kindness might smooth the rough corners of Robert's arrogance. She was glad William had consented, for his own sake as well as Robert's; were he not careful now, he might lose his son for ever.

The sharp wind was blowing sleet as they came into Dieppe; a wild sea dashed high, white as the cliffs themselves. She found herself wishing that William would not sail until the wind dropped. If he sailed now he'd be seasick and that humiliation he'd find hard to bear. Surprised, she found herself wishing he would stay one night more. For months before his coming she had slept in her lonely bed; now she must do so again. And the months between? Neither had taken much pleasure from the other. And the fault was hers. Under a show of submission she had deliberately withheld herself. Now, the time stretching emptily ahead, she wished she had been kinder, wished for one night more to show her kindness. Well, for that she must wait. When all was safe he would send for her into England. But how long must she wait? She was no longer young—thirty-six—all but. Not many years left to give joy to a man and to receive it again. Men were different; their time for enjoyment lasted longer. If William took a woman in England she could not blame him.

But for all that she was surprised at the anger that shook her at the thought. She tried to fight it down.

He was a man with a man's appetites. That he had been chaste all these months in England was, when she thought about it, surprising. None the less, if this husband of hers took another woman to his bed——

That blackness within the soul of which her nurse had spoken long ago, rose to poison her thoughts.

Fighting their way over the frozen ground she felt desire, unexpected, rise strong as sap. She cast a sidelong glance at William riding by her side. He was withdrawn; separate from her, already in England. And, already, she was missing him and not only in her bed. She was missing the importance of his presence and the colour he added to life—missing the progresses and the great church services; missing him in council so much more weighty for his presence; missing him, most of all, in her bower where she sat above her needlework and listened and gave advice.

Well, there would be compensations.

She looked across to Robert. He sat very straight, chin high; mounted, he looked to be tall, you could not see the shortness of his legs. But truly he was too fat; his father was right there! She must curb his appetite for sweet things before he lost that high and gallant look.

Robert turned his head. Before she could forbid it, the smile had flashed between them, uniting them in love… leaving William out.

Horses stepped gingerly upon the pebbled beach. The cavalcade stopped. At once Robert was off the mare and at her side; he took her by the waist—she was so small—and swung her to the ground. She saw William frown as he strode towards them; knew that he detested the lack of ceremony. Clearly, farewells were to be taken now; Robert made his father an awkward little bow and turned away. He disliked any sign of intimacy between his parents. She knew it; and now she was satisfied to let William go with little more than formal courtesies. Yet she called Robert back to hear her parting words; the boy must see that she honoured his father.

'May God bless you, my lord, and good health and luck go with you. And send for us soon—for me that lack a husband; and for the children that lack a father. We shall pray for you continually.'

Cold kiss upon cold cheek; the cold wind took them one from the other.

William had landed at Winchelsea after a rough crossing to find revolt in the south-east over. Kent and Sussex had come to heel; and with them, London. Aldred, archbishop of York, had stood for the King and brought the church solid with him. In Westminster William took homage all over again. He asked no question; he was gracious and they humble—but underneath discontent smouldered still. He was well aware of it. But fair words first; should they fail—the rod.

Secret as always, he was at his plans. He must appoint Norman bishops whenever opportunity offered; and, if it did not offer soon enough, he must, himself, make opportunity. At the head of the church he must have Lanfranc; and soon. Already he had put his countrymen in key positions—to rule cities, command castles; he must see to it that they outweighed the English on every council, yes, even in the witan itself. Meanwhile he must watch; watch the north, watch the south; watch the east, watch the west.

'Your father sets all to rights!' Matilda said, her boys about her. 'England is quiet. As for Denmark——' she smiled at the messenger; let him tell of their father's wisdom.

'Madam, he sent an ambassador into Denmark—a high prince of the church and an Englishman. He sent friendly words—from one lawful King to another; and with them rich gifts. Now, between the two Kings there is friendship.'

'To send an Englishman; it was clever!' She turned to her boys. 'Through your father's good sense danger from Denmark is passed.'

'For the present,' Robert said, slighting his father.

'He buys time,' she said. 'Now he is free to deal with the west country.'

'He will deal with it at once, Madam,' the messenger said. 'The west is in full revolt.'

'And the north?'

'Sullen, Madam. But quiet. The north can wait; not so the west.'

'Then it will be a winter campaign. Well, he is equal to it!' Robert said with some pride; she wished his father could hear him.

'Exeter's the plaguespot, Madam; a rich proud city.'

'Then it must be reduced!' Robert cried out. 'Would God I were there!'

'Your duty lies here!' she said; and for that gave her thanks to God. Time enough for warfare; he was but fourteen.

Every day brought news save when the winter crossing caused delay; then it would come all together like a story that is unrolled.

'The mother of perjured Harold is within Exeter. She whips the city to revenge with prayers and tears and bitter words. And with her is the woman that was his mistress; she and her bastard sons. Like hornets they sting the city to madness.'

'It does not surprise me,' she said. 'Exeter was, I believe, Godwine country.'

'Madam it was—and is; the family held great lands there. The city is dangerous because its strength is very great. And, behind Exeter stand the men of Somerset and West Wales...'

'The Welsh?' Richard asked.

'No, my young lord; English! Some call their land West Wales, others Cornwall. To secure peace in the west, the lord King must take Exeter.'

'He will take it!' Robert spoke still with that same pride. 'He never lost a battle yet; no, nor was he wounded ever, not so much as a scratch. He has his luck!'

'He makes his luck,' Richard said. 'He trusts, under God, to the work of his own head and hand.'

She nodded at that. 'Study your father well.' She spoke directly to Robert. 'And you, too, will be such a leader, one day.'

He shrugged, taking his leadership for granted. The responsibilities of that leadership he was, as yet, far from understanding; but he was beginning to understand that his father was a shrewd and devious man. He said, 'My father has all the pieces in his two hands. He leaves the north to destroy itself—each man at the other's throat; and those that could lead them in revolt, Edwine and Morkere, he keeps beneath his eye honoured—and close-watched.'

She smiled at that. 'There is yet another piece to be watched and one, we, perhaps, have forgotten; though I doubt your father will forget.' She turned to the messenger. 'What of Harold's widow, sister to those same earls? She was with child when last we heard of her.'

'Madam, she has dropped her burden—twin sons, no less; it is all of three months since. She is within Chester, the lord Edwine's strong city, she and her babes.'

'Would her brothers take up arms in her cause?'

'They would not, Madam. They fight only for themselves. Their sister and her babes may go hang themselves.'

'God grant it!' Rufus laughed.

William was on the march. Behind him streamed his armies—Norman, mercenary and English.

'But—English?' Robert asked. 'Dare he trust them?'

'Young sir, he is *the King!*' the messenger said. 'The fyrd must come at his call. It would be a rash man that would not come; nor serve him well. So, Madam, he is on the march. But first he sent to Exeter with fair words. Yet the city will not receive him, nor even pay the taxes which are the King's right. Well, they shall pay in another way!'

'Fair words!' Robert said, contemptuous, when the messenger had taken his leave. 'My father wastes time in fair words!'

'This calls for blood,' Rufus cried out. 'For blood!' his voice sharpened.

'He has put himself in the right,' Richard said. 'Now he may march; now he may punish!'

William was certainly punishing. He was burning, he was ravaging as he went. Towns and homesteads flamed to the sky behind him; food was carried away, winter grain destroyed. Shaftesbury was ruined and Dorchester; in Bridport not a single house was left—and that scarce mattered since there was no food either, nor any to eat it.

William had reached Exeter and was encamped about the city; from the walls the citizen hurled defiance.

'Madam, they rouse my lord King's rage with insult and foul actions. There's a man stood upon the wall with—saving your presence, Madam—his buttocks bare which he thrust towards the King. It was to show he held the lord King as nothing—*a nithing*; their word, Madam, of uttermost contempt.'

She whitened at that—and not only for the insult, vile as it was. Upon what innocent heads would William's fury fail?

Day after day; one day and another day and still the city stood defiant, impregnable. William, though no man might guess, was at his wits' ends; arms and food running low. How long could he stay encompassed by a hostile countryside? As long as the city defied him, so long he must stay. He dared not withdraw; news of defeat must destroy his legend, and the result—revolt; revolt everywhere. To save his crown he must take Exeter.

'The city has fallen,' the messenger said. 'The lord King gave orders to undermine the walls; and out poured the people like beer from a barrel when you take out the bung—old and young, women and children and priests, also, to beseech mercy.'

From the laughter in the eyes of her eldest and youngest sons, Matilda turned her own. Richard said, 'Pray God my father shows mercy.'

'Amen to that!' she said. 'And the old woman—the mother of Harold; and the woman his mistress?'

'Escaped by water; the river bounds the city on the west side. My lord King gave word to let them go. He had no mind, he said, to punish women—and one of them old and half-crazed!'

'I would smoke out the nest,' Robert said. 'What of the bastard sons?'

'Fled, sir; to Ireland, they say.'

'A pity!' Robert said.

'A pity, a pity, a *pity*!' Rufus echoed; his voice rose to a scream.

William had won. But how nearly he had lost! It suited him to be merciful. Free pardon for all—save for the fellow that had insultingly bared himself; he should be punished in that part he had so disgracefully exhibited.

William had left Exeter with a strong garrison to command it; he had left orders for the building of a castle—a hated castle; and he demanded higher tribute than had ever been paid before. Let them pay for their revolt! Now he was for West Wales; he did not intend to have a third revolt on his hands.

Again the march of armed feet; again the sowing of panic-terror long before he showed himself. Ravaging, burning, mutilating—so he quieted Devon and Cornwall.

All over England men trembled at the sound of his name. But they took heart also, because of the mercy he had shown Exeter. *Stark to those that defy him; to those that submit, merciful.* So he made his legend, lived his legend. Men would think twice before they roused his anger.

Returning glorious, he dealt with unrest as he marched; attentive to the faintest tremor he missed no sign. Gloucester, Harold's own city, came to offer submission, pay its tribute. Now he had the last of the Godwine lands beneath his heel.

So he took his way to Winchester, confiscating lands, demanding tribute, putting the English from their high places and leaving his Normans in their stead, placing his garrisons, raising his hated castles and laying his taxes; always and everywhere taxes. The country groaned beneath them.

By the end of March he had reached Winchester. Here he could rest; could give himself to the pleasing task of disposing of confiscated lands. Lanfranc's advice he kept in mind. Such of the English as had shown early submission and had proved trustworthy, should buy back some part of their estates. Such a one was Brihtric—the thegn; a prince almost, you might call him. His lands had spread through Gloucestershire, through Worcestershire to Dorset and West Wales. He had been foremost in the western revolt; but he had submitted early and brought lesser thegns with him. A man of power, a thegn of thegns to whom lesser men looked for guidance. His friendship was useful, needful, even. He, too, should buy back some land—at a price.

For the rest of the estates that lay still within his hands—he'd not be in too great a hurry to sell any part of them. He had first to learn whom he might trust. And, besides, he must reward his friends and repay himself—war is a costly affair.

His brother of Mortain, that bonny fighter, should have not only Devon and Somerset, but the whole of West Wales—that wild and distant land; a kingdom in itself. Henceforth it should be known as Cornwall; to call it Wales marked it off from England, inspired revolt. Robert would see that it gave submission to the King of England; a strong man Robert to keep rebellion down.

And more land for the two fighting bishops—brother Odo and Geoffrey of Coûtances. For them it was not only chieftains he would despoil, it was the church. Those that rebel against me, rebel also against God that put me on the throne. I take their wealth and give it to other priests that know how to obey Him, he said.

And now all was truly quiet, the country cowed beneath new masters ruling the great estates, by formidable castles everywhere rising. Quiet—for the present.

Now he would send for his wife and the children. Now, at last, this country should see the handsome Queen and the fine young princes with which he had honoured it.

XXIX

Spring in the year of grace ten hundred and sixty-eight.

William had sent into Normandy a great and noble company, both English and Norman, to bring the Queen with honour into England. She had won from them a grudging admiration. She was disarmingly small, she was sufficiently handsome—though not as handsome as they had been led to believe; she had a great dignity. The little English she had learned they welcomed upon her tongue and her desire to learn more they took for a sign of graciousness. And gracious she was; but already they felt about her the isolating dignity of a Queen.

Now, watching the cliffs of home fade behind her, and all the calm spread of water between her and England, she found herself wondering how she could endure to live from Normandy, for sixteen years her home. In Normandy she stood first—Madam the reigning duchess. In England for all her queenship she was, and must be, little more than a name. No longer young, she must learn to know this strange people and their strange ways. She must learn their outlandish speech which must always come slow and heavy to her tongue. Normandy was like a comfortable shoe; England the new shoe that pinches. She half-envied Robert left behind to sit with the council, to deliberate with them upon the well-being of Normandy and with his signature to head their decrees.

He was fifteen now and open to reason—except when led astray by those that, looking for favour, toadied upon him. Being left behind he'd been disappointed at first and inclined to sulk; he had wanted to see the great, the unique ceremony, that made his mother a Queen. But soon, with his usual good-nature, he was smiling again. In England what was he but his father's slighted son? In Normandy he was duke-regent. She was more disappointed than he; she longed to have her eldest son near when they put the royal crown of England upon her head.

Before sailing she had called her children to her to remind them of the part they must play in this new land if they were not to bring shame upon their father. They must be courteous to every man according to his degree; they must be proud yet not too proud, humble yet not too humble. Richard, she had seen, was the only one that understood his responsibilities in the matter; still, with the exception of Rufus—and vanity might make him behave—they did credit to their breeding.

William had hoped to meet them at Dover but news from the north had prevented him. Now, the Queen's party nearing London, he rode to meet them at the head of a great procession. There rode with him the portreeve, chief officer of London, together with all his officials; and with them William the Norman bishop of London and Aldred the Saxon archbishop of York. Stigand rode, too, uninvited and unwanted; William had judged it wiser in the present state of affairs not to forbid him.

When William saw her there upon the great horse he took again the surprise of finding her so little; always he expected—so erect her bearing—to find her taller than she was. With something of a shock he saw she was no longer the beauty he had married. She was, he saw—that first disappointment over—something better. She was a woman marked by high duties and cares of the state. She was still comely enough; and, for all her smallness, sat very splendid upon the great horse. Pride lifted him high. He had betaken unto himself this royal wife; bastard born he had raised her to a crown.

He had made great plans for the crowning. It should be at Winchester. London should see the Queen as she rode through; but it was the old capital, that had seen the crowning of the first King of England, that should see the crowning of England's first Queen. She should be crowned, as he had sworn, not as the King's Lady but as his Queen.

Crown a woman? Impious! Against the law of God that had made man the undoubted head of state, of church, of home. Such a thing had never been heard before! He smiled to himself remembering; smiled yet more, savouring the words he had added to the service, *chosen by God to be Queen over this people and hallowed by holy oils to share the King's royal dominions.*

But, for all that, he had no mind to be left out of the picture. His own crowning had been a hurried affair, difficult and dangerous. It would be well to remind these turbulent English—and his own Normans, too, for that matter, that he *was* the King. He had meant to let her take her crowning alone, her glory undiminished; but, for all his love of her, he could not do it. He must take his part in the ceremony; must sit beside his wife crowned and sceptred, holding the orb. A crowned King.

Maytime in England. Hawthorn and cherry; apple-blossom and plum. The sweet English countryside might have been her own Normandy— but it was not Normandy. Little Caen was dearer to her than the whole of this kingdom.

Hand-in-hand beneath the silken canopy they walked from the old palace to the abbey, richly clad and royal; behind them gravely followed the royal children. A fine sight, these last, but to the crowd, for the most part English, displeasing. These children set the seal upon foreign domination. What hope now of an English King? They stood watching, giving now and then a half-hearted cheer; and in their hearts they cursed him that had killed the best Englishman of them all, this foreign King that, in spite of his fine charter—his lying charter promising every man should inherit after his father—had dispossessed the rightful heirs and given England lands and English honours to his foreigners.

The abbey that had seen the crowning of great Alfred and of all English Kings after him down to the sainted Edward, stood ready to receive them. Hung with tapestries and with garlands of laurel and bay; a-glitter with jewelled crosses and golden plate, the abbey waited. In jewelled mitre and gold embroidered cope, Aldred, that should do the crowning, waited in the great entrance to receive the royal procession; behind him stood Stigand, not yet cast off, to play his lowly part. Behind them stood my lords the bishop of London, of Exeter, of Wells, together with the foreign bishops—my lords the bishop of Bayeux, of Lisieux and of Coûtances. Within the abbey each in his appointed place, stood such earls as had paid submission—Edwine earl of Mercia, Morkere earl of Deira and Waltheof earl of Huntingdonshire. And with them standing, also, the Norman lords dark and arrogant—my lord Robert count of Mortain, William FitzOsbern, new-made earl of Hereford, Richard of Brionne and many another that had followed their duke into England. Highest princes of church and state, both English and Norman, assembled to join in the crowning of Matilda, Queen of England.

To the sound of solemn chanting came William leading his Queen by the hand, behind them walking their children. A hero-King, a queenly Queen and royal children—and no-one to guess that, beneath William's exalted face, pricking the bubble of his immense pride, the thorn of his birth. A bastard to come to this!

He took his place robed and crowned in the great chair. And now my lord archbishop of York—and did he remember that so short a time ago he had crowned a King that lay sleeping on the high cliff beneath the stones?—took Matilda by the hand and presented her to the people, asking if they accepted her as Queen. And, as before, my lord bishop of Coûtances repeated that same question in French; and each time the concourse shouted *Aye!* And when the archbishop bent to place the royal crown upon her head, it was to William the greatest moment of his life; greater, even than his own crowning—for Kings had been crowned before but never a Queen. And there had been no wife, no children nor any assembly of ladies; there had been armed men only and a hurried crowning in the smoke of the fire and the cursing outside.

And so back to the palace for the feast. At the high table sat the King and Queen, on one side the archbishop that had crowned them, on the other Odo and Robert of Mortain. Behind the King's chair stood Richard; behind the Queen's, Gundrada. William had not been pleased at this last—honour belonged to the King's eldest daughter. 'Agatha is not strong enough to stand the long hours through,' Matilda had said when William questioned her choice.

'Then there are others more worthy than this unknown girl.'

'When many have equal right, a choice could make much bitterness. It is better so.'

Well, there was sense in that! It was his wife's day and she should have her way.

Below the royal table Rufus downed a little, seated between Agatha and Constance; the one very quiet, the other smiling and gay. For the rest, churchmen, lords and ladies sat each in his degree.

William had commanded that the Queen's title should be announced in true Norman style; and, since there had been little feasting at his own crowning, his own title should be once more announced. Let any man that resented the new King show it!

They were in the midst of the feasting when Marmion the King's champion rode into the hall. He was completely armed; with one hand he reined in his horse, with the other he lifted his sword. His voice rang through the great hall.

Does any man deny that our most gracious sovereign William and his wife Matilda are King and Queen of England? Such a man I pronounce a traitor and liar. And I, the King's champion, do challenge him in single combat.

To the Normans it was a known procedure; but the English looked from one to another. When would they come to the end of the outlandish ways of this foreign King? First the crowning of a woman; and now this strange, menacing behaviour?

There was no reply; nor any, it seemed, expected. The Normans sat upright, unmoving. Marmion repeated his challenge; and then once again. And since, answer there was none, turned his horse about and, in the silence broken only by the clatter of hooves; rode from the hall.

It was not only the King's title that had gone unchallenged; it was hers—her own. *Matilda Queen of England.*

She sat upright and royal and still. Saxons of princely blood served her upon bended knee.

Someone was kneeling, was offering her yet another dish—meat upon a platter of silver-gift.

Colour fled her cheek, her throat, her smiling lip.

She stared into the eyes of Brihtric.

He gave no sign of recognition. He had known of his duty tonight and had prepared himself. His face was quiet; the set of his jaw, perhaps a little grim for one who served his Queen. He had altered little, save that he had put on manhood and with it dignity. A prince among his people.

She forgot her husband sitting there; forgot the girl standing in her place of honour—place of the Queen's eldest daughter; forgot Gundrada, copy in little, of the man that knelt before her.

It was when he lifted his eyes to the girl that his face changed. She saw him stare as if he could not believe the thing he saw. The colour whitened in his cheeks, he swallowed in his throat. He knew the girl for what she was—his own.

The past all-but overthrew her as she sat, the ruddy, golden man kneeling before her. To this man she had surrendered her virginity against a promise—a promise he had dishonoured; and herself with it. That he had been a boy then and not his own master she did not, for a moment, admit. He had acted the man there in her bedchamber; but he had not been man enough to keep his word.

And even now she did not remember the dark, proud man upright at her side. She felt nothing, knew nothing but hatred rising deep within her; she tasted it bitter upon her tongue.

But still she bent a gracious head, smiling away the offered dish; beneath the table one hand clenched tight within the other lest she lift it to strike him full in the handsome face.

Brihtric rose, walked backwards and withdrew; he came no more with his service. Beside her William sat cold, indrawn; his very crown forgotten. She had not marked his keen glance from Brihtric to the girl behind her chair; she had not reckoned with those quick wits of his.

XXX

In the Queen's bedchamber Gundrada had unlaced the great robes, removed the jewels, combed and braided the dark hair. Now, alone and waiting for William, fear weighed upon Matilda; she paced from wall to wall.

Had William noticed anything of tonight's incident? She thought not. Her look of recognition he could not have seen; her face had been turned from him. But—might he not have seen Brihtric's face? She took herself carefully over the happening. She thought not. He had, she remembered, been talking to Odo. He could have no reason for suspicion; none. He would come to her as usual.

And there lay the cause of a deeper, almost superstitious fear. With Brihtric so shockingly alive, so shockingly near, to take another man to her bed was adultery. She could take no man—not though it were her own husband—until Brihtric was dead.

So just, so proper, so certain her decision; that it could arise from the blackness in her blood, the rage to destroy, against which her nurse had warned her long ago she could not believe. In all the years of her life she could remember no such madness; not when Brihtric had refused her, nor when Malger had spoken against her marriage, nor even when Cecilia had been taken from her. If there were blackness in those of Rollo's house, she had, she was sure, escaped it. In her decision there was no anger; it was decent, right and unassailable.

When William came she must put him off, for tonight at least; plead woman's sickness.

No need to plead anything at all. William, when he came at last, spoke no word nor made any move to touch her; he lay down stiff and cold beside her. He had seen; he had seen more than enough. Seen the stiffening of her whole body as the man knelt; seen the man stare at the girl behind the chair—the girl that was the living image of Brihtric himself; the look of astonishment and then of complete recognition. Suspicion had flamed and died and flamed again. He had come to her tonight hoping for some word that should prove his monstrous suspicion untrue. Yet, if she were innocent how should she guess at his monstrous thought? Innocent, she had no need to know. A careless word would clear the darkness from his mind.

There had been no word. He had come to her bed because it was his custom; a custom that, tonight of all nights, he did not choose to break; and, because he still hoped that at some moment in the night, she would speak. He could not, even now, for all his black anger, believe the thing he suspected.

And yet—those two. The shock that had passed between them; he felt it shudder still through his own body. And what of the girl, the Saxon-fair girl, that stood in the place of the Queen's daughter? A girl so obscure that Madam the Queen must never have heard of her... save for a reason.

Sitting there, robed and crowned, his life in ruins about him, he had remembered Brihtric's unwillingness to attend the feast; it was the King himself that had insisted. This prince of the west country, that had led his insurrection, should show honour to his Queen.

His rage shifted, centred upon Brihtric. The man had taken a woman and got her with child and ridden away. His rage shifted again. That was the nature of men. But she——! Night by night, lying beside her husband accepting his body and breeding his children. Hers was the greater sin.

When had it happened? He made a rough guess at the girl's age. It must have been when *she*—and he could not for very sickness admit her name—had refused his match, fearing, no doubt, a husband must discover her loss of virginity. And she had made public her reason—her lying reason—blaming his birth rather than her own lust. Yet, in spite of her insult, he had thought her honest; he had loved her, he had married her. A good marriage, he had thought. Now, suspecting a long deception, he forgot the long and certain kindness, the devotion to him and to his cause. This night—the greatest in his life because he had made her a Queen—she had ruined with suspicion of her unchastity and her years of smiling lies.

He would not touch her again, if ever, until he had dealt with the man. He had, indeed, the feast ended, sent for the fellow. He was gone; gone without his King's permission. That alone was punishable.

All through the long night bespoke no word, though he knew she lay awake. Did she lie thinking of the man, the first to take her body, long and long ago? Why had he believed that man to be the first? Had she other bastards besides the girl with the Saxon face? For this bastard she had done well—bringing her into her husband's house as soon as his back was turned. And the girl herself; did she know anything of this? He was forced to believe she did not. Though her parents had looked and trembled, her gaze had been untroubled. But, for all her innocence, his anger shifted to the girl. With her he would deal at once—give her to the meanest of his servants. But his anger should not stop at that. They should know, all three, the weight of his punishment.

The summer night came to its short end; though to those two, unsleeping, long and long enough. She came from the great bed, the long braids failing upon her nakedness and put her bedgown about her. She sat, heavy-eyed, by the window-slit through which the dawn scarce crept; she heard, without hearing, the clear flute of a bird. Blind and deaf to the outside world she was encompassed by disaster, locked within disaster—unless her own wits could find the key.

He knew. He had leaped to the thing that lay hidden between herself and Brihtric, the long-hidden thing. At the thought of his face when he had come into the room, of his brutal silence, of the way he had lain stiff and had not touched her the night through—he that was direct as an animal in his needs—fear was a sickness in her throat.

She had been a fool to give the girl such honour; but she had not been able to escape conscience in the matter. How should she—her other children honoured today—refuse this one child, this innocent child, some share in that honour? She had not bargained for the sight of Brihtric. So there Gundrada had stood, the living image of her father——

But not of her mother. Might she not have taken the girl into her household for the sake of old friendship; and for the sake of that friendship made much of her?

When she heard him move in the bed she turned her face from the window. She said, 'I have been thinking... the Englishman that served me at supper. He served me once, and then no more.'

Aye. He did serve you once; and that was once too many! He bit back the coarse and cruel jest; even now he was not sure.

'It was strange behaviour, so I thought,' she went steadily on; and when still he made no answer, 'There is something about the man I do not like.'

You liked him well enough once, and still he kept his silence; let her hang herself with words.

'A shifty eye. Never trust him. But—' and now unnerved by his continued silence, she was careful, indeed. 'It is not only a shifty eye, it is a lecher's eye.' She hesitated; staked all. 'Did you see, sir, the look he dared to cast upon me?'

'I saw no lecher's look; but, if you say so!' And it was as good an excuse as any; it would serve. Suddenly anger burst forth. 'But I saw the look he cast upon the girl, the bastard behind your chair!'

'Bastard?' her voice held nothing now but surprise. 'Did you say—*bastard*? The girl is daughter to Gerbod, the advocate of St. Bertin's, a good man and well-esteemed. He has no bastards, be sure of that; nor yet his good wife, neither. When she was young she served my mother well; as her son, young Gerbod, now serves you. It is on their mother's account that I favour the girl. It is not well, sir, to needlessly offend the good people their parents. Bastard—it's an ugly word.'

She saw the apple of his throat rise at the word. She said, 'To call a true-begot child, *bastard*—what shall the world think of you?'

He knew very well what the world would think. *His own bastardy eats like a maggot at his wits so that he runs mad with the thought.* They would mock at him behind his back since they dare not say it to his face.

Once they had dared. There swept over him again the misery of his childhood, of boyhood, of manhood; misery that, for all he had made himself a King, must go with him to the grave.

Because of that, whoever her mother might be—and of that he had grave doubt—he'd not punish the girl with her bastardy; whatever those two might have done she was innocent. But he must get her from his sight; without punishment or pain to her, get her from his sight.

Save for the first night of his crowning he had not come to her bed; for still he could not know whether she lied or not. He let it be understood that, in the great press of his affairs, he feared to disturb her.

On the seventh day he came to her bower. 'I have dealt with the man!' And he could not bring himself to name the name. 'I have disgraced and dispossessed him utterly—honour and lands, all!'

She said nothing. It was what she had expected; but he was not yet finished.

'Those lands,' he said, 'I give to you.'

'To *me*?' And now she was surprised, indeed!

'Who better?' And it was as though he said, *You know the reason.*

She said, since, after all, he had made no accusation, 'I cannot say my thanks—so rich a gift, so unexpected. Yet——' and she did not want this gift, she did not want it! All she wanted was the certainty that the man would never speak. 'His punishment is great, I think; the fault was small.'

'Small? You reckon it—*small*?'

'In coming no more to serve me?' She shrugged. 'Maybe the man was sick.'

'He looked upon the Queen with a lecher's eye!'

'Yes,' she said, and shrugged. 'I had forgotten.'

So far from forgetting, she remembered the accusation with satisfaction. It was near enough the truth—save that it did not go far enough. He had done more than look at her with a lecherous eye and nothing but his blood could wipe out the offence. The man must die. For, suppose, being stripped of all and having—as he thought—no more to lose, he should speak; tell the tale against her that was Queen of England? Would it be any less a scandal that the tale was old? If he thought he had nothing more to lose he was wrong; for had he not—his life?

That it was revenge; revenge alone that drove her, she could not still admit. She sicklied it over with the need for silence—and not her sake alone but for William's. How would it sound throughout Christendom that the King of England's wife had lain with a man and got by him a bastard? How would he endure it? And how would it seem to Robert? For the first time she thought of him, her beloved son. How would it seem to Cecilia vowed to chastity; to the rest of her children? The man had made his own punishment; he must die.

She said, 'How he looked upon me—I care not that!' and snapped her fingers. 'But, how he behaved to you—I care a great deal. It is this man, I believe, made trouble for you before. And will make it again—worse trouble, since now he has more cause to hate you. He will lead another rising, you will see. Unless—what have you done with him?'

'He's confined within his house at Hanleye.'

'His own house? It is not safe. Put him, my lord, where he can make no more mischief.'

He gave her a long look. Did she give herself away with eagerness against the man? Or had he, himself, been mistaken from the beginning? Once he had thought to know this seeming-candid creature his wife; now he wondered whether he had ever known her at all.

Brihtric was dead. He had been taken from his home to Winchester castle; and there within three days he had died.

'I find it strange,' William said; and he was, his wife could see, troubled. 'A man in perfect health—and dead!'

'How do you know his health, my lord? There are, besides, some that cannot endure to be confined; shut from the light, their freedom lost, they pine and die.' And prayed that William would never discover her hand in the affair. That she had done ill she could not believe. Rather, in saving her husband's good name, she had done right. And the man's death had been quick and without torment. It had been an easy matter. A word in young Gerbod's ear. *This Brihtric slanders your sister; even more, her mother. He names the girl bastard.*

And there was truth in it not as the young man understood it. She prayed—and she was not afraid to importune God—that William might not discover her part in the man's death. She did not fear God in the matter—He would understand; but she did fear William.

No need for her to fear. It was not possible to believe that, whatever might have passed between those two, she could have had a hand in the fellow's death. She had no opportunity—for where in this strange land had she the means? Nor had she the will—it was not in her nature. And more. Seeing the calm with which she took the news, he must ask himself again and again whether he had not misread the whole affair. He would ask her once and for all; once and for all accept her answer.

'This Brihtric; had you met him before?' He searched her with his eyes.

'Why, yes,' she said at once. 'He was a guest at my father's court.'

So! They had met, those two! But her frank acknowledgment; surely it showed her innocence.

'Was he anything to you?'

'To me?' Nothing in her lifted face but mild surprise. 'What could he be to me? I had forgotten his very name; would have forgotten him entirely save—' she played her dangerous game, 'like most of the young men he fancied himself a little in love with me. It was the fashion.'

'And you?'

'Amused; a little pleased perhaps.'

'No more?'

'My father's daughter—what could be more?'

'Much; had you wished it.'

'Nothing—however much I wished it. I was not for him. But I did not wish it.' Her nostrils flared. 'His birth; it was not equal.'

He would accept her word because he must. The man was dead. He would torment himself no more.

That night he came to her bed; she gave herself willingly. It added rightness to the rightness of her deed; as long as Brihtric lived she could not give herself to her husband. The man had purged his fault and her own with death.

When she was certain, she told William she was with child; and, in that moment of his joy, besought him for Gundrada.

'Give her to a husband, my lord; she's marriage-ripe. I promised her mother.'

He nodded his consent; it was still in his mind to clear the girl from his sight. He had brought himself to believe his wife innocent; but the girl reminded him all too much of Brihtric.

'I would have made her match at home,' she said, 'but you have carried the best part of the young men into England.'

'There are enough left.'

'She has—' and she hesitated, 'a fancy for young de Warenne.'

His own kinsman! He frowned at that. A man more loyal nor braver never stepped. He had given young William the castle of Mortemer for distinguished service on that battle-field; he proposed high honours when the young man should be older. He said now, 'He deserves better than a burgher's daughter.'

'Her father is more than that—this birth is good. And moreover he's a great lawyer, well esteemed. And wealthy, too. He would dower her well.'

'And de Warenne?'

'Willing enough. A handsome wife and a rich one; there's many a young man willing, and more than willing!'

'Then give her to one of them. The match is unequal.'

'Sir, the girl's heart is in the matter; and the young man's also; and her mother was my mother's friend. I am not one to ask for this and that; but my heart is in it, also. Shall you refuse me—now?'

She was carrying his child and it might be a son, a son conceived in England; an English royal prince—an atheling. His astute mind lost nothing of the importance.

Grudging and ungracious he gave her her way. It meant parting with de Warenne; he could not endure Brihtric's spawn under his feet. He would give young William a post far from the court; governor of a city, perhaps. He sighed. He was fond of his young kinsman.

Nine months to the day from the news of Brihtric's death his youngest son was born.

XXXI

She did not want this child; but she accepted it, offering it to William, a token of faithfulness, past and present. But William's joy knew no reason nor any bound. This child, conceived in England of royally-crowned parents, must be born on English soil—the atheling to bind up the wounds of the English people. She moved gracious, calm and kind; she was once more the admired, the trusted of her formidable husband.

Gracious, calm and kind. But, for all that, anger against William burned with a small, steady flame. He had filled her with a child she did not want but must welcome with joy, he had robbed her of the daughter she loved, he laughed at the wicked ways of his youngest son and ignored the real good in her eldest. And now he kept her from Normandy and from Robert.

She must go home. Robert was restless. He had been content to sit with her in council, to learn the work of government. He had enjoyed playing the young duke; but he had worked, also. She had seen to it that he was given due consequence; in her absence such consequence might well be lacking—his father's opinion of him was known. Now, she guessed, he played more than he worked; and of such games he might, at any moment, tire. He might run away, join in some mad adventure—in the east, perhaps, where some of his admired friends were already fighting beneath the Emperor's banner against the infidel Turks. It was the fashion. Everywhere in Christendom young men were marching to Jerusalem where the Holy Sepulchre lay dishonoured beneath pagan feet. Or, still worse—since it could bring no honour but only disgrace—he might lead some rising against his father. Sweet Christ, forbid! Yet it could happen. His friends were forever rubbing his anger raw.

And, for herself, she longed for home. She, too, was weary of playing her uneasy part, in this English land where, for all her crowning, a Queen could count for little. She longed to be in Normandy again; as soon as she had cast her burden she would go home, take up the reins again, keep Robert contented and safe. For Robert she had but one thought—to fit him for the place that must, one day, be his. To keep him close to herself, to stand, a barrier between husband and son—the would have laughed had she not been angered by so shocking a notion.

Edwine and Morkere had left the court—and no permission, nor any excuse. They had, William heard, ridden north; north to their earldoms. Well let them go! But, let them make the slightest trouble and he'd put them where they could make no more. They should rot in prison; he swore it. He had done his best to bind them in friendship; but, and he must admit it, he himself, was something to blame. He had gone no further in the matter of Edwine's marriage to Agatha. Matilda had been set against it. Her response had been the same as Lanfranc's; no doubt she had discussed the matter with him. 'Give them our daughter and when they revolt—as revolt they will—there's your hostage in their hands! And what shall you do then? They have you hip and thigh, unless—' and she'd been a little bitter, 'you care not at all what happens to the girl.' And had not added that, guessing what was in the wind, Agatha was crying herself sick at the thought. Yes, Edwine was handsomer, younger than Harold—Agatha must admit it; but more than golden looks was golden kindness. In Edwine's face she had found none. She was afraid of him for all his winning ways.

William had needed no telling; he knew all about Agatha's weeping; it moved him—as still it did—to anger. Daughters, he swore, were the devil! Though she wept herself into a fountain of tears still she must do as she was told!

Yet with Lanfranc and Matilda both in firm opposition, he'd gone no further with his offer; and now the two brothers trusted him as little as he trusted them. Well, they were gone and the tears might dry upon his daughter's foolish cheeks.

The flight of the two earls was only the beginning of his troubles.

Edgar the young atheling, also, had fled the court; Edgar that himself had besought William to take the crown.

'I treated him like a son!' William told Matilda.

Better than a son. You gave him lands and honours such as you gave to no son, not even your eldest…

'Edwine, Morkere and Edgar. They are part of a bigger threat, I see it now; threat from Scotland. The boy's there now. Malcolm promises to restore him to the English crown. The boy's a weakling. Malcolm means to rule from Scotland. But it isn't only Scotland and it isn't only the north!' He moved restless. 'The west country threatens again; the death of Brihtric didn't do me much good. More than half England's on the boil.'

'Half England may be aboil; but it isn't one big pot, it's half-a-dozen little pots. And it isn't the English people; it's the English earls. They still haven't got themselves a leader. Because of that Exeter fell.'

'And by God's Splendour, so shall every town that stands against me, north, south, east or west. This time I deal first with the north!'

She nodded, seeing the wisdom of that. But she was weary of this trouble-tossed country; she wanted to go home, to bear her child in peace. To say so plainly would but stiffen his obstinacy; she went to it roundabout.

'Sir, surely I should go home. We have left our own country——'

'England is our own country. With my sword I won it.'

She caught the note of anger and took her warning; she said, very careful, 'Sir, Normandy lacks a ruler. You and I away—we leave it to enemies without and within. The enemy without will not be slow. And the enemy within? At best laws will be broken and, as always, the strong oppress the weak. Who shall set it right?'

'Your son!' And it was clear he mocked.

'He is over-young to guide the council.' And she ignored his mocking.

'Then the council must guide him. You cannot go now. So much is surely clear. This child must be born in England. Such a prince adds to my authority.'

She said no more and he thought her content. But within her anger churned, bidding fair to destroy the goodwill between them; goodwill painfully built up on both sides. William and his authority and his ambition and his power! For these he would sacrifice everything—wife and children; the unborn child, even, upon whom he had set so much hope. She was weary of William and his harshness and his unloving ways.

William was marching north; as he marched, town after town fell into his hand, fell and was garrisoned; and to make submission more certain, stone-masons and carpenters left behind to raise his castles. And where submission seemed slow in coming, a little judicious burning and ravaging worked wonders.

Warwick surrendered without a blow. From Nottingham came submission; from Coventry and Leicester. Without a single pitched battle William had taken the midlands of Mercia.

Edwine and Morkere at the head of their armies submitted—and never an arrow loosed nor a sword drawn. Humbly they besought pardon; and that being granted—to the astonishment of those who, not yet taking the measure of this new King, mistook expediency for mercy—back they went, the shifty pair, into their gilded cage, their wings sadly clipped. For William took more than their humble submission; he took their proud castles and broad lands and made them his own. And there was no more talk of the King's daughter. 'So you may dry your tears, girl,' Matilda said; and then, a little severe, 'It is a daughter's part to obey her father. Next time your match is made, whatever you may feel, I expect a smiling obedience. And that is but commonsense. All your tears cannot bring Harold back to life; nor—your father's daughter—should you wish it.'

Without their leaders the northern rebels melted away.

'Your father is on the way to York,' Matilda said.

'The capital of the north—my father must have it,' Richard said. 'Pray God it submit first rather than last!'

But Rufus was gloomy. Too much submission already! Not enough burning, not enough bloodshed. And Robert had written with equal gloom; he was more out of love with his father than ever.

Richard's prayer had been answered. William had not yet reached York – long line of his castles rising behind him—when the city fathers met him with surrender; keys and hostages both.

'Now he has all three capitals in his hands,' Richard said. 'Who can stand against him?'

'And still he marches northward, to Scotland; nearer and nearer.' Rufus licked his lips. 'If I were Malcolm, I'd shake in my shoes.'

Malcolm was of like mind. He sent to William swearing to support the atheling no longer. Drive the boy out, he would not; he had promised shelter—word of a King. But there would be no invasion, nor any help, not so much as a word of encouragement.

No reason to march further. William turned his back; he had taken the eastern road and was marching south.

It was the same story; submission or destruction.

Lincoln had fallen. William burned a hundred or so houses to make room for his new castle; and, since there had been little resistance, granted land elsewhere that new homes might be built. His legend grew. *Debonair to those that fear him...*

Torksey had not listened. Now its inhabitants were dead or fled; its houses, its churches, even, burnt to the ground; never again would it stand, a busy river-town on the north road. Now its blackened streets, its burnt stubble reflected its ruin in the melancholy waters of the Trent. *Harsh to those that fear him...*

He had taken Huntingdon, he had taken Cambridge; and everywhere his legend preceded him. And always, debonair or harsh, he saw to it that the long line of his castles rose steadily.

'Your father is the greatest captain in Christendom,' Matilda told her children. 'He knows when to advance and when to sit still; when to parley and when to fight; when to show mercy and when to show none. He is a wonder of a man!' Love him she did not; but her pride in him was very great.

He had been successful beyond all imagining, but still the country was restless. He had expected it; he knew how to deal with it. His method was simple but effective. He would make it difficult for people to meet, to speak their words of revolt. He'd not allow any coming together after dark; the dark is a breeder of plots. By eight o'clock at night, summer and winter alike, every light, every fire must be put out. At eight, bells all over the land gave warning tongue. Had every light been put out? Every fire raked and covered? *Couvre-feu.* Thereafter, every man must remain within his own house. And for the disobedient, were it but in lack of care, fines and whipping.

Darkness, cold, punishment and fear. Fetters upon the land.

That year William kept Christmas in Westminster. Matilda was near her time; so great his pride in the child she carried he could scarce bear her from his sight. 'To play his full part this child must have the love of all my people. Here, in the south they know the promise of his birth—the English royal prince; in the north they do not know. So it is the north that shall see his birth, the restless north. His new-born hands shall keep my sceptre more surely than my sword.'

To take her, small as she was and no longer young—and child-birth at best a torment and a danger—to take her to the winter-bound north, the bitter, cruel north! Almost she hated him for it. But still she had her pride in him that he let nothing stand in the way of his purpose—to subdue this stubborn people. And, for that purpose, he would not hesitate to use both her and the unborn child.

The litter slipped and slid upon the frozen ground; within, Matilda sat wrapped about with furs. From the moment they had left Westminster she wished passionately, the journey well over. It had been in her mind to beg William not to let her make it; but pride held her back. If he would so use her she must be content to be so used. She sat pale and still; nothing but a tightening of lips betrayed discomfort. Every now and then he would ride up to see how she fared. She would stretch her mouth to a smile. 'I am well enough,' she would say. *If you lose the child and me together you well deserve it!* But that she did not say.

A long and tedious journey that grew always colder as they travelled north. They slept in monasteries when they must; but for a woman so near her time the comfort was small. They slept, for the most part, in towns, taking the best houses it could afford. Behind the show of loyalty, the concern for Madam the Queen, she felt hostility, the ill-wish. But Nottingham she would remember with some gratitude; seeing her so small, so weary and so near her time Nottingham received her with kindness.

Town after town left behind; and between towns—the waste of country where no man had ever lived; or the even more wasted country where once men had lived and which her husband had turned to desert. Of such devastation she had heard; but never with her own eyes beheld. She was not easily frightened; but, as the litter moved slowly along, she wondered that, in spite of their armed escort, no man burst from behind ravaged trees to pay a debt of vengeance, did it cost him his own life.

They had passed into Yorkshire. As far as eye could reach the moors stretched black, frozen, desolate. 'Tonight you shall sleep in York,' William promised. 'The softest bed, the warmest coverings!'

She made no answer; she did not even try to smile. But still she had fortitude not to cry out. The midwife that travelled with Madam the Queen cried out in her stead. At the first place they came to, town or monastery, or inn, even, Madam the Queen must stop—if she were not to give birth on the frozen ground. William would have whipped on the horses but the midwife, now in command, would by no means allow it; slow and steady—it was the only hope. Pale now as his wife, William rode by the side of the litter. Some times his lips moved as though he prayed; between pains she wondered whether it was for herself, or for the longed-for child. Had he been asked he would have been hard put to it to answer.

The walls of a small town rose blessedly before them; they rode through the narrow streets of Selby. The abbey church was not yet finished but the monastery, small and bare, stood ready. In the comfortless infirmary England's royal prince was born.

It was a hard birth—as for her it must always be; nor had the discomforts of the journey and the cold of the infirmary made it easier.

William took the child as yet unwashed and held it between his hands. A well-made child with a thatch of dark hair—a good head; it favoured himself. 'England's future King!' And he could scarce speak for pride.

'Robert?' she moved her lips about his name.

'For him—Normandy. Alas, my poor Normandy!'

'Richard?'

'A prince of the church. An archbishop, at the least. A Pope, perhaps; who knows?'

'Rufus?'

William's face softened. 'The crown goes by right of election. I fancy the English will want their English-born King. But, my little Rufus; there's a King for you! We must find yet another crown for him!'

She had used up her strength. She lay there thinking; of her three older sons Rufus was least fitted for a crown.

'This royal child, this atheling,' William said, 'is born in the north; he shall be christened in the south; so all may take their joy in him.'

She longed for the child to be christened in her abbey of Holy Trinity so that his sister, the little nun, might, perhaps, see him; or in Rouen or in Fécamp. Yet Westminster it must be; she saw that very well. But for all that she was weary in the heart and in the blood and in the bone of the way her husband's needs took priority of everything.

He was christened, the little royal prince, with all pomp at Westminster. William chose the name—Henry. Again she was pricked with anger. Her sons had been named, all three, for William's family. She had hoped to call this little one Baldwin. Her father had just died; he had left an honoured name behind him—Baldwin the Magnificent, the Great, the Just.

'Henry?' she said. 'A name neither in my family nor in yours; nor of any King of England.'

'I start a new fashion. The truth is I name him for the Emperor; a man of great power and well-liked by the English. So I please the Emperor and I please the English—two birds hit with one stone.'

And what of pleasing me? Even in so small a thing as the naming of her child he must weigh every advantage. In so sweet, so dear a thing, might he not have pleased the child's mother first?

This was the year of William's glory. He had crowned his Queen and his English son was born. He had put down the English; he had clamped his iron peace down upon the land. Throughout Christendom his name was on all tongues. His glory he shared with his wife paying tribute to her wisdom, her kindness, not knowing how surely he was losing her.

She was of all women in Christendom the most praised, the most admired, the most envied. But she was growing tired of it all. She had been ambitious; and still was—but not for herself; not for herself any more. She was no longer young, she was nearing her forties; she wanted to live in peace with her husband and children. Or, failing that, to live in peace alone with her children, looking to the welfare of her beloved Normandy. She was weary of battles and alarums; weary of the need to lay every tender thing upon the altar of William's glory.

XXXII

The year of grace ten hundred and sixty-nine.

For William the most victorious year; but not the most glorious. A cruel, hateful year; a bitter, bloody year.

He was holding Easter at Winchester, robed and crowned, as was his custom, when he heard the news.

Durham had risen; and, with it, Northumbria and north-west Mercia. Gospatrick, false earl, to whom William had given lands and honours, had fled; he was in Scotland with the atheling.

William sent for Robert de Comines, that stark man.

'I give you Northumbria for your own—if you can win it!' he said.

'I have put the matter in good hands,' he told Matilda. 'Myself I cannot march north; there's too much threatening in the west. And we haven't finished with the Danes yet. I brought Swegen off but for how long? Who knows when he'll strike?'

But, for all the gathering trouble, William showed never a sign of strain. He attended mass regularly, he received his reports, he sat with his council and he went hunting—a man must keep fit and take his pleasures while he may.

And all the time he watched and waited.

He had done well to send Comines. Wherever the man marched, fire and sword marched with him, fear and dread before him. He had reached the rebellious city; he was encamped before Durham.

The weather had turned enemy to the enemies of the King. Ice, snow and sleet; and food and fuel scarce.

He was at meat when the news came.

'Sir, the lord of Comines offers friendship and Durham has opened its gates.'

He was at mass when the next news came and did not rise until the service was finished.

'Sir, the lord Robert of Comines does not keep his word.' At the darkening of the King's brows, the messengers added hastily, 'And yet he keeps it, too! Himself he makes no move; he sits in the bishop's chair and his hands are clean.'

'And his men?' Matilda leaned forward in her chair.

'Madam, they do what they will!'

'They have brought it upon themselves!' William said. She made no answer then; but, 'The men of Durham kept their word,' she said when the man was gone. 'They opened the gates; they spilled no blood. It is their own blood that is spilt; treacherously spilt.'

He said nothing to that. A man must not belittle his captains.

'He will pay for this!' she said. 'And that's his own affair. But you; you will pay also. How should any man trust you now? Your name will stink of blood.'

It was the truth and he knew it; and she spoke for his good. But, for all that, he was not pleased.

News of Durham—the treachery, the savagery was out; reaction instant, was bitter. The whole of the north had massed. They had burst open the gates of Durham, they had put de Comines to the sword together with every Norman they could lay their hands upon.

And, to crown all, York revolted again. Angered by the bad faith of the Normans, sickened by the wanton burning of Durham and the cruel vengeance upon peaceful citizens, York, for the third time, had thrown off the foreign yoke. They had taken the King's garrison and killed its commander. Now they awaited the army of deliverance—Gospatrick marching from Scotland.

William took the news without a word; but the whiteness of his anger gave him away.

The next piece of news shattered his quiet; anger broke through, the man glittered like a diamond.

The men of York had asked help of the Danes; and they would get it. They had sent into Scotland for Edgar that they were calling King!

It was revolt with a difference.

'It is no longer this city or that revolting; this chieftain or that!' William told Matilda. 'They mean to rouse all England with the sound of a name. *Edgar King of England! I* am the King; the King of England chosen and crowned. *I!* And they shall know it!'

William Malet, governor of York, sent his urgent message.

'The army from Scotland advances to join the rebels from Northumbria. Edgar that they call *King* is in their midst—their hero. At every halting-place the English flock to join them. Send help at once or York is lost.'

And the north with it! There could be no more question. 'We march!' William cried out.

But first he sent his wife and children home. It was not safe for them; above all it was not safe for the new-born prince, the true atheling upon whom he had set such hopes. She took the news with a quiet face. She would not show him how she longed for home; longed to take her children away into safety—it was not only the new-born prince that would make a priceless hostage. But on her knees she thanked God.

She had one more reason. For all its rightness, the death of Brihtric weighed upon her heart. In that first outburst, fear had driven her, anger upheld her, justice consoled her. When, the outburst over, she should have come to true understanding of the thing she had done, pregnancy had insulated her from her own normal thinking. Discomfort to the point of pain—so small she was—blunted her feeling to everything except herself and William, her children and the unborn child. Now the child was born and she was well again she found herself dwelling upon Brihtric. His death she still held just; but justice, she found, was not sufficient. It was not so easy to kill a man.

During the day, her mind upon William and his affairs, she could, for hours on end, forget Brihtric; but at night it was a different story. He came back. Even with William sleeping at her side she was powerless to drive him away. She had known, at first, it was but an imagining that painted him so shockingly upon the darkness; now, so dear the appearance, she could not always be sure. As long as she lived in England she could not hope to be free of him; but when the sea lay between them surely he could trouble her no longer; across the sea his ghost could not follow. At home she would learn to sleep again.

In sorrow William let her go. She was his wife and there was comfort in her. That, against her will, she was being alienated by his ruthlessness, his starkness, he did not know. And if he had known? He would have sought to change her rather than himself. A man can be no other than he is.

It was a pleasant crossing in the midsummer weather. Her happiness was pinpricked by remorse for so gladly leaving William; she knew his loneliness. Save for FitzOsbern he had no friend. But it could not long cloud her happiness. She was going home. She had seen Gundrada married to the man she loved—a thing rare when marriage was in the gift of the King. For Gundrada she had done well.

Going home... and all her children safe; Agatha, unbetrothed as a child of eleven should be. Agatha, she thought, was showing signs of the réligieuse; as though love of Harold was turning to love of God. If that were so, it was still less forgivable to have thrust Cecilia into a convent so young; one child was enough to make William's peace with God.

She thought now with anguish that she had not seen the girl for three years. To herself—long and long enough; to a young child—eternity. Three years. And not one day when she had not missed the child; it was a grief that grew never less. She had waited—for the child's sake as well as her own—till she had learned to school that grief. She prayed, now, she had not done wrong; had not allowed the child to feel herself deserted.

Now she vowed to visit Cecilia at once; tell her of her father, of her own crowning, and of the new little brother, the Prince of England. She would beseech the girl's prayers for them all; and especially for William in constant danger.

But the wind that blew her homeward blew away her troubles. She was going home—home where she bore her honoured rule; where, though lost to the world, Cecilia lived; home to Robert.

At the thought of Robert her heart beat as though she were a young girl soon to meet her sweetheart.

She looked about her. Her little girls were clearly glad to be going home. Constance chattered joyously, Agatha, bright and calm, listened; she held the little chatterer by one hand, the three-year-old Adela by the other. The baby lay wrapped in milky content in his nurse's lap. Richard came running along the deck to tell her he was happy to be going home. He longed to see Robert. And he wanted to see Lanfranc again; and Rahere that tutored him and should tutor Robert and Rufus, also, save that they would never learn.

She cast a look at her third son where he leaned over the rail forever looking backward. He had wanted to stay in England. In Normandy Robert was everything, in England, nothing; the English scarce knew of his existence. But he, himself, was everything—the King's son. He wanted England for himself. Robert could have Normandy and welcome; Richard, whatever he pleased so long as it was not England. Woe to him that set foot in any place Rufus had marked for his own! She sighed for Rufus so young and already so ruthless. She would ask Cecilia's prayers for him also.

When she saw Robert waiting on the quay, the council behind him, she thought she must die of happiness. He had lost a good deal of fat; he had a look both alert and content. He had been restless, at first, in her absence, old de Beaumont told her later; but for her sake he had forced himself to the discipline of work and he had shown himself able. The council was beginning to regard him with respect; and, in that respect, he was finding respect for himself. She wished that William could see him now; and sighed that the boy was his best only when his father was away.

As soon as she set foot on Norman soil it was as though she cast off a pinching shoe. She healed herself in the air, the colour, the smells of

Normandy. She would go alone into the market-place to give herself the joy of hearing the broad tongue of the country people. It was joy to speak freely, to wrestle no more with the stiff English speech, to feel French free upon her tongue. When she went to mass, and especially in her own abbey at Caen she felt herself in God's especial care—the duchess that had given Him this so-splendid church. In Normandy she was at home; here she sat with her council whose advice she need not look upon with suspicion. For here, her nobles settled each in his degree, had little need, as with those adventurers in England, to turn all to their own advantage. In England she had been *the foreign woman that calls herself Queen*. Here she was Queen indeed; and more than Queen. She ruled Normandy. But more than anything, she was learning to sleep again. God had surely forgiven her; He was keeping the ghost where it belonged—in its own country where, God willing, she would never return.

She had seen Cecilia; yet she had not seen her, had not looked into her face nor held her in her arms. Hidden in the shadow of the duke's stall she had seen the girl come into the chapel; behind the long procession of nuns Cecilia walking alone. Too young to make her own vows, not yet accepted into God's service she walked, a child apart. A lost child. She was pale, she was thin; a white girl, a snowdrop of a girl, and like the snowdrop, head bent upon the young thin neck. One could not catch more than a glimpse of the hidden face; but the whole attitude, her mother thought, expressed less devotion than resignation. Resignation—at thirteen! Resignation of living, of loving, of her whole woman's life!

She felt her anger rising again, threatening to overthrow her; and with it rose dislike for William. If he must have a daughter to intercede with God for his cruelties, why had he not waited? Agatha would have done his praying for him. She had, her mother believed, already and in secret, vowed herself to God. Yet here, too, if ambition demanded it, William would not hesitate to destroy the fair pattern, his clumsy fingers tearing and tangling the threads.

Grief, anger and resentment seemed to taint the air, to spread in waves of violence. Disturbed, Cecilia had lifted her head. It was as her mother had thought; resignation—nothing more.

In the shadow of her stall Matilda felt her whole being dissolved into grief. Afterwards she sought out Madam the abbess.

'The girl is well enough,' the abbess said. 'She is thin? She is pale? What do you expect of a girl her age—a girl entering womanhood?'

'I have seen other girls her age, girls like a rose.'

'Shall you fault the lily because it is not the rose?'

'It is not a like case. The child looks not devoted but resigned.'

'That is half-way, is it not? She will grow into devotion, believe it. If I did not know it, I should not keep her here. But what is it that you desire for her? The world with its pains, its troubles, its misfortunes? Here life goes gently; with her it may go gloriously. She will win through to true devotion. I know the signs. It is a blessed state.'

'No doubt!' Matilda said, drily. 'Reverend Mother, I must see my child, hear from her own mouth she is happy.'

'Who is happy save that one who truly gives herself to God?'

'But has she truly given herself? My own eyes must see it.'

'Beseech you, Madam, leave well alone!' And then, 'I ask where I may command. In this place I bear rule.'

Matilda set her lips close; she made no farewell nor bent for blessing and so was gone.

The abbess looked after her. Madam the Queen of England had left it too late; she would never know now how the child had wept long nights through—weeping for her mother; weeping for her brothers and sisters, so that one feared she might die of her weeping. Well, it was all past and the child had found peace. God Himself had healed and strengthened the child; and one did not fly in the face of God, nor expect Him to do His work twice.

Without his wife, he was a lonely man; but she was safe—safe together with his children, with little Rufus and with Henry, child of his hopes. These English were savage; anyone among them might set his own life at naught could he strike at the foreign King through wife or child.

We march on York he had said and wasted no moment of time; long before he could be looked for he was battering at the gates.

He had sworn to teach York a lesson. But the slaughter he made surprised even himself. He was taken by a madness to destroy; it was as though he were possessed of a devil. No right, whether of church or state, was regarded; not even the sacred right of sanctuary. Those that sought it were slaughtered before the high altar.

Matilda went white to the lips when she heard it. William to do this! William pious son of God! She sickened at his monstrous cruelty; yet she pitied him with a pity that tore the heart from her body. He was throwing away the glory he had won. And more; much more. He was throwing away his soul. He was surely setting God against himself; for how could God forgive the slayings before His high altar, beneath His very eyes? She made offerings on his behalf, she doubled her prayers.

On York's first surrender he had commanded a tower on the east side; now he commanded another on the west. 'Twice this city has revolted; there'll be no third!' he told FitzOsbern. 'I leave you in charge. See to it!'

He was marching south again. Beneath its twin towers, beneath FitzOsbern's iron heel, York was safe enough. And those captains that had come marching from the north, their puppet King at their head, had gone scuttling back as fast as legs could carry them. He had but one regret. He had not been able to lay hands upon their atheling, their puny faithless fool! But, if they forced him north again—then woe to the north! He swore it by the Splendour of God.

XXXIII

In the late summer of ten hundred and sixty-nine the Danes came; the whole might of Denmark. Two hundred and forty ships carrying their fighting-men, their captain that mighty Osbeorn, brother to King Swegen. This Osbeorn, William reflected, was, in some sort, his own kinsman—son by a first marriage of that Estrith duke Robert had married; the mean shrew that had made bitter his father's life. Because of her his father had not been able to marry Arlette. If ever he met Osbeorn face-to-face, there'd be that score to settle!

Meanwhile in Winchester he watched and waited. Who knew, so cunning they were, where they would attach?

He was right. They did not, as expected, sail up the Humber to join those that had invited them. They attacked Dover. The English drove them out. William allowed himself a smile. The men of Kent preferred harsh law to no law.

The Danes sailed north, landing to pillage as they went. Everywhere it was the same story. In every town the English drove them out.

In the first week of November the Danes sailed up the Humber. Above the massed ships floated the ugly carrion-bird, the Raven of Denmark. The north received them with joy. All Northumberland, all Cumberland came to march beneath the Raven. And with them marched, also, the Scottish armies—English exiles thirsting for revenge, and the Scots marching shoulder to shoulder. And their mascot—though not their leader since leadership was not in him—Edgar the golden boy kept from his crown by the dark foreigner. Golden Edgar, royal Edgar, English Edgar.

And now it was a different tale! From every corner of England—from the east to whose loyalty William would have sworn, to the restless west; from south and midland, came the English to march beneath the Raven banner. And it was not only those with little to lose. It was great earls casting off their allegiance to the King and with it the rich lands they held of him—and chief among them Waltheof whom the English would follow wherever he might lead. And with them marched the thegns bent to regain their lands and honours; and, following them, the simple folk that longed to hear their own tongue honoured again and the hateful castles laid low.

And wherever they marched folk came out to greet their atheling offering homage, offering gifts, offering arms, offering themselves to serve the golden weathercock that hoped to set the crown of England upon his beautiful, unworthy head.

All, all converging upon York.

Do you need help?' William asked from Winchester; he had taken FitzOsbern from York to attack the west, if need be. William Malet, governor of York, laughed aloud. 'We can hold the city a year and more!' And gave orders that the ditches beyond the walls be flooded; and, as the rebels drew near, that the houses near the castle be fired. Between flood and flame, the enemy would be hard put to it to get anywhere near the town.

The houses by the castle; these, alone, to be fired. But what of sparks carried to do their damage unseen? The great minster caught and secretly smouldered. York burned like a damped-down fire.

Two days later the rebel army reached the city. Even from afar they had smelt the stench of burning, had lifted their eyes to the autumn sky heavy with smoke, black with fragments of charred wood. Bearing aloft the Raven banner they flung themselves to the attack.

Malet had laughed too soon.

The English within the city went over to the attackers. How could those be accounted enemies that had brought their atheling home? Against the leaping flames—for the wind changing had fanned the embers into life—the battle raged. Waltheof, sword wheeling above his head, blade running red, struck down countless Normans; above one hundred, the ballad singers sang. And where a man fell, dead or alive, the flames devoured him. That day, in the red and stinking light, above three thousand Normans died. To show their hatred of the foreign King, the walls were destroyed, and the castles cast down—those castles whence the foreigners had issued in their pride with whip and branding-iron to keep the English down.

'York is sacked, Madam; sacked and ruined,' the messenger said, 'it burns still.'

'And the church, the great church?'

'Burns also, Madam; but not I think beyond repair.'

'God grant it. A noble church; a fair city. I was there once before my youngest son was born. And now it is covered with ash, churches and houses open to the sky!'

'Deserted, Madam; its treasure carried away; the wild beasts roam the streets. The northerners have gone back home to lie snug against the winter; and the Danes have gone back to their ships.'

'Their *ships*?' Robert asked, very sharp.

'Their ships, my lord; not to their homes.'

'A danger still!' Matilda said. 'A danger and a menace.'

'They wait for spring and fresh chance to plunder—that is their purpose,' Richard said. 'Restore the atheling! The English are fools to believe it!'

'Put Swegen on the throne! The Danes would be fools to believe that, also!' Robert said. 'Their one desire is to embarrass my father and fill their ships with plunder. Well, he will send them packing.'

York has fallen. The foreign King could not hold it.

Mutterings and whisperings rising to a battle-cry. It brought the long-threatened trouble in the west to a head. Devon rose, Somerset rose, Dorset rose. Into Chester, where Harold's young widow lived with her babes, swarmed the English to hold the city; and everywhere the Welsh made their trouble. A very great rising to keep the country from the foreigner; to keep it forever English and free.

'The whole of England is in revolt!' Matilda cried out. 'The west risen to a man. Shewsbury attacked and Chester besieged. And the north, though it appear quiet, is tinder; and the Danes still lie in English waters. And your father must deal with them all!'

'He will deal with them!' Robert said and she was touched again by the pride in his voice. 'Would to God he would let me stand by him! If he would make me his knight—or his esquire, even—I would serve him as no man ever before.'

She looked at him with love. It was no idle boasting. He was a fine swordsman and fearless.

'My father would never need me,' he said, 'yet I am his eldest son.'

'That is why! You are needed here.'

But it was not the whole truth and they knew it, both of them. William would have none of Robert. *I cannot fight holding babes by the hand*; he had said that more than once, he, that at less than Robert's age had ridden to meet his enemies—and had beaten them, too. Could it be that in his secret heart he feared this young son might one day outshine his father? Or was it that, beneath his carping ways, he truly loved the boy and would not carry him into danger? Once she would have known; but it was long since she had lived with William quiet, as wife with husband; and he was no longer the man she had known. He was forging himself in the fire; burning away his softer parts. Man of steel.

Bit by bit he was putting down the revolt. Shrewsbury was loyal. Again and again the rebels threw themselves against the walls. They were forced to retire... but they left the city burning.

Exeter was besieged—Exeter that had once stood against the King with insult and defiance. Now it stood for him and drove the enemy away.

'Soon all England must bend its back before its master,' Robert said. 'But they take overlong to learn their lesson.'

'A hard lesson!' Matilda sighed, as often these days, thinking of the mutilation and the maiming; the poor wretches dragging themselves about, their life a pain and a burden.

'Better,' Richard said, taking the thought from her, 'to put an end to them altogether.'

'It is not our law to kill!' Robert told him. 'Nor would it suit the purpose—though I like it as little as you! a dead man is soon forgotten; but a maimed man—he's a workless man, a hopeless man; a burden to his friends and a disgust to all that look upon him. He's a warning to rebels——'

He stopped. Rufus was at his old chanting. Robert cuffed him away and Rufus cried out spiteful and shrill, 'I shall be King of England and then I shall cut off your head!'

'Robert will be your liege lord,' Richard reminded him. 'As for England—Robert comes first and after him—myself!'

'I will have England. I will *have* it!' Rufus threw himself screaming to the floor. His mother looked at him with disgust; the boy was fourteen! Of all her children he most needed a father's hand; of all her children he was least likely to get it!

William had quieted the west and with it the Welsh; now for the north— the tumultuous and savage north. There the Danes were encamped, their canvases crowded upon the wide estuary of the Humber. When he had finished with the north there'd be no rising there again—ever.

Horse and foot he set out making his forced marches in the clear autumn weather. *Punish, punish, punish.* The words beat through his head above the rhythm of his horses' hooves. Punish as never before. He had been over-merciful, overquick with the kiss of peace. He had ravaged only when necessity had driven; now he would spare nothing—nothing and no one. Every blade of grass should go up in smoke, every beast perish in the fire, the men of the north should drag themselves feetless, should clutch at emptiness with handless arms, should stare up at the sky with sightless eyes. They should crawl between heaven and earth like blind worms, their tongueless mouths crying out the punishments his hands had inflicted. But he was weary to the bone of the need to punish, God knew it! He had meant to secure this country in peace; and—sudden anger took him—by the Splendour of God, peace they should have if he destroyed all England to secure it! First he would drive out the Danes; then he would deal with this rebellious north.

The Danish ships lay on the northern bank of the Humber; wide estuary waters spread between them and the avenger. But when William found them they were disporting themselves on the southern bank; the river-mouth lay between them and safety. The avenger upon them, some crowded into the small boats in which they had come, or flung themselves into the water; others hesitated still upon the bank. Beneath a hail of arrows small boats over-turned, swimming men threw up their arms and sank; on the grass, bound men lay awaiting punishment. The pursuit of those on the other side he must leave to his brother of Mortain. Himself must march south at once. The midlands were in full revolt—he had just heard it. But when he had quieted the midlands, then, by the Splendour of God, he would finish his work in the north.

He had quieted the midlands. Stafford he had punished more than any city ever before, save only Torksey. Let every revolting city know what to expect! Satisfied he marched to Nottingham, that strong, obedient city, to rest and to watch; to watch Lindsey where still the Danish fleet lay, to watch York ruined but his northern capital still; to watch defiant Chester.

Rested, his plans complete, he turned again for the north. York he found smouldering still. Here a horse might stumble upon a hot cinder, or, the wind stirring, smoke blind a man's eyes. From the ruined city no-one came out to greet him; but little he cared for that—or so he told himself. He rode, head high, lest from the ruins eyes should watch, to the archbishop's palace—his headquarters. And here someone did wait to meet, though scarce to greet him.

It was the archbishop himself—Aldred, faithful friend; friend no more.

'Sir,' he cried out and he made no reverence to the King, 'when first you came into this land a stranger, and God saw fit to give you victory, I put the crown upon your head and gave you God's blessing. But that blessing you have turned to a curse. You that came as God's Servant have oppressed His church; you have broken the vows you made at your crowning. Now I take away the blessing and put upon you a curse.'

He raised his hand, his lips moving the while; and, before any man could move had turned and gone.

It was Lanfranc that brought the news to the Queen.

'My lord the King cannot take this curse easily,' she said and she was as white as bleached bone. 'In his own way he truly loves God. What he will make of this curse, or what this curse will make of him, I do not know.'

'This archbishop is over-hasty!' Lanfranc said. 'My lord King lays a heavy hand upon the people; but what else can he do? He must show himself master or all is wasted. What is begun must be finished. For all his holiness the archbishop is not a wise man.'

'He cares little for earthly wisdom when he speaks for God!' she said, white and shocked and stubborn.

In this one thing, at least, William's wife knew him. He would not take Aldred's curse easily. It lay upon his heart. He gave no sign; but he sent in secret to Aldred to make his peace and to name his price. But peace had already come to the good man, from a higher King. The curse remained.

On her knees Matilda besought God for William; but above the words of prayer her thoughts clamoured. *This curse he will remember always. It will lie heavy on his soul. It will drive him to fresh cruelties, for what has he to lose being already cursed? A mortal wound he would bear unflinching; but this is wounding in his immortal part. That, save God help him—must spell his ruin.*

She pitied this burden upon his soul. She gave more gifts to her abbey, more to the poor, she asked prayers for his soul's good that, in some way, the curse of the dead man might be lifted. Should she, asked herself, go into England to be with him? And answered her own question. He would not allow it; she was a hostage to fortune. And, moreover, she was needed where she was; to know that she kept peace and prosperity at home strengthened his hand.

But it was not the whole truth. Had she loved William, or had she even kindness enough, nothing would have prevented her. She would not go because of William himself. Reluctant, she faced the hard, essential truth. His ever-growing cruelties, necessary though they might be, were cruelties still; and they sickened her. Pity him she did; yet she knew some repugnance for one cursed of God. Of her own accord she would never set foot in England again.

William spent a few days in York to assess the damage and to give orders for instant repair to wall and castle; thereafter he marched north.

The northern rebels had gone home; the Danes had either sailed or lay quiet in their ships. As far as Scotland the north lay open, defenceless. Yet he was sworn to punish—and he would keep his word. Blood spilt now would save blood spilt tomorrow. But his deadly anger, as he rode, might have warned him that punishment could be less policy than revenge.

He rode unhurried at the head of his cavalry, the infantry steady at their heels; villages and farms burned behind them; a reddened sky announced him. On the ground, marking the way he had come, the maimed lay bleeding into the burnt earth. He would send ten miles out of his way that the meanest homestead night go up in flames; and the smoked-out inhabitants come running upon his swords. And it was all done with the most scrupulous care. No pity to be shown to old or young or sick on pain of death. And no plunder. Everything to the flames—beds and tables, pots and pans, carts and tools—all piled together and burnt; and the livestock wild with terror went also to the fire and the stench of their burning hung heavy on the air. Never had there been massacre so cold-blooded, so orderly, so horrible—or so piteous. When he turned south again the whole of the north from York to Scotland lay waste.

Matilda took the news in silence, lips close-pressed lest horror break forth in cries. She was the daughter, the sister, the wife of men well-pickled in blood; but this went beyond all telling. She tried to close her mind to the horror, to tell herself the thing was needful; Lanfranc the holy man had said so; but not this; not this!

None left to till the soil; and, if there had been—the seed destroyed. Neither sowing time nor harvest time in the burnt desert. And the wild beasts roaming, possessing the empty cities. And in the once-tilled fields, those that had escaped the sword, old and young together, lying down to die, their only hope that death find them before the wild beast.

She was to cry out in greater horror still.

Hunger-maddened, the northerners were falling upon such corpses as the wild beast had not found, and, like the wild beast... like the wild beast...

In a Christian country under a Christian King, man eats man. Dear God to what are we come? What darkness in William commands this thing? Is the curse of Aldred already at work... or is it that older curse, the blackness in the soul of the house of Rollo?

She was taken with horror of William. Yet, she asked herself, weeping, did not she, also, inherit that same blackness? Had she not herself brought about the death of a man? She had considered—did consider—that death just; William, also, considered himself justified. And who, save God, shall judge of justice? *But Sweet Christ, so to waste the land that human flesh feeds on human flesh!* She was torn between horror of William and pity for William. She might long to comfort him; but she must, she knew, shrink from the touch of him. He was great, he was glorious; yet still she could not endure his touch.

Taking his way south William was bitter.

They had forced him to their punishment, the treacherous northerners, the northerners that had intrigued with Scotland, that had brought the red-handed Danes to fight against the King; their chosen King. The kiss of peace they had turned into the kiss of death—death of men, death of land and death of cities. He hated it as much as any man. But they had forced his unwilling hand... and he forgot a certain horrible pleasure in the work. He was, he knew it, the most hated man in Christendom. But those that prattled of his cruelty, did they think it had been easy for him to lay waste the fruitful land—his fruitful land? Or that anything but dire necessity would drive him to make this winter campaign? Let them try it for themselves those that lay snug abed; let them face ice and snow; and so bitter a cold that hands froze to swords and the skin came away leaving the flesh raw.

And now the weather was worse still. Snow froze upon snow; the roads were slippery as glass so that men and horses slipped and broke their bones and must be left to lie where they had fallen. As they came further south, the ice, they found, had melted. But it was no warmer; it was colder rather, the last warmth sucked from the air to melt the ice that ran in torrents so that man and beast must wade knee-deep in bitter water. And, without ceasing, icy blasts cut through armour like swords and chafed the flesh beneath so that men bled as from a battle-wound; and harness galled the poor beasts so that they could scarce lift a foot.

So slow the march, food began to fail; without a word the King took less than his share. In blinding rain that froze upon frozen snow, more and more horses slipped and must be killed. Soon, it was not only the injured beasts that were eaten, but men killed those uninjured—though to eat horsemeat was by the church forbidden.

On paths all-but inaccessible they slipped and slithered; they sank into bogs, clambered over boulders; sometimes they must stop to clear paths or to make new ones. Then the King himself bent to the task, frozen hands about the stones. If he spared not others, he spared not himself. He was a man. His followers must give him that!

When they reached York at last, they found that the masons had wasted no time; yet still the city was a doleful sight. Castles and walls had been rebuilt but the most part of houses lay in ruins still and the smell of soot and the piles of wet ash were scarce cheering. But, for all that, William sat down to his Christmas feasting. In the half-destroyed minster he thanked God for victory; victory against a defenceless people. He made what pomp, what cheer he could; he must show all Christendom his vengeance was right and just.

For all his praying, for all his feasting and fine words, it was a festival without cheer.

XXXIV

In the new year Waltheof came to York to crave pardon. William looked upon him with bitterness—this man that, with those same hands clasped now for mercy, had slain uncounted Normans. He looked upon Waltheof with hatred—and gave him the kiss of peace. It was expedient. He gave him also his young niece in marriage; Judith, daughter of his sister Adelaide and count Lambert of Lens. She was of his own blood; Rollo's blood. Let Waltheof seek to betray his King a second time—and she would not hold her peace. And for a second betrayal—death; death the most shameful. Even as William bent to the kiss of peace he swore it.

All England lay beneath the King's heel; except Chester, the proud, strong city that had never submitted. Chester must be reduced—and not on the score of submission alone. Within its walls lived two fatherless babes that must never grow to be men; true-born sons of Harold that had been crowned King. Those boys he must have.

Chester so troubled him that he could not wait for spring. In early February he marched. Between York and Chester lay wild moor and bare mountain, hill and dale where wild beast roamed. The countryside was still winter-bound, rivers locked in ice, mountain paths lost beneath snow, and such tracks as there were all-but impassable. It was the same story as the march from the north. Bitter winds chafed flesh raw, horses fell and had to be put from their misery, tracks must be cleared with bare hands. Hail bruised them, snow blinded them; and now, as they moved westwards the ice in sheltered spots had melted, rivers ran in full spate; and these rivers they must cross. The horses refused and must be abandoned; on foot like the rest, William led the vanguard. When courage failed in the men, the King's voice rang out to raise the heart; where he led the men followed. A man to die for, his Normans said; a man to die with the English said. And both spoke the truth.

The wild and dangerous country lay behind them; spring was gentle as they came into the rich lands about Chester—the royal valley, William called it. He gazed upon the city with a calculating look. It was strongly garrisoned, walls and gates well fortified. To take it would not be easy

The most obstinate, the most formidable, the most bitter siege he could remember—England or in France. But the city fell at last. It fell at last. He thought, exulting, *The work begun at Pevensey ends here. All England is mine.* It was his; but only through fear could he hold it. He gave the old orders. Mutilation. Mutilation. Mutilation. Mercy shown too soon is no kindness. So he justified himself; and did not know that the rust of cruelty corroded the clean metal of his soul.

Into Chester Castle he strode—and no-one to announce his coming; and into the lady's bower. And there he found Edith, the young widow, quiet at her needlework; and quiet she stood up. Without haste she made him a reverence. She was fair enough, he saw, in the Saxon manner he was growing to hate; she had more than a look of her brothers whom no man could trust.

Sudden anger took him; anger because of what she was—widow to Harold that had played him false; sister to false Edwine and Morkere; mother to twin boys whose claim Englishmen, in their hearts, held greater than his own. He was a chaste man that had never taken a woman save his wife; now, anger rising in a flood, he was tempted to take her as she was, to humble that English pride of hers; to put such punishment upon her as she would never forget. Commonsense, stronger than anger, told him this was no way. Rape; it was nothing less. He—a Christian King; God's soldier! How would Christendom speak of him. The thought put an end to his punishing desire. He wasted no further look upon her. He said, 'Madam you are free to come and go as you choose. But you must leave your hostages behind. Where are your sons?'

She that had been courteous and quiet, was shaking now, he could see, for all she strove to hide her fear, the trembling of the fine white hands. 'My lord King—' she said; and then no more.

It pleased him that she—who but for himself would now be Queen— acknowledged him lord and King. He saw that she had no words with which to plead for her children and that pleased him too; she and hers had worked him sufficient harm. He knew, for certain, that, had she believed it useful, she would have offered herself there and then—her body for her children. But she, like all Christendom, respected his chastity.

She began again. 'My lord King, life has gone bitter with me; and bitter indeed!' And now he saw how grief lay upon her like a blight; she was younger, even, than he had thought—twenty perhaps; if so much. 'I was a child when they gave me to lord Harold. He was a great man, and good; but he loved one woman only all his life—and I was not that woman. And he was old; the youngest of his sons older by far than I. I was put into his bed; no time for courtship, nor yet for the kindness that should be between husband and wife——'

'Time enough for your purpose!' He interrupted, brutal, remembering her sons.

'I bore my children in anguish—body and spirit, both. And in danger, also; a hunted beast driven this way and that to seek safety. The children—they are all I have in the world.'

'Your children!' He was impatient. 'To the English a hope; to me scarce that——' He smiled; his smile, she thought, more dreadful than his frown. 'Some hazard, maybe. I am a man that recks little of danger but I'll not run to meet it, neither!' And then, because there was some kindness in him even now, he said, 'Madam, I must have the children, yourself must see it. They shall come to no harm. I swear it.'

She sent him a long look, as though she would read his very heart. She could not trust him. As long as his crown was safe, her children might be safe; but no longer. She said, since there was nothing else to say, 'Where do you take them?'

'To Normandy. You cannot suppose I should leave them in England.'

It was commonsense—and she should have expected it; yet still she could not restrain her anguish. 'Shall I see them?' she cried out. '*When* shall I see them?'

He shrugged. 'Who knows?' Suddenly he lost what little patience he had. 'Enough, madam. Bid the nurse bring the children.' And when she stood and made no move, cried roughly, 'You had best make haste. My men may not be so gentle.'

She rang upon a bell; and presently the nurse came bringing the little boys. Three years old, he judged them to be; fair and sturdy and friendly children that showed no fear of the big dark man. They had so clear a look of their father that hatred rose within him. He could have struck them where they stood smiling; and did not care that she saw his anger.

She knelt between them, an arm about each young child; she held them lightly lest they sense her grief and be afraid. She told them they were going with their nurse and must be good; she would come when she could. She dropped a light kiss on each young cheek and they went obedient, not knowing they would see their mother never again. She stood very straight, as beseemed the wife of Harold and there were no tears. She had behaved seemly, he must admit it. He gave her a bare salute, signalled the nurse and so was gone.

He had got both Chester and the children. He gave his orders for the building of yet another castle and appointed his own governor to the city.

He should have been satisfied; but Chester had defied him, Chester had wasted his time and patience. It was not the city alone that went up in smoke; the peaceful land for miles about he burnt and ravaged. The homeless streamed southward to beg their bread.

'Is there never to be an end?' Matilda cried out to Lanfranc. 'Never an end to the burning and the maiming and the punishing of the innocent along with the guilty? It is not only the north, it is not only the midlands; but he has so wasted England that from every corner they come in search of food.'

'It is always so with war,' he said. And though he sighed she could not think he was deeply moved. This Lanfranc was as ruthless as William himself; but in the man of God, ruthlessness was disciplined. Anger—the urge to punish, would, at times, drive William; Lanfranc, never. Expediency together with his Father in Heaven were his gods.

The next messenger brought further news.

'One hundred thousand, Madam, so they say, perished in the open fields for the crows to pick; and, as many dying of hunger. Madam, I have seen them, their feet cut to pieces on the rough roads and the stink of their hunger crying out their need. And Madam, there are some that have sold themselves into slavery.'

'Their free bodies for a little bread,' she said; and it was as though she wept.

She went to her chamber to pray. She was pious rather than devout; but now she sent her soul out in prayer for the country that suffered beneath William's hand; and thereafter she prayed for William, himself, that cared not at all for the suffering of men, nor for their hatred; whose own children were strange to him; and lastly she prayed that her own cold heart might warm again to him; for with hatred, dislike and coldness all about him—God help him.

William regretted the need for punishment but the country had forced his hand. The English had revolted against the King God had given them. When he punished it was not only the wrong against himself but the wrong against God. He had dreamed of a rich and peaceful land; that it was, instead, poor and despoiled was not his fault. To show leniency was to flout God's mercy, to invite yet more rebellion. So now in the midst of the devastation he had made William praised God.

Now that the country lay quiet, he would keep it so. His laws were to be obeyed. And woe betide that man, English or Norman, that thought otherwise. Nor was he satisfied with the church. It did not, he considered, give him sufficient backing. Whenever a see fell empty he had filled it with one of his own Normans; but there were not, at present, enough of them. And these English bishops were difficult; inclined to be rebellious and they influenced their priests. Time to send for Lanfranc! And—the sudden thought fired him—Lanfranc should bring the Queen with him; yes, and the children, also.

Heavily occupied with warfare that took mental and physical toll, he had not, as yet, had time nor inclination for women. There were women enough for his taking; but he was King. He was William; he was chaste. Yet, since that day he had stood face-to-face with Harold's young widow, thinking for one mad moment to take her body by way of punishment, the flesh had pricked. A chaste man; but fully a man. Now he wanted his wife for the comfort of his body as well as his soul. And he longed to see his children again. Ill at ease with them he was; but still he was proud of them; proud of them all except Curthose, that stinging nettle. He worked for them; their welfare and his own were one.

Stigand had been deposed; not by will of the King but by judgment of Rome—the only judgment Lanfranc could accept. The way to Canterbury was clear. But for all that he played humble. To be so great a churchman was not for him! 'With great respect to my lord the King of England, I serve the King of Heaven first. I serve Him best here, within my own abbey,' he told the messengers. And not for all William's requesting, nor all Matilda's pleading, not for the synod of Norman churches, nor even for Pope's legate would he consent. He stood there eyes down, arms folded within his sleeves, refusing. Matilda suspected that, give him but the right excuse, he would find his duties to the King of Heaven chime with those to the King of England. She sent for the old man Herluin abbot of Bec, that had first accepted him into the life of the cloister. When the old man commanded him, Lanfranc could, he said, no longer refuse. To Herluin he owed, after God, his first obedience. Eyes downcast still, he accepted.

In the early summer of ten hundred and seventy, the ship carrying the King's desire sailed. It carried Lanfranc; it carried the Queen and her children; all except one.

Robert must be left; and now he was more than a figurehead. He was needed and he knew it, and was well-content. Now he not only sat with the council, he spoke to the council; and it did not always agree with him, still it listened with respect. One day Normandy would be his own; *was* his own—as long as his father kept away. To him, when his father had first gone into England, the oath had been given, every vassal swearing fealty during the duke's absence. England he did not want. He liked smiles about him and not frowns; goodwill and not fear. He would fight if he must—and to the death. But he liked the tournament better; he liked the splendour, the ordered rules, the good fellowship... and especially he liked the presence of the ladies. He preferred it to the hunger of warfare, the misery of women grown ugly with defeat and hatred. Normandy, he believed, would always be easy to hold—and forgot who had made it easy. Normandy was his; his own right. He loved it and was by it beloved. He prayed, with passion, that his father would never come back. More than the waters of the Channel flowed, and would forever flow, between father and son. They would stand one upon one shore and one upon the other; they might call but the distance would be too great for their voices to carry. They would never draw near again.

Crossing in the sweet summer weather, Matilda sighed over the son she had left behind—Robert taking the easy way and believing it must always be easy. Life, alas, would teach him his lesson—but at what price? What, she wondered, would William think of these other children? He was a man hard to please. She looked at them now, all save Richard wild with excitement at seeing England again; England where they were all royal princes. Richard took his pleasures with some dignity; her eyes rested on him with pride. Sixteen; and the image of the young William, old de Beaumont said; but a gentler image—his life had gone gentler. Twin lamps, she thought; but Richard gives a clearer light.

Rufus; in the last few months he had grown somewhat but it was clear that he, as well as Robert, would make short men; and, if they didn't take care, fat men! They were clearly brothers; but while Robert looked open and friendly, Rufus looked shifty. She had done her best for him but it was little enough. She prayed he would not grow in viciousness.

Her little girls were debonair but strong-willed; and the gentle Agatha the most strong-willed of them all. She had set her heart on the religious life and said so. *Once I was betrothed and once all-but betrothed; but I was never given. God does not mean to give me to an earthly groom.* What would William say to that? *One daughter I have given in ghostly marriage; for the rest I have my plans.* Certainly he would dispose of them as best matched with his ambitions.

As for Henry—scarce two years old and sharp as a bodkin but show-ing, even at this tender age, a passionate, unequal spirit; what would his father make of him? She hoped William would be satisfied with his children; he'd get no more, though he didn't know it. The midwife had told her so after Henry's birth. It was a secret she cherished; she wanted no more children. Always she had known, more than other women, the misery of pregnancy, the danger of actual birth; and now she was no longer young. Once, of her own secret will, she had refused him more children; now, loving him so little, giving him so little, she could not, in conscience, have refused. Well, the matter, praise be to the Virgin, was out of her hands.

Should she tell William? To him childbearing in a woman was essential; without it a woman was scarcely a woman. To tell him would take something from their relationship—and there was little enough left! On the other hand, not to tell? He was a proud man; to find his virility in question was a thing he could not endure. She must wait and see.

She found William grown grimmer since his return into England; eyes and mouth still more guarded. And, though he moved quickly enough, he had, in spite of the rigours of the winter campaign, grown heavier. He looked upon her with pleasure; she was handsome still, her looks those of late youth rather than early middle-age. There was no grey in the dark curl of her hair and her figure was trim. There were lines about mouth and eyes—lines proper to her age; but, and this he did not notice, no lines of laughter. She was gracious as ever; and she was royal—a Queen every small inch of her. For him nothing had changed. This was his wife; and he had been without a woman overlong. The long campaign over, he was aware of his need. Had she not come now he must do as other men—take another woman to his bed.

From the moment of their meeting she had felt uneasiness against him harden. They were changing, both of them. To him, as he grew older, to shed blood seemed more natural; to her more abhorrent. Between them flowed rivers of blood. Yet to sleep with him did not disgust her. He was all a man—and she a woman. To take a lover was not in her desire. A man might take his harlot but a woman must be faithful. She was the guardian of her husband's honour and of her children's name. Since she must never take a lover, for her own comfort as well as his, she accepted William. If her kindness for him was less, still she had loyalty unswerving for his interests. She remained in the eyes of Christendom the perfect wife.

They spent easter in Winchester. Here, though she feared him no longer, she could not but think of Brihtric and pitied him in his nameless grave when the spring winds blew fresh and sweet; and pitied herself that had been driven to so dark a deed.

In Winchester she had a visitor. A woman hooded and cloaked; young and sturdy and fair in the Saxon manner. She, that might have been Queen of England, fell on her knees before the woman that was Queen.

'Madam Queen, I was wife to the lord Harold.' And her very quiet showed her desperation. 'I am the mother of two sons; little ones, Madam, that are not above three years old.' She took in a deep breath as if to steady herself. 'They never had a father; they have no-one but me. And I? Life has gone hard with me and I have nothing but them. Madam Queen, you are a mother, also; but your children have not been taken from you——'

'I know what it is to have a child taken from me,' the Queen said.

'Then, Madam, pity me. That your husband should be King, I lost my husband. To keep him King, I must—unless the Queen help me—lose my children.'

'It is necessary,' the Queen said. 'I cannot help you.'

Edith took the news quietly; she had never had much hope. It was a last bid—if not for the return of the children, then for their safety. She said now, 'What will come to them, lacking a mother? How shall they fare in enemy hands?'

'What shall come to them, who can say? No man can foresee fate. But our own doings we can, for a little, foresee. I promise you, as far as a human creature may, your children shall come to no harm.'

'Madam the Queen promises.'

'I have said it.'

'For that God will surely bless you. Where, Madam, do you take them?'

'Home with me. They shall be bred as princes of a royal house.'

Edith said, very low, 'It is more than I had hoped. I had thought... prison; shut from the light of day. It has been done before, even with such little ones.'

'What I have said I will do.'

'Madam, there is one more thing. Shall I see them—ever again?'

'In England, no. But when there is trust between my people and yours, you shall come to Normandy. When that may be—who knows?

But this I do know; your children shall be brought up with my own. I pledge my word.'

'Madam, have you seen my children?'

'I have seen them. Their father's sons. They look to make brave men.'

'May I see them... once?'

'If you have courage. But they must not see you. It would cause them distress; and my husband is not patient with children.' It was a clear warning.

The Queen rose and led Edith to a window. The narrow slit focussed the picture clear and sharp. Outside on the bright spring grass four children played—Adela, the little Henry and the two others; two small dark heads, and two of bright gold—the twin boys Harold and Ulf.

Edith stood hands pressed to her mouth to hold back the weeping; and all the while she looked at her children as if she could never be done looking. Matilda said, gentle, 'They fretted a little, at the first; but they are brave children. Their father would have been proud. Are you satisfied?'

Edith looked at the children playing together. 'I am satisfied,' she said.

Matilda guessed at the crying of her heart.

XXXV

'The church is a stumbling-block to peace,' William said. 'These English priests—their stomachs are too proud!'

Matilda nodded, remembering that Aldred, even Aldred that had crowned him, had thereafter cursed him.

'These English bishops! They do not deny the Pope's supremacy, but they do not affirm it neither. They take their own quiet way. Now we must see to it that all churchmen acknowledge the supremacy of Rome.'

'It could lead to trouble,' she said, 'sir, leave well alone.'

'I do nothing in haste. A see falls vacant, I fill it with my own choice, good Norman, good priest, good scholar. Well, I've done that before—but not systematically, not invariably; I left Stigand in his office, I left Aldred; left too many to make their mischief. But I'll leave no more. There'll be no exceptions. Nor shall I always wait for a see to fall empty! If a priest displease me—out he goes! And it will not be bishops and abbots only; it will be every priest, however humble. And every priest however high, however low, I shall myself appoint. So I bring this stiff-necked people beneath the Pope's yoke. And, since I am the Pope's favoured son—beneath my own yoke.'

'Complete obedience to Rome! Here, in this country, you set a precedent.'

'I implement what should be already here.'

'Complete obedience to Rome!' she said again, remembering their own disobedience and its dire consequences, 'it could be a rod to a King's back!'

'Not to mine. As to my successor—if he's a weakling, he deserves all he gets!' And if she was thinking of Robert she had her answer pat. 'As for me, I have Lanfranc to keep the balance even. He's to be supreme head of the English church.'

'York is equal to Canterbury.'

'I put York lower; a little lower.'

'Thomas of York will not submit.'

'He shall submit!' William smote fist upon palm. 'It is needful for the peace of the country.'

She took his point. Let William get his way in this and—should the north revolt again, its capital at least should never again play traitor. Its archbishop, under submission to Canterbury, must forbid it, must punish with all the severity of the church any that dared take arms against the King. Subtle! The idea, she fancied, was Lanfranc's—and not only for the sake of peace. He was one to stand supreme, to demand complete obedience from the entire English church. But why should York give up his equal place?

'York will refuse!' she said.

'Let him try! If he appeal to Rome—then the Pope is my very good friend. If he appeal to my council of bishops—they know which side their bread's buttered. He might as well save his breath!'

And so it proved! A domestic affair, the Pope said; settle it among yourselves! And certainly the council of bishops knew which side its bread was buttered. Now, for the first time in her history, England acknowledged one supreme head of the church in England. Canterbury.

He had the church settling nicely under his thumb; now for the law. He had thought to put the country under his own Norman law; he saw now that it would not do—he was beginning to know this people! It would give rise to resentment, perhaps to actual defiance; English law was bred in their bones. The obedience of this people he must have; their love he could never win and he must do without it. But all the same the knowledge pricked. By the Splendour of God he had done this people some good!

It was Lanfranc that suggested calling a full witan.

'Sirs,' the King told them, 'I mean to rule this land by the laws of the late good King. Therefore let twelve men in each shire declare what those laws are; thereafter we shall write them into a code. And that code shall be the law.'

It was a sop; and no mean one.

'You have done well,' Matilda said, 'but still it is not enough. If you want true peace in a country you must set its heart at rest. That cannot be when you have two peoples in one land; and those whose land it once was, bound, for the most part, serfs to their conquerors. You, yourself, sir, make the division. It was needful—but still a breach; that breach you must heal. You must encourage friendship, you must encourage marriage between our two peoples.'

She saw the suggestion displeased his high Norman pride.

'It is the only way,' she said. 'Already you have recognised it. You would have given our daughter to Edwine; you have given your own niece to Waltheof. It is the surest way to wipe out difference.'

'They were special cases.' Clearly he was displeased. 'What shall we call them, these half-breeds—English or Norman?'

'Your loyal subjects,' she said.

He had his Norman priests, his Norman councillors; he had Lanfranc. Now, in every shire old laws were being collected. Soon he would sit with his council to do as he had promised. He would do more than he had promised. Where the law pressed too hard he would lighten it; but where it did not enough protect the people he would make it heavier, putting the fear—if not of God—of the King into robbers, rapers and murderers.

The English feared their King; they complained, with reason, against his harshness—but they were beginning to say that a man might go the length of the land his bosom full of gold—and go in safety. It was not true; and it never could be true; but it did show which way the wind of justice blew.

For all his pride in his wife he was disturbed on her account. She was gentle, she was patient; she listened, she advised—and always she put his interests first. In bed she submitted, but without pleasure; he was man enough to know it. But why? What had he done? He was forty-three and virile; as capable as ever of giving pleasure to a woman. He would hurl himself upon her, take her with a passion that was almost rage; but he kindled no response. Unsatisfied and savage he would tell himself, to hell with chastity! He'd take another woman, two or three; as many as he chose to satisfy his hunger and to teach her a lesson.

But, as long as she was with him, he could not do it.

And he was more than ever troubled on account of his eldest son. Rufus was always running with a tale—Curthose was lazy; he would not rise in the morning, would not attend the council until business was all-but done. He cared only to hunt; and to sleep with girls. And, seeing his father's anger at that, proceeded with his embroideries. 'Curthose says that, when he comes into England, he'll have English wenches; he'll try them all. High or low, they're all cattle, Curthose says...'

And moreover Curthose had said slighting words about his father. *He doesn't understand the laws of chivalry. He's more butcher than soldier.* No-one but Rufus had heard him; yet it sounded like Curthose and it wasn't a thing a child could make up for himself—of that William was certain. He must speak to his wife on the matter. She'd hear no wrong of her eldest son, that he knew; especially if it came from Rufus. But whatever she might think she'd allow nothing to stand in the way of her husband's wishes.

She listened in silence. 'Rufus is jealous,' she said at last. 'There's the truth plain and simple! Robert is the eldest. He is co-regent with me; and there are other privileges the others cannot share. Rufus is not only jealous; he's untruthful; and that's all there is to it!

'Robert is proud of you. You should hear him talk of your victories. It would be well for you both if you let him stand by your side in battle.

Well, you have refused him! If he did, indeed, speak those words—and none but Rufus ever heard them—then you must take some blame; it could be Robert's pride in you gone sour!

'As for sleeping with girls—' she shrugged, 'he's a young man!' But she had spoken to him more than once on that matter and would do so again as soon as she was home. 'Give him a share of fighting and he'll have less time for girls! It isn't Robert you should watch; it's Rufus!'

'You see no harm in your eldest,' he said, sour.

'God forbid I see harm where there's none. Or that I see no harm where there's much. Watch Rufus, I advise you!'

'God forbid I see harm where there's none!' He flung her own words back in her face. 'Think of Rufus and take your words to heart.' He turned on his heel. So withdrawn she was, so inimical, he scarce knew her. Till this moment he could have staked his life that, come what might, always she would put his interests first. He would stake it no longer. It sharpened his anger against Robert and against her—against her, also. It was a thorn to fester. Yet, since all Christendom praised his wife, his own pride must keep that praise bright. And besides he loved her; she was all he had.

Whitsuntide found them at Windsor. She was still gracious; yet still withdrawn, so that at times his resentment would burst out into violence over the smallest thing. He was, at times, unjust; he knew it. When he put himself in the wrong it angered him yet more. She made no complaint; always she showed herself friendly—that and nothing more. He found her friendship useful even while he resented it; he made full use of her commonsense and the wisdom her years of ruling had brought. His own wits were good enough, none better; but anger, he knew it well, could overthrow him, drive him to deeds better left undone.

She was not happy here in England still less was she happy with him; that he knew, also. Well, he would win her, make her his own again; all should be as before—he swore it and did not understand that she never had been his. He would give her such honour as no King's wife had known before. In Normandy she signed all ducal decrees but never in her own right; she signed as regent. Now, although her position did not demand it, she should sign the royal decrees of England. It must cause amazement; but no matter. Her name should stand with his.

She accepted the honour with grace; but she wanted to go home;

home to Normandy and to Robert—and to her quiet bed. In bed, at least, she thought, rueful, any woman could serve him better than she had done. And for his counsel he had Lanfranc; they were of like mind, those two!

'A woman, when she is wise, sees deeper than a man,' William told Matilda. 'You were right; though I did not want to believe it. Two separate peoples in one land—two stools between which a King must fall; and not all his just laws will save him. There must not be two stools but one, one stool only, on which he may sit firm. We must encourage marriage between our two peoples. There must be—' his mouth was wry, 'respect one for the other. We can learn from them, simple as they are; and they will learn from us. They will grow into our tongue and into our ways; so we shall hold power and keep it.'

'I doubt, sir, that these English are as simple as you think. But one thing I don't doubt—their quality to endure. It may be that, in the end, it is their tongue will prevail, their customs endure. Maybe they will hold the power; and keep it.'

He bit upon his anger. 'There could be, which God forbid, something in what you say. But not if we walk with care, talk with care, act with care.'

She saw, in the days that followed, how together with Lanfranc he kept careful watch; he boasted that, like God, no sparrow fell but he marked it. Now it was no longer a question of an earldom or bishopric fallen vacant; it was as he had promised. Let a mere sheriff die or a simple priest, even, and his place was filled by a Norman. And, when it suited the purpose of those two they did not wait for death; a charge—not always true—would be made and the man of their choice step in. And sometimes a post would stand empty until their own suitable candidate appeared.

All going quiet and smooth.

And now the vow that William had made on Senlac field was to be honoured—the building of a great church worthy of a great victory.

'To build such a church might rub old wounds sore,' Matilda said, 'unless it is a church in which to pray for the souls of those who fell at Senlac; all of them, English as well as Norman. Such a church and such a praying might be balm upon sore places.'

'It is a church to bear witness to my victory,' William said, stubborn.

'Let it stand witness to your mercy. As for victory—it is not yet won; nor shall it be by fighting. Victory is yet to come.'

He said nothing to that. But he sent for his masons. On every other point he was adamant. The great church must stand upon the very spot where victory had been won. It was bleak? Let the monks light their fires. It lacked water? Then let them drink wine. It lacked stone? Then let them set up their engines, haul it from wherever stone might be found. He brushed aside all objection. The high altar must stand on that same spot where Harold had raised the *Fighting Man*.

Peace, order and prosperity steadily growing; and yet, underneath it all—distrust, resentment. How long would peace endure?

It was a question Matilda asked of none but her own heart. Well, they would know how to deal with every contingency, those two, William, and his other self Lanfranc. It was no longer her business—her business lay in Normandy. She was—and she could scarce believe her joy—going home!

XXXIV

She was home again. No more need of continuing subtleties, continuing watchfulness; nor any need to fear the mutterings beneath men's breath. Home again in a land where no Queen ever wielded so much power; where her children felt themselves free of the iron will of their father—even Rufus glad to be released from his show of obedience. And Robert's joy equalled her own. As always he had met her in love and high pomp; as always he took on stature when she was at his side, bore himself with a more princely dignity, worked harder, and forgot for days on end his love-songs, his ladies and his light friends.

It was autumn; it was Christmas. In the peace of Normandy she felt herself renewed. She was not long to enjoy her peace. In February, Maine broke into sharp and sudden revolt.

Revolt in Maine, Maine that had sworn fealty to her eldest son! It must be crushed at once. William had the most part of his armies in England; she was forced to send to him for help.

Intent still upon his watching of the north and the Danes, William could not come himself; he sent, instead, his finest captain—his sworn brother, FitzOsbern.

FitzOsbern, to his own surprise, found himself seduced from his lord's affairs. But then the temptation was great—the offer of a handsome bride together with a count's throne; no less than the throne of Flanders. He turned his back upon Maine and marched for Flanders where Matilda's orphaned nephews were being kept from their inheritance by their mother. They were over-young, she said; until they were old enough she should rule in their stead.

Ruled by a woman! Flanders would have none of her. They offered the empty throne to their late lord's brother. But—give up her new-seized power? Never! She had besought help of FitzOsbern, that noted fighting-man, offering herself in marriage—which she had every right to do; offering the throne of Flanders— which she had no right to do at all.

FitzOsbern was dead, fallen in Flanders. He had been sent to fight for his King; he had fought for himself instead. He had turned his back on duty to win himself a throne. He had lost his life instead—a life he had no right to throw away on his own business. And he, had done his lord a worse disservice still; he had lost William the friendship of Flanders.

William was overthrown by the tide of his rage; but, the storm, at length, subsiding, he remembered the man himself—his sworn brother to whom he was bound by the blood of a father murdered for his duke; remembered also that FitzOsbern would come no more; never again would he feel his friend's handclasp nor hear his voice.

In his desolation his anger turned upon his wife. FitzOsbern had been sent to fight for Maine and she had allowed him to meddle in Flanders instead—Flanders that was no longer her concern. That his anger was unjust, that no power save his own—and perhaps not even that—could have stopped FitzOsbern, he did not care; his anger must out. The fault was hers. Through her Maine might be lost... and he could not leave England.

He could not leave England. The peace Matilda had, in her heart, questioned, was breaking. Once more the western sky was stormy; and, in the north, made blacker yet with promise of Scottish help.

And then, suddenly, shockingly—revolt in the Fens.

The last piece of news was, at first, unbelievable. Revolt in the north and west was nothing new; nor were threats from Scotland. But Ely. Peaceful Ely where the monks in their great abbey cast their mild influence, praying, always for peace! But did they? *Were* they men of peace?'

And suddenly Edwine and Morkere were gone; escaped from their gilded cage—and not hard to guess why! And now, to add to his troubles, the Danish fleet he had allowed to winter in northern waters appeared in the waters about the Fens.

'Sir,' the messenger said, all breathless with his haste, 'the Danes have been received at Ely with great joy. There's no more talk of the atheling; 'I think they have forgotten him. But there's talk—and much talk—of the Danish King——'

'And what do they say of him?'

'Sir... that he is to take your crown.'

Willliam stiffened in the great chair. His face had sharpened; it had taken on the white and luminous look of his deepest anger.

The messenger stopped, not daring to speak further; but William signalled him on.

'To Ely run all those that are discontented; and, sir, there are not a few—earls and villeins, gentle and simple, rich and poor. And the monks egg them on; they have left the cloister, they share camp with the rebels. They sleep, they eat, sword in hand.'

'A rabble!' Robert of Mortain spat with contempt.

'Sir, it is, alas, no such thing. They have a leader that all obey; and one, sir, not to be despised.'

'His name?' The King's voice burst forth harsh and guttural.

'They call him Hereward.'

'I never heard it before!' William said with deep contempt.

'Who is this Hereward?' Odo fingered his swordbelt.

'My lord bishop, who knows? Some say this and some say that!

A gentleman of good birth—on that they all agree; a thegn or earl. An outlaw some say; they say it was the late holy King sent him from the country, the man's own father beseeching it. For this Hereward, though then a boy, was already a man of blood. But sir, whatever he may be and whatever he has done, he is leader now. The people turn to him as a god. And, indeed, he stands, so they say, as though he were indeed a god, a great golden man——'

'I fear no man,' William cried out, 'nor any god—save One. By His Splendour our right shall be our might!'

Edwine was dead. It was Lanfranc that brought the news. 'He fled, sir, to the rebels in the Fens. Thereafter he went on a secret mission to Malcolm of Scotland. The first plan stands. This Hereward will have no Dane as King—none but a true born Englishman. The lord Edwine was on his way to ask the Scots together with the men of the north to join the rebels in Ely and put the atheling on the throne.

'But on the way he was recognised; it is the penalty of handsome looks. He had but twenty horse and he must face a hundred. Well, but he gave a good account of himself! He cut his way through and would have escaped; but three men went behind him and hewed him down. Sir, those three stand without to speak with the King.'

'Let them come in.'

So in they came, three men together; and he in the middle carrying something beneath a cloth. 'Sir, behold the traitor!' he said and withdrew the cloth.

William stared at the golden head now black with blood; head of the man to whom once he would have given his daughter—thanks be to God, he had not!

Sudden anger seized him; the black anger of his middle years at the sight of Edwine slain. 'He should have been more dreadfully punished, to drag out his maimed and wretched life in the sight of all men and manhood together destroyed.

He looked at the three before him, the severed head between them. He spoke quietly enough. 'No man may kill save at need. One hundred men against twenty; you had no need. You have broken the law.' And now his voice was thickening, growing guttural. 'I pronounce you outlaw—all three. Now there is no law to protect you; any man may hunt you as he hunts the wild beast, to do with you what he will.'

Afterwards Lanfranc, that had read the cause of his wrath, said, 'Sir the punishment was right; but the reason—the reason was wrong.'

There were many, Norman as well as English, to weep for Edwine; not because of his goodness but because he had been handsome and debonair.

Agatha, the King's daughter that had been all-but promised to him, did not weep 'God Himself saved me,' she said as once before. 'This second time he kept me safe. His Will is clear. I am to wed Christ alone.'

Matilda said, 'It is not for you to interpret God's will. A daughter leaves that to her father; she obeys his will believing it to come from God.'

Agatha said nothing; she had more than a look of her father.

Of Morkere, equally false, came news. He was at Ely with the rebels.

'Revolt against me is revolt against God. To such impiety I shall make an end!' William swore it. 'An end to false Morkere; an end to all rebels chiefly those that calling themselves priests set themselves against His Anointed. And most of all an end to this Hereward himself!'

He was on the march for the Fens where, like ravens themselves, greedy for pickings, the Danes were massed; where the English, gentle and simple, were gathered; and where Hereward, that strong man, that mysterious man, stood—the symbol of freedom. The *Fighting Man* come again; and this time in the flesh.

It was the most difficult, the most exasperating, the most exhausting task he had ever undertaken. It was defeating—suppose one allowed one's self to admit that possibility. It was worse, even, than the winter campaign in the north. Here a man must watch his every step; in this water-logged land he might sink to his thighs—and lucky if he sank no further. No road through these accursed marshes; no way at all a man could see. As his armies struggled painfully in the bog they were picked off by the arrows of the rebels.

Nothing for it but to build a causeway through the swamp.

'Sir,' his masons told him, 'it will cost lives; many lives.'

'That is expected in war!'

They were building the causeway; they were laying down trees and sacks, cinders and boulders—anything to make firm the base. A man at work is unarmed. It cost as many lives as a battle. Inch by inch it grew; yet, for all their guards, more than once Hereward came forth in the night and destroyed the work so that all was to do again.

'This Hereward!' cried out William of Warenne to whom the King had given Gundrada for wife. 'A man never knows where to find him. He is quicksilver. You think to catch it between finger and thumb. And when you look—gone!'

And, indeed, he was like quicksilver; or like a spirit that knows no chains of the flesh. He was here, he was there; he was punishing every city obedient to the King—cities as far from Ely as Peterborough and Norwich; and was back again before any man knew he had gone.

The causeway was growing. In spite of every set-back, growing. It was five hundred paces, it was a thousand, two thousand paces... it was five thousand paces—enough to reach to the heart of the rebel camp. And seeing this, the monks of Ely that had blessed the cause, that had eaten and slept sword in hand, deserted. It was their duty, they said; they feared for their abbey. 'They fear more for their own skins—and with reason,' William said. And the Danes, too, deserted; and this time they went home. No more lingering in English waters; and that to William was a clear sign of success.

Dogged and bitter Hereward's defence. Others had followed deserting priests and Danes; and what use a handful of men, be they never so valiant, against an army well-found? But still they gave good account of themselves. Here died William Malet that even the English praised; for in his own arms he had carried Harold to his resting-place under the cairn that faced the North Sea. Here in the bogland he came to his death and many another with him so that the marshes ran with blood.

The revolt was over. Hereward had escaped, no man knew whither.

'If I were my father,' Robert said, 'I would seek him out wherever he is...'

'and I would seek him also!' Rufus interrupted. 'And I would cut off his hands and his feet; and I would——'

'...and I would take with him the oath of brotherhood!' Robert ignored Rufus whose eyes were pricking with red light.

'Such a brotherhood would honour them both,' Richard said, like Robert in love with chivalry.

Morkere came crawling with his submission. William gave him the kiss of peace; but he did not mean to keep it. The man was false. He should hang from a tree—a shameful death.

It was Matilda that won his life.

'My lord King gave the man the kiss of peace,' she sent her urgent message to Lanfranc. 'That promise must be kept—not for the traitor's sake but for the King's.'

It was good sense and it sent Lanfranc hurrying.

'The man has betrayed me three times!' William said, stubborn. 'Let him go free and men will mock at me!'

'Will they not mock more saying you broke the given word?'

'There's reason in what you say! He shall go a prisoner to Normandy—and there he shall rot to his death!' Words choked in the King's throat. 'There he shall rot to his death!'

The rest of his punishments William did not spare. He took no life by execution; but the maiming and the branding and the unspeakable dungeons of his castle prisons made many a man long for a quick, clean death; their miseries must satisfy even Rufus. The monks of Ely together with their abbot he drove away; they might starve, or come to their death any way fate pleased; for they were declared outlaw—and any man might hunt them. He gave orders for the immediate building of new castles and the strengthening of the old. The land was ringed about, was menaced by his castles.

But Hereward had slipped through his hands.

Hereward was a free man—as long as he could keep himself free. He took to the woods; an outlaw. To be an outlaw was nothing new to him—but a man grows older; and he longs for the freedom to come and go—and no price upon his head. And especially in the sharp cold of winter he longs for the comforts of hearth and home.

He did not forget the King; and the King did not forget him.

Here, in the woods, with such few as remained faithful, he did not cease from harrying those towns in the King's obedience. From Warwick to Peterborough—fire and flame and blood. Men dreaded his coming; children awoke crying in the night, his very name a warning and a dread. Town after town suffered beneath his swift and savage raids, and the disaster he left behind. But though there was a price upon his head—and a handsome price—he never came into the King's hands. No Norman ever caught so much as a glimpse of his heels; and no Englishman ever betrayed him. Luck and love he had them both.

The lady Elfrith, as English as himself, loved and in the green wood married him. She was debonair, she was very rich; and because of these things, but chiefly because it made sound commonsense to the King, she bought her husband's freedom. But it was the man himself with his honesty and his courage and his strength that bought friendship from the King.

In Normandy Robert cried out with pleasure at the news and longed to see the man; and Richard, too, was pleased. But Rufus turned aside and spat.

XXXVII

The fighting at Ely was over. But still there was unrest on every hand. Nothing a strong man couldn't deal with—but even a strong man may tire. And William missed FitzOsbern; it was like a sore socket from which a tooth has been torn.

Trouble in the west he would leave his brother's capable hands. Robert would put down the revolt if only to save his own broad lands. The trouble in Scotland William must deal with himself. Malcolm, false to his oath, had crossed the border. Those loyal English that would not march beneath his banner he had carried off as slaves. That any man should dare lay hand upon William's subjects to make them slaves! He choked upon the thought. There remained the trouble in Maine. Matilda must deal with that until he was free. Business with Malcolm came first.

Marching, marching in the autumn weather, his armies moving solid across the face of England. Marching through the midlands his own hand had punished—that punishment clear in burnt fields and new stark castles. The towns were quiet now, prosperous he would say; surely it justified his severity! As he went, he caught clear evidence of growing tolerance between English and Norman. Here and there a man might turn to mutter beneath his breath as the King and his armies rode by—it was only to be expected. But some of the English were speaking a sort of Norman-French; and though his own tongue could not deal with the stiff English speech, some of his younger men were more successful. When he lodged in a town he found there had been some inter-marriage; and even where there had been none, still the children played together, their speech a lively mixture of both tongues. He did not doubt that, in the end, his own tongue must prevail.

Marching, marching; through the north himself had savaged; across wild moors, across burnt farmlands where men should be busy about the harvest; but now nettles grew through ruined door and window. For leagues on end, not a soul to be seen; and when they halted for the night, they must light their fires not so much for cooking or for warmth as for fear of wild beasts destruction had brought from the woods to roam countryside and town.

Marching, marching; across the border and into Scotland. Here, in this very country, his own loyal English dragged out their lives as slaves, their women raped, their children dead. He remembered Malcolm's vile game of skill—young children tossed into the air to be caught again upon the spear's point. Even a seasoned soldier might puke at such vileness. He gave his men their head. Through the Lowlands and crossing the Tay, he left behind him the bloody trail of fire and sword.

Marching, marching, blood and fire all the way until Malcolm himself appeared—Malcolm that had been hand-in-glove with every rising in the north, to whom Edwine had been riding on that secret mission, traitor to traitor; Malcolm that had pressed the atheling's claim, Malcolm now bending the knee and offering his hostages, and swearing to turn the atheling out of Scotland.

Goodbye to Edgar's hope of a crown!

The west subdued and Scotland subdued—now for Maine. But winter was shutting down on land and sea; and he and his armies needed rest. He must wait for spring; it would save time in the end. In spring he would sail; in spring march into Maine, and, while he was about it, he would punish Anjou, also, that had fermented the unrest.

And he would see his wife again; he found himself wondering how it would be when they met again. They were growing apart; he could not but realise it. That his ambition which had brought them together was now putting them apart had no place in his mind, nor the fact of their long absence from each other. A man cannot be forever at his wife's apron-strings; she must know that for herself. Let her be thankful that he had uttered no word of reproof in the FitzOsbern affair—he had not forgiven her for that; nor that, because of it, he had lost the friendship of Flanders, of her own brother.

This growing coldness on her part was difficult for him to put a finger on. She was as careful a listener, as wise in advice, as eager as ever for his success. In bed she had never refused him; but she had not shown herself willing, neither... and there was no sign of another child. That irked him. She had reached her fortieth birthday; she had not spared herself in his service and she had borne him many children—these things he took for granted. These last years she had lived, for the most part, without a husband; What then? That should, in his opinion, make her more eager.

For himself he had managed well enough; he had been faithful. He had gone without strange women in his bed; but now he was in his mid-forties and desire pricked. In his court there were women aplenty but upon none had he ever cast an eye; nor had any—save one—dared to lift an eye to him. But that one woman had done more than raise her eyes. She had offered herself—the fine, handsome woman—her whole voluptuous body for the taking. He did not care for large, over-ripe women; he liked them delicate and fine—and he liked them modest. Of all women he disliked Adelaide de Grantmesnil most. He had not forgotten those early days when she had thrown herself at his head—she, the wife of his boyhood friend; nor how her tongue had been lewd about his bride so that he had been forced to send her from the court. Nor had he forgotten her husband's faithfulness in the English adventure; how Hugh had written from banishment asking that he might serve his lord. Hugh had done good service at Senlac; and, for that service, been created Earl and Governor of Leicester. Take the wife of his faithful friend! Had he been mad with desire, still she had gone free of the King.

Now, once more, she was at her tricks. She saw the King's restlessness and understood it. A fine man needed a fine woman. That wisp of a creature, the Queen! Her lewd fancy played again. The King had never known what it was to take a real woman; she would show him.

Adelaide de Grantmesnil was stupid as well as shameless; to a man, until now, severely chaste—an offence. He cautioned her in a few well-chosen words and commanded her husband to keep her from the court.

In one thing she had read the King aright. He wanted a woman; and he wanted to beget children—to know himself virile still. Once he had sworn to beget no bastards; now he was not so squeamish. A bastard could do very well for himself. As for his wife—she had appeared to have no use for a man in her bed and must take the consequences.

He had bedded with a girl; a fine, small creature, and, a virgin—he'd not lick the dish after another man, not he! Her name he could not recall, but she was daughter to Ingleric, one of his clerks; the father, himself, had brought her. The girl had been unwilling; well, he favoured modesty in women and liked her the better for it.

The girl was pregnant with his child and his virility established. He would not, at present, claim the child; he had no wish, needlessly, to antagonise his wife nor blot his fair picture in the eyes of Christendom. Nor had the girl; herself, wish to boast; far from being honoured to carry the child of her King, she was, incredibly, ashamed. He'd tell her father to marry her off; himself, he'd wait till the child was born. If it were a fair boy, he'd claim it; for a girl he had no use! The boy, so he proved worthy of his sire, was none the worse for being a bastard.

William was riding to Canterbury; he had taken this way often of late. There was much to discuss with Lanfranc concerning the spring campaign in Maine and the government of England during the King's absence. Odo should be named regent; a name only. Lanfranc should hold the secret power—the one man to administer justice free of corruption and to keep peace without cruelty. He could, of course, have summoned Lanfranc to London; but Canterbury was convenient to Dover where the fleet lay.

Agnes, daughter of the canon Robert of Canterbury, was young and she was kind. She had a veneration for the King, though she was frightened of him—the great, stern man, thick in girth and enormous in height. And she pitied him, too; a lonely man, his wife and children across the sea. And a harassed man—enemies all about him. But she pitied him most because he was sometimes a bad man—a bad man that meant well.

When she saw the sad, stark man ride by she would make him her deepest reverence. And he, noting the kind and pretty child, would send her a smile; or, he would stop to enquire of her father whom he knew and liked. He would as soon have slept with her as with one of his own daughters.

In the opinion of the lady Adelaide de Grantmesnil the King was riding too often to Canterbury. Consulting Lanfranc! If that were all why did the archbishop not wait upon his King in London? And why did the King stop each time at the canon's house?

Forbidden the court she decided to visit her kin in Rouen; and there her tongue began to wag. *The King has deflowered the daughter of a priest of Canterbury. To take so young a virgin—a man of the King's years! The court is shocked and the church is shocked!*

Matilda, at whom the gossip was aimed, did not believe a word of it; though every prince took women to his bed William's chastity was renowned in Christendom. Even, a young man with his bride, he had shown no pleasure in love-play; had shown nothing, indeed, but the urge to satisfy his need and to beget children. How should she believe that such a man would take a virgin for his light pleasure?

But, the tale ever-growing, she must think again.

Men, they said, had greater need in such affairs than women. That there had been little love-play in William's bed might argue an urgency in him, an animal's direct need. Deprived of his wife through his own ambitions, unsatisfied through her own unwillingness, might he not have taken the girl?

She could not drive the girl from her mind. Sitting in council, dispensing justice from her throne; even upon her knees, she found herself wondering who had heard the tale and whether, believing it, they smiled behind their hand. Had her sons heard it; and what did they make of it? Did Robert shrug because to take a wench—or two or three—was the way of princes; or did he regard it an insult to his mother? An insult Richard would certainly regard it; it would anger him for all his gentleness. Rufus would enjoy it and Agatha shrink from it in disgust. The others were too young to understand.

The more she dwelt upon the hateful tale the more likely it seemed. A man deprived of his wife had taken another woman to his bed. No great surprise there. *But the man is my husband; mine! Once all Christendom rang with the tale of our faithfulness one to the other. What shall Christendom say of him now?*

Against her better judgment she commanded my lady from the court and too late regretted it. Banishment lent edge to the tale. It was whispered in every corner, sung, thinly disguised, in every ballad. Impossible for the Queen, even if she would, to forget it. Anger, ever-growing, took precedence of everything; of the conduct of Normandy, of the troubles in Maine, of her love of Robert—of that, even.

From the depths of her being that root of blackness—of which her nurse had spoken long ago—rose and thickened and grew ever more strong. She could taste it, bitter as vomit upon her tongue. Her anger against her husband was sufficient; yet it was less than her anger against the girl. He was, after all, a man with a man's needs; but she? Lecherous daughter of a lecherous priest—for her no word could be too evil; no punishment too dire! Shame upon the priest, her father, that flaunted the fruits of his lust within the very precincts of the church. It was a Christian duty to remove the fruits of that sin.

She tried most desperately for justice. Had she been blameless in some such matter, the faraway girl that had been so incredibly herself?

The matter had been quite other; that girl had given herself in love and on the promise of marriage. She had taken no woman's husband, nor looked to reward from a King. She had been innocent and betrayed.

The memory served only to exacerbate the anger that already possessed her—anger that left her with no hope of rest until it was satisfied.

The priest's daughter was found hanging from a tree in her father's orchard; they had not, at first, recognised the misshapen thing that swung hamstrung in the wind.

William sickened when he heard. Mutilation was the natural result of revolt, of treachery, of crime; on occasion he had himself stood by to see it done. But an innocent so hatefully murdered! The work of a madman; no man else could put his hand to so foul a work. But, though he set his officers to enquire into the matter, he could learn nothing.

Matilda, too, was sickened when she heard and almost equally perplexed. In the shocking reality of the girl's brutal death she thanked God she was innocent. She had prayed for strength to overcome her anger. Righteous or not, she wanted no more blood on her hands; and so had come to terms with the matter.

She would, quite simply, remove the girl; put her where no priest of Canterbury be tempted to follow his canon's example, nor the King's eye dwell upon her. She had sent a fellow—one of her own bodyguard—to remove the girl; to take her into Surrey with the request that Gundrada do with her what she would—put her into the kitchens or about the pigs; or, if she prove a harlot still, give her to the soldiers.

What had happened that night? Had the fellow tried to have his way with the girl? And had she resisted, not finding him to her taste after the embraces of a King? And had this been the fellow's revenge? A soldier in William's armies was no stranger to mutilation. Matilda did not know; she did not want to know. She had asked no question. And, now, thanks be to God, the hand that had performed the deed, the tongue that could have spoken, lay rotting on some field in Maine.

Now she must forget the matter. First she must confess her part; and then, conscience dear, go about her duties.

She had confessed—and no mention of William. There was no penance. The priest's daughter had been an incitement to sin; to remove her from the sacred precincts was right and proper. The girl's unfortunate end did not concern Madam the Queen. Since she could not entirely acquit herself, she performed her own penance, said her prayers, gave her alms. Her soul was clean. Why then in the sleepless night did the misshapen thing rise before her? And why did one other stand by her side; and both shrouded and dead?

William was startled by the change in his wife. Yet, what change? Her hair was as dark, her figure as trim with small high breasts and narrow waist. But for all that she was different. When she smiled, her eyes remained untouched; set, as it were, in a smiling mask. And the eyes, themselves, were different... troubled eyes; as though they looked inward upon herself and did not like what they saw. In bed he found the difference, too. A little while ago she had submitted; without pleasure, but still submitted. Now she denied him; not in words but with her whole body. A woman of iron lay beneath him.

She could not help it; the thing was beyond her. She would vow to be kind; to be, at least, submissive. But when he came to her bed her whole body stiffened against him, lay cold and rigid as a dead woman. Now it was more than withdrawal; it was repugnance; repugnance that came from more than his cruelties, more than his infidelities—for beside the priest's daughter, another name was linked with his; the clerk's daughter that carried his bastard. It was more than all these things. Through him she had done violence to her inmost spirit. She had meant to punish a sin, to remove a cause of sin—that, and that alone. But through her a life had been taken; horribly taken; she felt the mark upon her, body and soul.

Yet still, since his pride would allow of no cause for gossip, he came to her bed. But now there might have been a sword drawn between them; a sword he made no attempt to cross. She was old, she was unwilling; he need never go short of a woman.

She knew well that she gave him licence to seek his pleasures elsewhere. But now she did not care. The shock of the girl's death had purged her of jealousy. Yet the purging brought no relief. She felt herself but half a woman; she was aware that so William regarded her too.

But still they were close-bound; in their interests indissoluble. They worked together, took counsel each of the other. Together they planned the campaign in Maine, together made their public prayers, went on progresses; on all occasions showed themselves hand-in-hand.

Impossible for the world to guess there was little kindness between them. Robert knew it and was not sorry; he had heard the tales about the clerk's daughter and about the priest's daughter and about other men's daughters. A lusty young bachelor might divert himself with his ladies, but his father was another matter; he wronged his wife—and that wife Robert's mother.

Now, more than ever, Robert roused his father's anger on mere sight. He exacerbated the husband's anger against the wife—this son had stolen affection that was his father's due. And the short dark boy was perfectly of the house of Baldwin. Nothing at all about him of the house of Rollo, so that William would ask himself, at times, whether Robert was, indeed, his own son; he had never entirely rid himself of suspicion concerning Gundrada.

In Richard, too, he knew some disappointment. He could not but be proud of the handsome lad so completely of Rollo's house. And the boy was brave enough; but still too much of a scholar. He'd never make a soldier until he had grown another skin.

If Robert died tomorrow, Matilda thought, his father would be relieved. If Richard died, he would hardly notice it. For both there would be a fine procession and a great church service; thereafter William would turn, not without pleasure, to set his third son in either place.

For Rufus was still the favourite. He offered, as ever, immediate obedience—and went away tongue in cheek to do as he chose. More than ever he pricked his father against Robert nor did he spare the youngest. 'Some fool has made my brother a little crown,' he said once and smiled to think it was no fool but his own clever self. 'And now he forever cries out, *The crown of England is mine. I will have it of my father!*' And did not say that he, himself, had taught the child. William's face darkened; and, indeed, he had heard the child for himself and did not understand it was nothing but play to the four-year-old. Yet he had great pride in his youngest son; already he could read and write; and his body was as quick as his wits. He could run faster, throw further than any boy his age. But—and Matilda could have told him—the boy was wily beyond his years. Already he could lie with a smile; he was more dangerous than Rufus that betrayed himself by a shifty eye. Henry was a child not so much greedy as careful, forever counting his small possessions; he would—if aught were mislaid—accuse with violence anyone at all and demand punishment. A passionate child that could dissemble well.

Henry would lie or make mischief for gain, or because he could not deal with a problem beyond his tender years. But Rufus made mischief not only for gain but for love of it; now he told how—his father being absent—Morkere had been given the freedom of the castle and beyond. 'He may ride where he will. If he choose he may ride away before any man can take him. My mother talks much with him; she is, they say... overkind.'

William bade him hold his tongue. But Morkere was removed from the kindness of old de Beaumont and fettered within a dark cell and he never knew it was the laughing boy, the friendly boy, that had put him there.

And Rufus was mad with jealousy of the two small boys of Harold. Matilda, as she had promised, played a mother's part to them. Five years old; and as like their father as a small pea to a large one. Rufus could not look upon them without hatred. Fate with her chopping and changing might yet put one or other upon the throne himself coveted.

'My mother favours the brats of traitor Harold,' he told his father. 'With my mother they are always right—and my brother Henry, wrong. They are everything and he nothing. They are bred, the Saxon brats, as though one or other shall be King of England.' And noted with pleasure the darkening of his father's face.

Matilda was stricken when she heard that William had removed the two little Saxons from her care.

'You dishonour my word!' she cried out.

'You had no right to give it. They say everywhere that you favour these brats at the expense of our youngest son; that, give you your way, and one or other of them should be King of England.'

'Who says so?' But she could make her guess. 'To such arrant nonsense I'll not reply! But, so much is true! The little Saxons are more often in the right, because they have accepted the discipline of right behaviour. It is a discipline our son has not yet learned. They are, alas that I must say it!, braver than our son, more truthful. But Henry has great gifts; he is cleverer, by far, than either of them. As for his faults, we shall, please God, amend them. And, for the next King of England—pray God it be long before we see him! But whichever of our sons it may be, to mention the little Saxons in the same breath is a great nonsense.'

And, though she begged and prayed him to honour her word, he took the children away. When next she heard—from Rufus all agrin—they were lodged with the turnkey in the old castle of Caen—dark, half-ruined and a grim place for little ones. They were no longer dressed according to their birth; a little freedom they had, but at night they slept upon straw on cold stone.

That William should visit his anger against their father upon these two innocents, that William should break her vow to the children's mother, that he should take the word of Rufus before her own, filled her with shame. It was an added cause of estrangement between husband and wife.

XXXVIII

They were on the march for Maine. William rode ahead with Hereward. He had brought Hereward not because he did not trust him but because he did. There were many English in his armies and he had appointed Hereward their captain; a bold stroke and justified.

Riding, it came to him with a sudden desolation that he was growing tired. Would it never stop, the need for bloodshed and the punishment?

A man grew no younger; he wearied, at times, for the quiet hearth. But how soon a man may age! It was not more than seven years since he had set out on the English adventure—how young, how vigorous he had been! True it was that in a few short years a man grows old. FitzOsbern would have understood; but FitzOsbern lay beneath the earth. Well, what a man begins he must finish!

He turned to Hereward. 'All this trouble comes from Fulk of Anjou. His heart bleeds—he says—at the sight of Maine beneath the Norman heel. He'd prefer, naturally, to see it beneath his own! So he sends men into Maine, sends arms, sends gold.'

'It shall not help him!' Hereward said.

As they rode they heard how the Mayennais and the Angevins had driven the Normans from Maine with most brutal savagery.

'This shall not help him neither,' Hereward said.

They rode steadily, Hereward alert for signs of the enemy; William sunk in gloom. He was remembering his eldest son. Curthose had begged to be allowed to ride with the army. He was, incredibly, twenty; old enough these four years to ride with his father. William had refused him—and no word wasted. He wished now he had been kinder.

'When will my father stop treating me as a child—a tiresome child?' Robert demanded angry, sulking. 'I am old enough to fight—old enough to have an establishment of my own, come to that! I am still, it seems, in leading-strings; and all Christendom laughs at me.'

'When a man goes to war he knows not what fate will bring. You are the heir—must I say it again? He has no mind to have you killed; or worse, perhaps, taken as hostage. The second complaint she ignored; but for all that her heart was with him in both.

'I wish to God I were not the eldest son!' But even in that moment he did not believe it. But to fight beside his father, to win a word of praise—even now it was his heart's ambition. He followed the army's route as if his life depended on it.

William was making for Fresney, first city on the line of march. He was at the old game of burning; it was a game that never failed. Before ever they reached the walls, town and castle had surrendered. At Sillé it was the same. He had scarce deployed his forces but there was Hugh de Sillé kneeling in the dust.

All the way to le Mans, city after city surrendering. Everywhere the city fathers coming out to meet William, to kneel in the dirt, to offer their hostages, their gifts, their prayers for pardon.

With constant news of victory, Robert grew ever more bitter.

'I should be there!' he cried out. 'Maine is mine. It was given me—a betrothal gift. If the girl died it was not my fault. The land was given and nothing can take it from me.'

'Your father will see to it that you get your rights!' his mother said.

'No need for me to skulk beneath my father's cloak. I am old enough to fight for my own!'

William was nearing le Mans.

'It will not surrender,' Robert said. 'Not le Mans, not my proud city!' It was clear he wanted the city to defeat his father. It was partly anger against William; Partly pride to see his capital glorious.

William was actually before le Mans.

'It will never surrender!' Robert cried out.

'Sir, it *has* surrendered,' the messenger said.

Lip caught between his teeth, Robert bit upon disappointment. To make it yet more bitter, Rufus cried out, 'Wish you joy of Maine, brother! These Mayennais—men that fear a cut finger. Cowards, all!'

Seeing the rage flame in Robert's eyes Richard spoke for him. 'You'd not be in such haste to see your own blood flow!'

'Dare you doubt me?' Rufus cried out. 'Much you know about blood— you priest! Prick yourself and it's not blood we'd see but water!'

'Shame upon you all so to celebrate your father's victory!' Matilda said, very sharp. She turned upon Rufus. 'To speak so to your brothers, do you *dare*! One day you'll say the thing that can never be forgiven; and then blood will surely flow; and it could be your own blood; your heart's blood! Now you can ask pardon of your brothers; and you shall do them some service, whatever they shall ask of you!'

Rufus sent her an ugly look; he made no answer.

'Now every city in Maine, great or small, hastens to offer obedience,' the messenger said. 'Outside my lord King's tent their banners wave; and every man he has let to go home in peace.'

'Peace!' Rufus smote fist upon palm. 'There is no peace—unless it be sealed in blood.'

'Get from my sight!' his mother cried out. 'I am sick to death of you and your talk of blood.'

'You'd not say that before my father!' He tossed his yellow hair and his eyes sparked red with anger; he hated the whole world.

'You are too old for a whipping,' Matilda said, 'but you are spoiling for a fight. Robert, take your brother and teach him a lesson.'

Afterwards she thought she should not have done so. There was sufficient bad blood between them; but the boy needed discipline and there was no way else.

It looked as though Rufus was right.

Fulk of Anjou had no intention of letting Maine pass into Norman hands. Angevins and Bretons solid behind him he marched; and Maine, ashamed of the humiliating peace, rose again.

Twenty thousand men riding into battle against William; thirty thousand, forty thousand, sixty thousand. How many no man could say!

'He will deal with them all!' Matilda said and prayed that it might be so; he was no longer a young man.

'The enemy, the great enemy, the twenty thousand, thirty thousand, sixty thousand—where are they now?' Robert cried out, joyful. 'Deserters all! Gone like snow before the sun!'

'Now my father will punish the men of Maine—your men, Curthose!' Rufus made of his speech a double insult. 'They did not die in battle— but now, by God, they'll wish they had!'

'There'll be no punishments, young sir,' the messenger said. 'My lord the cardinal Hubert has made the peace.'

The movement of anger did not come from Rufus, alone, it came from Robert and from Richard also; she felt it rise strong within herself.

'It is a question to be settled by the sword!' Robert cried out. 'And not by any meddling priest. Peace!' he rejected it—an obscene word.

'The terms of the peace?' she held herself in to difficult patience.

'The count of Anjou to be recognised—overlord of Maine.'

Robert leaped up burned white with rage; even his eyes had lost their colour. In spite of every difference he was undoubtedly his father's son.

'I am to tell you, lord Robert, it is but a manner of speaking. You shall be true ruler and lord of Maine. You shall take the oath to the lord

Fulk to save his face; for that and that alone. But it is nothing, nothing; your father makes you his promise. When you come of full age—which shall not be long—you shall rule in Maine. Meanwhile your father takes possession.

His father to take possession; he himself to do homage to Fulk!

'I'll not do it!' Robert cried out. 'Maine is mine. Do homage for what is my own, accept it as a vassal—never!'

He was not wrong there, his mother thought. He should have been present when the peace was made. It was his right. *But William… William over-rides the whole world!*

'Maine is my brother's own right!' It was Richard that spoke. 'Yet, it is wise, maybe, to sacrifice something for peace.'

'Peace!' In the mouth of Rufus the word was once more obscene. His lips had lifted above his teeth; he had a dangerous look. 'Peace never came from weakness. I tell you there'll be no end to the risings, the treacheries, the stabbings in the back!'

'Your father will deal with it!' Matilda said, weary.

Does he mean to stay in Maine forever?' Rufus said; and then with sudden viciousness, 'My father grows an old man!' And there was contempt in his face.

Robert for all his just anger shows no contempt; Rufus for all his smiling obedience shows his true self. A pity their father cannot see them now! Matilda's sigh was deep.

Robert had taken the oath to Fulk. It was Lanfranc come all the way from England that, at last, persuaded him. It had not been easy. Lanfranc had dwelt on this great chance, not to be missed, of visiting Maine that was Robert's own; the need to see, and be seen. 'And if you take this oath—which can mean as little as you choose; for consider how little your father is bound to his own overlord—then all others must take the oath to you. And it is their oath that counts, that makes you lord of Maine.' And he had dropped a sly word on the need of fine clothes for such an occasion. He knew Robert's weakness; knew, too, that William's parsimony kept his children far from fine.

Now Robert was back in Rouen and full of himself—Robert, count of Maine, crowned and acknowledged. As for old Fulk—overlord, so called; he didn't look to last long! Always inclined to arrogance in spite of his easy ways, he swaggered in his fine clothes so that Rufus pretended to vomit at the sight of him. His mother longed to counsel the modesty of a more proper pride; but to humble him in his moment of glory was not the part of wisdom. She was increasingly troubled about him. She had found it useless to discuss his faults with his father; William's response had always made it seem betrayal; now, Lanfranc so providentially at hand, it seemed more betrayal not to seek help.

'You see him, my lord archbishop; he has courage and kindness. He shows, I admit it, an unbecoming pride; but that is because his father forever puts him down too much. For that same reason he is not firm in his purposes. Obstinate he can be; yet a word, and not always a wise one, can change his set mind. He has not been allowed, my lord, to be sure of himself. And if his father is harsh, I am, maybe, too fond. His duties he does well enough; but always his father's return robs him of self-respect and throws him back. And now the ceremony at le Mans has gone to his head; he forgets, for the moment, that it was done over that same head. He has done homage where he had done better to fight for his rights. He is count in name only—and is like to remain so as long as his father lives. And if my lord King will not let him play his part either in war and peace, what does that make of my son but a painted popinjay? And if my son fight for his right—son against father—what then? I foresee trouble and great trouble.'

'These things are in my mind, also,' Lanfranc told her.

'In the matter of Maine I will do my best. But he must do his. Let him show himself more stable of purpose; let him pay as much attention to the business of state as to his ploys. Let him not be led by dissolute friends nor run to feel under a pretty petticoat. Above all let him not press for an establishment of his own. It is his right; but I doubt it wise. Let him please his father in these things and all may be as you pray. For pray, Madam, and never cease to pray; for always the first word and the last word and every word is with God.'

XXXIX

'I strive to the uttermost for an ungrateful people!' William strode restless about Matilda's bower where she sat stitching a fine shirt for Robert. 'My will is to rule in peace; a strong hand but just. But what's a man to do? These English have, forever, the itch to rise.' She sat quiet, drawing her needle through fine linen and let him have his say. 'I hoped for friendship between my two people, I thought I saw some signs. But now I must punish rebellion and friendship is spoilt.'

'You must blame our Normans for that! You talk of justice but I hear tales of confiscation, of imprisonment and of maiming without reason and without mercy. I hear of English girls hiding themselves in convents—the only way, it seems, of hiding themselves from the lusts of beastly men. And he that should put down such evils, himself points the way; he is the fountainhead of oppression. I mean, my lord, your brother Odo—that man of God!'

'I know it,' he said.

'It seems, my lord, you are needed in England.'

'I am needed here.' *Do you hope to rid yourself of me; you and Robert, together?*

You are no longer needed; by your own choice you have divided yourself from Normandy. Robert and I are capable of ordering affairs. But Robert you never trusted; and because of him you no longer trust me...

Between them the wordless speech.

'I cannot leave Normandy,' he said. 'In Paris Philip watches with a jaundiced eye; the peace I made with Anjou and Maine galls him. And your brother stands with him in this.' It was clear he blamed her still for FitzOsbern's folly.

But for all that he took her advice. He crossed into England and with Lanfranc laid down severest measures against those that broke the law. Nor could any man whatsoever hope to escape just punishment; his rank would not protect him. High earls were censured, bishops urged to greater care of their flock, Odo received sternest warning; he was, moreover, to hold himself obedient to Lanfranc, that in the King's absence stood in the King's place.

As to his own affairs, Ingleric's daughter—whose name he still forgot—had borne him a son, a fine red-headed boy; the child was christened with his father's name. William left her—no longer unwilling, since to bear the King's son was an honourable and profitable business—pregnant once more, with his injunction to do as well as with her first.

And now he must leave England in haste. Edgar the atheling was once more making trouble. He was sailing for France; Philip of France and Robert of Flanders had vowed to make him King of England.

'Let my enemies do their uttermost!' William told his wife. 'God is on my side. He sent His storms and the fool has been wrecked. And where do you think? Upon the coast of England! Now we shall have him caged; fools the English may be; but not fools enough to take him for King.'

Edgar had managed to make his way back into Scotland but Malcolm had had enough of him. 'I take this wreck to be a sign from God,' he said. 'Do you, also, take it so. Make your peace with William. Offer humble submission and he'll forgive you.'

'He is not renowned for mercy.'

'Your memory is short. Already he has forgiven you three times; and will do so again. It will please him to show himself merciful to Christendom.'

'It galls my pride.'

'Without pride a man may live; without his head—never!'

Edgar was William's guest; a bird in a cage that would never fly free. William was content; he had never killed a man in cold blood and did not intend to start with this pretty fool—they had been playing at hide-and-seek too long. Surely, Edgar, fed fat with content, would never again hazard his tender carcass in the fight.

Matilda looked upon their visitor with the love-hatred she gave to all handsome Saxons. For all her soul's cleansing, the first sight of such a one troubled her so that for nights thereafter she awoke from uneasy dreaming. But she commanded that he be given pleasant quarters; and he dined in the King's hall—though never at the King's table. He was given a pound weight of silver, every day, for his needs, and he had freedom—within limits—to ride where he would. And if he sickened at times of his pleasant captivity and wondered whether death upon the battle-field might not be even pleasanter, no-one knew or cared.

All his enemies caged and not one shall escape—Edgar and Morkere. And the two little boys... dead now for all I know; and for that, I will never forgive him! Matilda prayed for the children. It was the only thing she could do for them; but for Morkere and for Edgar, traitors both—she did not care how soon they should die!

In the white light streaming from those pale eyes the messenger felt himself shrivel to a pea. Beneath the fall of her cloak Matilda laid a warning hand upon her husband; he ignored it. He was nearing fifty; and, anger, ever more easily roused, grew ever harder to shake off.

'He disobeys. He dares!' William's voice came clotted thick with anger. 'Roger of Hereford that I honoured for his father's sake—does he think that for the sake of dead FitzOsbern I'll stomach open disobedience? He dares, my back turned, to give his sister in marriage to Ralph le Gauder against my express command—le Guader, liar, rebel and traitor. They shall pay for this, both of them! Hereford I shall strip of all his lands; as for this Guader—this *Wader* as the English call him—he shall wade without his head; I swear it!'

She made no more than her first attempt to curb his violence; her own anger was as great. This marriage spelt danger to him; their open disobedience made it clear. Between them Roger of Hereford and Ralph le Guader, earl of East Anglia, held too vast a stretch of England.

When the messenger had gone William rose and strode about the room. 'To give so much land in one place—it is not my way; not my way at all! I have been a fool! But how should I think FitzOsbern's son to be a traitor? As for the other—him, too, I honoured for his father's sake that died for me! Sons of loyal fathers—and traitors both!'

'You do well to punish them,' she said. 'And not only for disobedience in this affair. Were they faithful to you as the sun, still they make bitter trouble for you, both of them. They oppress their vassals, they ill-treat their villeins, they show justice to none. And they speak with too-loud a mouth against their King.'

'This marriage!' William cried out, raging still. 'Had they sense to keep it quiet, there had been less offence. But no! There must be a bride-ale, feasting and drinking; the guests the highest in the land; princes of church and state gathered together in disobedience to their King. And chief among them—Waltheof!' He choked upon the name. 'Waltheof that I pardoned for treachery and for the slaughter he made at York; to whom I gave my sister's child together with the earldom of Northumberland. If there's not treason here I never smelt it in my life.'

'The letter?' she reminded him. 'The letter the messenger brought?'

'From Lanfranc. Read it!' And his anger was too great for his own slow stumbling upon words.

'You are right,' she said. 'Treason was spoken; and much treason. Roger of Hereford whipped them on to revolt. He said…' she stopped. William, all impatience, signalled her on.

'He said—' she dared not look at William, *'The King is a bastard, unworthy by birth to wear a hallowed crown. Such a sight is displeasing to God.* Then, le Guader took up the tale, *Displeasing to God—and to men no less. All men would cast him off. Both here in England and in Gaul, also. Maine, Anjou and Brittany are all set against him. The King of France, his own overlord, hates him so also the count of Flanders that is own brother to his Queen—if Queen she can be called…'*

And now she came to a halt; and when it was clear she must read the rest of it, she took in her breath and read, *'And not these alone; but his son, his eldest son hates his father and wishes him dead…'*

She heard his breath draw in and out with rasping gusts. And, since he must hear the whole of it, she read on, *'It is right and pleasing to God to take the crown from his head. And now is the time.* But sir, it seems they were drunk, for they hiccoughed and belched.'

'And how did he answer this, Waltheof, the traitor?'

'He spoke as a true man should. He said, *God forbid I should so stain my honour! I say No. And, for yourselves, I warn you! Such enterprise needs caution. You are not yet ready.'*

'I do not like his speech,' William said at once. 'He said *No*, for himself only. I doubt his faithfulness. It was rather he feared to be linked with drunken louts. Give him suitable company and he'd rebel fast enough. For note, he did not try to dissuade them. He warned them, only, to caution. No, I do not like it!'

'He warned them to caution, as I think, sir, to gain time.'

Waltheof, himself, appeared in Rouen, a little troubled but a cheerful man. 'William received him coldly.

'Sir, you have heard the tale from the lord Lanfranc; and it is true; for I, myself, told him. But, I pray you, sir, remember they were drunk.' And he was, it seemed, pleading for them—as though he held himself free of all blame in the matter.

'I cannot hold you guiltless, either,' William bid him. 'The marriage was forbidden; there's the first treachery. Everyone that attended it is guilty also. Remember it. Why did you not come to me at once with the tale?'

'Sir, they were *drunk*! When they came to themselves they besought me to say nothing. They bound me by an oath.'

'Such an oath is treason,' the Queen said.

'Madam and lady, were I minded not to swear, there were plenty to put it out of my power to speak, ever; then you would know nothing. So I judged it wiser to wait upon events. But when I saw the wine was out of them and still they held by their plan, then I was much troubled. I had sworn not to betray them; but then I must betray my King to whom I had sworn the greater oath. I sought counsel of the wisest man in England—the lord Lanfranc. But even before he spoke I knew my answer. He told me I must cross to Normandy at once and tell you all I know. And this I have done, beseeching, sir, your forgiveness.'

'I forgive you.' But forgiveness was not in eye nor on mouth. Yet, for all that, William made much of Waltheof binding him in friendship as he had bound Morkere, as he bound Edgar. One more bird in his cage! Matilda thought; but this man is honest, is good.

To Normandy came further news.

My lords of Hereford and of East Anglia had called upon their vassals; and le Guader, since he was half-Breton, had called upon the Bretons. And both of them upon the Danes.

'The English would be fools, indeed, to rise against me for such wolves!' William paced Matilda's bower; he was both anxious and irritable. 'And, as if I haven't enough already on my hands, there's trouble again with Curthose.' And still he used the old slighting name.

'You should expect it!' she said.

He made no answer and stormed his way out.

Robert had passed his twenty-first birthday. William had not kept his promise—nor seemed likely to keep it; and Robert was bitter. His friends forever urged him to march into Maine and take his own. Richard considered his brother ill-used but counselled patience; and Rufus never ceased his taunts—no new thing that!

But—and this was new—now the youngest joined him. Two sons against two sons; and their mother, as usual, taking the part of her favourite! Only to be expected, William thought, in his turn bitter, making nothing of his own broken promises. Well, he'd no time to deal with the matter now; the business in England came first.

News from England was good; as good as William himself could have desired.

'Sir and lord, Roger of Hereford has been taken. And le Guader— quick his tongue to utter treason, quicker still his feet to run away. He has fled into Brittany and those that trusted in him are left to bear punishment.'

'Punishment!' William cried out. 'Where it is not enough my own hands shall add to it.'

'Sir, it is enough; every town, every road, bears witness.'

William was for England to clear up the mess his rebellious earls had left behind.

'What of Waltheof?' Matilda asked.

'Goes with me. Let him face the rebels; so we may come at the truth.'

'He has already told it. Lanfranc vouches for him.'

'I judge for myself; I do not trust the man.'

'I think, sir, you should. God knows I have little pleasure of these English; but the man is to be trusted. Moreover he threw himself upon your mercy and you granted it.'

'I must have him where I want him—between my two hands.'

'Lay a finger upon him and you may rue it.'

She had said the wrong thing, and, too late, she knew it.

'Rue it? I rue nothing. And justice I mean to have.'

'Then, sir, see that it is justice. But if, in spite of all, you doubt the man's honesty, then mercy is better. He is a man well-esteemed—English and Norman alike.'

He made no answer. She stood there silent willing him to show, if not mercy, then, at least, justice. She cared little for Waltheof for her husband's well-being she cared a great deal, even more she cared that his dishonour should not stink in the sight of men.

He bade her Farewell; and, even at the last, it was her hand, only, he saluted, having still his anger against her for the sake of Robert.

A smooth crossing; and the King walking with Waltheof, very friendly, arm about the earl's shoulder. But, the moment they set foot on English soil, William turned himself about. 'Arrest that man!' he commanded.

Ralph le Guader was safe in Brittany and his bride with him. Roger of Hereford and Waltheof lay in prison to await the winter gemot. In Rouen Matilda waited anxious for the outcome; and her anxiety was all for William.

Roger of Hereford came first to his trial. His guilt was clear. He was condemned to prison—lands and honours forfeit; a life sentence.

'It is not enough! Robert said. 'The sentence for high treason is death.'

'Cod grant he show mercy in the right place; Roger of Hereford deserves none!' Matilda said. 'A stark man, your father; yet he can not endure to take the head of FitzOsbern's son. He cannot forget the friend of his youth.'

'Cod will remember it for righteousness!' Richard said.

'So back to prison goes the traitor, with—if I know my father—a hint to the gaoler not to be over-harsh!' Robert cried out, goaded.

But Waltheof was a different matter. Waltheof should stand, a warning, to all rebellious English. The man's head he must have! William vowed it. In all his years, however angered, however justified, he had taken no life in cold blood; Norman law and his own conscience forbade it. One killed the enemy in battle; one commanded a maiming knowing that blood must flow, to end, very likely, in death. But by no direct word had he ever commanded the shedding of a man's life-blood.

But, for all that, this man's head he must have. Waltheof was innocent; or, if not perfect in innocence, very near it. In this last revolt he had taken no part; he had, indeed, spoken out like a true man. And, more; at the risk of his own life he had warned the King.

But it was not only this last thing William held against the man. How could he forget that, with his own hands, Waltheof had made a massacre of honest Normans? And, before that, he had been close-leagued with the traitors of the north. On all these points William's mind was clear. But other thoughts were less clear; were scarce thoughts but unconscious memory pricking. Punishing Waltheof he punished Brihtric... and Matilda had asked mercy for Waltheof. All unconscious, he punished her, too.

The winter gemot could not decide upon Waltheof's guilt. Pentecost came round; in Winchester the gemot met again. Many held by Waltheof's innocence; but many knew the King's mind in the matter and hoped to do themselves some good. It was Waltheof's wife that turned the scale—Judith, the King's niece, whose marriage had so honoured the accused man.

Waltheof's guilt was found; his, sentence spoken.

Matilda was stricken when she heard the news. The man was innocent... but the witan had known the King's mind in the matter. She feared for William; for the bitterness this must rouse against him and for the tarnishing of his good name. But, most of all, she feared for William himself. Before ever the gemot had gathered, he had, in cold blood, decreed the man's death—a thing he had never done before. This, let him say what he would, he could not take this lightly. She feared some corrosion of the soul.

Robert received the news with something of triumph; justification to himself of his father's bad faith. When he would have spoken of it, she refused to discuss the matter; faithfulness to William demanded it. Robert's anger had swollen into an abscess; she would not press upon it. The bursting of the infection could prove dangerous.

They had taken Waltheof's head—not within the city nor yet in the full light of day. On a hill without the city in the dark of the morning, lest his countrymen make a bid for rescue, they took away his life.

Matilda knelt before her altar; she could not pray. Her heart spoke its own words and it was as though she spoke to William. *You have broken the law of your own nature. You have taken a life in cold blood. What is happening to you? Growing older in years do we grow older in cruelty?* And remembered her own cruelty to the canon's daughter. *Oh William, to this deed, what end? You have made of this man a martyr. Now there will be miracles—that is the way of men; miracles that shall testify against you, that shall make enemies for you and troubles without end. William, William I fear for you...*

She was right about the miracles. The first occurred in the moment of death; not in dying but in death itself. Waltheof knelt before the block, the headsman stood above, dreading the stroke. It was his first execution;

in ten years no such stroke had been given. *Lead us not into temptation*, Waltheof prayed; the headsman, courage already on the ebb, dared wait no longer. The lifted sword fell. The bloody head rolled; *deliver us from evil*, the dead lips said.

XL

Ralph le Gauder whom the English called *the Wader* would never again hear his honoured name mutilated by their clumsy tongue. Count Howell of Brittany, his kinsman, made much of him—le Guader had revolted against the detested Bastard. Howell gave him lands, and riches to go with them. He had his life and he had his wife—and what was honour but a word?

Roger of Breteuil, once earl of Hereford, that deserved to die, lay in prison; an easy confinement—if a man may endure to be confined. But indeed, William would have had him out long ago had the young man's arrogance allowed it. Yet still William hoped to release him. Let the young man show some small sign of regret and he should be free. At Easter, when he had been confined a year, the King sent him a gown and cloak rich with embroidery and lavish with minniver—fit for the King himself. Let Roger accept it with a word of thanks—or even with no thanks at all—and he should be free. Acceptance of the King's goodwill; it was all William asked.

The prisoner said no word save to ask that a fire be lit in the courtyard; and into that fire went William's gift—and with it William's goodwill.

'By the Splendour of God,' William swore when he heard of the insult, 'he shall never come forth as long as I live!' But the two small sons, Roger and Reynold, he ordered to be nurtured as befitted their birth.

This you did not allow to the children of Harold in spite of my vow. Matilda heard her thoughts as clear as though she spoke to William herself. *Now one traitor lies in comfortable prison until it shall please him to come forth; and the other flaunts himself in Brittany. And the truest man of them all, Waltheof, lies in the ground... holy ground thanks to the monks of Croyland that begged his body. And every day the tale of miracles worked at his tomb grows. William, do you heed no counsel but that of your own angry heart that bids you destroy the innocent… and yourself may be; yourself, also?*

She was seeing more of William these days. His duties kept him crossing and re-crossing the Channel; he was in Normandy almost as much as in England. With all the coming and going she could not but catch some whisper concerning him. The woman that had given him a son had now given him a daughter; another woman had borne the King a son. Beyond the prick to her pride his infidelities concerned her little; she was surprised to find how little she cared. The shocking death of the priest's daughter had purged her of jealousy and anger; nor, in this chastened mood, could she blame William overmuch—a man in his prime bound to an unwilling wife!

'I have put an end to revolt in England!' William said. 'My princes are submissive; and all the people high and low are obedient to my laws. Now murder is less, robbery less, rape less. My punishments bear hard upon these things. Now we may look to a long peace.'

'Yes,' Matilda said, 'you have made good laws.' *But you, yourself? You do what you will; the English will not soon forget Waltheof—murder if ever there was one. And all beneath the cloak of law. There is no peace in England. There is submission, only; a hard and bitter submission.*

'I am good to those that love God,' he said. 'I honour the church with rich gifts.'

'As long as the church obeys you!' The words were out; too late she wished she had left them unspoken.

'What else?' His lifted brows showed surprise.

She said nothing. *But let a priest so much as frown upon you and you sack his church and cast him out to beg his bread.* She sighed, wishing her thought and tongue less quick; wishing she did not see him so clear. Once she had accepted the faults along with the man; now she could no longer accept them. Yet—faults of a strong man; she must still admire him.

Suddenly she was sorry for him because he was so strong—and yet so weak; because all men must bend their back—but not their heart. For who, among them all—his wife, his children, Rufus even, loved him? She was desolate for him. She longed, since she could not love him as a wife, to counsel him as a friend, to warn him, against his cold heart that

273

he might prepare some comfort for himself at need. But the years they had been apart were too many—and he was the man he was.

That Easter Cecilia took her final vows. She was twenty. And now it came sweeping back, Matilda's old bitterness against William, the more bitter because the moment had come; and because she had thought herself resigned. But when she saw the girl so young and already remote from life, the old wound bled afresh. She wanted to cry out to the girl, the girl with the consecrated look, *You are too young, too obedient to your father.* But she knew well the answer. *I am obedient to my Father; one is never too young for that.* It was too late; ten years too late.

She stood there, Matilda Queen of England, duchess-regent of Normandy, in the beautiful church her husband had enriched with the spoils of England. About her stood her sons and daughters—princes all. Beside her, her husband royally crowned, ruddy and growing stout; a man well-satisfied, reassured because he had given his girl—a hostage to God. *But suppose He demands that we be, each one of us, our own hostage—and no buying ourselves off?*

She looked again at Cecilia. At this moment the archbishop was presenting her to God. She could not endure to see so unearthly a look upon a face that had not time nor chance as yet to judge between earthly and heavenly good. She could not endure to look upon the child nor yet upon the husband that had done this thing. But now they knelt to pray; she put her face into her hands... and her hands were wet with tears.

William was restless and withdrawn. He made his swift journeys into England and his swift returns. In neither land could he know peace as long as le Guader lived safe from the vengeance of great William that no man had flouted and lived. He could not forget the man living at his ease in Brittany; he brooded on his anger, reciting punishments for the traitor. Not death. Death was too easy, too sweet, too final. Revenge worked in him like yeast.

And for FitzOsbern's son kindness, too, had turned to hatred. But still the children were bred as princes; but, of the children of Harold William never enquired, taking it for granted that no man dared defy him. But he had reckoned without women—without one woman. Matilda took the children from the dark cell. In captivity they must remain; but now it was in honourable captivity, bred as becomes the sons of Kings. With her own

274

children they were not bred—so much of her vow she did not dare, but far from the court where William was not like to come nor Rufus carry his tales; and where she might visit them in her husband's absence. Of his other captives William did not enquire, either—save to see to it that Morkere's chains were not too light nor Edgar's cord too long.

Never an easy man to live with, these days he was hard and hard, indeed. Some comfort he still found in his wife's presence; but it was a dumb comfort. He rarely spoke with her now nor asked her counsel. Cold to her as to all, censorious and unloving to his children, he yet accorded her all courtesies due to his Queen, so that if not heart-to-heart, they went still hand-in-hand.

His own loneliness he was beginning to know; how could he not, when every day he and she moved further apart? He tried to win her again and did not understand that she had never been won. To win a woman—he did not know the way. Now he tried to cross the drawn sword; but it was overlate for that. He had never known tenderness in making love and even now he never asked if she were willing. It was his right; she recognised it as well as he. His loveless lovemaking, her rigid submission, exacerbated the difficulties between them. In the end he let her alone. She thought of him constantly, guilty that she could do so little to ease his burden. She saw him active as ever—mind and body; but he was growing heavy. He ate little and drank less, an abstemious man; but his middle years were upon him. That fine lean body was turning to fat.

Ralph le Guader was in the city of Dol, so close to the Norman border that William had one of his white rages when he heard it. But it was not only his anger against the man; the lust of battle was upon him as in the old days; the driving need, in these middle years, to crown himself afresh with laurel. 'Howell of Brittany breaks the peace we made together; he cherishes my enemy. He, too, shall pay for it! I shall thrust through to Dol.'

And suddenly he saw Normandy as a lusty man thrusting to the rape of Dol.

'I shall take Dol; aye and more than Dol. I shall take all Brittany if it please me. Howell shall rue the day!'

He was on the march—his cavalry, his foot-soldiers, his baggage-trains, banner and pennant gay against the sky. He felt a young man again.

Matilda watched him ride out. *He feels a young man... but he is not a young man.* Yet for all that he was a strong man, a soldier of experience and unsurpassed skill: and one that had never known defeat. She could not believe he would know it now. But all the same she prayed for his success.

Outside the walls of Dol William was encamped. So great his armies, so rich his furnishings, so mighty his engines—the city might well tremble. But, within Dol, Count Howell laughed; he knew what William did not know. Two great armies were marching to his help; from one side Philip of France, William's overlord that should be bound to his aid and was now turned enemy; from the other Alan Fergant, Howell's son and heir to Brittany.

Two great armies marching, converging.

Sweet Jesus help him, he is no longer young. Let him not be shamed! Matilda prayed.

Let him be beaten; let him learn he cannot do without me! Robert prayed, hopeless for who could conquer the unconquerable?

For the first time in his life William sounded the retreat.

'He couldn't get away fast enough!' Robert said, contemptuous. 'Tents and arms and engines—he left them all behind. He cannot cover the loss with ten thousand pounds weight in gold.'

He gives no thought that his father is humbled. Matilda looked at him with reproach.

Robert did not even mark it. 'Had I been there he had not failed. It is the beginning of the end for him!' He swaggered a little.

He does give thought and rejoices. For the first time since childhood she bade him hold his tongue.

The beginning of the end. That Robert had spoken it in anger made it no less true. She grieved for William, his pride laid low. She dreaded the homecoming for him, and for them all.

But he returned very cheerful. 'I have turned an enemy into a friend. A wise man—if he cannot win by force of arms—must win by force of wits. Howell has a son, we have daughters; I offer one of my girls to Howell for his heir. He is well-pleased.'

Matilda nodded her approval. She was very willing to give a daughter in marriage; marriage was a woman's natural state. She had no false notions about love—Brihtric had cured her of that long ago. The meaning of a woman's life lay in furthering the good of her husband and children. If she found happiness therein, she was fortunate; if not, she must accept her lot, thankful not to be left a barren tree.

She said, 'This Alan Fergant; they speak well of him. The girl that gets him to husband may feel herself lucky.' *...unless she feel the call to be bride to Christ, to Christ, alone.* 'Which of your daughters?'

'Agatha, naturally.' He showed some little surprise.

She said slow and careful, 'For my part I say Constance.'

'Agatha's older.' And now he was surprised indeed.

She said—and it was best to let him have it plain, 'Agatha's heart is set upon the religious life.'

'One daughter is sufficient.' And he showed no interest in Agatha's heart.

'It is not wise to urge her now; she needs time.'

'She's had time enough—full nineteen. Constance is but fourteen.'

'Constance is more than her age; Agatha's less. Agatha's still in bud; Constance already in flower.'

'A flower, indeed! Enough to turn any man's head.'

'Give him Constance,' she urged.

'Well, you should know best!' And it pleased him to be gracious.

She said, her point gained, 'But a betrothal; a betrothal, only.'

'It suits me well; I have yet to prove Howell a true man. But a betrothal gilded enough to keep him firm in the matter. A rich dowry in gold and jewels.'

Howell was well pleased with the bargain. It meant keeping William out of Brittany; and the dower was rich and the girl handsome and of pleasant humour—he'd be sorry to deliver up his son to a shrew. And she came of high lineage; second cousin to the King of France, niece to Robert of Flanders... and daughter to a bastard; but a glorious bastard; he was well content. There was talking of adding Chester to the dowry.

Robert said no word to his father, good or bad; but when he confronted his mother he was white as ash where the flame burns hottest. To him—the eldest son—no honour in England had been given. So far from honouring him, his father was keeping him out of England, was deliberately putting the succession out of the question. So white, so intense his anger, he had the incandescent quality of William himself.

Angered by the injustice as much as Robert himself, she yet tried to calm him...The city had not yet been given; maybe it never would. And, if it were? Little good would Alan get out of it—Robert knew his father by now! Robert did. So far from calming him it caused a fresh outburst... Robert burning still with the rape of Maine.

William commanded his eldest son to the betrothal-feast; but Robert was gone no man knew whither. Now William had a fresh grievance and no small one. 'My son shames me with open disobedience, and open rudeness to my guests. And which shames me more I do not know!' Now he was set more rigorously than ever against his son. Never in this life would he forgive him.

Between the two Matilda was torn; a tearing that kept her from sleep and slowed the pulse of living. Robert had good cause for anger; yet, a little patience and all might yet be well. But the young had no patience and Robert least of all. *When the good time comes may he not be eaten by disappointment to a shell of his true self?*

At the thought her heart stood still with misery and fear.

For William she knew equal misery, equal fear and a most intolerable pity. He was growing old and altering for the worse. Ever since Waltheof died she had seen it. The sacking of the north, the cruel death of hundreds, did not weigh as heavy upon him as the death of this one man. *Sacking is a hazard of war; but the death of Waltheof that trusted in the King's word—there is betrayal to fester in his heart. In the face of men he must affirm the rightness of that death but his own heart knows the truth. Does he confess it in his priest's ear? Or does he brazen it out with God?*

At the thought of this last corruption her fear for William multiplied; she could find comfort nowhere.

William was back in England; Robert came home again full of rancour still and well-primed with tales against his father.

'He will set England to rights with good laws! He will stop robbery and violence. I could laugh if I didn't want to puke. Everywhere they talk against him! They call him a tyrant who burdens the English with taxes so that the very ground groans beneath his feet. He's richer than any King in Christendom; every day brings him in more than a thousand-and-sixty-pound weight of silver. And me—his eldest son!' He turned about to show the shabbiness of his clothes. 'And where does he get it from? From the churches he sacks, from the English he robs and from his everlasting taxes. Oh yes, something he gives in alms; it makes a good show. He's like the man in the old saw—he steals the goose and gives the giblets in alms.'

'The giblets must be worth something!' Rufus said, mocking. 'As for the goose—you'd not quarrel if he shared it with you!'

Robert ignored him. He turned to his mother. 'My father says he loves good men; believe me, he loves his beasts better! Let any man, however good, wound one of the King's deer—though it be by mischance—and he must suffer. He is driven from home; and his wife and children with him!'

'Since when have you been so tender?' Rufus mocked still.

Robert went on speaking to Matilda and to Richard as though Rufus did not exist. 'They say, everywhere, he loves the tall deer better than his own children. He could well do that! He wastes no love on us; as for his beloved deer—it's all one! He kills and eats them at his pleasure!'

She was shocked at his bitterness.

'And this new hunting-ground, this new forest he's made for himself—as if he hasn't hunting-grounds enough already! It's the scandal of Christendom!'

She said nothing. She would not criticise William to his sons; but she felt it deeply, this wanton wasting of good land. He turned to Richard. 'Our father has destroyed farmlands and houses and churches—thirty miles in length, they say, and as much again in breadth. All laid waste—sixteen parishes! Did you know that? Men driven from their homes, churches level with the ground and all that he may amuse himself when he visits Winchester. Oh the good son of God!' Robert's laughter was edged.

'You'd be well-pleased to hunt in this new forest!' Rufus said.

'Not I! Already they are prophesying evil from it; evil for my father and for us.

> William's forest is William's bane,
> There shall sons of his house be slain...

In England, so I'm told, they sing it everywhere!'

'Let it not concern you!' Rufus said, spiteful. 'You are not like to come there!'

'Nor you, neither, unless Robert choose!' Richard said, very quick. 'He's the eldest—remember it!'

'England may yet be mine,' Rufus said, mocking and spiteful, still. 'Remember the prophecy!'

'Are you not a son of the house?' Richard asked. 'May it not concern *you*?'

Rufus only laughed the more.

XLI

William had taken Richard into England. Though no word had been said, Richard, it was clear, was to have the crown. The English might prefer Henry but Richard was his father's choice. Rufus he loved; but Richard's virtues he recognised—gentleness the one fault. But William would see to it that all softness was rubbed away; William would make him fit to be a King.

She let the boy go since there was no help for it; but she was troubled for Robert's sake. Yet, if Richard was to have England it was right he should see and be seen. And certainly he was the better choice. He had a clear honesty and a patient judgment; he had values of the spirit that, for all his piety, William lacked; and that—she sighed—she feared Robert lacked. Richard was compound of all the best of Edward the holy King and William himself. He would make a noble King.

Robert was angry but scarcely surprised that Richard had been chosen. England as well as Normandy should, come by rights, to the eldest son—halves of the same empire. But with him anger rarely lasted; and, on the whole, he was relieved. Give him Normandy and Maine with it—and he'd not complain. And moreover, England beneath his father's dark shadow was no place for him! As long as his father stayed away life was good.

But Rufus was eaten with bitterness. He was unbearable these days with his sulks and his jeers and his sly violence. When his father returned he would play the lamb again.

Matilda sat upright and stared at the messenger. At her feet her daughters wept; and eight-year-old Henry, brimming eye and stiff lip, tried to play the man. At her side a stricken Robert held her hand, his own cold; cold as the dead. But Rufus, for all his decently solemn face, could not forbid some joy. He was the second son now and England must be his!

For Richard was dead. In the new forest he had met his death.

When the messenger knelt before her she had guessed by his habit and bearing at some misfortune. But this she had not dreamed—how should she? Richard so young! She had not, at first, made sense of the message; the words had run meaningless through her head.

'...he was running down a stag at full speed; he was laughing I saw him for myself. And, Madam, as he rode, a great branch of hazel swung into the mare's eyes so that she started and fell... and my young lord beneath her. We carried him back to Winchester and, for all his pain, he made no moan. You might have thought he slept, save that his eyes were wide.'

Richard's eyes... his kind and gentle eyes.

'We put him in his bed and there he lay... and, Madam, death was in his face. But still he neither groaned nor sighed nor showed a sign of fear. It was my lord bishop of Winchester shrived his soul.'

'Shrived his soul?' she cried out wild; for suddenly the meaningless words had run into a pattern... and the pattern was death.

William's forest is William's bane.

Above her anguish she heard the man speaking still.

'They gave him the last sacrament and he took it, knowing full well what it was. And then he said *Jesu* and smiled and fell back upon the pillow. Madam, his sweet soul is in heaven; and in England, never was such mourning for any prince.'

She lifted a hand as though to push away the words. Robert put his arm about her and led her from the room.

She had thought to know grief when Brihtric had left her deserted and with child; she had thought to know grief for Cecilia mute and obedient to her father's oath. But grief such as this she had not imagined—death of a child she had borne. She could not, at first, face the finality of death but must put it into words to make it credible. *My son is dead...* the most shocking words a mother can say. *My son is dead.* She was filled not only with anguish for her loss but with anguish of remorse because she had not loved him enough; the dreadful, tearing anguish of remorse.

In her chamber hung with black, she shut herself from all eyes; she could not look upon Robert to whom she had given Richard's share of love; still less upon Rufus who, for all his tears, could not hide his joy. Nor was there comfort in her daughters. She was angered by Agatha's belief that Richard was best in heaven; nor could she endure Constance and Adela with their swift changes from tears to laughter—and more laughter than tears, as should be in the April of their years. Only Henry she would have kept by her, treating him as though he were a little child so that the sturdy boy struggled and fought to be free and she was forced to let him go.

She began, a little, to accept her loss, to go about her business, but her anger against William was not less; it was deeper, harsher, for very acceptance of her son's death. For that William must bear the blame. Had he not made his accursed forest her son would be alive... still alive. With his lust for ambition and his lust for pleasure he had robbed her of two children.

Richard was dead and buried and his soul in heaven; and life must be lived. She went through the motions of living; she took up her duties, played her part. But all the time her heart was bitter against William; it was a thing she could not help, nor try to help. Already he had robbed her of two children; now he was driving away a third. And without that third she could not endure to live.

For now her love turned yet more strongly to Robert—the more because she knew his faults and loved him none the less; they were part of himself. But she knew his virtues and they, also, were part of himself. If he broke his word it was because of the generous spirit that promised more than he could keep; she knew his kindness and his courage. He was debonair and loving; and he was her son... her eldest son. How, Cecilia lost and Richard dead, could she without Robert endure to live?

She was a changed woman. William saw it when he came home again; home without his son. Once he had been startled by some change in her—a change he could not name, could not put his finger on so nebulous it was. Now he was shocked to the core of his being. Her hair, her dark hair, was streaked with grey, the lines on her face deep-etched. She had grown very thin; and the elegance of her small frame was lost in a new shrunken look. She did not see it for herself, he thought; or, seeing, did not care—her clothes hung upon her. The line of the jaw had sharpened; like a blade the bone thrust forward. There was no colour in her face—neither cheek nor mouth; and the eyes, overlarge in sunken sockets, lacked light. She had some beauty still; but it was the beauty of an old woman. In the sombre black-and-white of her mourning she looked nunlike; but there was nothing nunlike in bitter eye and bitter mouth.

He pitied her. The emotion so strange to him, so rare, made his own heart ache. But then he was, himself, scarce recovered from shock—the sudden death of the little-known son whose princely virtues he had learned too late. Their shared grief—though she, he knew, bore the heavier part—the memories of their young days made yet more poignant by her changed looks, filled him with tenderness. The man that knew little of pity pitied her now with intolerable pain.

She thought he was marked not at all by the death of his son; his colour was high as ever and he had lost nothing of his flesh. Anger flamed still higher against him—the red-faced corpulent man. He had never been a tender father; not even to Rufus—indulgent there, perhaps, but never tender. He would get over Richard's death soon enough—if he were not over it already. One child more or less—what did it matter to him? Yet for all her anger she greeted him seemly; she was well-schooled to all courtesy. Nor could her pride endure that any man guess her bitterness, that gossip should make it a cause of scandal against them both.

His new and hurtful tenderness he had no words to speak. He said it, instead, with gifts of land, with jewels, with ornaments for her church; every way but the right one. Had he shown kindness to Robert he might have won her own kindness. The first night of his homecoming he turned to take her in his arms; she lay stiff and cold. It was like lying with a dead woman.

Things were worse than ever between father and son. To Robert's anger on his own account, was added anger because of his mother's grief. She had spoken no word to blame his father; but once she had cried out, 'The forest, the accursed forest! If he take you into England keep from the forest. Keep from it Robert, keep from it Rufus, keep from it Henry! It means to have all my sons!'

'The forest, the accursed forest!' she cried out again and wrung her hands.

'Never blame the forest; blame him that made it!' Robert said.

Rufus carried the words to their father who openly reproved his eldest son. A public rebuke—and at twenty-three; duke-regent and heir! Now Robert carried himself insolently towards his father; a flaunting arrogance to cover his hurt. William was not likely to make allowance for youth; himself had never time to be young. He put it down to a wicked heart and all Richard's virtues rose up to blacken Robert. There were times when he wished his bad son dead in the good son's place. Robert knew it and his mother knew it. It did not make things sweeter.

It was a habit that was growing upon William—this reproving of Robert in open court; it was as though he must prove to all, the rightness of his disapproval. It was embarrassing, and not to Robert alone; it embarrassed everyone—except Rufus. There was much sympathy for Robert, especially on the part of the younger courtiers. And always those that professed to be his friends hounded him on to rebellion.

There was one unpleasant scene when, in open court, William rebuked his son for extravagance, and Robert's anger matched his own.

'See for yourself if I go as befits a great King's son; or, indeed, the son of a simple gentleman!' He turned himself about that all might mark the shabbiness of his clothes. 'You keep me so that I haven't a sou in my pocket and you talk of extravagance! When you went into England you named me heir of this Normandy; and, later, co-regent with Madam, my mother. That is all of ten years ago. Yet still you treat me like a child and keep me as a beggar. Well, sir, I am no longer a child nor satisfied to be a beggar!'

'Watch your tongue, Curthose!' was all his father said.

Curthose. Again *Curthose*! It was this father of his that had given him the name that had spoilt his boyhood pride and sickened him still with humiliation. And though men no longer dared speak it to his face, still his father used it to take down his pride; and Rufus cried it jeering and even little Henry would shout *Shortshanks* as the eldest brother went by. Now the slight, added to all those his father had put upon him, stung him unendurably and he cried out, 'Normandy is mine. Already our lords have sworn fealty, and that by your own command——'

'Normandy is not yours yet—have the grace not to long too open for my death. It must, alas, be yours in good time. Or bad time, rather; for this poor country. Pray God it be long in coming. You are not yet fit to rule!'

'There are plenty will give you the lie to that!' And he cared not at all that he spoke to his father and King. 'This ten year and more I have played my part. I have learnt my trade and done naught amiss—go ask my council! Well, if Normandy is yours, keep it; and England, too! But Maine; Maine is mine. Thrice it was given me—once by gift of dowry; and once by voice of Maine itself; to me the lords of Maine swore the oath; to me and not to you. I promised to be their good lord, I, I and not you! And the third time? I received it at the hands of Fulk of Anjou; I took him as suzerain; it was your wish. I swore the oath for Maine to him and not to you; and he will protect me at need. Maine is mine.'

William was whitening now but still he held himself in to patience. He said, quiet—though the guttural thickening of his voice spoke its warning, 'Maine is mine. By strength of arms I took it, by treaty kept it. I am not one to strip before I go to bed. As for your oath to Fulk—a gesture, a gesture, only, to save his face and prevent more bloodshed; you knew it then and you know it now! Hark ye, Curthose! It is not what I want nor yet what you want; it is what events put upon us. No man may have Normandy while I live—let me be never so willing; no, nor Maine, neither. Only with the strength of the first and the goodwill of the second can I hope to hold England. God Almighty gave the crown to me and I must keep it lest His Anger fall upon us all!'

'It is useful to throw your meanness upon God. You would not cast a man a clout though he should die of cold. Is it His fault, also, that I am so poor I cannot even pay my servants?'

'It is not His fault, nor mine; but yours, yours alone. If you did not let your money fall to the ground for beggars to pick up, nor throw it away upon those you are pleased to call friends, you'd have enough and to spare! But you're a sieve; money flows through you like water. Your servants I shall pay; those that serve must have their wages. But for you and your mischief-making friends—not a sou. And on these same friends—friends, God save us—you'd do well to turn your back. A pack of idle fools that turn you from your obedience to me—and not for love of you; but for love of themselves and what they can get out of you!'

'Sir, have done with your lectures. I am no longer a child—though you seem not to know it. I ask you, sir, a plain question. Do I get Maine or do I not?'

'Never while I live; must I tell you again? It shall come to you, and Normandy with it, when I am dead and not before. And God pity them both when you come to rule!'

'Then I'll not stay here to crawl for such pence as you think fit to throw at me. You may be lord of Normandy, you may lay hand upon Maine, you may be King of England, but before God you haggle over pence like any peasant. I'd say you shame your birth—save that it is already shameful.' And he flung himself out, which was as well. Had William laid hand upon him then he must have killed him.

To no-one, least of all to his wife, did William speak of the heartless insult; he could not bring the words to his tongue. All his life he had borne the stigma. He had thought with his victories and the glory of his crown to wipe out the stain. Now it sprang forth as fresh and shameful as ever; and it was his own son that had put it upon him.

There was a patched-up peace between father and son. Matilda together with de Beaumont had contrived it and William had allowed it. For the first time he needed his eldest son—though he would die rather than admit it. There was need to punish Routrou, count of Mortagne, for his insolent raids. Routrou was strong and he was powerful... and William had not forgotten Dol. Though untried in battle Robert had, in jousts, proved himself fearless and skilled; he had also friends and followers to lead into the field.

Robert, for his part, was ashamed of the taunts he had flung at his father. But he'd not apologise; he believed them deserved. The quarrel had gone too deep and he no longer had any wish to fight beside his father. Yet, to please his mother, when William marched, Robert marched with him.

William made no comment; he did not show by so much as the lifting of an eyebrow that he was glad to have his eldest son with him. He had taken the two younger boys also—he felt he wanted them with him; the death of Richard had shaken him. Rufus should serve him as esquire in the field; during the fighting Henry should be left in a safe place.

Matilda had cried out against the plan. 'Take Robert; it is his duty and his right. Take Rufus; he is old enough. But Henry—such a little boy! Leave him with me.'

'Leave him to hide behind your skirts, to be spoilt and made a fool of like Robert! He'd not thank me for that!'

She'd been stung by his ingratitude. 'Robert can speed an arrow, lift a sword and wield a mace better than the best. And that you may be glad to find out soon enough!'

He had kissed her hand and she had wished him Godspeed; but, for all that, the Farewell had been cold. Now William and Robert rode, grim-faced, both. Robert had offered no apology; until he had done so his father would not be appeased. Robert, too, was angry. He had offered his service—and his life with it; seemingly it was not enough.

Rufus, observing how it was between those two, smiled. This patched-up peace could not last long. He had but to play his game aright to play Curthose off the board. And the game was simple—to plague his brother, until, temper flaring, Curthose did, or said, the unforgivable thing. And that would be the end of it!

Rufus put it to Henry as a game; for all his tender years Henry saw it was no game at all. Let Curthose offend their father beyond forgiveness—and one son's loss was another son's gain; and that gain not necessarily Rufus's. But, if nothing came of the matter he was still child enough to enjoy ganging up with Rufus and annoying fat Curthose.

As they rode the two boys kept close at Robert's heels teasing and taunting. At night they were at their tricks—water in his riding-boots; his hose hidden or his gloves. They kept his temper forever on the boil.

In the village of Richer where they must stay several nights the trouble came to a head. William and Robert lodged in the castle; Rufus and Henry down in the village. But the boys could not be kept from the castle; and there, without pause, they continued their teasing. As mosquitoes infuriate and draw blood—so these two. And the more Robert showed his anger, the more gleeful they.

It was the day before the march. When the boys came up to the castle they could not find the object of their attentions. Well, he was bound to appear some time! They sat in an upper chamber playing at dice and glancing now and then through the window-slit.

They were weary of gaming and glancing when they espied their quarry at last—Robert walking between his friends, the de Grantmesnil boys. A few steps along, in the privy, stood a pot half-full. Rufus went quickly to the privy, he was laughing when he came again to the window. Robert, at that moment, lifted his head and received the contents of the pot full in the face.

He stood rigid at the insult; not so his friends—they, too, had been splashed.

'Do you mean to pocket such an insult? Shall you do nothing at all to those young devils that plaster you with filth?' Ivo asked.

'They mean to show their contempt!' Aubrey wiped his face with his hand. 'Unless you have a care they will filch everything from you—your birthright and your honour!'

'You must deal with them at once!' Ivo looked up from rubbing at his cloak, the soiled grass still in his hand, 'or you can never lift up your head again.'

Already Robert had come to himself. Friends at his heels, he was up the winding staircase and into the room. So white, so wild his face that, before ever a finger was laid upon him, Henry was crying aloud for help; Robert lifted a punishing hand, while the de Grantmesnils dealt with Rufus.

The noise disturbed William in his nearby chamber. His bulk filled the doorway, his roar filled the room. He asked no question. He saw Rufus standing between the two louts, saw young Henry crying beneath the hands of insolent Curthose. It was enough.

'My eldest son!' William made of the words an insult; the de Grantmesnil boys he ignored. 'Must you be forever at your horseplay? Are you not ashamed to lay hands upon a child. You shame your knighthood, coward that you are!'

Robert looked full at his father that, asking no question, assumed, as always, that his eldest son was wrong. He was here to fight for his father, to die for him if need be; and his father named him coward—an insult no man, be he knight or swineherd, should pocket. In that look was so much of wounded pride, of contempt and hatred, that William was taken aback. He would have given much to have the words unsaid; but to ask any man's pardon—least of all pardon from this son—was not his way. He turned about and left them.

But, for all that, he was troubled. He had asked no question, listened to no complaint. And Curthose, not even his worst enemy—had he an enemy—could accuse him of cowardice. Nor, for all his failings, had he any bullying or spite in his nature. He must, William vowed it, be fairer to Curthose, more patient.

Too late for any show of kindness Robert was gone. He had stolen away in the night; he and his friends—good fighting-men all!

Roger of Ivry, commander of Rouen castle, sent his urgent message. The young lord Robert and his forces were camped about Rouen to take the town. All was under control—town and castle well-fortified and faithful. Would the lord King send his commands?

The lord King's commands were immediate and clear—the traitors to be arrested; on no account must the lord Robert be allowed his escape. Reinforcements were on the march.

Outside Rouen the besiegers saw William's armies marching; a formidable array spread upon the countryside. Against so large a force the small band, for all their courage, could not hope to stand; nor could Robert allow his friends to be cut to pieces in his private quarrel. He ordered the retreat.

He had lifted his hand against his liege lord and King. He was an exile now, his life forfeit.

XLII

Matilda wept for Robert. Once she had found it hard to weep; since the death of Richard, she found it all too easy. Her son was in exile—how should she not weep? He was penniless; had he place to lay his head, his gay and laughing head? Within her, bitterness piled upon bitterness against William that had robbed her of three children. Her anger, her misery she hid, as ever, beneath her mask of courtesy; but she spent more time in prayer and she never smiled.

Robert was safe. She could not give enough thanks to God; she even smiled a little. He was safe in Château-Neuf, he and his desperate young men—the noblest blood in Normandy. There was William of Breteuil whose father lay still in prison. 'Traitor son of a traitor father,' William said. 'It is well FitzOsbern is dead; his heart would have broken for this!' There was Robert of Belesme whose grandfather Talvas had cursed the infant William. 'Traitor grandson of a traitor grandfather—it is to be expected!' William said. There was Ralph of Conches and, of course, the de Grantmesnil boys; there was Hugh whose castle this was, and a score of others. Hugh had not only put Château-Neuf at Robert's disposal, but Raimalard and Sorel also—border castles all three; indispensable for the swift raid, the swift return.

William gave no thanks to God for Robert's safety. He wanted his son in his own hands; not to make an end of Robert—the boy was still his son—but to make an end of revolt. Now he must hire yet more mercenaries, comb Normandy for those that had not yet marched beneath his banner. Normandy, it was clear, was not with him heart and soul; he had been away too long. Men resented his harsh look and his closed hand; Robert with his easy charm had taken too many hearts.

Robert's armies were growing. From Brittany, from Anjou and from Maine they marched, bitter all of them against the man that had beaten them. Philip of France, too, was supporting Robert with men, with gold, with promise of friendship. 'A man's a fool to trust him!' William said. 'Your son, Madam, had best beware!' Grim he was and threatening; shocked that his son should lift an impious hand against his father.

William came to terms with his old enemy Routrou. Together they fortified castles on the Norman border overlooking Raimalard where Robert was now ensconced; and sat down before its walls.

In Rouen Matilda waited for news; news that, for her, could never be good. Between husband and son she was racked. To William old loyalty kept her true; but for Robert she agonised; and not the least of her fear was lest God should strike him down for his impiety.

Robert's bad news began to come through. No help had come from Philip—nor was like to come. *A man's a fool to trust him!* It looked as though William were right! Robert's funds were running low: now that he had nothing to give, those that had flattered him were stealing away in the night. He was losing not only his friends but his trust in men.

Robert had thrown up the game; he had stolen out of Raimalard, he was a wanderer again; Robert heir to Normandy, born of such pride, such love—homeless. Yet still she had news of him. He was in Flanders; her brother, God be thanked, had received him kindly. Another cause for thanks she had; William had returned to England. Perhaps now her son would come home.

But Robert did not come home. Restless and disillusioned, he was wandering again. Unable to eat or sleep for anxiety she lived for the news. He was in Swabia, he was in Aquitaine, he was in Gascony;

everywhere he was received with kindness and with rich gifts; hearts were gentle towards him because he had been harshly treated, the debonair young man. 'But Robert is Robert; he'll never have a sou in his pocket,' she sighed to Constance.

Constance was sixteen now, betrothed but by her father's will, not married. A girl to be trusted—shrewd wits and a loving heart; Alan of Brittany would get him a good wife! To her sons she never spoke of Robert lest Henry, childlike, let slip a word; or Rufus send across the sea to make his mischief. Richard she missed with his kindness and his wisdom; but she ate out her heart for her darling, her first-born son.

She was in her chamber alone; it was dark night. In the cresset a torch flickered; the tapestries stirred in the draught that blew under the door. She had dismissed her women and Constance had gone to her bed. She was unwilling to seek her own, dreading the long hours when she lay defenceless to her fears. Thinking of Robert, as always she must, she knelt to pray for his safety; it was when she rose from her knees that the knock fell upon her door. Given permission to enter, the serving-man said, 'Madam, there's a monk from Trèves desires humbly to speak with you.'

It was nothing strange for a priest to seek out Madam the Queen; her pious and generous hand was always open; but the hour was late... and Robert had lately been in Trèves. She began to tremble. News of Robert? Was he well? Had he money in his pocket? Had he friends. Was he... dead?

The monk came in quietly and stood facing her; beneath the drawn cowl she could not make out his face. A short man he was, thickset; and carried himself unlike any monk she had ever seen... a soldier's bearing... a prince's bearing.

Her heart's beat shook her head to foot so that she could scarce find strength to take a forward step. But still she had presence of mind. She lifted the hasp of the door and pressed the spring-bolt home.

And now he was in her arms, her Robert, her son, her best-beloved. She set her jaw but, for all that, the tears ran down upon her face and upon his. She saw—when she could see clear again that he was tired, that he was hungry, the plump curve of his face fallen into folds. She struck upon the bell and, while he stood hidden within his cowl, ordered bread and meat and wine.

As they carried the food in at the door, the old man Roger of Beaumont came in; he wanted a word with his lady before the council sat tomorrow. He peered at the visitor; his old eyes were none too good and the cowl confused him.

'My lord,' she told him, 'my brother of Trèves commends himself to me. He sends to ask how I fare.'

That her brother Eudes was archbishop of Trèves, Roger knew well. 'God be with you,' he greeted the visitor.

The monk hesitated. 'And with you, sir,' he said at last.

So! Eyes might deceive him but ears—never! He gave no sign that he knew his young lord; but his thoughts, twisting this way and that, all-but overthrew him. His first duty was to his duke. But he had served his lady long... and he loved Robert; the day the child was born, his own hands, stronger then, had held the little one. And he pitied the boy, also. Dissolute and lazy, yes. But who had made him so? Surely his father had much to answer for! That a boy on the run should steal in to see his mother—what harm in that? As long as that *was* all! Roger would keep his old eyes open; he would say nothing, unless he must. If there were more to it—then he would speak. There was no need; within the hour the monk was gone.

Madam the Queen-duchess was short of money; yet her revenues were no less and always they had been sufficient. Now she was cutting down expenses; she was borrowing money from this one and that—old Roger knew it as he knew everything, she had borrowed from himself, even; he had given the money with some pricking of conscience.

The great jewel she wore always at her throat, she wore no longer—old Roger marked it; marked, too that, save for the rings of her betrothal and marriage, the long, fine hands were bare. She was sending large sums to Robert—the old man knew it; had tracked down the hand by which it went. Why did the young man need so much money? Extravagant and dissolute he was; but he could not need so much that his mother must strip herself unless... Was he once more gathering an army to march against his father, his liege lord and King?

A true man dared hesitate no longer.

William had arrived in Rouen all unlooked-for. Matilda's heart shrivelled to a pea. Why was he here? What did he know? What could he know? What could anyone know? She had not seen Robert since that one night in her chamber. No-one had seen him there but herself and the old man Roger—and the old man had not known him. But still her fears persisted.

William's jealous eye noted at once the bare throat, the all-but ringless hands. Nor did she wear the jewelled circlet that bound her veil; and her dress, over-plain, was unfitting in his Queen. 'We like to see you fine—as our Queen should be!' he said when he had kissed her cold cheek. 'Put on the gown I sent you at Easter; it is stitched in pure gold—and the work itself worth more than that!'

He could not possess himself in patience until supper to prove her; for still he hoped against all hope that de Beaumont was wrong. His wife, his faithful wife and Queen a traitor! Roger was a very old man... but Roger was no fool. And Roger loved his lady; and particularly he loved Robert. Roger would not have spoken unless he must.

For supper she had changed her gown; it was finer than the first, but still not overfine. 'The gown you sent is too heavy,' she said. 'The gold weighs me down... and I have not been well.' And that was true enough; grief had pulled her down still further.

He knew now, as dear as if she had spoken, that she had sold the golden gown. Selling his gift, the gown that had embraced her own body, she had insulted them both; it was his first thought. And, hard on it, How much did she get for it? It had cost a pretty penny, he'd hesitated over the price; he was not one to throw money away!

He said nothing till they lay in bed together; and even then he did not say all he knew. 'Your son's a traitor and I forbid you to help or comfort him in any way. Such help, such comfort, is treason.' And when she made no answer save in the stiffening of her whole body against him, he added, 'Disobey me in this and you'll regret it—you and he, together. By the Splendour of God I swear it!'

That he should speak to her of disobedience and threat of punishment, shocked them both—a sign of how far they had gone one from the other. And still she made no answer—nor was there need. Each knew that nothing on earth should keep her from succouring her son.

She sold no more of her jewels—she had little to sell; nor any more of her rich gowns. But a coffer of gold pieces that stood in her bedchamber was empty; he knew it though she had bound it with seals—it was light in his hands. The discovery sent him raging anew.

'A faithless wife is her husband's curse. And where should faithfulness be found if not in you? You have been dearer to me than my own life. I trusted you with everything; everything I had—with my secret counsels and with the government of this, my Normandy. I trusted you with the best part of my treasure and I made you a Queen. And how, how have you repaid me?'

She said very steady, 'I never betrayed the smallest part of any trust. No secret of yours has ever passed my lips. I love this land; I have governed it the best I may. If I have done ill then punish me as you think fit. You made me a Queen—' she shrugged, 'and little good I got from that! As for your treasure, I have parted with nothing but what's my own. I——'

Cold and savage he interrupted. 'You help them that plot against me. You give gold and jewels, yes and your rich gowns, also, to those that buy arms against me. You strengthen my enemies every way.'

She said, 'Not your enemies. Robert; Robert, only. And if he's your enemy, who made him so? He is my son; my first-born son. Do you wonder that I love him with all my heart? I cannot keep my heart from such loving, by the most High I swear it. If my Robert were buried deep within the earth end, by shedding my own blood, I could bring him back—be sure I'd do it.'

He said sour and uncompromising, 'And my blood, too, I make no doubt! And much good he'd be to you or to himself, or to anyone at all resurrected from the dead.'

Anger took her that he ridiculed her love for her son; she thrust it down. 'Sir,' she said, 'shed your blood? By Christ I could not do it. But for myself, I'd not hold any suffering too great for his sake. You cannot expect me, sir, to sit here in comfort while my son's in dire distress. You cannot, you should not expect it; no, nor lay such commands upon me!'

His face now was bleached with anger save for the red patches that, with increasing years, stood out upon his cheekbones. He said—and the thickness of his voice warned her, 'I will deal once and for all with this traitor son! And the first thing is to cut off his supplies. So! I deal first with the fellow that does your business. Blind he has been to his duty to me, his lord; therefore he shall be blind, indeed! He shall lose the sight of his eyes. I know the man; he cannot escape.'

Now she was as white as he; the sight of her anguish enraged him yet further. He dared not stay lest he lift his hand to her. He flung himself from her bedchamber; nor would he come here again, he swore it, until he had brought her to her knees.

Samson the Breton received her urgent message at once; he had been waiting, within the very castle, for her orders. She was somewhat relieved when she heard that he had reached the abbey of St. Evroult and there found sanctuary. And though William's soldiers surrounded the abbey to break sanctuary and take the man, the abbot swore no less than the truth—he had no Samson within his walls. That he had a monk new-received and tonsured, he did not find it necessary to say.

William's baffled anger fell back yet more strongly upon his son, his graceless, disobedient son—and not a little of it upon his wife. That his anger was just and well-deserved angered her the more. In both of them anger fed upon anger.

With Robert wandering the courts of Europe there was little point in staying to punish him. In England William was needed. He flung himself off with scarce the courtesy of Goodbye.

Robert was weary of wandering. He was resolved to hazard all upon Normandy and Maine. They were his and he would have them! He was in Paris now, imploring help of the French King.

'Philip of France is a bad overlord to my father!' Rufus cried out, red of face and eye. 'He has lent my brother the castle of Gerberoi!'

Matilda knew well the point of that. Gerberoi stood in Beauvais on the border to threaten Normandy.

In early December Robert marched into Gerberoi at the head of his armies—men from every part of Gaul; men of high nobility and simple soldiers; young men looking to win honour and the rewards that go with it; and mercenaries concerned with pay and booty here and now.

William took the news with a white and furious face.

So! They had broken the pact they had made with him—Brittany, Anjou and Maine, all three! And—as he had prophesied—his suzerain in Paris was aiding his enemy. Nor was that the worst of it. From Normandy, itself, marched an army seduced from loyalty to their true duke. Well, the more fools they! Let them see what Curthose would do for them—Curthose, the faithbreaker. What part had Matilda played in this? Had she worked against her husband? For all her passion for her son he could not believe it. But, if she had sat back and done nothing—it was treachery enough.

Anger corroded in him like acid as he gathered his armies; in late December, he sailed. His ships, tossed upon the winter sea, carried his engines, his fighting men and his horses; carried his armourers, his carpenters and his masons. Ten sixty-six in reverse!

Landed, he wasted no moment of time. With that disconcerting speed of his he dealt with his own border-castles, seeing to it that they were well-garrisoned—men, food and arms. Thereafter he proceeded to Rouen for the Christmas festival; time he considered well-spent. If a man did not remember God then God would not remember him.

The festival brought little peace and no happiness to husband or wife. Even Rufus, that took pleasure in other people's quarrels, was subdued.

William continued bitter against his wife. He could find no proof that she was in any way helping her son; but still she spoke no word against the traitor, not though he was in Gerberoi to threaten his father in arms. Nor did she say one word to wish her husband well. Even in this last thing she failed him; wretched, she knew it. But how could she say the words that, wishing him well, wished ill-luck upon her son? With regard to Normandy, William was right; a son had no right to snatch at his father's shoes while still his father stood in them. But in all else William had put himself in the wrong. With regard to Maine—wrong; with regard to his treatment of the boy—humiliating him more than a young man could or should endure—wrong, wrong, wrong!

Between the two her heart was torn—for Robert whose life had been made wretched by his father; and for William because he was not the man he had been—a hard life had taken its toll. At Dol he had suffered his first defeat; what if he should be defeated now, again? What if this time he should suffer that defeat at the hands of his son—his young, despised son? That he—proud conqueror—should be so humbled, she could not endure to think. But—if William won? It could be prison for Robert, prison for life. And, in William's first anger, it could mean more than that. Anger against his son was now a madness in him; with his own eyes Robert might suffer the punishment meant for Samson.

At the thought of Robert blinded, her blood turned to water.

Robert was sending insulting messages to his father; certainly he knew how to draw blood with stinging insult. *Why do you play the laggard? Do you fear your son, the lad you heap with humiliation? Come great conqueror and see how you fare!*

William took the insult quietly; deaf, you might think, save for the bleaching and blotching of his face. He made no answer—save to gather yet more men, more arms.

The Christmas festival duly honoured, William rode out. Rufus who had won his spurs—the young Sir William—in proud attendance. From the battlements Matilda watched them go; neither turned to see if she were there. The heavy winter sky promising snow, the iron trees and iron roads pressed upon her heart. God knew how this would end! William, she saw, sat his horse erect as ever; but it had not been easy for him to mount; nor, once mounted, did he show himself supple, giving to the easy movement of his horse. He was stout and stiff in the saddle. Thirteen years ago it had not been so. At Senlac, unhorsed, he had, with all his armour, clambered upon another mount, and yet another. If now he were unhorsed—what then?

Outside the walls of Gerberoi William lay with his armies; three whole weeks in the bitter weather playing his patient game. Cat and mouse.

It was not clear, after all, which was cat and which mouse. It was Robert that, with sudden, unexpected sally, pounced. As the enemy poured out of Gerberoi, William marked a man vigorous and bold; saw how he gripped his stallion between strong knees that he might better use his hands; marked, where the fight was hottest, the man's blade went circling above his helmet so that his path was cleared by those that fell or fled before him. Who the man might be William could not know; but the man was a challenge. In William the lust of battle rose, the need to make an end of the unknown warrior. Urging his horse forward he could see beneath the helmet's rim only the gleam of shadowed eyes; the nasal hid the nose, cast into shadow the mouth and thin, chain mail hugged the ears. A man might as well be covered, altogether, William thought, irritable; he should have his name writ large upon his shield—if one could read!

But whoever the young man might be, William wished he had such a son instead of fainéant Curthose; he wished, even more, he had this young man to fight beneath his own banner. Well, since he could not, he must make an end of him—while Curthose, no doubt, slept still with his paramour. Two bastards he had got out of her already! The thought of Curthose spawning bastards as lazy as their father set William's teeth grinding jaw on jaw. Let him but get into Gerberoi and he'd teach his son a lesson he wouldn't forget in a hurry.

The thought sent him spurring forward, digging without mercy into the beast's flanks so that they ran with blood; Rufus, the new-made knight, could not keep up with him.

A figure so commanding and so fierce invites combat; William rode taking blows that rained upon him and giving more than he got. His sword broke in his hand; standing to the attack of half-a-dozen, his shield-strap broke. Useless shield, useless sword flung among the dead, mace lifted, William spurred towards his man; Rufus, slightly wounded, followed hard on his heels.

Rising in his stirrups, the unknown warrior William sought surveyed the field. It was Robert, not abed with his sweet-heart and fired also with the lust of battle. He could see the rear of his father's forces breaking in confusion. If he could put fear into those that pressed forward and force them, also, to fly, his father's van would be unprotected. And there lay victory. He spurred forward.

A tall, stout horseman, mace uplifted, barred the way. His shield was lost, his breast uncovered, his scabbard empty; but the deadly mace could do sufficient work. Robert lunged in with his spear; felt it pierce through the chain mail, saw the mace go hurtling through the air. The stranger's mount twisted sideways and fell; the man thrown clear lay defenceless on the ground.

Robert lifted his sword for the coup-de-grâce. From the helmet of the fallen man a thick voice roared. *A moi. Au secours. A moi!* He knew that voice.

In this moment of victory all anger was gone. Shame fell upon him, and a mysterious wounding tenderness for this man that, in all his battles had never been wounded till now… at the hand of his own son, his despised son. Rufus came spurring with uplifted sword; Robert struck it from his hand and signed to his brother. Together they lifted their father upon Robert's own horse, together led the wounded man from the field.

In a quiet place, victor and vanquished looked each upon the other.

Robert said, 'Sir, forgive me. I did not know you! As God hears me, I would never lift a hand against my own father.'

'You have lifted it!' William said; he spoke as the dead might speak. 'And for that I put my curse upon you. From this day forth you shall know neither victory nor happiness! Be very sure that God will hear me. Do you think He will forgive this two-fold sin—a murderer's hand lifted against your father and His anointed?'

Robert turned about in silence, victory turned to gall. Fight for his rights he must; but lift his hand against his father's body—that he could not do. He would take the field no more this day.

William rode back to Rouen—a man ashamed. His son, the light and lazy fainéant, had defeated him. So stark his face, so iron-bitter, no man dared to speak with him; not even Rufus, who in his father's defence had received a first wound that burned and throbbed.

In Rouen William waited for the next move. *Robert the Conqueror*—were men already calling him that? Surely now he would press his victory further! But from Robert no word.

'He has left Normandy; he is with my brother in Flanders,' Matilda said; she had a sick look these days. 'He is shaken to the heart that he lifted a hand against his father.'

'And his King!' William added, bitter. 'And well he may! I will never forgive him—not in this life or the next!'

Robert, in Flanders, felt the weight of his impiety, the weight of his father's curse. Bowed with melancholy he resolved to fight no more. He had been lucky at Gerberoi—or had it been luck? Had it not been the devil luring him to destruction? Even now he might have had that sacred blood upon his hands—that doubly sacred blood. A parricide and regicide all men, nay God Himself, must shun.

His pockets were empty again. He could not, for shame of his deed, ask his mother for more. Without money, his armies were melting away; and, as before, it was not only the mercenaries—that he might expect; but his friends as well, his fine friends. There, at least, his father had been right. He dared risk his luck no further against the formidable man that could use his tongue as mortally as his sword. A father's curse; to such a curse God must surely listen.

XLIII

Robert sued for forgiveness; there could be none.

William let both facts be known. But that his son had so sued strengthened both pride and self-righteousness. Since Gerberoi he had tormented himself with a question. *Is Curthose a better man than his father?* Robert, admitting his fault and praying forgiveness, had answered him. Had Matilda entreated now, his pride restored, William might have listened. But she had done with entreaty. That she asked no favour angered him the more.

'Your son's a coward,' he told her. 'Fighting goes to his head like strong drink. When the drink's out—courage goes with it.'

She said no word to that. She knew the wound to William's pride; a wound he must staunch as best he could. Robert, she thought, had behaved with chivalry... or had it been with lack of purpose? At Gerberoi he had held the whip; why had he not used it? Filial respect, surely, stayed his hand; that and that alone! But, whatever the reason, the whip had passed into his father's hand. William would see to it that Robert would take his punishment not in the flesh alone; but in the spirit also.

'I'll not forgive him so long as I live!' William repeated it to all that came urging him to forgiveness—friends and nobles, councillors and priests. Roger of Beaumont, very old now, went down on stiff old knees.

'Sir, all my life I have served you. I held—and do hold—your honour and well dearer than my own. And so I pray, hear me. Our young lord has been led astray by worthless friends; now he repents with a humble heart. He swears to carry himself like a good, obedient son——'

No, William said. And *No!*

Hugh of Grantmesnil came with Roger of Salisbury; their Sons had been foremost in revolt. He looked upon them with a jaundiced eye, knowing it was less his son for whom they pleaded than for their own. Forgive one—forgive all!

He said, 'Do you dare plead the cause of a traitor? He has made such mischief against me that father fights against son and son against father!' He took in his breath remembering how bitterly this was true. 'He has stirred up countless enemies against me. At home he seduced from their loyalty the best of my young men; abroad he has raised up armies to trample the sacred soil of Normandy. And why? Because he cannot wait till I am dead! I'll hear no more. Already I am too merciful; by the law of God and man he deserves to die.'

He had listened to them all unmoved; or so it would seem. But here and there a word found its mark so that he remembered that youth should be allowed some foolishness. And he remembered also that day at Gerberoi. *He played the loving son. He wept; he set me upon his own horse and led me from the field.* For the first time it came to him that Robert might have led him into Gerberoi instead; might have made him prisoner, demanded ransom on his own terms.

And how did I answer him? I cursed him, my son, my eldest son? And he remembered his pride in that birth and Matilda bearing herself as though she carried the lord of Heaven.

Yet, for pride, he could not yield; not to the prayers of his people, nor to the unspoken grief of his wife nor to his own conscience. A man never to yield though he cracked his own heart.

It was the Pope that saved his face. From Rome came intimation that it would please His Holiness to see Normandy made whole again. And to the Pope he must listen. A King, however glorious, must obey the voice of God. To Flanders went the letter signed with William's large and clumsy cross commanding Robert home,

'...where I shall grant you everything you may reasonably expect from a father that is consistent with the duty of a King...'

Not a loving message; but it would serve.

Matilda came to thank him and to ask forgiveness for aught she had done wrong. He was glad to be on better terms; glad, also, to show her some kindness. He was more than ever troubled by her looks. It was not only that she was thin and pale and old; it was that she had lost her proud air. She that had always held the world between two firm hands looked now as though life itself was slipping from her. It came to him with sudden shock that she was a sick woman. The thought was unendurable. They had drifted apart; but she was still his wife, the dear companion of his youth. Though he gained all Christendom and lost her, it would profit him little. For the moment he almost believed it. Now when he asked of her health she smiled, 'You have made me well!' And, indeed, it was as though he had given her back her life.

Robert was in Rouen. To show goodwill he came, neither friend nor soldier at his heel. For his mother it was as if the gates of heaven had opened. But with his father it was the old story. William's heart hardened at the mere sight of him. In vain he reminded himself that, in all honour and tenderness this son had saved his father's life. He could remember only that against that father Curthose had lifted his hand; that while this son had sought his blood, the other, for this same father, had shed his own. Rufus was not only the son of his flesh but the son of his spirit.

What now? Matilda asked herself, again despairing. Robert was home again; but for all the good he got from his father he might as well be away.

News from England was bad. Troubles in Normandy had kept William away too long. There had been a rising in the north; my lord Odo, earl of Kent, forgetting that he was also a man of God, had put it down with a most bloody hand; not only with blood that must be shed in such a case, but with blood of the innocent. 'Nor, sir, is this all!' the kneeling messenger said. 'Every day there are executions in the name of the law.'

'It is forbidden!' William cried out in a dreadful voice. 'Forbidden save in the most rare and especial case; and then it is the King that commands, the King alone.'

'But for all that, sir, men and good men die by rope or sword. Sir, the lord Lanfranc humbly beseeches you to return at once!'

Bad news; and worse at its heels.

It was not the north alone; it was the whole country in revolt—north to south, east to west, all, all enraged by extortions, by torment, by executions in the name of law.

'And sir, I speak by command of the lord Lanfranc. Since my lord Odo is the King's brother and stands in a high place, there are some to believe that it is by your goodwill he carries himself thus. Sir am bid to say it—your brother will lose England for you. I have also, a letter for you.'

'Read it!' William said when the man had withdrawn. Matilda cast a troubled eye over the writing; she said, 'Our brother, it seems, has run mad with ambition. He means to be Pope—no less.'

He said, when at last he could speak for surprise, 'Some rumour I did hear, but could not credit it. Truly he runs mad.'

'He has, so Lanfranc says, bought himself a palace in Rome and furnishes it fit for an emperor. He sends vast sums of gold to buy himself favour. He bleeds England dry; not only by the death of good men, not only by the draining away of gold—which is a country's life-blood—but also by draining away soldiers, English as well as Norman. He plans to take St. Peter's throne by force.'

He robs England of her defending armies. He could not speak, so monstrous the thought, so dire his rage.

'The country is in revolt and open to invasion.' She spoke knowing his mind in this as well as her own. 'Certainly, sir, he will lose England for you. Put him where he can make no more trouble.'

'A bishop elected and hallowed!' He threw out his hands. 'What man would dare lay hand upon him?'

'It is not the bishop that does these things, God forbid! It is, sir, the earl of Kent.'

He looked at her; his laughter rang out. By the Splendour of God, this wife of his was still without her peer! It was only afterwards he remembered that once, offering such exquisitely subtle advice, she would, herself, have laughed. A pretty laugh she'd had, low and charming. How long since he, or any other, had heard the delightful sound?

Odo had already embarked, he and his armies; he waited but for a favouring wind.

'By the Splendour of God,' William swore it, 'I will make an end to this mad priest. Curthose, here, shall come with me.'

They were taken by surprise, both mother and son; and neither was willing. Once they had asked nothing better; but not now, not now. She distrusted the uneasy peace between father and son, nor could Robert find the contemptuous nickname reassuring. More even than Robert, she feared proximity between those two—spark and timber. Nor had she forgotten the old jingle; it had, in her mind, taken on the doom of prophecy. Already she had lost one son in the accursed forest.

She had thought never to entreat William again; yet, for all her appearance of quiet commonsense, her words were urgent with entreaty. 'Sir, I beseech you, leave our son behind. Yourself away, we need him here; you have always said it. This is his rightful place.'

'His rightful place is where I put him!' William said, sour. 'Here's England in revolt and Odo making trouble; and, as if I haven't enough on my hands, Malcolm must add to it—it is of course his chance! I need every strong arm I can get. Curthose has won some fame as a soldier—no doubt you have heard it!' he said drily, remembering Gerberoi.

Robert came to take his unwilling Farewell. 'Here every man is my friend; in England I have not one.'

That is why he takes you with him. She bit her tongue upon the words. She held him close and then at arm's length that she might see him clearer; but still she could not see him dear for tears. 'My son!' she said, and thought of the sickness in her breast of which she spoke to none and of the weariness that dragged at her limbs; and thought of the new forest that awaited her sons. 'Shall I see you ever again?'

'I'll be back and soon.' He attempted to be cheerful. 'There's talk of my sister Agatha. She's to be Queen of Spain, I hear. I'll be home for her betrothal.'

'Before that!' she cried out, knowing the girl's aversion from marriage and the strength of that young will. 'Before that, I do pray!' She took him in her arms again and held him close, crying out against William; and crying out against the new forest.

'You trouble your heart with a piece of nonsense,' he said, 'you that all men praise for wisdom!'

'It is the part of wisdom not to question such sayings, lest we learn the truth to our grief,' she said, stubborn; and would not let him go until he had sworn never to go near the forest.

She stood on the battlements to watch them ride out; and though William did not turn his head, Robert looked back; and back again. She stood there until the turn of the road took them from her sight; and went within to find Rufus raging that he had been left behind. He should have gone with his father; it was his right because England was his right! As for the old prophecy, he could afford to laugh at it. It referred to those that had no right to be there; these the forest would certainly destroy. For himself he had no fears.

XLIV

William, taking the spray upon head and shoulders, was all impatience. At dawn he saw his brother's ships crowding Southampton water and ground his teeth at the sight. They out-numbered his own. Well, for all that, he would deal with them! By the time his flagship had slipped into harbour, the rest of his fleet lay across the harbour-mouth—the way to the open sea, blocked. Odo neatly trapped.

Odo was commanded into the King's presence; a command he could not but obey in face of the escort sent to fetch him aboard. Not greatly put about, save at delay to his plans, Odo obeyed. A King, however great, could do nothing against a hallowed bishop. In any punishment, William must first consult the Pope—and William had no case. The defence was simple. *I had no intention of crossing the sea. I was cruising in English waters, I was on the look out for the Danes. It was my duty.* And what could William say to that?

It was a point William had already taken; he did not intend to submit the case, and himself with it, to the ruling of Rome.

Face-to-face with William, Odo was confident still. No court in Christendom could convict him except the court of Rome—and there he had bought himself friends enough! But when he heard that William was calling a witan of those aboard together with what dignity the Isle of Wight could afford, then Odo was more troubled than he cared to admit. Yet still he was far from fearful. He had but to refuse to recognise the jurisdiction of the court. Simple as that!

Not so simple after all! Refuse to recognise it he might; but for all that he must appear. Physical force, were he so unmindful of his dignity, must constrain him.

'Sirs,' William addressed his witan, 'before I crossed into Normandy I left the government of England in the hands of my lord archbishop of Canterbury and my brother, the Earl of Kent.'

Earl of Kent; no mention of the bishop of Bayeux. Odo shifted uncomfortably on his feet.

'Affairs in Normandy kept me longer than I had thought; and, indeed, I had still been there but for news I received of my brother's conduct. Never such a tale of injustice, of unlawful executions. All executions, as you know—and he knows—are lawful only by command of the King. And to the tale of his crimes he adds a last. The armies I left for England's defence he has taken from their duty. He carries them across the sea in the mad hope of securing for himself the triple crown.'

The triple crown! William read amazement in their eyes and in the indrawn breath.

'Sirs, this last is the worst of all his crimes. To rob this land of its defences, to leave it open to the enemy—what is that but treason—the blackest of treason? Of this treason his ships crowding upon the water bear witness. Sirs, consider these things and tell me what I shall do with him!'

It was as he had feared. Not one dared answer; not though many here had suffered Odo's oppression and had been loud in complaint against him. The man was answerable to the Pope alone.

Since no voice spoke in the silence, William strode forward and, himself, seized Odo by the arm.

Odo said, proud above his fear, 'You dare not lay hands upon a priest.'

'I have no quarrel with any priest,' William told him. 'But with the earl of Kent I have great quarrel. To him I entrusted the safety of England; and that trust he betrayed. Odo, Earl of Kent, yield yourself to justice.'

Against that no man could speak; not even Odo himself.

'It is my will,' William addressed the witan, 'that he render account of his stewardship.' And commanded his brother to be conducted to Rouen and there imprisoned; and not in honourable custody neither, but in close confinement lest he incite others from their duty to the ruin of two countries.

To William, relaxing in his favourite Winchester, appeared his other brother, breathing forth reproaches. Robert of Mortain went away with a flea in his ear; and the promise of trouble for himself if he did not hold his peace. My lord of Mortain made no answer to that; but, as he went, he murmured in his throat.

Another name added to those whose goodwill he had lost! He took himself over the list—his wife estranged, his good son Richard dead, his bad son, all self-will and threat, only too much alive; one brother imprisoned and rightly so, and the other turned from brotherly love and fealty to his King. Where would the next blow fall?

In Rouen Matilda asked herself that same question. She grieved for William—a man hard to love; to like even. She pitied his loneliness, she wished him well; yet, in spite of every effort, her anger smouldered still against him. How could she forget the loss of two children—the living and the dead? How forget he had taken Robert from her; Robert the sole comfort and reason for her life? And how long would that life last?

Autumn of the year ten hundred and eighty-two; and things easier for William. The Pope had not shown himself affronted in the matter of Odo; it was, after all, the Earl of Kent that had been corrupt and not the bishop of Bayeux. And William had sweetened his Holiness with flatteries and with gifts and with a show of humble obedience; that danger was passed and Odo secure in his uncomfortable prison. His removal, had gone far to reassure the English; they were settling into acceptance. Scotland, alone, brandished the sword.

William sent Robert.

Now why? Matilda wondered. Her son, though fearless in the field, was not experienced in the stratagems of war; his behaviour at Gerberoi showed it plain. Chivalry might applaud; but scarcely his captains, nor his armies, nor any man of commonsense. Why then had William sent him to Scotland in full command? To give him a chance to show his worth? Or to get the boy out of the way? He had more than once lamented the fate of Normandy under Robert. Robert, dead in battle, would clear the way for Rufus and Henry—the one in England and the other in Normandy; and a soldier's death would go far to sweeten disappointment in his eldest son. Not hard to believe it of William, that stark man! She prayed for Robert's safety; prayed that he would satisfy his father—if that could be done.

Rufus and Henry, also, awaited news from Scotland. They, too, were perfectly aware of the involvements. If they prayed at all, it was not for Robert's success.

There had been no battle. Malcolm and Robert had found themselves of a like mind. In Scotland they had met; Malcolm had offered, and Robert accepted, surrender and hostages.

'We have only your word for it!' William cried out, brutal, and did not care who heard. 'Where is the peace signed and sealed? Where are the hostages?'

'Between honest men a word is enough; the hostages follow. There'll be no more trouble; that I promise. And, moreover, I have strengthened our defences in the north. Sir, I have commanded the building of a castle upon the Tyne. It will keep the north quiet; and it will keep out the Scots.'

'I wonder you should wish to keep out your friends, your honest friends!' William said, jeering and sour.

Feeling a fool and resenting it, Robert said, sullen, 'It was not for myself, sir, but for you. As for my new fortress, it will, I fancy, make you a new city; the men are at work, and they have brought their wives and children. Already the place is busy; men speak of it as the New Castle.'

'I sent you to fight not to play at building!' William's voice was thick with contempt. 'By the Splendour of God you should be ashamed!'

'I will never take by blood what I may take in friendship!' Robert cried out. 'I am a soldier; and I have proved it—as you, sir, have good cause to remember!' And now he, also, did not care who might hear. 'It is yourself, sir, that should be ashamed!' And, no permission given, flung himself out.

William commanded him back; nor would he allow Robert to leave the court. Angered at that last undutiful speech, he kept pricking at his son, pricking and flicking. Robert tried to keep the peace; he had spoken undutifully and he was sorry. But soon, pride rubbed raw, he had no regret at all.

In Rouen Matilda heard how William continually slighted his son, commanding him here and there as though he were a child; and how Robert endured it—as he must, in a foreign land without a friend. How would it all end? Her heart burned against her husband.

The breaking-point had been reached.

William had commanded Robert to marry the daughter of Waltheof. She was young, she was well-favoured, she was rich.

Robert refused.

And he is right, Matilda thought. It is no match for the King of England's eldest son; no, nor even for the future duke of Normandy. If William hopes to make amends for Waltheofs death, let him do it like a man; admit the wrong and compensate the family. Let him not drag Robert into the matter.

William went on commanding and Robert refusing with ever diminishing courtesy until, at last, refusal took the most inexcusable form; even Matilda must deplore it.

'I'll sleep with her; but I'll not wed her.'

He was sorry before he had finished speaking; not for his rudeness to his father but because he had offered insult to the family his father had so injured, and, in particular, to an innocent and virgin girl.

'Get from my sight!' So harsh, so guttural the voice, it was scarce to be understood; but for all that the meaning was plain. 'I'll see your face no more.'

'The loss, sir, is yours,' Robert said, very clear; he made a low and mocking bow and turned his back upon his King; and upon England.

And now his mother had yet more cause for grief. Robert had put himself in hazard of his life. Without permission he had left the court. He had left, not the court alone, but England, too. His father could—did he choose—charge him with treason. Now, in peril of his life, her son would not dare come home. For, though she, herself, were so disloyal as to harbour him, someone—and it could be Rufus—would make it his business to inform William. William would certainly demand punishment; and whatever that punishment might be, her own eyes must see it carried out. That she should punish her beloved son—neither she nor Robert could endure it.

Robert did not come home; not even, as before, by stealth. But she had her news of him—he was in Paris, Philip's honoured guest; he was drinking too much, gaming too much, wenching too much. He was sick to death of his father—he let it be known; sick to death of Normandy where he dared not stir a finger without reproach, where he counted less than Rufus, less than young Henry, less than his sisters, even.

When would she see him again? Ever? Once more—symptom of her sickness—she was losing weight. Gowns already taken in at the seams hung loose upon her. She was hollow-eyed, she was tired, she was without hope. *I am sinking into the grave; I shall see my son no more.*

The thought was more bitter than death itself. *If I might see him once, once only, I should be well again*. But in her heart she knew her sickness to be mortal. It seemed to her a monstrous thing that she should die and see her son never again.

XLV

The year dragged on. England was a sad place; a land of famine. Bad weather and poor harvests were, only in part, responsible; much of it had been brought about by the burning and pillaging of Odo; and some of it—though not even in confession would he admit it—by William himself, laying waste farm and field both for punishment and for his own pleasure. He was glad to return to Normandy. He had had trouble enough with his eldest son; now for his daughters. In them he would find pleasure and profit.

Two daughters to be given in marriage. But not Constance.

'Six years since she was betrothed,' Matilda said. 'How much longer must she wait?'

'Till Howell of Brittany dies. I don't trust him. If he break faith—we break the betrothal; a marriage we cannot break. Besides, it is fitting that Agatha marry first. She's all of twenty-five. I never expected an offer for her now; let alone so good an offer. At her age a girl's already given to a husband. It is gratifying that our girl will be a Queen. Queen of Spain!' William said.

She made no answer. Her heart was hot that he so coldly regarded his children. Agatha must be married against her will; Constance, though deep in love, must still be kept from her marriage. Neither made complaint—Agatha because she knew she was meant for God and not even her father could stand against Him; Constance because she would not willingly grieve her mother. Without Constance she would be lonely indeed; Constance had the listening heart. Agatha's heart was all on heaven, Adela's on her own pleasures—it was natural; at seventeen one should be gay. But it was wrong to take advantage of the girl's kindness;

one must learn to do without her—it could not be for long. She must see that her good girl married before her own eyes could close in peace.

She said now, 'Constance must wait until her older sister marries—well, there's justice in that! But that her younger sister should wed first—it's neither just nor right.'

'I marry my daughters when and where I must!'

'It is not right; it is not just,' she said again, quiet and obstinate. 'Already Constance has waited long enough.'

'I had to wait; and so did you. Believe me—love will wait!'

'It may cool.'

'That's nothing new.' He sent her a meaning look. 'Well, hot or cold, they'll marry when it suits me and not before.'

She looked at him with dislike because he rode rough-shod over his children; but she looked at him with pity, too. What would become of him when he grew too old to impose his will? With neither love nor obedience from them how would he fare then? Already the dark red hair was grizzled and he had grown stout; but for all that he was vigorous and strong—a fine figure of a man. He will outlast us all, she thought; and sighed for his coming loneliness.

When Constance heard that Adela was to be married before herself she burst into sharp anger. She had been betrothed six long years; she rarely saw her betrothed; she loved him with all her heart—and she was twenty years old. Girls married at seventeen, at sixteen, at fifteen! Yet she had endured the years with patience... *a little longer, a little longer* they said; and always it was longer, and longer still.

'Is there no end to my waiting? And is my little sister to be married first? It is not right, it is not just! But when did my father ever concern himself with right or justice? Our eldest brother could answer you there! Me he keeps from the promised marriage—and that is bad. But Agatha he forces into marriage—and that is worse. For Agatha can give herself to no man; she has vowed herself to God. To violate Christ's bride—it is blasphemy and God will not allow it!'

She turned her dark and stormy eyes upon her mother, read distress there and bit upon her anger. Her mother, it was clear, could do nothing in either matter. High spirit and high temper might have carried her to protest to her father; pride held her back. His indifference bridled her proud tongue.

It was Agatha the gentle, the obedient, that could not be bridled; she had her father's own unassailable will. She had given her eight-year-old heart to Harold; a child's heart. Whether she might have come to love him with a woman's love is doubtful; she held virginity a holy state. But there had been—in her own eyes—at least—a betrothal and Harold had come to a violent death. When, a little later, there had been talk of betrothal to Edwine she had prayed that God would show His Will in the matter—and Edwine, too, had died—a violent death. She had been frightened at first, at this answer to her prayer; then she had commanded her courage. God had shown His Will. She had said then, *I will never marry a man. I am for Christ; for Christ alone.* Now she was saying it again; repeating it with the gentle, untired obstinacy that marks the saint.

William was as tireless in obstinacy as she; though less gentle.

'One daughter given to God is enough!' he told her.

'Sir, shall you measure your gifts to God?' and she was gentle still.

'I gave Him my best.' He was himself surprised that he troubled to answer the unimportant creature.

'Who shall judge of best?' It was Matilda that interrupted. 'My eldest daughter went unwilling but obedient—obedient to you and not to God; she was too young to choose. But Agatha is old enough to know her mind. She burns with desire for God.'

'Then she must learn to burn with desire for a man!' he said, brutal; his nod dismissed the girl.

To his wife he could not, for anger, speak. One girl given to God was enough; he could afford no more and she knew it! He needed his daughters; needed them to tighten the slackened bonds of friendship; to buy more power.

She said, not content to leave the matter, 'A father has rights over his daughters; and nine times out of ten such obedience is right; the tenth time it is wrong. This is the tenth time. It is not only wrong; it is impious. I have seen her on her knees beseeching God to take her to Himself; I have heard her crying out, her voice all choked with tears, *I am for you, Seigneur, for you, alone!*'

'Then we will leave it to Him!'

The marriage-treaty had been signed and sealed; the jewels chosen, the tailors busy about the wedding-garments. 'It is all useless,' Agatha said, standing patient while they pinned and cut, 'you would do better to give the money to the poor.'

Matilda tried to show her how acceptable to God a married life could be—if one made it so. 'To do His work we must please Him and not ourselves. You would choose the cloister but how if He choose the world for you; the world of wife and mother?'

She cried out at that. 'I shall live and die a virgin. I have vowed it.'

'Then you had no right. A daughter is her father's property; she is his thing until she weds.'

'I am God's Thing, I beseech you, Madam, speak again for me. For if I am not God's Thing then I am no thing, no thing at all!'

In that same church of Holy Trinity where Cecilia had been promised to Christ, Agatha was wed by proxy to Alphonso of Spain. She was white as the white gown she had chosen; there were no tears nor any mark of tears. 'It is as I said,' William was complacent. 'She is resigned; this tiresome virginity of hers will melt in the warmth of a man's bed.'

Matilda said nothing; it was too late. And certainly the girl appeared resigned. Maybe William was right. But for all that she could not drive from her mind the sound of the girl's voice beseeching God to let her die before she was deflowered.

Making her Farewell Agatha said, 'Goodbye, sir, Goodbye, Madam. I shall see you no more. But you shall see me; and sooner than you look for.'

William gave no sign that he had heard this singular nonsense; and, though her mother besought her to explain her words, Agatha only smiled.

Within the week she was back; and they learned, mother and father, both, the meaning of her strange words. It was her confessor that told the tale.

'The first day Madam the Queen of Spain sat her horse though towards evening she tired. The second day we saw her drooping a little. So we lifted her into one of the carts; but for all the summer weather, and for all the warm coverings we put upon her, she lay and shivered. On the third day they came to call her; but already God had called her... to Himself.'

A second child dead. Through William's obstinacy, his ambition, his cold heart—a fourth child forever lost. Nor could she entirely acquit herself. She should have stood with her daughter in this. But, stand against her husband? Once, perhaps; but not now. She had not the strength—neither mind nor body.

She shed no tears; not even while they prepared the bride's body for her last rest. But when they told her of knees that should be round and soft, hard-scaled from kneeling, then she wept; wept for Cecilia and Robert lost; for Richard and Agatha dead. And she remembered the anguish of body with which she had borne them; now it was her heart that took the torment. She envied Agatha quiet in the grave.

Another marriage and this time with great rejoicing; Adela was to marry Count Stephen of Blois. He had seen the girl at William's court; and it was this girl or none. And she was willing. There had been some secret understanding between them, Matilda thought. Wise, then, to keep it secret; William tolerated no understanding but his own. For the first time she allowed herself some joy in a child's future.

But she missed the girl; missed the gaiety, the bright laughter. And Constance these days could give little comfort; she stood, indeed, in need of comfort herself. It was unjust, it was cruel, to let her go unwed.

Again Matilda opened the matter with William. 'I wish, with all my heart, to see Constance married before...'

'Before?'

'...it is too late.'

He let out a great laugh. 'She's young enough and she's lusty enough. She'll last!'

But I am not young and I am not lusty... and I cannot last. She said nothing, unwilling to say the words that must harden fear into fact; but her hollowed eyes spoke something of her meaning.

'Do you talk of yourself? Come now! Small you may be; but tough—tough as a riding-boot. You'll see us all into our graves.'

She recognised fear beneath this jeering. She said, 'It is of Constance we speak; not of me.' In spite of herself something of her distress broke through. 'But I am tired. I have much upon hand and heart; too much.'

He could not remember having heard her complain before. Yet he could do nothing. Her hands he could not lighten; here in Normandy he could not manage without her. Nor could he lighten her heart, either.

To send Constance into Brittany while Howell lived was the act of a fool; to give his girl a hostage into Howell's hands—he dared not do it! Once this wife of his would have seen that for herself; now she could see nothing but her children and what she called their happiness.

He said—and he spoke as to a foolish woman and not his clear witted wife, 'You should have one daughter by you to be your comfort.'

'What comfort to see my girl unwed? I am not one to fasten upon the young, like a bat to suck their blood.'

'The girl shall marry in good time; and that time you must leave to me! She's young enough and handsome enough to wait; and I'll not stint her dower.'

'Will you think upon it?'

'I have thought.'

Useless to say more. She grieved for him as well as for her girl, pitying him that he could not put by one jot of his ambition to pleasure his wife; nor cared that he left his daughter to wearing disappointment. A sense of failure weighed her down. Once she had advised her husband and he had listened; now he listened no longer. In her weakness she had betrayed her daughter.

When we are dying we live our whole life through—so they said. She was slowly dying; and slowly she was reliving her life. In present fear and present pain she lived again that other fear, that other pain—anguish in the flesh of that first birth; herself a child—fifteen, no more. And thereafter, anguish of the spirit when they had taken the child away. Torn body and soul she had longed to die. But it had passed; and this, too, would pass. All, all would pass... when life itself was passed. Yet, while still she lived she could not now forbid her thought from Gundrada; must know how it fared with her, must speak at least her name. All these years, in the full pressure of her life, she had been content to know the girl was well enough. Now, in the face of death, the first anguish of parting rode her hard; a longing not to be denied.

When, at last, she brought herself to question William, he answered shortly, speaking less of Gundrada than of her husband.

'She is well enough—or so I hear. We see nothing of her at the court; nor her husband, neither. They live for the most part in the country—he looks to his earldom. He promised well once; now, he's something of a clod. He married the wrong wife!'

He blamed her still for that! She cared not at all as long as all was well with her girl.

'They are happy? She was my waiting-woman once,' she excused herself.

He shrugged. 'Happy enough; but clods, clods both!'

'Have they children?'

He shrugged again. 'A litter, so I hear—the great strapping wench.'

For the moment she was overcome with longing to see Gundrada's children, flesh of her own flesh. But the moment passed; she was too weary. Gundrada was happily wed; it was enough.

By God's grace she had not failed her first-born daughter; but what of her first son?

For Robert she fretted unceasing—a fretting that wore away her life. She never saw him; he wandered still. He was in Lorraine, in Germany, in Aquitaine; he was in Gascony, and once, at least, in Italy. 'He tried for the hand of the Countess of Tuscany, but she has more sense!' William let out a great laugh. 'She's no mind to see her gold poured down the drain nor yet to join herself to an idle fool!'

Anger took her that still he so heartlessly despised his son nor cared at all for the hurt his coarse words inflicted. From Robert himself she never heard; dependent upon hearsay, she gathered each word like water in a desert. She had not seen him since the day he had ridden with his father for England and turned and turned and waved his hand. Perhaps he meant it to be so; perhaps he did not mean her to see him, the marks of dissipation clear upon him. Better so perhaps...

But she ate out her heart for her eldest son.

In one thing William had read her aright. The once wide-ranging mind that had shaped policies of state, concerned itself now with little more than the well-being of her children; the hands once strong to hold the reins of Normandy, worked now to shape their happiness. Sickness and weariness had reduced her.

She was increasingly concerned about her last will and testament; she must make it soon; yet she had the same reluctance to making her will as to speaking of her sickness. Robert was away; how could she bring her death so near? Yet her mind played, unceasing, about the matter; she must, for all her love of Robert, be just. To him she must leave little;

already he had had more than his share. Normandy and Maine must come to him; he would—if he had learned his hard lesson—do well enough. To Constance, William had promised a rich dower—and Alan Fergant was a rich man; she'd need little when she was wed... *when she was wed*. For Constance she must still work, force William to name the wedding-day, though doing it she spent her last strength. Adela's husband was very rich and her dower generous; a jewel as keepsake would suffice. But Cecilia? To the girl herself she could leave nothing; yet the great abbey that housed her pure spirit should receive yet more gifts, more treasure.

Cecilia was much in her thoughts these days. She longed to see her daughter. Not to speak with her; they could say little to each other, either as mother and child, or woman to woman. The distance of time, the difference in their way of life, was too great. But merely to hear her voice, to see her face-to-face; it was all she asked. The longing was terrible, not to be denied. Yet still she fought her longing... *She left me a little girl; now she is a woman. And all these years I never once looked into her eyes nor touched her hand. I dared not tear the plaster from the wound lest we bleed to death—both of us. But now? Sixteen years is a long time... a long, long time... and there is not much time left.*

Sixteen years. Often she had seen the girl from a distance; from among the sea of faces, anonymous each one beneath the concealing habit, one face alone had drawn the mother's eye. Each passing year had seen the round and childish, grow thin, grow pale; had seen the child, the girl, the woman. At first it had not been a happy face—that was a thing to break a mother's heart; to make it hard to forgive William. She had seen that face grow into acceptance; now it mirrored only serenity. It was no longer the face of Matilda's child; it was the face of a saint. The old abbess had planned for Cecilia to take her own place. '...not because you built our abbey, Madam, but because she is an ornament to the church. She is matchless in virtue, in learning and in humility; and, not least, Madam, she is greatly loved. God knows I am weary and long to rest; but still I pray Him not to let me die till she is old enough to take my place.'

Ageless in serenity, perfect in prayer, matchless in virtue... and twenty-six years old! All this Cecilia had gained; but what had she lost—and did not know her loss?

She was growing weaker still, thinner—if that were possible. But still she had a certain beauty; beauty of bone showing clear beneath the thin flesh. Still she attended her council; she might just as well have stayed away, so difficult she found it to fix her attention.

William came from England with a new project; he was full of it. His *Great Survey* he called it.

'I must know everything that is to be known about England. I must know at a glance who holds the land and how! I must know my resources in land, in iron, in men and gold. I must know what I may command in war, if war should come.'

'Yes,' she said, 'Yes, you should do it.' But she could not keep her thoughts on his Great Survey. They were bent upon her own problems—upon her children; and, at the moment, chiefly upon Constance. The good child was growing bitter. *Keeping her here he takes her from me and so I lose her; her, too.*

'...divide the country into districts, in each district my officer shall enquire...'

'*Yes,*' she said again; and '*Yes.*' But her mind was too weary, too absorbed to hold this great, this alien idea.

'...every town, every village. They shall report who held the land in the time of the late sainted King; and what was the value then and what now...'

'*Yes,*' she said and again, '*Yes.*'

He went on talking but before he had finished she had forgotten the beginning.

He had gone back to England to carry out his project; he had taken his young princes with him, Rufus and Henry—and Robert wandered still in the courts of Europe.

All her children gone; all save one daughter that longed to be gone also. Was this the end of all her anguished child-bearing? What had she to show for a life that had begun so fair?

She heard her thoughts speaking within her head clear as a bell.

I was beautiful they said, I was noble; I married the foremost prince of Christendom and in that was my undoing. For I married unloving and lying, to escape the price of my sin with Brihtric. But I never escaped it. I paid for it with my happiness; and with a man's death upon my soul.

And even now she did not think to call it *murder*.

My sin with Brihtric and the long lying thereafter; it closed up my heart within a tomb; the cold, unloving tomb. And so I failed William that loved me once; and as I think, loves me still... William that I never loved nor tried to love. I have failed him as I failed my children, every one.

Gundrada, child of my sin, I gave into the hands of others. That she had a happy childhood was not my doing. That loving and beloved she married the man of her choice was God's kindness to her and to me.

I would have stood in the way of Cecilia's immortal soul, deafening God with prayers that she should not renounce the world. Yet she is a saint. And from this same world what did I get but heartache and weariness of the soul?

And Robert, for whose lack I waste into the grave. What good thing have I done for him? A weak nature; but I did not seek to strengthen it. Rather I yielded to it, giving him his way in this thing and that. And now he wanders an exile and a beggar. And I must die and see his face no more. And that is my punishment; and I must not complain though it is harder than I can bear.

Of Rufus I dare not think. Why did his childish faults harden into viciousness? Because his father was too fond; and I not fond enough. I did not love him enough. And so for his failings I must take my blame. Twenty-seven and vicious; dear God, how vicious! My little Rufus, my gold-and-ivory boy that trumpeted the way to England.

And Henry. A child I do not know. Secret eyes hiding the secret thoughts. Secret and smooth and cold, save when rage most shockingly breaks through. Like a cat he'll always fall on his feet. Marked for success. Yet love and true happiness I doubt he'll ever know.

And, for the rest, Agatha had to die before she could give herself to God and I could not save her. And Constance wanders through this great house and wearies of me because we keep her here where already the younger generation treads hard upon her heels, my bright, my beautiful girl.

To all my children I was forced to play father as well as mother; and in both I failed. William should never have gone into England—though for that I take my blame! He had done better to stay at home.

What use the crown to Robert? He'll never wear it! To Agatha and Richard that lie in the grave? To Cecilia that shall wear a brighter crown?

What use Rufus may make of it I do not like to think; or Henry, so cold, so secret and so violent.

What use? What use?

XLVI

Weariness and pain her constant companions. She was dying but she would not admit it. Death she did not fear; but uselessness, helplessness, death-in-life—these things she feared and greatly feared. Her council besought her to rest; but for her there could be no rest. For Robert she pined with increasing grief; she never heard from him, she did not even know where he might be. It was a constant, gnawing grief, this longing for the sight of his face. Nor was there rest for the body, either. In William's absence she must still be about his business. She had commanded that no word be said to him of her condition. What was there to tell? She was tired; when there was time she would rest... a long, long rest. And soon. She was nearing fifty; a good age. And her life, though it had been spent in soft places, had been hard; it had wasted her, body and spirit. Her body she could still flog to its task; but the spirit she could no longer drive.

The longing to see those she loved best in the world was unendurable. Robert it was out of her power to see; but the need to see Cecilia was a wound that bled. Well, it must bleed. To disturb Cecilia's hard-won peace after the years of silence—not even her own dying could excuse it.

The year of ten hundred and eighty-three moved slowly, moved inexorably on. To her that, in her sickness, must gather what pleasure she might through her eyes, it was as though she had never looked at the world before; there had not been time. This was the last time she would behold the spring and summer—she knew it; the march of the months towards winter sleep must bring her own sleep; and from that sleep there could be no waking.

The ice melted and spring was bright in the land. And still she fought against her desire to see Cecilia; and Robert wandered still. She would give the heart out of her body, her outworn heart, to see him again.

Roses were out, pale cups sparkling with dew; and apple-blossom— would she ever see the rosy fruit? The fields were starred yellow and white and red. In the clear running water women bent at their washing—as once her husband's mother had done; she envied them their strength. But even now there was little time to stop and look; she must drag herself to the council chamber. But even there her mind wandered to her children; though sometimes it wandered back to her own childhood, her own girlhood. Sometimes she talked with her mother in her mind, *You should not have let me run from my sin. You should have forced me to pay the price.*

That sin has been paid for; and all your sins, her mother said. *Cecilia has paid for them.*

She cried out at that. She did not want the girl to take her mother's sins upon young shoulders; but it was part of the punishment and must be accepted. And, hearing her cry out and seeing the pale lips move, one man looked at another. She has some great sin upon her, some said; and others, What sin—the virtuous god-fearing lady? No! She is dying of a broken heart; the lord Robert has broken it.

One day in early October, when the longing to see Cecilia was no more to be endured, she visited the abbey of Holy Trinity. If she must not see the girl face-to-face nor speak one word, then surely she might find some comfort kneeling in the chapel where her daughter prayed. She walked the short distance, feet dragging among the fallen leaves. In the abbey fields the haystacks stood golden; in the orchards apples were ripe in all-but bare branches. She stood for a moment looking; she must savour to the full this last golden autumn. She went in at the church door and, lost in the shadow of a stall, knelt.

The place was empty save for herself; and for a nun that lay before the high altar, arms outstretched so that she made of her living body a cross. Oblivious of the presence of another, she lay prostrate, unmoving.

Her sins will be forgiven, they cannot be heavy or many, the Queen thought. A life offered to God is a blessed thing. But my sins, for all my praying, cannot be forgiven. For God, though he be compassionate, is yet a God of justice.

Time hung silent, unmoving. The nun rose, silent as a ghost; only the slight shifting of light and shadow betrayed her movement. Matilda's weary mind had long left her prayers; it was grief to her that she could not, save for a few minutes, fix her mind upon God. The nun stood for a moment and lifted her head; the transfigured face shone with joy.

It was Cecilia, the child for whom she had wept and prayed; for whose sake she had first let her anger fall upon William. She knelt there fighting her craving to speak with her child, to touch her hand, perhaps. To kiss that transfigured face she would not dare; how should she dim her young saint's happiness, drag her back to the world by the weight of a mother's tears?

She knelt still in the shadow, her face hidden. Cecilia, as she passed, said *God bless you*; and made the sign oft he cross upon the bent head.

Matilda lay upon her bed. *My child has blessed me. In the name of God she blessed me.* She lay there smiling because God had allowed her to hear her daughter's voice again, the voice with the blessing.

They had sent for William; she was glad of it. So many things to say; and chiefest, *You were right about Cecilia—and I was wrong.* But before he came she must dispose of her possessions; she must not grieve him with the plain fact of her dying. Let him find time to reconcile himself. She sent for the abbess of Holy Trinity. 'I have little to give,' the Queen said, 'yet there are still gifts to be made.'

'You gave your most precious thing when you gave God your daughter.'

'I was unwilling, God forgive me.'

'But you *gave*. And that is the main thing.'

That, too, she would tell William when he came.

'My son Robert had the most part of my gold; and my jewels, also. To him I give what little gold I have left. He will have Normandy; it should be enough. Rufus, also, will be well enough—England is for him. To my son Henry I give all those lands that belong to me, including the lands of my morning-gift, with exception of the manors of Felstede and Pinbury; they are in England and they are to come to God, to your own abbey.'

'Does the lord King allow it?'

'They are my own; he will allow it. Felstede and Pinbury—have you the names?' and waited for the abbess to write them down. 'And there are other lands also...' She lay there trying to recall their names. These, most of all, must come to God, lands stained with Brihtric's blood. If she could recall their names she would take it a sign of God's forgiveness.

'I cannot remember the names,' she said and raised a distressed face. 'They are in the west country; in England. The King gave them me when I went for my crowning. He will know. These, above all, I give to your abbey.'

'Yes,' the abbess said. 'Yes.'

There was something too soothing in her tone; it was as if she talked with a child. The Queen cried out, wild, 'The lands of the west must come to the church; it is to save my soul.'

The abbess looked upon the sick woman; eyes, experienced in human suffering, saw marks of great sorrow, great remorse. 'I will tell the lord King,' she said, 'there shall be nothing forgotten.'

'For the rest—it is little enough. I give my cloak with the English embroidery to your abbey; there's none finer in Christendom, it is worked in pure gold. It will make a fine cope for shoulders more worthy than mine. I give also my golden girdle set with jewels and bearing the royal emblem. These things I did not dare give my son; I am glad now, for I can give them to God. The girdle shall carry the great lamp that hangs above the high altar; it is very strong. I give, also, for that same altar, my candle-sticks of silver that were made at St. Lo; you will know them because the smith's initials are scratched upon the base. Do you write all this?'

'Madam, I do.'

'I give also my crown and my sceptre——'

'Madam, have you thought? What might my lord King say to that?'

'They are mine to give. Once we spoke concerning them, my lord and I; and it is allowed. I give, also, to your abbey, my cups; every one, both silver and gold. The gold ones I never used; you will find them in their wrappings still. And, lastly, I give you those lands in Quetchou and in the Côtentin that are not already willed to my youngest son. The list is here, under my hand. And now, reverend mother, will you pray for me?'

Matilda abbess knelt by Matilda Queen and covered her face with her hands. When she had made an end of praying, the Queen said, 'Will God, do you think, forgive me?'

'If you repent with a true heart, be sure He will forgive you.'

When the abbess was gone the Queen lay back upon her pillow. Now all was done, save for one thing; one thing alone. She prayed to live until William came; there were things that must be spoken between them.

Lying there her thoughts ranged back over their life together, zig-zagging, erratic as a butterfly. And now she remembered some thing she had forgotten this long time... the tapestry; the great *toile* of the duke her hands had never touched. It was to have ended with William gloriously crowned; it ended, instead, with the flight of the English at Senlac. The drawings for the rest of the tale had been made; but Odo had never found time to command the stitching—overbusy always, with his fighting and his plotting and his rebellions. Now he sat in prison and time hung heavy on empty hands. Well, maybe it was as well the work had stopped; as well not to have set down in pictures, for all the world to see, the things William had done—the burning, the mutilating, the sacking of cities. Without pictures to remind them, men might, one day, forget.

She lifted her head and requested the nun that sat by her bed to order the tapestry to be brought. Two men came carrying a chest and set it down. They lifted the bale of linen, unrolled it and held out the innermost strip. The nun lifted the Queen upon the pillow that she might see better.

So! The pieces were not yet stitched together! She would ask madam abbess to see it was done; the nun should carry her message. The next moment she had forgotten it.

She gazed upon the heavy linen strip; its width was twice the measure of a man's foot. The colours were beautiful—blues and greens, yellows and red and grey. The grey she noticed was not quite black; black would be too heavy. It was just dark enough to throw up the soft bright colours; she was enough of a needlewoman to appreciate that. Odo had been wise to commission the work in England. The drawings were lively so that men and horses seemed to move, ships to sail upon the sea; a picture book to be read as well as looked at, the lettering clear and bold.

She lay there looking and living it all again.

Once more Harold took leave of the holy King; the King wore his crown and sceptre. She sighed upon the picture of Harold, remembering his high and handsome look; the little picture could not show it. No wonder Agatha had given him her child's heart. She sighed again for Agatha, dead.

Now Harold and his friends set out for Bosham. High-stepping horses. Too fat to move! Robert had said and laughed aloud. Now Harold was on board ship. The unknown monk in England must have loved ships; he must have known how to handle them—maybe he had been a sailor before he'd become a monk. There the men sat at the oars, the steersman at the tiller. The wind must have changed; for the men were no longer rowing; the sails were full and the waves swelling.

Picture after picture in fine bold stitches.

Now Harold was swearing the oath. He had shaken with fear, he remembered; she had seen his hand. And no wonder. That oath broken must bring doom upon the perjured man. In the picture he wore a short tunic; he had, she thought, come in from riding. He held his hand over the relics—the hand she had seen shake. William sat on his high seat wearing a long gown—a true Norman. And that there could be no question ever, the writing said, in the Latin tongue, *Here Harold swears the oath.* Well, no-one could question, ever, the act of swearing. But might they not question William's honesty? Might not their hearts be with Harold for the oath that must be sworn... and broken?

Picture after picture. They had reached England, they had brought the horses from the ships. They had all disembarked and were preparing to eat; there was the meat turning on the spit. William sat at a round table on the seashore. But it was Odo that sat in the middle. He was saying grace, one hand lifted in blessing, the other held the wine cup. She looked at it a long time. It was perfectly Odo—the full and fleshy face, the cold eye, the sensuous underlip; beneath the cloak, undisguised—the coat of mail.

Picture after picture. The fighting at Senlac. The Normans were losing heart; Odo was cheering them on. The writing said so very clear. Too much of Odo in these pictures. She had said so at the time, had sent him a message; but he hadn't listened. So there he was still a little larger, a little more important, than anyone else—even William.

Picture after picture. Her eyes were growing heavy. She saw them not as pictures now but as patterns; the colours were beautifully laid together—a pattern like music, like notes in a song. The unknown monk must have been drunk with colour. Here a man in red mail sat a blue horse; a man in blue mail sat a red horse. It didn't take from reality; rather it gave added liveliness.

Picture after picture. Her eyes were so heavy now, she could see no more; not even the bright soft pattern of colour. The nun made a sign. The men moved softly bearing away the chest.

Beneath closed lids her thoughts came and went. The *grandetoile* was unfinished; her mind finished the tale.

William took the crown; but that is not the end of the story. He neglected his children and he neglected his wife. How should a man in such glory have time for commonplace things? That glory I shared. I lived glorious; but I lived lonely. I might have taken a lover; there were plenty to creep into my bed but Brihtric cooled that itch for ever.

I have been faithful but William has not. I could not expect it—a man without a wife. Yet if he truly loved me, why did he not keep me by him in England? He could have found another to rule his council—this last five years Robert certainly. But those five years—what use to him? I was no willing wife. So he sowed his random seed and begot his bastards—he that swore never to put a bastard into the world.

Yet he did love me—still does... in his way. One might call him more faithful than I. In the body he betrays me but never in the heart; faithless yet faithful.

She lay still, considering this man of contradictions; sleep overtook her at the thought. She awoke her thoughts clear and full still of William and his contradictions. She took up the tale in her mind as though she must see him clear; must set him before others before her mouth should be sealed in dust.

He has great principles of justice; yet when need drives, he is unjust and unashamed. Well, it is a need I know for myself; but then I never boasted myself of justice. But am I the better for that? Is it not better to keep justice—a light before one's eyes... though sometimes the light burns dim? She did not know. That matter was too hard. One thing she did know—William was no hypocrite.

He speaks of mercy and he means it, too; yet when need or anger rides, there's no cruelty too great. He loathes the shedding of blood; yet he has shed blood to flow in rivers.

He is truly a good son of the church; but let the church offend him and—like any other enemy—she is plundered and burnt. And his people—the English. No-one must plunder them save he, himself. He will beat the last penny out of them as women beat dirt from their clothes.

She shook a restless head over this strange, stark man she had once thought to wind about her little finger.

But he is a great man; with all his faults, in Christendom the greatest. Right? Wrong? Who shall judge him? He lives by the law of his own nature. A lonely man; dear God, how lonely!

She was taken with a most passionate longing to stay with him, to be with him in his need. She had thought herself done with earthly wishing; now passion of this desire shook her body and soul so that she lay shaking in her bed. *God let me live until he needs me no longer. Let me not leave him to such loneliness as he has never known. Loneliness; You know it is a terrible thing.*

Lying there weeping and beseeching she saw how it must be with him and could not, for pity, endure it. Anger in him would harden. Already he had chid away his children. Robert he had lost for ever—the one son with kindness in him. Rufus, if he might gain by it, would betray his father to his death. Henry would calculate to a hairsbreadth the advantages accruing from that death and would rush from the death-bed to weigh his gold and measure his land as soon he would do at her own. Richard and Agatha; she must rejoice at their death though once she had wept tears of blood. They sat at God's footstool and He would incline His ear. God must have loved these two above all her children. From Adela, happy and distant, William could expect little; a gift maybe at Christmas or on his birthday—if she remembered it. From Constance, unless he let her go now, there would be nothing but hatred. For the sake of Constance, and for his own, he must live till William came, beseech him once more for the child's happiness.

But one child would remember her father. Her pure prayers would rise to heaven; nor would they cease until the child herself ceased—Cecilia, her mother had once thought sacrificed; the one living child whose kindness was sure because her happiness was sure.

The last of her hardness against William melted from her heart.

She must see him, warn him, make him understand the need to be easier, kindlier; warn him against his angers and his terrible pun-ishments—punishments that tormented not only the condemned, but himself, himself also. He was no longer young; and such punishments turned back upon himself, bit into him with a remorse he did not always understand, and that must sap his strength. No longer young nor active nor strong, he must learn to set his soul more truly upon God. And that could be only when he had learned to set it upon mercy and justice... and upon love. And, if love were too hard a thing, then upon kindness. And this he must do for his own sake.

If she could make him understand these things then her life would not be complete failure; she would die content. If not—the thought of his loneliness, his helplessness, surrounded by enemies in his old age, must trouble her in the grave.

The second day of November in the year of grace ten hundred and eightythree.

When William came into the room he was shocked by what he saw. That she was tired, ill even—for that he had been prepared. That she was dying, had never for a moment occurred to him. He looked down at the pinched face, at the light body that scarce lifted the bedclothes. Always she had been a little thing; that she was so small he had forgotten. Hair hidden beneath a cap as white as her cheeks, the nose sharp in her face, gave her the look of one already dead. The eyes he had loved above all things in her, lay shuttered beneath bruised sockets.

She heard him come in and lifted her lids and he was taken by despair. The eyes were strange to him; eyes of a child, a troubled child—of Cecilia trying to understand what it was he wanted of her. *But it is not the face of a child; it is the face of my wife and she is dying.* Almost he could find it in his heart to weep, this man of iron. Jaw grated against jaw; it was overlate for weeping.

She was going to speak; he felt within his own body the effort with which she drove herself to the task. He did not want her to waste her strength; yet, with all his soul, he longed to know what it was she was so desperate to say. It was long, long since they had spoken their hearts in kindness one to the other; and, if not now—then never.

His will urged her on.

She let out her breath on a sigh. The things about kindness and loneliness were too hard to say—too hard. She must leave them awhile. But about Cecilia she must speak; it could not wait. *The thing I held against you all these years has turned to blessing.* The thought was clear in her mind.

'Cecilia.' The name breathed through the quiet room. She could say no more. Her dimming eyes could make out little more than the bulk of his body in the darkening room. Yet still her mind was lucid. She knew she could not make him understand; even, dying, she knew his mind. He believed that now, even now, in this last moment, she held Cecilia against him. Tears trickled down her wasted cheeks.

He sat there, unmoving; bitterness as well as grief tore at his heart.

She must leave Cecilia for now; later... perhaps. For Cecilia all was done and nothing could alter it. But Robert; Robert and Constance. Robert must come home again; William must forgive.

Home... forgive.

She set her mind upon the words. She began again; so faint her breath, he must kneel to hear.

'Robert,' she said, 'Robert...'

Anger swelled his bitterness and grief. She was dying, unforgiving still of himself that had, by the Splendour of God, done his best for her, and for them all; yes, and for her bastard, too. She was dying... and nothing in her heart but reproaches. He had loved her. God knew how much! He had asked no question, ever, about her bastard, though, in his blood, he had known the truth. He had made her no reproaches, though another man might have put her away. All these years she had lied by her silence; but he had given never a sign of the thing he knew, had never, save in the secret places of the heart, held it against her.

That this secret withholding had worked its mischief he did not, even now, understand; nor that her one act—and even he could not call it infidelity since then she had not known him—was little enough to set against his own infidelities; was less still to set against her long faithfulness to his good.

Once she would have taken the thought from him, answered the thought. She could do so no longer; it was finished. There was one thought in her mind; one only thought.

Robert. Again she breathed his name. She wanted with most urgent desperation to tell him Robert must come home. But there were no words and no strength.

She lay silent; and now there was no thought, either. The clouding mind remembered one thing, one thing only. Not Robert. But the long loneliness; but whether it was her loneliness or William's was not clear. Loneliness. It was scarce a thought, scarce an awareness, even. It was a sense, a weight, a burden.

'Lonely,' she said, 'Lonely.'

He took it an accusation. He said, knowing she could no longer hear, and less accusing than trying to make his own heart clear, 'You never loved me. You were courteous always and kind sometimes, but you were never loving. However you might hide it, there was never love. At first I did not know it; and when I did? A man, I thought, could rest on your kindness. Now, dying, you take even that kindness from me, unforgiving for Cecilia, unforgiving for Richard and for Agatha; most of all unforgiving for Robert.'

Anguish burst from him in a groan. It was such pain, such agony body and spirit, he thought his heart must burst.

She neither heard nor saw; yet she sensed his despair. She made a movement of the hand towards him. *William...* the sound just breathed in the room; it was as though already she were a ghost. *William*; and she had never called him that before. In her mouth now—though neither could know it—it was a word of forgiveness, of tenderness; of love.

He knelt there fighting down his tears—the great, strong man that, since babyhood, had not wept; his father had never allowed tears. *You must never cry; you must show yourself stronger than all men because you are a bastard.* Even now, his wife dying, the wife he had so loved, though that love he could never show, he must not weep. Let grief be what it might, still he was a bastard and bastards must not weep.

She gave a sigh; so faint a sigh, yet it took the last of her failing breath. She fell back upon the pillow.

He knelt there looking into the half-closed eyes, the eyes he had so loved; honest eyes that had yet lied throughout all their years together. But that mattered no longer; it had all happened long and long ago. God that he might have those years again, show her that beneath his iron face he had loved her truly and for ever!

He shifted on stiff knees; he was no longer young and he had grown heavy. He put his face in his hands and prayed for her soul.

He raised his head at last and looked at the dead face sealed into a smiling wisdom; peaceful and remote. She had gone from him for ever. He wished, with agony, she had said those things she had tried to say. Always she had spoken with wisdom; those dying words of hers must have helped him to carry his burden. He felt strangely weak, the big, stout man kneeling there, as though all strength had left him. And now the tears, so long forbidden, had their way. But not for long. Even as the short November sunshine struck upon his tears to make a halo about her dead face, his father's words rang again through his mind.

He set his jaw so hard he felt the bone must snap. He lifted a hand to wipe away the tears. She lay there still and smiling and again unhallowed.

He rose, stiff; he turned and went to the door. He felt rather than saw how those that stood about waiting for news of her they had loved, made no movement towards him. More; they shrank back, made themselves non-existent before him.

Alone he strode through the emptiness they made... the emptiness himself had made; foretaste of the years to come.

SOME BOOKS
CONSULTED

Bloch, M.	*Feudal Society* (1961)
David, C.W.	*Robert Curthose* (1920)
Douglas, D.C.	*William the Conqueror* (1964)
Freeman, E.A.	*The History of the Norman Conquest of England* (1867–79)
	The Reign of William Rufus (1882)
Galbraith, V.H.	*Literacy of Mediaeval English Kings* (1935)
Haskins, C.H.	*The Normans in European History* (1916)
	Norman Institutions (1918)
Lennard, R.	*Rural England* (1959)
Planché	*The Conqueror and his Companions* (1874)
Poole, A.L.	*From Domesday Book to Magna Carta* (1951)
Round, J.H.	*Feudal England* (1909)
Schramm, P.E.	*History of the English Coronation* (1937)
Stenton, F.M.	*Anglo-Saxon England* (1947)
	William the Conqueror (1928)
	'Norman London' (1934) Historical Association Leaflet
	The Bayeux Tapestry (1957)
Strickland, Agnes	*Lives of the Queens of England* (1840–9)
Vinogradoff, Sir Paul G.	*English Society in the Eleventh Century* (1908)

CHRONICLES AND DOCUMENTS

Anglo-Saxon Chronicle, ed. J.A, Giles (in Bede's *Ecclesiastical History*, Bohn edition 1847)

English Historical Documents, 1042-1189, ed. D.C. Douglas and G.W. Greenaway, 1953

Florentii Wigorniensis Monachi Chronicon, ed. B. Thorpe, 1848-9

Select Charters, ed. W. Stubbs, 1913

Polydore Vergil's *English History*, ed. Sir Henry Ellis, 1846

Ordericus Vitalis, *Ecclesiastical History of England and Normandy*, trans. T. Forester, 1847

William of Malmesbury, *Chronicles of the Kings of England*, ed. J.A. Giles, 1866

William of Poitiers, *Gesta Wilhelmi Ducis Normannorum*, ed. J.A. Giles (in *Scriptores rerum gestarum Willelmi Conquestoris*, ed. J.A. Giles), 1845

Vita Haroldi, ed. W. de Gray Birch, 1885

Master Wace, his Chronicle of the Norman Conquest from the *Roman de Rou*, ed. E. Taylor, 1837